I0647900

Journey of a Thousand Truths

By

Lazette Gifford

Journey of a Thousand Truths
A Conspiracy of Authors Publication
www.aconspiracyofauthors.com
Copyright © 2020, Lazette Gifford
ISBN: 978-1-936507-94-8
Cover Art Design: Copyright © 2020, Lazette Gifford
Thank you to Design Cuts for making so much fine material available. www.designcuts.com

First Print Edition, March 2020

Thank you to whatever muses are still playing through my mind, baiting me with such lovely ideas even after so many years.

TABLE OF CONTENTS

The antelope strides out across the field, his step steady, his head high. He moves with purpose, but he knows not where he is going. -- The Art of Ata

CHAPTER ONE

A legend walked through the door of the Lost Way Inn.

Oh, not the cautious young man himself, but rather the blood that ran through his veins. The illustrious Prince Zaron was the grandson of two contending barbarian conquerors who had finally ended their wars when neither the Tiger of the East nor the Wolf of the West could get the better of the other. They'd sealed their peace when the son of the East married the daughter of the West. Despite a marriage as tumultuous as the battles their fathers had fought, the pair had produced three daughters and one son.

What brought that renowned son to my humble inn worried me so much that I almost stared at him for too long. A quick glance around the crowded room showed that no one else had recognized the hooded figure. I'd had only a brief glimpse of his face and identified the boy I had known so well until five years ago. Besides, he looked remarkably like his father, whom I had served for ten years until he had been executed for treason.

That the boy came here was a reason to worry.

"More beer, Mai!" One of the regulars reached out and caught my arm in his spindly fingers and made as though to pull me down into a kiss. He knew better than to catch hold of my dress, at least, which had gotten fingers broken. He stank of the fish he worked with all day. "More beer!"

The customer, Old Lomin, was a happy drunk who frequented the Lost Inn at least once a moon. I signaled one of the others to bring him another pitcher of beer while I threaded my way past a dozen other tables. Zaron had barely paused at the door; he moved as though he knew the place, scanned the room once, and headed for a small table at the back wall. I had been wending my way there as well, laughing with customers, pretending that there was nothing wrong.

I didn't want Prince Zaron in my inn. I had stopped serving the royal house when his father, the son of the East, had been taken up for treason and killed. Zaron's mother mistrusted everyone who had served her husband. I was lucky that I'd made provisions to escape the moment I saw the way the dice were rolling. Not many others had survived her cleansing of the guard. After a few months in hiding, I had presented myself as one of the many widowed women who had taken up a business in Willoway City. Few knew the truth about my past -- and Zaron should not have been able to find me here.

Unless....

I reached his shadowed table ahead of any of my people, which was not unusual with the place so busy tonight. Prince Zaron looked up at me with such relief that I felt a shiver. His face appeared to be pale and damp; he must have rushed to this place. He also kept that long braid of hair, which surely would have given him away, tucked not only into the cloak but also under the shirt beneath. Nothing he wore looked to be of royal weave and embroidery and the shirt fit him ill.

No boyish lark had sent Prince Zaron out into the poorest part of the city to find an old friend.

He didn't waste my time.

"My mother and sisters are dealing with demons," he said softly. Far too cultured of a voice for this place. He knew how to keep his voice soft, though, having grown up at court. "They intend to kill me, the Grandfathers, and take the rule. They will destroy everything."

I blinked several times. Someone came closer, but I had made certain I stood at an angle and blocked the view of his face. Oh yes, the old ways of the court came back too quickly.

"We have beer of three levels," I said, sensing the person within hearing range. "May I suggest the golden?"

"Yes, thank you," he replied. Still too cultured, but I didn't think anyone would take note of someone being politer than most of my customers on such a rowdy night.

I didn't dare stand over him for much longer. I lowered my voice. "To the outhouse after the next bell. If anyone goes out before you, wait for the following bell."

He bowed his head in agreement. I sensed a weariness in him that came from more than just a jaunt through the city. What he had said -- well, I was not surprised about the Queen and the Princesses. I didn't even doubt him.

"Soon," I said and walked away.

I made my way past the tables and friendly customers, though I became far too aware that they were all strangers to me, even after all my years here. My real past had walked into the inn, and nothing that had happened in the last few years seemed important now, except for links I'd kept to two others from the palace. I had lived a dream in this place that had never been my true destiny. The moment *Prince* Zaron entered through that door, I had known in my heart I was still a guard of the Royal House.

I gave his beer order to Jana who was the least observant of all my girls. Then I went to the kitchen and viciously chopped vegetables for the next day's food, though I suspected I would not be around to cook it. The scent of onion and peppers filled the air, along with the lasting hint of the fried fish we kept warm for those who came here late to eat. I purposely took a position where I couldn't see the boy because I would stare, despite knowing better.

"Ah," Danisin said as he came in the back door with a bag of rice over his shoulder. He dropped it onto the table and eyed me with a slight frown. "Old Han make another play for you, did he? I'll just stay clear of that knife."

"Ha." I chopped some squash, and then turned to him. "I may have to leave for a while."

Danisin nodded and asked no questions. This wasn't the first time I'd left on other business, though the reasons before this had never been so dire. I suddenly remembered what the boy had said. *Demons?* I chopped more onions, and Danisin went about the work of preparing for the late-night business. We had worked well together.

A bell rang as the nearest temple and counted the quarter-hour. I saw movement toward the backdoor -- the boy in his cloak still. I chopped another carrot, watching to make certain no one followed him, and then I went out, all the while aware of Danisin's curious stare.

Zaron had taken a spot by the high fence that protected the inn's garden. He stood in the darkest shadow he could find, his cloak pulled up around him. I automatically bowed my head -- old habit when seeing royalty -- and checked the outhouse to make certain it was empty. When I came back, I put the lock down on the Inn's door so that no one else could come out. I crossed to Zaron with my anger starting to bloom into a righteous rage because he had come here and upset my usually quiet life.

The rage died when he looked up at me again.

This was not the boy I had left behind five years ago. Zaron was nearly twenty, and he looked far too much like his father had at that age: a thin face, high cheekbones and dark eyes. Those features were all that I could see in the darkness.

More than the age and resemblance stopped my ill-timed rage, though. His face showed damp with perspiration, his mouth set in a tight line against obvious pain, and his right hand pressed against his left side. I instinctively pulled the cloak back and could see the bulge of cloth and a dark circle that had to be blood.

"What in the name of the Forgotten Gods --"

"Endris sent me," he said and drew his hand away from the wound; he stood straighter and doing his best not to show any pain.

"Ah, Endris," I said with a slight snarl. "He wouldn't have sent you unless --"

"He's dead," Zaron said. He gave a bow of his head as my heart missed a beat and I shook my head in denial. "I'm sorry. He managed to get me away from the others. Hasana killed him."

"I assume you mean your sister and not the Goddess of Mercy."

"She thinks she's the Goddess incarnate. They all think so -- Mercy, Abundance, Hope. Mother convinced them --"

His breath caught, and I put a hand on his shoulder when I feared his legs would give way. He looked startled; no one touched the prince without permission. I almost bowed my head and apologized.

"No matter," he said. I wasn't certain if he meant that I had touched him or the story about his sisters. "Endris sent me because he said you should know. He said to tell you about the demons and to say that it is a truth unwritten."

I had not expected those words despite the situation. My breath caught. Zaron nodded and seemed to understand the importance of the statement. Then he did something I had not expected. He stood up straighter -- he'd grown as tall as me in the last five years -- and gave me a nod that was clearly meant to be a sign of farewell.

He had not come here looking for my help. He'd come to deliver a message from Endris, and nothing more.

I could let him walk away. I won't say wisdom made me catch hold of his arm before he turned. Maybe I only wanted a chance at redemption and to do for Prince Zaron what I had failed to do for his father. I could not save King Yasidin on that fateful day, but now his son fell into my hands, and I felt as though I had a chance for redemption.

Strange how the call of duty came back so strongly at that moment.

"We have someone else we must see," I said and looked around, preparing for our departure.

"I have told you all I know," Zaron replied. He sounded weary, and his hand went to his side again, no longer trying to hide his pain or weakness. "You do not need me. I'll go now while I still can. They won't find me near the inn."

Those were the words of wisdom.

I didn't listen to them.

"No," I said. The prince frowned. "You must trust me, Zaron."

"I always did," he said, which I think he had not meant to say aloud. Zaron had always been taciturn when it came to expressing trust or emotions. I blamed that on his ruthless mother who had been unhappy at the birth of a son. She had wanted her eldest daughter to rule, but both Grandfathers had wanted a grandson to fully unite the empires. Personally, I thought the Grandfathers were fools. The princesses had been ferocious little beasts from the start, while Zaron had tended towards a quiet and retiring nature. The two old battle horses should have stuck with the girls.

The Grandfathers ruled the empire, East and West, on either side of Willoway and the lands around the city. They clashed still sometimes, but now it was war of diplomats and not soldiers. Where East and West met, and this fine city, the new ruler was to be born and fully unite the two lands. Zaron should have been that ruler.

"Stay with me," I said. "I'll put you somewhere safe for a few minutes. I'll join you soon, and we'll leave before the hour bell."

I saw worry in his eyes, but he had no other hope except to trust me. If Zaron left and headed out on the streets, he would collapse, and he would either die, or he would be found and killed. If he came with me, we risked being caught together, though.

"Captain Mai --" he began.

"I will not let them take you alive."

His eyes widened this time. We knew what could happen to people who fell into his mother's hands. "I -- yes. But you -- "

"Oh, they won't take me, either."

"You shouldn't --"

I pressed him back against the fence and stared into his dark eyes. Dogs barked somewhere down the street and doves took to the air, flying south to north overhead. I could hear things that were not normal out on the street, but he would not realize it, having rarely left the palace.

"Tell me that there isn't more at stake here than you and me, Prince Zaron. Tell me that the story about your sisters and the demons is not true."

His face paled and he gave a slight shudder. I feared I had hurt him with that sudden move, but I did get his attention. He took a deeper breath, his eyes tracing the path of more doves before he looked back at me. "It is true. You're right. This isn't about the two of us. Endris sent me to you for more than a message, I think. What should I do?"

I took him to a corner of the small yard and put him between two sheds with a crate he could sit upon and the high fence at his back. "Stay here. Rest. I can't simply go rushing off, but I won't take long. Not much past the next bell at the most. Will you be all right that long?"

"Better for resting," he admitted. "Thank you."

He'd always been a polite boy.

I gave a quick nod and headed back into the building. Danisin still worked in the kitchen, stirring water and rice into which he dropped a few herbs. I gave him a nod and went on through to the common room, pulling a few coins from my pouch and then placing them carefully on the table where the boy had sat. Jana would find the money soon enough. She was good at spotting coins, and she knew better than to pretend someone had slipped away without paying. I poured the beer down by the wall -- lousy waste of the good stuff, I mused, then I left everything for Jana to clean up.

I had to hope no one else had taken much notice of the odd customer. A glance across the place showed that they were all regular customers tonight, intent on their drink and their arguments. I put my worries aside behind a mask of genial pleasure as I greeted patrons, broke up an argument that had almost gotten out of hand, and managed to keep only a mildly curious look on my face when four of the city guard entered the inn.

I had suspected the guards had been out and were the ones who upset the dogs and the doves. They were moving quickly through the area to be here already.

"Problem?" I asked, directing the question to the woman who seemed to be their leader.

"Lookin' for an escaped prisoner," she said with a bit of a snarl. I couldn't tell if this was what she had been told about Zaron or if she used it as a cover. "Tall young man, thin. Wounded."

I looked around and shook my head. "Not in here. Not many strangers in tonight."

All of it true. If one of the guards happened to have a truth charm, I had to be careful of what I said.

They walked around the room. One checked the outhouse. I stayed by their captain, wondering if I could take her and the others -- if anyone here would help me.

The man came back in and shook his head. The guards left.

I got more beer for a couple grumbling customers and spent most of the rest of the hour doing my usual work. Then I took the journal of this week's business and headed upstairs to my room. "Take care of things, Danisin."

The older man gave me a worried nod. He knew something must be going on and those words meant he wouldn't likely see me for a while. I wondered if I would ever see him again. Or my wonderful inn. I had come here to hide, but the years had been good. For a moment I resented that Zaron --

No. I was still the person I had been when I served his father. I would not turn my back on my duty now.

I grabbed some bread and cheese and went to my upstairs rooms, sat at my desk for a little while and worked on the journal. As I had expected, Nuar came upstairs no doubt to ask me an inane question. Not a very good spy was Nuar. I knew he worked for the Spotted Pot Inn which was not far away.

"Yes?" I asked with a bit of a snarl at being interrupted. I had left the door open on purpose, though. I didn't want him hanging about in the hall, trying to listen. I didn't have time to waste.

"Anything else you want me to do?" he asked, looking around the room. He must have expected to find the escaped prisoner sitting in a chair by the window. I had the door open to the sleeping room as well. Nothing to hide here.

"Have you suddenly learned to read and write?" I asked

with a wave of my quill and a little splatter of ink across the desk.

"No, Mai," he said with a pretentious bow of his head. "I am not given to such greatness."

I already knew he could read and write, in fact. He'd copied and passed on a recipe for a unique beer that I had purposely left out to test him. The Spotted Pot had lost a lot of business over that one after a few patrons drank the stuff.

"You can leave for the night," I said with another wave of my hand. "And shut the damned door behind you. This is giving me a headache already. How could we lose so much income in one week? I'm going to have to find a cheaper source for the grain and rice. Go, go."

Nuar had barely hidden his smile at my mention of loss of income. That would be a lovely little tidbit for the Spotted Pot. It also set the stage so that I could be away for a few days looking for new supplies. Nuar dutifully closed the door behind him. He'd be heading out in a few minutes, his work here done. Oddly, he was much better at waiting on customers than he was as a spy. At least he didn't shirk his work as Jana sometimes tried to do. I gladly paid him for it.

I waited until the next bell. By then I had a mental list of everything I needed from the room. I had a pack in the closet, always ready to go. I'd learned that trick the night Zaron's father had been taken and I had to scramble to get anything that I could salvage out of the palace. Most of the rest of the guards hadn't survived. Some of them had died trying to get Yasidin free from the Queen's men, even knowing they were going to be killed in the attempt.

I would have -- should have -- been one of them. Instead, I had survived because I was not there to join the initial madness. I'd been working with the City Guard for a few days while we sorted out a sticky problem about precedence between the soldiers of the Tiger of the East and those of the

Wolf of the West.

I had heard there was trouble at the palace and had rushed back to see the Queen's Guard drag Yasidin away, leaving a trail of dead behind them. Nearly everyone I knew had died in less than an hour. There had been someone else I'd known in the castle, though, whom I hoped had not yet been killed.

I had gone back for Tansa. Maybe we should have tried to grab Zaron then, too -- but that would have been suicidal, and besides, Zaron still had Endris, whom I trusted. I'd gotten Tansa away, though -- our own personal victory on a day of disaster.

I grabbed the food I'd just brought from the kitchen, the pack from the closet, and the swords and their harness from behind a hidden panel. I had not worn the two blades in a long time. They settled across my back with a familiar weight, and the pack dropped over the harness, so only the very edge of the pommels remained within sight, and those I had long ago wrapped in cloth so that no metal reflected the light. The night had gone dark and foggy. I hoped that we would mostly go unnoticed on the quiet streets.

I climbed out of the window, spidered my way across the uneven outer wall, and down into the yard. I looked back once to the window and the inn and bade farewell to that life.

CHAPTER TWO

Fog spread across the little plot of ground, like cold fingers reaching for him. The place reeked of the outhouse, garbage, and muddy earth; not a place for the Prince Heir to stop and rest. Not the place for him to die.

Za had not wanted to sit still because that gave him time to think and remember what had sent him to this place, and to locate someone he had never expected to see again. The fog moved ghost-like and dragged him back to the events of a few hours before.

The battle had ended.

"Captain Mai," Endris had said, his breath rattling as he fought to get the last words out. "Go to her. Say it is a truth unspoken."

Za had started to protest, thinking Endris had already slipped beyond reality. Undoubtedly Captain Mai had died with the others --

Endris lifted a bloody hand to Za's forehead and gave him the information by magic.

And that had killed Endris, the only friend he had in the exquisite Summer Clouds Palace.

Oh, the man would have died anyway. Za knew that logically. Yet in his mind, his only friend had died to try and save him, and Za still had no doubt that he'd be dead soon as well. He'd gotten this far. He'd given the message Endris had passed to him. He had told the very much alive Captain Mai about his sisters and mother.

What more did this woman want of him?

Mai had been a soldier he had trusted when he was younger, but she should have been dead years ago. She had deserted him --

Endris had still trusted Captain Mai, and she did not seem willing to give him up.

The door to the inn opened and a man in the gray of the city guard stepped out into the yard, giving the area a quick glance. Za knew that if he moved, then everything would at least be over. No more games, no more lies, no demons to face.

The guards would not just take him, though. They would drag everyone from the building in with the prisoner and they would all face the Queen's justice. Captain Mai would have survived for nothing.

Za remained still, holding to the *Art of Ata*, the practice of being nothing while accepting -- feeling -- all the world around him. Endris had introduced him to the older holy man who had been his teacher for the last few years. His mother had let the ancient priest come in and out of the inner court, showing her piety to the outside world -- but she never believed in Ata. From the start, Za had found the meditations helpful in a world filled with stress. Now he practiced holding the stillness within and making himself no more than shadow while the man checked the outhouse, cast one quick glance around the yard, and went back inside.

Once the soldier closed the inn door, Za leaned forward and found that he could no longer remain seated. He slid down to the weeds and curled up in his borrowed cloak. The ground felt hard, and a small rock pressed against his cheek. If he died here, he had to hope that Captain Mai would find a way to remove his body without drawing attention. He didn't want to make more trouble for her.

"Prince Zaron."

He sat upright with a start, expecting trouble for having slept when --

"Oh Gods," he whispered. Not in the palace now, but not anywhere better, either.

"Can you stand?" Mai asked. Za couldn't see much of her face, except for the jut of her nose and the slant of her brown eyes. He thought she frowned. Strands of her dark hair had come loose from the mass she had tied up in a bun, like a commoner would wear her hair. "Prince Zaron?" she said again.

"Not the name to use," he replied, pulling the strands of his mind back to this strange reality. "Za. Just Za. No use to take any -- any chances."

He got to his feet. It was, he realized, a show of pride rather than wisdom. The movement had pulled at his side, and he nearly went down again.

"Knife?" Mai asked as she rose gracefully to her feet again, despite the pack -- ah, and the swords, too. Good.

"Claw," he corrected. Her eyes went wide. "I did mention demons."

"Yes, but I thought --"

"Metaphorical demons?" he asked and gave a grateful nod when she took his arm, helping lead him the way she wanted to go, which was not back to the Inn.

"Well, at least not demons actually *here*. I want to know -- but no, not yet. We must be careful."

Za had considered that demons might have followed him, but he managed to get all the way to Mai without being killed, and nothing found him even when he had stopped moving. Zaron had feared they would have the scent of him after the wound but --

"My beloved sisters don't dare turn the demons loose

yet," he said in a near whisper. "They wouldn't want the people to know, at least not before they are ready to take on everything. That's why they haven't caught me."

Mai nodded with grim-faced agreement, the moonlight catching the look from one step to the next. They walked along the fence behind the inn, and she pushed at a section that slid aside, leading out into a narrow alley. Rats ran, one dancing over the top of his foot and he stopped a shudder after the first startled gasp. This was no time to revert to the pampered prince.

"This way," Mai said, though she had spent a moment looking one way or the other as she slid the fence back into place. "I'm not certain how many guards are out looking for you. I also don't know what would happen if they found *you* out on the streets. You can't be mistaken for an escaped prisoner."

"Perhaps," Za said, and then held his breath while they climbed over some debris that had been tossed behind a fence. Mai cursed softly and helped him as best she could. "Perhaps they only want me spotted so they could send ... others to take care of me. My mother does not fully control the City Guard, but she does have ... have people within the ranks."

"Yes," Mai agreed and looked pleased that he had sense enough to think of that possibility.

"I should like you to get me away as best you can and then for you to go back --"

"I'll do what I can," she replied, cutting him short. "I know my duty."

"You left the service --"

"But I did not abandon my oath," she replied, her voice quiet but steady. She made less noise than he across the debris. "And that is why Endris sent you to me, you know. Rest a moment. I'll check the end of the alley."

Captain Mai had changed from the polite, well-trained

guard who had stood by his father at every event the prince remembered until his father died. She would never have spoken to the king that way, and Za watched her with a slight frown.

Saving my life, despite myself.

Za leaned against a rough wall and watched as she moved to the fence that made a dead end of the filthy alley. He was not surprised to see her push another section of wood aside with her foot and then kneel and look out. His side ached at the sight. He wasn't sure he would be able to crawl anywhere.

Blood had soaked the cloth at his side, but he knew the wound could not be bleeding too badly. Painful, though. It must have caught muscles because every time he took a deep breath, it hurt like the first cut. Za didn't want to go on -- especially since he had no idea where she might take him. Za supposed he should have been paranoid, but she hadn't turned him over to the guards.

"Now!" she whispered.

He stumbled forward, got down on his hands and knees, and slid through the small opening. He tried to get out of the way before he collapsed on the other side. She came out as well, grabbed him up off the ground, and got him moving by the sheer force of her will and some curses he'd never heard from the Royal Guards before.

Za held his breath and forced his legs to walk, one step after another. The world around him blurred, the colors melding into bright spots of fire and cold blue seas. Neither appealed to him, and he might have complained --

"Rest," Mai said. She pushed him into a corner between two buildings, made sure he had his back to a wall, and then stepped away. "I won't be long."

The moment of panic as she abandoned him passed quickly; he hadn't the strength to sustain any worry, and he felt grateful to have stopped moving. He took a deeper breath, a hand to his side, and tried to think clearly. He didn't know where he was or where Captain Mai meant to take him. Za suspected that he ought to care, but he wasn't certain why. He could not fight the demons if he went home. Nowhere else mattered.

He didn't go to sleep this time, but he did pull back the *Art of Ata* once more, letting the calm settle over him. He had never attained the higher powers that the Master had hinted at -- the powers where one could draw power and objects from the real world. He could, however, control his own body. When Mai returned -- he hadn't been confident she would -- he stood up straighter. She gave him a nod, relief plain in her face.

"Not far. We dare not go straight in the front door, though. I'm going to take us a longer route and up to the side door."

"I can't go much farther," Za admitted, though he proved steady enough as he pushed one hand against the wall and stepped away.

"I know," Mai replied.

No walkways here which meant they were well into the poor quarter. The sounds were alien, the scents foreign, even though he was no more than five miles from the Summer Clouds Palace. Lights flickered, but he couldn't focus beyond Mai walking to his left.

"I would expect more people about," he said and stumbled along with her steadying him every few steps. He probably looked like a drunk. He knew people watched from shaded windows. Maybe being drunk wasn't too bad here.

"The guards scared them all indoors," Captain Mai explained with a quick glance at a dark alley. "That's good, really. We don't want anyone getting close to you. You look far too much like your father."

Those words surprised him. "I do? I wouldn't know.

There are no portraits of him left in the palace."

Mai glanced his way, and for a moment he saw a whisper of anger on her face. Za hadn't considered how some people might still be loyal to his dead and disgraced father. Had Endris been one of them? Had he missed a chance to understand --

Now was not the time to seek answers about the past. He tried to guess where they might be. He didn't know most parts of the town well --

Yes, he did. The information must have come from Edris at the same time he sent Za to Mai and implanted the path to take there. The magic had so surprised Zaron that he'd not explored what else might have come with that dying gift. For a moment, he saw a map of Willoway in his mind, but he still had no idea where they were since he'd paid no attention. Fool, he supposed.

Za looked for landmarks, but his eyes seemed unable to focus beyond the most immediate area. Better, he supposed, to concentrate on each step, so he stared at the ground instead.

They passed a few people, all of them peasants with their heads bowed in perpetual humbleness. The helpful fog made them look like two more locals, hurrying on their way through an unpleasant night.

A group of four city guards crossed the road hardly more than a hundred yards ahead of them. Mai slowed but did not stop, and then turned down the path where the guards had become indistinct shapes in the fog. Za felt a surge of worry, but he did not slow. Mai moved at a sedate pace, the shadowy guards walking farther away from them, lost in the fog. Mai and Za turned off to another street of closed doors and shuttered windows covered in rags of cloth. They were still in a poor area of town, and the scent of cheap food cooked on braziers within those walls nearly made him ill.

"The gods have been with us," Mai muttered. He wouldn't

have said the same, walking now with a hand on his side and his breath catching again. "This way."

They turned down a dark alley where no light seemed to reach, and the fog grew even thicker. Rats ran again; Za had expected them this time and didn't even shudder. Amusing how fast one could get used to something out of necessity.

"Almost there," Mai said. "Let me do the talking."

He didn't argue, even when he saw the building. *Especially then*, in fact. Mai had brought them to the Lightning Company Mercenary Headquarters, a place he never would have gone to in search of help.

A strange place, with elaborate decorations everywhere, and none of them having to do with war. Generations ago, this had been a temple to Aia, the goddess of hope, and the structure had sat well outside the city walls. However, the city grew and grew, and finally the priestesses had abandoned the building and moved to the Summer Cloud grounds -- and lost touch with the people. That the mercenaries could take over such a structure probably meant terrible things for the people of Willoway.

Though Za admitted that he felt a touch of *hope* as they neared the old temple.

Mai walked up four steps to the side door, nodded to the guard on duty, and signaled Za inside.

CHAPTER THREE

I had feared we might not make it this far.

Worse was the nagging feeling that this wasn't the place to bring our fine Prince Zaron. Maybe we should have stayed at the Inn. After all, it had already been searched. Ah, but I didn't trust all of my employees, including Nuar, of course. My doubts plagued me, but I didn't slow, as I held his arm and led him through the maze of halls from the side door and up the back stairs, though he did stumble on the steps. I wasn't certain he knew where he was when we finally reached the commander's office.

We had passed only four people. I was not -- at least officially -- a member of the mercenaries, but they knew me well here. Everyone moved out of our way with curious glances at my still hooded companion. Let them think he was the escaped prisoner the guards searched for, but I wasn't ready to give up the worse truth yet. Besides, something this serious couldn't be my decision.

The commander's door was painted with the lightning emblem of the Mercenaries. I knocked loudly, having learned better than to just walk into this room.

"Enter."

Zaron frowned. Hadn't he known the leader of the

mercenaries was a woman? Maybe not. While they were stationed in Willoway, under the careful watch of the Queen, Lightning rarely worked in the city. Like all good military people, they kept quiet about their own affairs.

I pushed the door open, and we walked into the well-appointed room. Cushioned chairs sat in front of a large cherry wood desk covered in delicate animal carvings that held the piles of papers in place. A sword hung over the back of the commander's chair. I glanced at Za who looked ready to collapse.

The commander looked up from her writing. Her short dark hair stood up in spikes, a style she'd taken up in the last few years and seemed to fit with her personality. A scar traced a pale line down the left side of her face but did not ruin her delicate beauty.

"Sit down," she ordered with a wave of her hand.

I pushed Za towards the chair, and he sat with little grace, leaning forward and his hand on his side. I thought the wound must be worse -- but no. He was staring into the commander's face.

"Kintansa?" he whispered.

She smiled. "Quite a change from your father's favorite concubine to this, eh?"

"But --" His breath caught as he moved. Kintansa frowned. "How did you survive? How did you get *here*?"

"Mai got me out," she said and gave me a fond smile.

"You've changed," Za mumbled. He looked as though the latest shock might have been too much for him. "The Queen doesn't know."

"Your mother? No," Kintansa replied with a snarl. Then her head tilted as though she were only now looking Za over as well. "We hide in plain sight in front of her. She keeps a spy in the building, but he never knew me at the palace. Are you going to tell her? It might win you some favor."

"No."

The answer had been absolute. I noticed how even Tansa didn't doubt him.

"Tell me why you are here," she said, looking at him.

"I really don't know," he replied. "Captain Mai brought me. I assume for a reason --"

"Tell her what happened," I ordered.

Prince Zaron frowned, probably because he didn't do well with orders. If this had been his father, he would have clamped his mouth shut and probably not spoken for the rest of the day. Prince Zaron, though, told the tale, and without any embellishment. Tansa's eyes widened as he explained about his sisters and the demons. She cursed when he said Endris had died.

"Damn him. I told him a thousand times that he needed to step down and join us." She scowled at Zaron as though this was all his fault. We both knew Endris would not leave the prince. Then the look changed. "Clawed by a demon? They often have poison, though that might only be in a bite. You need care --"

"Carefully, Tansa," I said and reached across to grab her arm as she started to stand. "I know you trust your people, but this is a delicate damned mess that could bring the queen and all her allies -- human or otherwise -- down on us."

"Yes, yes," she said and pulled free. "Not the company medic. He's new. Sirma. His father was a medic, but he doesn't like the work. He knows it well enough, and he's been with me almost from the start."

I knew Sirma. He'd sewn up a cut in my arm a year ago and asked no questions at all, despite that I was not one of the Lighting Company. Za looked at me and apparently found no reason to argue. I thought he might be beyond coherent thought by now. His eyes appeared glassy and a little wild.

Commander Kintansa went to the door and cracked it

open. "Sirma!" she shouted. She didn't wait for an answer. People would pass that order on through the building until it found the man, who would get up here as quickly as possible. No one made the mistake of keeping the commander waiting. She had barely crossed back to the desk and sat down when I heard someone running in the hall, a pause, and then a knock.

"Enter."

Sirma stepped in and saluted -- hand to heart with a bow of his head. His dark hair had streaks of gray along the edges, and his eyes squinted slightly. He'd left the field, most of the time, for work behind a desk in the last two years. Since then he had put on a bit of weight. By no means fat, though. He'd always been far too thin.

"Commander?" he said with a glance to me and the other guest, who still sat with his hood up.

"Bring a report to me. I don't care which one. Also, bring a med kit, but don't let others see. I have a cut for you to deal with, but we must do so without any show."

"Yes, Commander." Barely a glance at the stranger in the chair whom he could not clearly see.

He bowed and left again. Za had turned his head and looked at the closed door, pensive now. The rest was doing him good.

"I do not want to draw all of you into my trouble," he said. "Endris sent me to give Mai the knowledge of -- of what had happened." A slight movement sent his eyes fluttering this time, but he held on out of pure stubbornness. Oh yes, very much like his father. "I was surprised to find her alive. Surprised to find you, Lady Kintansa. Pleased, really, for both of you. But I had not meant --"

"You had meant to give me the news and go off and die," I said. Tansa's eyebrow rose, and I gave her a quick nod of affirmation. "We might need more information, you know. We had better get him to the bed, Tansa. Sirma will need him to be laid down anyway."

Kintansa still frowned, but I could see a hint of curiosity in her face. We'd had little reliable information from the inner palace for the past three years. Endris had still been at the compound, but he hadn't been invited through the inner gate for quite a long time. We'd known something must be going on.

I had never considered demons. The Queen and her daughters had never been my favorites, even when the girls were young, but dealing with demons seemed excessive. I didn't doubt anything the prince had said because I had known them well enough. As insane as this might sound, I knew it to be true.

"How did they find contact with demons?" I suddenly asked.

"I don't know." Zaron did his best to stand on his own, but I caught his arm before he fell. "They didn't ask me to join in."

"Ha," I answered. I could feel his clammy skin beneath the ruined silk tunic the prince wore. I was lucky I had gotten him to this building before he collapsed. "Not far now, Za."

He bowed his head, nearly tripped, and then somehow forced himself to go on. His father had been that stubborn. I wondered what he had acquired from his mother. Certainly not her temper.

"Clear the blankets off," I said to Tansa. "There's no reason to ruin them."

She gave a grunt of agreement and tore the blankets back. The sheet beneath was beautiful silk, but more easily replaced. I pulled his tattered cloak off and threw it down on the bed and then helped Za to sit on the edge of the feather-stuffed mattress. He hadn't the strength left to stay there. Kintansa caught his legs, and I lowered his shoulders. He shuddered at the movement but made no sound.

Tansa went back to the other room, leaving the door open only a crack. I stood by the bed, watching our unusual guest. His eyes had closed, his breathing sharp little gasps that could no longer hide the pain. Endris had always said --

The loss of Endris struck harder now that I had time to stop and think. His death left an irreplaceable hole in our group. We would never be able to fit someone else into the palace city to keep watch over the Queen.

I wanted to mistrust Prince Zaron and blame him for my personal loss. I'd had only two true friends from the palace.

A knock on the door was followed a moment later by Sirma's appearance in the outer room. He shoved a stack of papers into his commander's hands and started to the bed.

"This is the escaped prisoner the city guard is hunting?" he dared to ask.

"He's the person the guard is hunting. He's not an escaped prisoner," I said. There was no use pretending anything but the truth. Sirma had his first clear look at his patient, and he stopped, staring down at the form.

"Prince Zaron," the man said softly. The patient twitched at the name.

"He needs our help," Kintansa said and put a hand on the startled man's shoulder. "And I trust you."

This was why she had done so well as the leader of the mercenaries, I realized. She not only knew how to handle her people in battle, but she also knew what to say to them at times like this. I would have ordered the man to get to work, and damned what he thought personally. I didn't have the patience to deal with people who questioned what I wanted. I thought I had been better back when I served in Summer Cloud Palace and the enclosed small city around it. We'd needed to be polite there, stuck in a small place with others we didn't want to annoy.

Sirma pulled a chair over to the side of the bed and began

removing the cloth at Zaron's side. I watched and grimaced at the sight of the wound which appeared far worse than I had expected. This wasn't a mere scratch that bled a bit; the claw had gone through skin, muscle and even gouged bone out of at least one rib.

"What in the name of the Gods --" Sirma mumbled.

"Demon," Kintansa answered.

He looked at her, his face going white, and then nodded and went back to work. Steady hands. I began getting the shakes. We'd had a long, arduous journey to get Zaron here. I realized that we'd had more luck than we deserved. I should have found a better way to transport him, hidden in a wagon or --

No matter. We were here. Kintansa went back to her office, and I followed, dropping into the chair before her. We'd have to clean the other one of the spots of blood.

"What is going on, Mai?" Tansa asked, though softly. We'd kept the door open to the bedroom, and I could see Sirma working steadily away without a pause. Good man. "Mai?"

"I don't know any more than what he's told us," I replied. I felt a slight surge of annoyance, mostly at my own past mistakes. "That's more than what Endris had said in his last report. I didn't take him seriously, you know. He'd been talking about strange things at the palace for a long time."

"He had," Tansa agreed. She sat back in her own chair and shook her head. "He sent the prince to you. He put this into your hands."

"And I brought him here because I knew I could not handle this trouble alone."

She snorted and stared at the wall, and her face grew pensive. I wondered if she wished Za dead and an end to that part of the trouble, although his death would be of little help if all the rest of what he said proved to be true.

The cut in his side seemed to be confirmation. I had never seen any weapon or natural animal that could do the kind of damage I'd seen there. So, at least for the moment, we had to believe that there were demons involved.

Kintansa glanced at the bedroom and then turned from the doorway and looked back at me. Something had softened in his face. Did she see his father -- to whom she had been concubine, but well loved -- in his face? Did she remember the prince as a child, somber and quiet, and very good with book learning?

"The Queen and her daughters want to rule," I said and leaned forward. "That's no surprise. Involving demons, though, means they intend to rule far more than Willoway and Summer Cloud. He said they intend to take on both Grandfathers."

"They'd be fools to --" She stopped and reconsidered the words. "Demons would give them some unusual power, but what would the demons want in return?"

"A foothold here," I said and felt a shudder. "My father always said that the demons wanted access to this world, which is a fair, beautiful place compared to the hells where they reign. Maybe we can tame them."

Tansa snorted again. We both knew the tales taught to children about what the evil demons had done to our world in the past. I wondered if the Queen and her daughters knew the tales, and if like the worst of the story people, they simply decided they would do better than anyone else in the past.

Kintansa looked over the report Sirma had given her and I sat quietly trying not to fidget. She made a few notes on the pages. I had nothing to do except to fret and wonder what we were going to do with the trouble in the other room. I did not look that way. I contemplated what I could do to get back to my lovely inn and leave all of this in Tansa's hands.

But the boy had come to me, and I had felt the call of

duty.

Sirma came out. "He's sleeping. That's best. He needs to be watched, but if I stay, someone is going to get suspicious."

"I'll sit with him," I said. I tried not to distrust Sirma who was going to be out of our reach and could do anything he wanted.

"If his fever turns worse, send for me. If there is sudden bleeding, send for me. If his breathing is worse --"

"I'll send for you if anything looks odd," I offered.

Sirma gave a nod of agreement.

"I'll call for you in a couple hours to go over the report again unless there's a change we don't like. Then I'll call you sooner"

"Yes. Good." He looked back through the door to the bedroom. "I have the feeling we're going to be in for a lot of trouble before this is done."

"Maybe. Maybe we'll just slip our fine prince back out and let him fend for himself," Kintansa replied. "It all depends on what we find out."

Sirma nodded again and left the room.

I got up and went into the bedroom. Tansa followed me, and she stared down at the prince as I pulled the plush chair from beside the wall. I sat down with a sigh that mixed regret and frustration. Her hand rested on my shoulder, drawing my attention.

"I'll have my nightly reports about the Summer Cloud soon," she said. "We'll see if there is anything unusual in them. There is really nothing we can do until we get confirmation of what he's told us."

"You don't believe him?" I asked, surprised.

"I don't believe anything until I've heard it -- or can piece it together -- from other sources. And if it is true, should we go rushing off to fight the royal family and the demons? I am not going to waste my people on a hopeless cause."

"Yes, you're right. I hope I have no reason to regret bringing Za here."

"No need for regret." She bent forward and kissed the top of my head, surprising me with the moment of intimacy. Tansa was always shy about showing her romantic side, and I would have thought the prince, even unconscious, would have inhibited her. "I am glad you brought him straight to me. I'd much rather know what's going on before demons become manifest and walk the city. We can make decisions based on the information and plan for actions. Without Prince Zaron, I fear we might not have learned about this mess until far too late."

"Lightning Company would not be safe," I realized. "They wouldn't want an independent force loose in the city."

"Which means we are already not safe," Tansa said with a nod. Her hand still rested on my shoulder, and her fingers tightened. "I need to let my people know that something might be amiss in the city tonight and to take care."

I nodded. Tansa went off to her work, and I sat with the boy. Oh, not a boy anymore. He'd grown in the years since I'd last seen him. I thought I had gathered enough about his personality in the last couple hours to know that I could trust him. I hoped so. We were going to need his help before long. Only he could tell us anything about what we faced.

The night sounded quiet outside the small, barred window. I knew that would change.

CHAPTER FOUR

Zaron came awake slowly to a soft and warm bed, but not his bed. It held the scent of jasmine and pine. He moved slightly --

The pain brought him fully awake with a start, but he still didn't know where he was or how he'd gotten here. Something wrong, and that was enough to induce panic in anyone from the palace. A royal prince did not wake up in some unknown place, injured --

Demons.

The memory of the dark, sinewy creatures with blood red eyes and claws like curved daggers drew a different gasp from him. If they had taken him --

Captain Mai sat by the bed. She watched him with her face devoid of emotion except for a narrowing of her dark eyes.

"Are you awake, Prince Zaron?"

"Yes," he said softly with a look around the room. "I don't remember --"

"Commander Kintansa's bedroom," she replied, not waiting for him to say more. He wasn't used to being interrupted, but just now he didn't mind. "I brought you to the mercenaries, assuming they were the only help we really had in the city. The city guards were obviously already working for the Queen, even if they were not fully aware of what they were sent to do."

"Yes," he said. His head pounded. His hand brushed against the soft mattress and fine sheet. "I would not have expected such luxury from the Commander if I had not known she was Lady Kintansa. I'm glad she survived. She was never as mean-spirited as the others."

"True," Mai agreed and smiled. "I have a little wine. Not as good as you are used to --"

"I'm not a delicate child," he replied, but without any bite to the words. "Endris and I slipped away sometimes. I suspect I've had worse -- worse wine than anything you have here."

"Endris was a good man," she said and helped him to sit; she held to him until he was able to stay there. "We'll miss him."

"They took us by surprise. Aia shouted from the end of the hall for him to come to help her. I meant to go to the stairs and head up to my room. The stairs were about halfway down the hall. By the time I got there, I could hear the battle and rushed in to help. Kwana and Hasana stood on the far side of the room with Aia. They were smiling. I only then realized we were fighting monsters. A dozen or more. There were arms and claws everywhere."

Tansa had heard the words. She came to the room and leaned against the chair, either weary or trying to look less imposing, he supposed. "How did you get free?"

"Endris," he said, and his breath caught again, but this was for sorrow. He'd never had a friend except for Endris, even though the man had been at least a decade older than Za. "He'd already lost one leg -- just cut off, and bleeding so much -- No, I'm alright. He had fallen, but at that moment he lifted his hand and tossed a light into the air. I'd already been wounded. Not as bad as he --"

"Bad enough," Mai said.

"I never realized he knew magic," Za confessed. He sounded more amazed than upset by that part. "Neither did the demons or my sisters. They all ran screaming. Endris grabbed my arm, shoved cloth against my wound and whispered more magic. I don't know how he had lived that long. At the very last he gave me the message -- gave it by magic along with the way to find Captain Mai. Then he died."

He had not meant to show much emotion at the end, but he felt warm tears on his cheeks. For a moment, he thought to be embarrassed, but neither of these women begrudged him the pain that he felt for the loss of a friend. This was not the palace.

A strange pair of women. He was slightly more clear-headed now. Finding his father's favorite concubine at the head of the most notorious, ruthless mercenaries made him suddenly doubt his own mind. Perhaps the demons had done something to him besides the wound.

There was a dire thought.

"What's wrong?" Captain Mai asked, a hand holding his arm.

"I don't know that you are real," he replied. "And if you are not -- what have I given to the demons? The two of you, here like this --"

"Do you remember when your father brought me home?" Kintansa asked. Her voice still held a touch of the accent he remembered, the musical notes of the far south.

"Oh yes. That was a day one could hardly forget given the reaction from my mother."

"Very diplomatic. Yes, it was quite a scene. The Queen was not happy. I had to pretend to many things that day. Your father had seen me riding with my brothers on a hunt. He went straight to my father and bought me."

"I didn't know," Za said and bowed his head. "I never

knew much about him at all."

"He was not an evil man," Kintansa said and softened that blow. He had tried to think his father a good person. "He was given to taking what he wanted -- like me -- but compared to others, he was not a bad person. He was certainly never a traitor."

That brought a look of surprise from Za. He had never expected to hear those words from anyone since the people he knew always had to be wary of the Queen and her spies. "Then why was -- oh, I know. My mother arranged it all. I knew it even then, but I kept thinking I must be mistaken because he was a powerful man and only a powerful truth could bring him down.

"Or an even more powerful lie," Captain Mai said. "You need to rest. You're trembling. Here, I'll place the pillows, so you can recline. You just need to rest while we speak."

He obeyed, too weak, tired, and hurting to complain about their care. His mind kept wandering as well. He remembered his father dragged away by the Queen's people. That was the only clear memory he had of the man.

"I wasn't like the others, you know," Kintansa said as she sat on the arm of the chair by Captain Mai. "I had already seen the way matters would go with your father, but he refused to acknowledge it, no matter how much I tried to warn him."

"You escaped before anyone could come for you," he said with understanding.

"Not on my own. Mai came for me. I never would have made it out of that maze without her help. I'd only ever gone in once to the women's quarters and never out again. I thought I would go mad trapped in those walls."

He nodded, knowing the feeling as well.

"Do you believe us real?" Captain Mai asked with a tilt of her head.

"I don't know yet," he admitted. "I might as well continue

along the path I've taken so far, though. After all, this is a place of hope, isn't it?"

"Wise," Kintansa said. "And I'll tell you what we've learned in the last five hours while you rested. Yes, it is dawn already. I'm glad you got the rest you did."

"Ah, but I took your bed --"

"We were not going to get any sleep anyway," Kintansa said.

He looked from Mai to her and back, putting that last piece into place. They both watched for his reaction. "You are lovers, and that is why Mai came for you when my father died. That all makes sense now. What has happened?"

"Several frightened servants have already spread the tale of a battle in the heart of Summer Cloud," Mai said, taking up the tale. "None of them saw it, though some reported a bright light and screams. They thought it was fire at first, and many ran -- but they came back eventually and found only Lord Endris's mutilated body. Many of them left the palace city immediately, and the wiser ones didn't even stop until they were out of the lower city and into the wilds. Everyone knows that what happened there was not natural. Your disappearance has been noted. Some claim you are in hiding, but a few say that was not your nature, and that something has happened to you, as well."

He hadn't expected anyone to stand up for his honor. Had some of the servants thought that well of him? He'd tried not to be as cruel and demanding as his sisters --

"What of the princesses?" he asked.

"They and the Queen appeared before the Upper Court in the middle of the night -- quite an unheard-of event. The Queen claims that Lord Endris was dealing in magic and it may have turned on him."

"A little truth with a lot of lies," Za replied. "She has always been good at that sort of manipulation. No truth charm would find fault with that answer."

"That's about all we know," Mai said with a wave of her arm. "The guards are still looking for the missing prisoner, but more than a few people are starting to guess that they're really looking for you. We have to trust Sirma and the others who saw you not to give you away --"

"I should not be here," Za said. He felt a surge of worry again. "There's no telling what sort of trouble I might bring --"

"We're ready to move you out if we need to," Kintansa replied.

"You don't owe me --"

"Maybe not," Mai agreed. He wasn't used to people not letting him have his say, but it seemed to be happening quite a bit lately. "Endris sent you to us, and we owe him. While I suspect he sent you because he was your friend, I think he also knew that you would be needed to deal with this trouble."

"I can't see how."

"Some paths are not as clear as others," Mai replied. She stood and stretched. "I'll get us all breakfast and see what's being said among the rest of the company. Then we'll think about what to do next. The best you can do, Prince Zaron, is to rest so that you are at your best when we have to move."

He did not argue. He suddenly remembered how his father had argued at every suggestion some days --

Zaron had grown up in a different world. His father had fought battles with the Tiger of the East, destroying whole villages, fighting the western enemy to a standstill in a battle no more than a hundred miles from here. Willoway had been the summer capital of a vast empire of its own, all gone now, subsumed into the world where two enemies stood guard over the line that divided them. It had held so far through all his life, despite the treason of his father, who was beheaded at his mother's orders.

He looked at Lady Kintansa, remembering her with long

hair, beautiful silk dresses, and exquisite fans that hid her face; Zaron had thought her a shy creature. Now he wondered what those fans had really hidden.

"What do you want from me?" Zaron asked.

Kintansa blinked and frowned. "I'm not certain yet, but you are far too valuable a piece in this game to toss aside. You spent time with Endris if nothing else. You might have information we need from what you have seen. If the demons are real --"

"They are," he said, feeling a bit annoyed that they didn't believe him.

"Yes, I fear they are," she agreed. "I would rather they were some sort of magic, something a touch less troubling than to think the hells are opening to our world again. My people had many legends of the Devil Days. I do not want to see them return to kill and destroy again. I don't want to see them breathe in the souls of their victims and grow wild with power."

"How did they come to the world before?" Za asked. He had leaned back, tired already, but anxious to hear the story. "I know so little --"

"Your people call them children's tales," Kintansa said with a snort of derision. "They never wanted to think there was anything greater than them."

"My father's people? Or my mother's?"

"Both," she said. "Your mother, though -- she was always open to new paths that led to power. She hated that people went to your father rather than her, so she had him destroyed. She never understood that they went to him because she was unpleasant and not likely to help them anyway. Does hearing this bother you?"

"No. It confirms and fills out most of what I'd already known," Za said. "We were never close. I didn't spend much time with my father, either."

"No, you didn't," she said, reminding him of the time she'd been at Summer Cloud as well. "And no one was close to your sisters. They were always destined for something great and could not be bothered to deal with the rest of us."

"And now ... how can they think this is going to help them? Never mind others. They never cared about anyone else. How can they think demons will give them what they want?"

"I don't know. I had never thought they were such fools, Prince Zaron. And now we must deal with their mistakes. I fear we are in for a war, my friend. A long and bloody war."

CHAPTER FIVE

As I headed down to the common room to grab some food, I started trying to sort out the story I would tell the others. I wasn't ready to admit we had Prince Zaron, but there was bound to be some question about whom I had brought in last night, especially with the rest of the rumors flying. Everyone knew something had happened at Summer Cloud Palace.

"You came in late last night, Mai," one of the women said almost immediately as I moved into the line to dish up some food. I didn't know this one's name, but I gave her a nod. "Didn't expect you today, but with everything going on --"

"What have you heard?" I asked, grabbing up a platter and three plates. She took note of that and frowned. "Anything we should know about?"

I was not officially one of the Company, at least not as far as the lower recruits knew. Sirma and a few others knew I'd taken my oath from the start. I even had the lightning tattoo on my shoulder, but I kept it hidden.

The woman frowned, but Kisi, standing behind her in the line, gave me a nod. He'd joined over a year ago and stuck with us through the tough first few months. A lot of the younger ones came and went, a few months with the mercenaries fulfilling some childhood dream of adventure. Sometimes they even got more adventure than they expected when the company went out to take part in some battle along the border. The last time a local lord had paid the mercenaries to clear out a nest of robbers in his hills. That had been in early spring. Summer had passed. We were looking at the long autumn and I prayed for a short winter.

Kisi maneuvered in around the other woman, and she went wandering off while I made a show of choosing the right food. The Company ate well. Tansa always made certain of the supplies.

We had not mentioned to Zaron that we'd left Summer Cloud with more than the clothes on our back. She'd had jewels, of course, but we happened to raid a couple other rooms on the way out.

Kisi moved closer and his voice dropped. "They're looking for Prince Zaron."

"Who is looking for him?" I asked, putting scrambled eggs on all three plates.

"Everyone, as far as I can tell. The Palace Guard is out. They are going to have heard you brought someone in last night."

I nodded and did not deny who we had in the room upstairs. Kind of useless now, I realized.

"People are saying he called up demons to kill his mother and sisters."

That finally drew an emotion from me, along with a snarl and a curse. Kisi looked surprised. "They need to look elsewhere for the link to the demons," I said softly. I had not expected this and for a moment had considered ignoring the demons. Better to start pointing things elsewhere.

"I had the same feeling," Kisi replied. He glanced around the room, crowded with most of the Company who showed up for the first meal of the day, even if they lived outside the building. "We'll let you know when the guard comes near. You had better be ready to do something."

I nodded, got the rest of the food and carried the platter up to the room while I tried to think my way through this situation. The best answer, I supposed, would be for me to take the prince and leave again. I wasn't sure what I could do with him, though.

I did not want him to fall into the hands of the palace guards and go to face his mother's justice. Maybe that was because I had not saved his father -- but even so, I thought the boy deserved better.

Sirma was in the room when I came back. He looked at the food and nodded.

"Yes, that's good. I've done what I can for the wound. It will take some time to heal, I fear. Go easy for the next few months --"

"Somehow, that doesn't seem likely," Prince Zaron said with a touch of humor I had not expected.

"Less so with what I've heard," I said and put the plates down. I gave mine to Sirma. "Eat that. I'll share with the commander and get more if we're still hungry."

"What is the news?" Kintansa asked with a frown. She could tell it had to be bad.

"The Palace Guard is out looking for Prince Zaron who has been accused of calling demons to attack his mother and sisters."

"Ah," Za said. He had the plate in his lap where he sat. I suspected he had never been so informal at a meal in his life -- or maybe that wasn't true. There had been Endris to teach him how to be less of a prince. "Has anyone wondered why I would do such a thing?"

"I am sure a lot of people have wondered," I said. "But they also know something odd happened up in the palace last night. Word will have spread that I brought someone in here, too. Kisi, and probably a few others, have guessed who it was."

"So, what do we do?" Sirma asked.

"We hide the prince until we get him out of here," Kintansa replied. "And I need someone who was so drunk last night, they wouldn't remember how they got back here. Try Elmas. I have a report on her already in the files from last night."

"I'll see to her and get her up here," Sirma said.

I liked this plan. Prince Zaron looked uncertain, but he didn't argue. We also had a place to hide him. We'd used it before, and no one had found it yet.

We ate the food. I wasn't very hungry, so there was more than enough for the two of us. Sirma went off to get Elmas. As soon as he was gone, Tansa and I went to the bookcase against the far wall and pulled it out. The small room inside was well appointed. The last person we'd hid here had been a visiting diplomat. We'd had him tied up and blindfolded though, so he never appreciated the room.

"Best to get you in here now," I said as I came back to the bed. "Finish --"

"I'm done," he replied. "I really can't eat much right now."

I didn't argue. The prince looked feverish, which I didn't like. Sirma had been worried about a fever. We wouldn't dare leave him alone for very long.

Za said nothing as we got him up although I could tell he held his breath against the pain. He let it out again when we lowered him onto the daybed where he could recline comfortably. I pulled the blanket up over him.

"It won't take the Palace Guard long to come looking in this building," I warned. "We're always high on their list at the best of times."

"But you and the Lady --" he said, worried. "The Palace Guard might know you!"

"Your mother did us the favor of replacing all the guards within the first year after your father died. These soldiers are completely loyal to her, of course, but they are limited in what they know."

"Yes. True," Za agreed. He closed his eyes for a moment and then focused on me again. "I will try to remember anything else that might be of help."

"Thank you."

He appeared startled by those words. Maybe he hadn't thought he could help us.

"If you hadn't come to me last night, we wouldn't have known anything until someone said *you* had called demons," I reminded him. "And while we might not have believed this -- I tend not to believe anything the Queen says -- we still wouldn't have had a clue about the real trouble."

"Yes. True." He lifted his head and looked steadier. "I'll be fine here."

We left him to his thoughts and pushed the case back into place. The room had heat and air. With the lock in place, the bookcase would not budge, even if someone thought to try and move it.

Oh, we'd had people checking things out before. The moment they saw the panel that led to the bedroom, they tried every panel in both rooms, but none of them gave way. A second little trick hid the small cubby hole of a room. The bedroom had a closet, but it was in line with mirrors which made the spot seem far larger than it was.

Sirma arrived a little later with a surprisingly drunk Elmas. The woman looked startled and swayed as she tried to salute.

"Take her on into the bed," Kintansa ordered. "And sit with her."

"I slipped her a bit more before I brought her up," Sirma admitted as I took hold of the young woman. Such a waste; if she'd just stayed out of the alehouses, she would have done well with us. I helped Sirma get her situated and the sheets turned enough to hide some blood -- but we did not change them. Best if they look as though they'd been slept in all night.

As I had expected, the Palace Guards arrived within the hour. Word came up only a little after we'd gotten Elmas into the bed. The officious bastards escorted our own guards into the building and put their own outside all the doors -- at least the doors they knew about -- and thought they'd sealed us inside the building. We'd let them believe so in the past. The ploy worked well.

It didn't take long for Kisi to escort the leader of the group up to the room. The Captain had been here before; an unpleasant man who glared, steel-eyed, round-faced, and sneering. He'd put on weight, and he didn't look happy to be out chasing around the town a little after dawn.

"One of your people brought someone in last night --"

"A drunk member of the Company," Kintansa said with a wave of her hand to the bedroom. "She's soon to be released from service."

"You always bring your drunks up here?" he said with a snort of disbelief.

"Ask my people if I do," Tansa replied. It was in fact, something that had happened more than once in the past. "If they've been warned about getting drunk and continue -- yes, they come here, and when I'm sure they're sober enough to understand, I pay them off and release them from the Company. I believe we might have had this conversation before?"

His lip curled upward into a more impressive snarl. The man had made a fine art out of snarling.

I stayed in my seat and let Tansa handle the fool. I didn't have the patience for him. Tansa stayed in her chair and continued with her work. Although he had never introduced himself, I knew he was Captain Gar, the son of a nobleman.

His father had bought him the appointment, but except for how he felt about the Company, he didn't do too bad of a job. Like most nobles, though, he distrusted soldiers for hire -- right until they were needed. We'd helped with riots two years ago when the food supplies ran low, and the Queen didn't want to distribute grain. She'd hated that the Company made a good name for themselves, and we'd been harassed even more since then.

They checked the walls of course. I was tempted to tell them we'd added another wing and a floor on top -- but Captain Gar had no sense of humor. I kept quiet. He checked Elmas himself and came away with a deeper scowl, as though no one had ever been kicked off the Palace Guard for bad behavior. Oh no, they were perfect.

He couldn't fool me. I'd been one of them, though he didn't know it.

Elmas became coherent just after he'd left the room. I could hear her mumbling for a moment, wondering where the hell she was -- and then she gave a surprisingly anguished cry.

"Oh hell, no, no, no. I didn't --" Elmas stopped when Commander Kintansa came into the room, and I followed, not trusting myself alone with the others. Gar moved to the door. "Commander -- by the Gods, known and forgotten, this was not what it seems. I went home, but my mother had died last week, and no one told me, and -- and --"

I had a moment when I thought she lied, but that passed. Her face had gone white. I feared she would be ill, but she got control. Her head bowed.

"I will take my things and go," she said with the kind of sound I'd heard from people heading to their executions.

"No," Kintansa replied. Elmas looked up, her bloodshot gray eyes blinking in confusion. "I'll look into your story, and if it is true, we are all allowed those moments of despair --"

Gar made a sound of disgust behind us. I turned, but

Kintansa touched my arm, and I clamped my mouth shut. I supposed we didn't need a disagreement in here, especially one that might end up with fists or weapons.

Gar pushed his way into the room. "How did you get back to the Company Building?"

Elmas blinked several times. She looked at Tansa as though she had not understood. "I don't remember. I went from one place to another -- I think I remember someone finding me and bringing me here."

"Were you in a hooded cloak?"

"I could have been stark naked for all I remember," she replied with a snarl of anger. Clearly, she was not in the mood to be interrogated by the annoying Captain Gar, but she must have also realized that there was something important going on. She pulled her anger back. "I have a cloak. I don't know if I wore it or not."

"I will need --"

"You will need to get out of the Company House," Kintansa said. Her voice remained calm, but we all knew she'd had enough. "As you can tell, she is not the prince."

"You know whom we seek," Gar said as he backed out of the room. He didn't like to take his eyes off Tansa, but I thought there was something predatory in that stare today.

"All the city knows, and probably villages within fifty miles by now. Was this supposed to be a secret? If so, I think your people need some training."

The snarl came back, but he ordered his men out and followed them. Tansa and I did not leave him to rifle through her papers on the desk. His hand had reached, but finding us following him, he turned and stalked way, slamming the door as he left.

"Let them get downstairs, and then make certain they leave," Kintansa ordered. I gave a salute and went to the door, listening for them to go down the stairs. Tansa went back into the bedroom to no doubt lay down the rules one more time with Elmas. I had the feeling she was going to listen this time.

She had done us a good deed, even if she didn't know it.

I went out into the hall. The window at the end let in the gray light of a dull autumn day. I thought there must still be fog, though I couldn't see it through the thick panes that distorted the view. The stairs were empty, so I went down halfway and listened. They were still on the second floor.

"You'll have to talk to the commander about that," someone said. That was the reply everyone was supposed to give for anything about the Company.

Gar cursed. Then the Palace Guard kept going down. I followed just out of sight from that flight to the next one. When I reached the main floor, they were heading for the big double doors that led outside, and I watched them leave without ever looking back.

We had pulled it off, at least for the moment.

CHAPTER SIX

Za had heard sounds in the other rooms. He remained still, hardly daring to breathe for fear he would draw attention. He heard voices, one louder and more demanding -- a voice he knew, in fact. Captain Gar had arrived to search for him.

Gar was his mother's pet. Za wondered how much Gar knew about the truth. The man was often in private conferences with the Queen and her daughters. He might be in league with the demons as well, though at least he hadn't brought them here.

Had anyone noticed how the prince had been gradually cut away from anything having to do with the rule? Oh, he was sure the servants knew. They were far more observant than Lords and Ladies sometimes. As long as Prince Zaron appeared at the official court functions, none of the nobles would care what happened inside the closed doors of the palace buildings.

Be still. Be calm. Return to the Art of Ata.

The calm settled over him, and he breathed easier. He didn't like the dark, though--

A light appeared over him. No, he denied. I did not create a light.

The room went dark again. Only the fever, Za told himself. Or the touch of the demons. He calmed again, and this time he did not wish for light or anything else.

Eventually, the wall opened, and Mai looked in at him. "Doing okay? We need to keep this closed for a while still. Too many people coming and going."

"I am fine," he answered. His voice even sounded steady.

"Let me get you to the privy now," she said and crossed quickly to the daybed. Za didn't argue and was glad to see there was a door to the little room at the far corner of his small hideaway. He went in and was back out as soon as possible. She took him back to the daybed and helped him settle there. He tugged at his braid, which had gotten caught and pulled. Parts of the hair had worked free, and he wondered if they would braid it for him again. He could do it himself under normal circumstances, but just now he needed both hands to hold to the cushion, so he didn't fall.

"Take him some water," Kintansa said. "Quickly."

Mia brought in a goblet of water and sat it on the table by the daybed. Za gave a nod of thanks, and she slipped away again. The wall closed.

The room was not entirely dark. A slit of light came from above the bookcase and though it wasn't much, he could gradually make out the rest of the room. He sat on a daybed with a small table beside him, and there might have been a painting on the far wall, which made him think the room had a lighting source somewhere -- but he was not ready to get up and look for it.

Ata.

Za focused on the breathing first, pushing aside anything that interfered, from random thoughts to the pain in his side. His thoughts cleared as his breath settled. He could count his heartbeats -- still too fast -- and gradually felt the muscles in his body start to relax.

He sat up, crossed his legs, and rested his palms on his knees. With his eyes closed, he slipped farther into a trance, his inner mind directing all the power it could to heal his body.

He sat for a long time.

The bookcase slid away once more. Za looked up.

"Ah, so that's how you made it this far," Sirma said with a nod of appreciation. "You practice *Ata*. Quite a surprise for someone in the royal family, let alone the heir."

Za unfolded his legs and moved to rest against the curved pillows. He felt better.

"Endris brought a holy man to me at least once a week. It was our secret for over three years. Master Drital said I had gone as far as I could with him a few months ago. Now I'm on my own path to what truth I can serve."

Sirma pulled a chair over from by the open bookcase and sat down. "You know that *Ata* is considered a peasant practice, and not worthy of consideration by those of higher standing."

"I heard such from Master Drital," Za replied and even smiled a little, remembering such a conversation. The aches were coming back again, and he'd broken out in a sweat. "But he taught me despite that I was not one of the worthy."

Sirma gave a little choked laugh but nodded. "*Ata* has helped you control your body so far, but you can't use it for much longer without requiring a long, quiet rest. You've managed to divert energy to healing wounds, but you don't dare keep up that practice. Your body will give way otherwise because the energy to heal still comes from within. You could suddenly collapse, and that might be dangerous if you are not in a safe place, and catastrophic if you have pushed your body beyond where it can recover."

Za bowed his head in agreement. He'd heard these things from the master but had never thought he'd need to put such knowledge to use. Now he wondered if Master Drital -- and probably Endris -- had known more about his future than they'd told him.

Or maybe they'd expected him to see what was happening. Za felt an unexpected welling of embarrassment that he might have been so blind. He thought back to when Endris had first brought Master Drital. He'd thought the guard only wanted to keep a young, energetic prince busy and out of trouble. Endris might have been surprised at how well it worked. *Ata* suited Zaron very well. He preferred quiet and inner peace since there was so little of either in his outward life.

Over the last couple years, all the servants he'd had for most of his life had *retired* and been replaced by people his mother had appointed. He'd never doubted what it meant; she wanted closer watch on him and better control. She had known he spent time with Master Drital, but she might not have realized it was for lessons in *Ata*. Queen Taranis would have used that against him and called it treason to associate with the lower class. His father had learned that too late.

"Prince Zaron?"

"Za," he corrected. "My apologies. My mind wanders."

"You have a serious fever," Sirma replied. He lifted Za's wrist and felt the pulse. "And your heart is racing. Mai is bringing some broth for you to drink. I won't insist on anything else yet, but you do need more strength."

"Yes. Thank you. What time is it?"

"After midnight. You've been here a full day, but...."

"But I'll have to leave soon," he said. "I understand. You cannot keep slipping food to me and sneak in to check without others noticing."

"The risk of someone realizing you are here is too great a threat. They'd kill the entire Company," Sirma agreed.

Mai, coming into the room, made a sound of protest. "That's no reason for us to avoid doing what's right," she said and handed the cup of broth to Sirma.

Sirma reached into a pack at his side and pulled out a small packet and dropped the contents into the broth, swirling it around before he handed it to Za.

Za took the cup and sipped.

"You are very trusting," Sirma said with a surprised look and a shake of his head.

"You have far easier ways of killing me," Za replied. "If you wanted to render me helpless to hand over to the Palace Guard, it wouldn't take much work. I either trust you or try to escape. Should I?"

"Try to escape?" Mai said. "From the headquarters of the Lightning Company? You think you could?"

"I escaped from Summer Cloud Palace," he reminded her. "And in worse shape, than I am now."

Mai started to speak. She stopped. "Let's not try that test and see if you can do it, shall we?"

He offered a slight smile and drank the rest of the broth. He'd been hungry, but it was all he could do to get that bit of liquid down. He laid back without being ordered, already weaker than he had expected. The fever bothered him, too. Za knew he would have to recover if he was going to --

Do what?

He hadn't thought beyond surviving. "There are still the demons," he said. "What can we do?"

"I don't know yet," Kintansa said from the opening where she had lingered, watching over them. "I am trying to find out what I can."

"Carefully. If the queen thinks I am here --"

"Oh, the queen herself gave me a reason to look, you know. She and her people are the ones who brought the idea of demons loose in the world to the public, and the public is not taking it well. Whether the people think you were dealing with demons or she was -- there are rumors about both --

hardly matters at this point. My company needs to know all we can learn in case we have to fight them."

"Ah. True. My mind is addled."

"Sleep now. True sleep, Prince Zaron," Sirma said as he stood again. He pulled the blanket up over him. "The fever is going to get worse, I fear. The gods know what got into that wound, both from the demon claw and from all the time you wandered around the city. We'll fight it back. For now, you need to rest."

They left him again. The light in the outer office remained on, and he heard movements now and then. He went to the privy once, quiet as a mouse, and then back to bed.

Nightmares woke him several times, and he was less certain of his surroundings and safety each time. He could not tell the time, how long he'd slept, whether the monsters that had come for him were real or not.

When Mai finally came back in, he thought she looked worn. He wondered if any of them slept at all.

Kintansa followed her inside the room.

"We have broth for you again, Za," Mai said.

"No --"

"Yes," she replied. "No arguing with us now, not if you want to know what's going on outside this room and this building."

He frowned. Mai had to help hold the cup -- a rude, chipped thing of clay -- as his hands trembled. He sipped. It tasted good, but he still had trouble drinking it all.

"Thank you," he said. His voice sounded rough.

"Here is the news, Za --"

"Mai," Kintansa began to protest.

"I promised him. I won't go back on it. We might want his cooperation later, so it is best to be open and truthful from the beginning. Besides, it's important he has some idea of what's going on out there."

"True," she conceded. "But give Za the short version."

"Riots," Mai said, a shorter version than he liked. She looked at him for a moment and then continued. "Mostly in the market area and down by the port. Kintansa went out with some of the Company and helped get things settled. The people of Willoway are in an uproar -- but not for the reason you probably think. The Queen has ordered the guards to search through every house in the city to be certain you are not hiding. If you are not found, she says that she will start executing people at random until you are turned over to her."

"But --" Za said. He shook his head feeling the certainty of disaster lurking just beyond these walls. "But I might already be out of the city, for all she knows!"

"Yes, that's true," Kintansa agreed and seemed pleased that he'd figured that much out. They must have thought him a fool or a child. "The people know that truth, Za, and they're angry at her. She wants trouble, Prince Zaron. She wants enough trouble, I suspect, that the demons will be happy."

"Twenty hells," he whispered and wiped his hand across his forehead. The fingers came away damp. "If the queen turns them loose, people will think I did it to save myself."

"Yes," Mai said. "We have to get you out of the city."

"No. You need me to go out there and stop this." He started to get up but didn't get far, even before Mai put a hand to his shoulder to stop him.

"Your appearance will only mean your death," Kintansa explained. She came into the room and helped settle him onto the narrow daybed, the pillows pushed up around him. Za didn't have the strength to protest. "And after you died, she'd turn the demons loose and say they still came from you and are avenging your death. She's made certain that you will be blamed, no matter what happens."

"Then it hardly matters --"

"The truth matters," Kintansa said, her voice steady. He

looked to her, uncertain of what she really wanted. "You saw the truth. You know the truth. We need to get you somewhere so that the truth will count for something."

Mai gave the commander an odd look, but she said nothing.

"You also know the truth," Za protested.

"We know what you told us," Mai corrected. "But we could not swear before the gods that this is true."

He started to protest and then stopped. They meant that a priest could not force the truth from them because they only had what they believed. If he went before a priest --

"Get me to the temples --"

"Not here in the city," Kintansa replied with an interruption that almost won a curse from him. "You would never survive to take the oath. Rest for a while, Prince Zaron. We might all have to leave in a great hurry. If she plans to execute people, the Company will not be safe."

Captain Mai and Lady Kintansa left the room, but Za did not go back to sleep for some time.

Ata was called the Path to Truth. Right now, his sense of *Ata* told him to rest and continue with these people and hope to make a chance that his useless death would not.

CHAPTER SEVEN

We settled the prince so he could rest, and then sealed him into his hidden quarters. Kintansa went back to her desk, looked it over, and shook her head. She took me by the hand and led me to our bed. We curled up together, holding each other tight -- and I slept better than I had for weeks. Exhaustion had won this round.

We woke and dressed in clean clothing, preparing for what I hoped would be a better day. I washed my hair as I looked out at the gray-washed world. Clouds had moved in, and with them a sharp wind that I could feel around the leaded glass. I could see clearly only out of the very center of the window, but all it showed me was the fall of rain and a vista drenched in water.

"Maybe the weather will keep most people in today," Tansa suggested as she pushed her own hair up into spikes. She sounded hopeful. "We need at least one more day of calm."

"You mean that Prince Zaron needs it."

"Yes," she agreed. "The rest of us could pack up and be gone from one bell to the next quarter if we had to. We've always been prepared for it, given our precarious position with the queen. However, getting Za out -- that's becoming more and more dangerous. I don't know who among our own people we can trust."

"I know," Mai said. She put a hand on Tansa's arm, a silent reassurance that she would do what she could.

"I am going to prepare for us to leave," Tansa decided with a quick nod of her head. I hadn't wanted to hear those words and I snarled at the bookcase. "Not Za's fault, my love. We'd have been going anyway, given the circumstances. He just gives us a cause to fight for rather than simply retreating from the field of battle without ever understanding what we face. The Queen is not going to hire us, you know, and that means she'll count us as an enemy. The city is going to hell. It makes sense that we leave."

"Where will we go?" I asked.

"I don't know yet," she admitted. "Some of that, I think, is going to depend on the prince."

I nodded. "I am going out to check things. The rain is a good cover. If it looks bad -- well, I suppose we better be ready. How could that woman be even this much of a fool!"

"She's going to look like the bravest of us all, staying behind and holding out against the demons and the horrible peasants, while the rest of us run for safety. At least that's what she'll claim unless we can get Prince Zaron somewhere where the truth will help. Be careful out there today. And take some of the jewels -- no, do it. We need to spread them out. If you are halfway across town and we need to leave the building, I don't want to think you'll be without funds to get out and join us."

"The guards at the gates are not going to want any of us to leave and risk the Queen's anger."

"I know."

I nodded and drew one of the ugly, dark cloaks out of the closet. It rested heavier on my shoulders than it should have been because there were jewels sewn in the seams, though not in the hem where it might catch. The shoulder pack I took was the same.

"Should I look in on --" I said with a wave to the bookcase.

"I'll make certain he has breakfast. Sirma will be here soon to check the wound. He's worried about the fever. I don't think Prince Zaron even realized we were there that last time we checked on him."

I nodded agreement, no less assured. I was going out, I knew, to escape having to deal with our guest. I didn't want to care about the damned Prince Heir -- but then I thought about how he had reacted to this business, and how his concern had always seemed to be for others. He was not like his mother and sisters, and as much as I still idolized his father, Za apparently cared more for the people around him. His father had never showed much concern others, even if he had been better than most.

I left Tansa's office with a final nod but no words of farewell. I hated saying such things in times where the conditions were volatile; I'm not normally surreptitious, but it always felt like a bad omen to say good-bye in times of danger. The halls were busy today, and some of the guards were just getting in from their patrols outside the building.

"Nothing to report," Elmas said before I could ask her. "Except that it is damned wet. No one came near the building. I think they fear what we'll do under the circumstances."

"I'd like to think someone out there is wise enough to worry," I said. "I'm going back to the inn for a few hours."

"Be careful. Be *damned* careful."

I nodded and went out the side door and it closed behind me with a loud thump.

Not an omen. Not a sign that I was cut off from them.

The Lost Way Inn was the best spot for me today. I could get some news there -- poor me, off in Kira village when all hell broke loose here, and only now able to get back in; it was a simple enough tale. Danisin would wonder at the truth, and I might even send him on to the Company today. I'd warned Tansa that I would someday, and this might be the only chance we had. He'd make an excellent mercenary. Besides, the Company always needed good cooks.

The streets ran with water and debris, and the entire town stank. If it rained for much longer, the rivulets would grow and sweep all the refuse away to the river. I snarled and sidestepped everything I could, pulling the cloak up and the hood over my head. I barely avoided a patrol of unhappy City Guards who probably would have liked to grab anyone right now. I didn't see any of the Palace Guards, but that wasn't a surprise. They wouldn't come out of Summer Cloud until the weather turned better.

The rain fell harder. Maybe it was the gods doing us a favor since I didn't think there would be much trouble from the townspeople in this downpour, though the city might float away before too long. One had to be wary of gods acting in the world. They were made for grand gestures, and a city destroyed by a flood to stop the riots might suit them very well.

I almost slipped, grabbed at a pole, and it nearly gave way as well. Somehow, I kept to my feet. I mumbled a curse and started to move back out along the path --

I smelled something odd. Something *wrong*.

A heartbeat later I heard high-pitched singing -- or so it seemed at first. I threw myself into a shadowy corner by the nearest building out of pure instinct, even before I realized the sound was the terrified screams of people. The mass of bodies came towards me, and their unholy screams sent me scurrying as far into the corner as I could get, rolling into a tight ball. I didn't want to look. I didn't want to see what was happening --

I still watched through the slits between the fingers that

covered my face. The people ran like a multitude of rats before a herd of cats. Mindless; I saw three fall and were trampled beneath the crowd that followed. The screaming never ceased, though some gasped for breath before they began again. I could barely see the faces since they stared ahead, mindless with their fear.

The odd scent grew stronger, something like fire and decay, and with it came a palpable sense of wrongness so intense that I tried to batter my way through the wall to get away, hitting it with hands and feet, pounding as I started to scream. Run -- I had to run --

No.

Some little whisper of sanity caught hold in my brain. I thought of Kintansa who would need to know about this. I thought of Prince Zaron who had warned us about the demons. I could see them now, moving just into sight; huge, dark creatures with snake-like bodies, long and twisting, but moving on four limbs, each ending in hands that were mostly claws and so sharp that they beheaded people with a single swipe. The monstrous long heads had huge, hinged jaws. The demons grabbed at the nearest humans, devouring parts of them.

And on their backs rode Hasana, Aia, and Kwana, their silk dresses immaculate, their hair worked into fanciful styles, and their faces fixed with smiles that would have been better shown in a hall filled with adoring subjects, rather than a place where those people ran in terror and died by the teeth of their mounts.

I wanted to run. I wanted to scream. I slapped my hand over my mouth so hard that my lips burned. I burrowed back into a ball, and I stayed there, expecting to be found. Stayed. Listened. Waited long after silence filled the street.

When I moved, I realized that no one else had come by me, despite the time I'd spent curled up and afraid. The scent still filled the air, but it wasn't as strong or as troubling as before. I shivered, but I made myself stand and step away from the wall. My knuckles bled and hurt where I'd pounded at the building. At some point, I'd been ill, but the rain still fell in copious amounts and washed me clean.

It had not rained enough to do the same for the street. Pieces of bodies laid strewn across the road and up against the buildings. I walked over an arm, a leg, and a head with the mouth still wide in a silent scream and the eyes bulging with fear.

I needed to get to the Inn. I could sit down there, rest, recover before I --

I stopped, and a new fear nearly overcame me.

The demons had been heading westward, towards the Lightning Headquarters.

I spun, tripped over a leg and fell. Mud sucked at my clothing, and I could smell blood now which had overcome the other scent, even as I moved after the creatures. They'd been gone a long time. The dead lay everywhere along the path and I wondered if anyone had survived.

The trail led straight to the building.

I didn't know where the demons had gone. I saw no sight, sound, or scent of them. They had been here, though. Bodies laid everywhere, and I feared if I looked closely, I would recognize some. The double doors had been torn from the frame and tossed aside. I saw no movement inside.

I stopped. I wanted to drop to my knees and never move -- or else trace those monsters and kill them. Or let them kill me. I wanted to run away before I learned --

I had to know. I went across the road, up the steps -- past the head of Jandrin, who must have tried to hold the doors. A dozen other bodies had been tossed around, with pieces of more still at the doorways and --

And a vast skeleton lay stretched out across the inner hall, claws dug into the floor. Fragments of arrows and swords lay all around it, but one sword must have gone straight through the skull into the brain. I could see an odd spider-web design of cracks through the bone, all radiating around a nearly perfect slit that could only have been made by a good sword.

So, they could be killed.

The mass that had been the living creature had disappeared, though a gray ash seemed to have fallen all round it. The demon's bones filled the entry hall all the way to the stairs, so that I had to crawl over them.

I made my way along the edge, careful not to touch the bones. No sign of life clung to them, but I didn't trust --

"Captain Mai."

Elmas stood a few feet beyond the skull, her arm in a makeshift sling, a cut still bleeding down the side of her cheek. Her face seemed a decade older than she had been when I had last seen her.

"What -- how --" I said. My voice sounded hoarse, and the words didn't want to come out.

"You better get upstairs. The commander will want to see you."

Kintansa still lived. I didn't ask about wounds. I didn't ask about the other dead, though I saw some even here on the steps -- Andan, Camtis, Geja -- I rushed past them and up another set of stairs, these free of bodies. Sirma stood at the top of the steps and moved out of my way. He looked bleak, but then anyone would have here. It didn't mean Kintansa --

I did not knock. The door stood open anyway, and a small crowd had gathered inside. I hadn't heard the angry words until I stood at the edge of the opening, unable to see --

"Get the hell out of my way!" I ordered.

People leapt aside.

Kintansa sat at her desk, a bandage around her head, her left hand swathed in so much cloth that I feared for the damage. Then I hardly realized that Prince Zaron stood behind the Commander's chair, for whatever trouble that might mean.

"Praise all the gods," I said, my heartfelt words silencing the start of more protests. "How did you kill it?"

"Perseverance," Tansa replied. I saw relief in her eyes as well. "And, I think, insanity -- though you'd have to ask Za that one. He's the one who put the sword through the creature's head."

I glanced at the prince. He looked feverish, and the blood on his chest appeared to be his own -- but he remained steady on his feet and met my look with a nod of relief.

"What happened to the princess?" I asked.

"Princess?" Kintansa looked startled.

"There were three demons, and each had a Princess riding on them," I said. I did my best to keep my voice calm, but Tansa looked worried; she knew me well. I swallowed and continued. "Out in the streets -- people running and screaming. The demons brought madness with them, and they killed ... I don't know how many. Hundreds that I saw, and maybe thousands of others for all I know. The Princesses were sitting like goddesses on the finest mounts. I can't say they controlled what the demons did, but they were certainly part of it."

"We heard the sound," Tansa said. "And saw the crowd coming. Tried to hold at the door, but the demon knocked it open. The demon made a sort of high-pitched sound, but we only heard it once it was so close. Many went insane at the sound, but a few of us stood at the stairs. I don't know how we did it, Mai. I really don't. I wanted to run and scream with the others, but --"

"But you are the Commander of Lightning Company," I said. I dared to put my hands on her desk and lean there, almost too weak to stay to my feet. "Discipline. I think that's what saved me as well, though it was harder out there by myself. It took me too long afterward to think clearly enough to realize the direction they headed. I'm sorry --"

"You couldn't have done anything except shove a sword up its ass."

I unexpectedly gave a little laugh and saw a better reaction in some of the others, too, though Prince Zaron looked startled and blushed.

"I was -- I was coming back to the building," Kisi said. He looked pale white, and I wasn't certain he knew he had been wounded. One of the others had wrapped up his shoulder and neck. "I saw -- I thought I saw people, flying upward as though on a gentle wind, going to the roof of the warehouse. But I thought I was crazy. It drove us all crazy."

"It did," Kintansa agreed. "We cannot stay here. Get your things. Pack up weapons and supplies. Do it as quickly as you can. Za, sit down. Mai, tell me everything you can remember."

I watched Za, hoping he understood. If he argued with her now, the others were not going to trust him. The boy was smart, though. He gave a bow of his head and crossed to the nearest chair and dropped into it. He had paled and he still bled.

And he had killed the demon.

I feared that I might be the only one without an injury. I tried not to be embarrassed -- or angry. The others left the room to do as Tansa ordered``. I heard whispers of anger, of sadness -- I heard people crying as soon as they were no longer in the presence of the Commander. This was going to be hell.

"Mai?"

"I'm sorry I wasn't here," I said softly.

"That's not something to apologize for, you know. You survived, as did I, thanks to Za. As far as I can tell, those people who were in here in my office are all that's left of the Company.

"No." I felt the world go out from under me and I caught

hold of the desk to stay to my feet.

"Mai -- *Mai listen to me*. It's a damned good thing that you aren't injured, at least not badly. We need you."

Kintansa was admitting to her own weakness and asking for help, though not for herself. I took a deeper breath and nodded again.

"Where are we going?" I asked.

"North to the mountains." She moved her hand and winced. I wanted to cradle her in my arms and take her somewhere safe -- but there was no such place. The mountains? Why would that stop the demons? They would follow -- they would find us again. Za's fault. They were after him --

Or were they?

"They didn't know the prince was here, did they?" I asked as I pulled a chair over to the desk and sat. I fought to keep my voice steady.

"No, they didn't seem to know, and since he leapt forward and killed the thing, I don't think the Queen could have learned. We can't be certain with magic involved. I think though --" She stopped, glanced at Za who looked too pale. "I think destroying the demon frightened the others enough that they left rather than risk another battle and lose another one."

"They could only get one inside at a time," I said. "Aren't we safer here --"

"They'll destroy the building," Za said. "I imagine they're planning on how to do so even now."

Of course, he was right.

"Tell me what you saw out there," Kintansa ordered.

I focused on her and told the tale. They had seen much of what I had, except for the Princesses and a few of the other small details. I could hear the others out in the hall; they were getting organized and heading downstairs. We would be leaving soon.

Sirma came to look over both the commander and the prince. I went off into the bedroom to get -- I didn't know what. How could we leave this? The room was lovely. Should I pack the little porcelain animals? Should I wrap the elegant gown she'd saved, but never worn again, after we left Summer Cloud Palace? What about my old uniform, still hanging in the back corner of the closet?

That one, yes. It might come in handy if we needed some authority. I grabbed it out and tossed it on the bed. I got some warm clothing for both of us -- and I wrapped the little glass animals in shirts and pants and packed them all carefully into the bags we would carry. I pulled both up on my shoulders and headed into the other room.

Tansa was on her feet. She'd shoved papers into a case that would go over her shoulder. Her hand had been re-bandaged, and I could see the fingers now -- all of them there. She had a cut on the leg, too, but she didn't seem to have trouble walking.

Sirma still worked with Zaron. The prince had leaned back in the chair, and Sirma carefully placed a few stitches to close the chest wound. Za's side bled again, as did lesser cuts on his face. He didn't wince as the needle pulled the skin together, but I thought it might be because he was too exhausted and weak. I watched Sirma finish. Then he packed a few of his bandages and herbals into a pouch and handed that over to Za to carry. The prince changed into a different tunic, this one plain cotton with no embroidery. His cloak lay across the back of the chair where he sat. We had to get him out of the building and out of the city, but there would be problems.

"The moment Prince Zaron steps outside, someone is going to recognize him," I said. "Especially since the Queen will have people especially looking for him. Even beneath that cloak, all it will take is one glimpse of his face or that braid."

Tansa put three knives on the desk. "We'll have to run

that risk. We'll put him in with the rest of the people, while you and I draw most of the attention."

"People are going to panic, seeing us leave," I said.

"They are already panicked. We can't help them, and we can't stay here, Mai."

"I know. The Prince --"

"You should leave me behind," Za said. For a moment his eyes closed. I feared we would be carrying him out -- but maybe we would do better disguising him that way. He looked back at me again. "If someone recognizes me, it will just be more trouble."

"Chances are that they won't," Tansa replied. "Just keep that braid hidden. Since the royal family is the only one who wears their hair like that --"

"Only the males," I pointed out. Za had picked up the end of the braid and looked it over. A great deal of hair had come free and he frowned as he tried to tuck some back into the tie.

"I always wondered why you have the braid," Sirma said with a slight frown.

"My grandfather -- my Eastern grandfather -- insisted I have a braid since it's a sign of power in his lands." He gave up and let the ragged hair fall back over his shoulder and down to his waist. "My mother threatened to cut it off so that I could not be emperor. I'm sure she intended to if I ever got close to that position."

"Ah," Tansa said with a nod. "I think I remember something about the practice. Take one of the knives, Za. I know you can handle weapons but be careful. I keep my knives very sharp."

"Do you? Good."

He picked up the knife closest to him, pulled the braid around and hacked it off at the back of his neck.

His dark hair fell in feathery black strands back around his face.

We all three stared at him in shocked dismay.

He held the severed braid in one hand. "We better not leave this here." He shoved the hair into the pouch Sirma had given him.

"Prince Zaron," Sirma began, his voice trembling this time.

"It is the best way to make certain I am not recognized," he said. Hair fell over his face and he brushed it back. His hands remained steady. "This will take time to get used to, though."

"Let me trim some of the hair around your face," I said, recovering before the others did. "And then we had better leave."

CHAPTER EIGHT

The hair tickled at the back of his neck. Za brushed at it again, his mind thinking it was an insect of some sort. He wondered if he would ever get used to having shorter hair. It fell into his eyes, brushed against his neck and ears -- and was the best disguise any of them could have devised.

He hadn't looked in the mirror before they left the building. Za knew he would not look like himself. He didn't even move like himself. Everything ached, and he'd stumbled along like a lame man.

Ata, he thought. Pulling back the path was more difficult than an afternoon exercise. He had to keep moving or he risked not only his own safety, but also the lives of everyone who stood with him.

The others knew who he was. They glanced his way sometimes, and he didn't dare look into their faces. Someone had shoved him once. He had fallen to his knees, cursed, and got up again. He didn't try to find out who had knocked him down. No one repeated that pettiness.

He just kept walking with the rest of them, though the soldiers increasingly moved away so that he walked alone. It might not even be because of who he was, but only that he was not one of them.

"This won't work," Mai said. She took his arm. "Come over with Tansa and me. Kisi and Sirma are there, too. You won't look as odd as you do by yourself."

Za thought he ought to argue, but he wasn't certain why. For a little while, he had considered going off by himself. They really didn't need him, and he hated that he needed them instead.

"Za," she said and pulled at his arm a little.

He went with her. It would have been harder to argue. They were still in the city, though he could see the gate not far ahead, along with the crowd gathered there. Za found himself increasingly grateful that Mai had pulled him over to stand with them.

He didn't think they realized, but he had *never* been out in a crowd of commoners before, let alone people who were this upset. The sounds filled him with apprehension because he had no idea how to deal with people who were not under his command. Za had been dealing with people like Mai and Tansa without a problem, but these strangers -- these *angry* strangers --

Mai might have figured out how he felt, probably because she'd been a high-ranking guard at the palace. She moved closer to him and signaled Kisi around to the other side. The taller man still glared for a moment, but then he appeared to remember his duty, if not to Prince Zaron, at least to Mai. Zaron had figured out that Captain Mai held a high rank in the mercenaries, too.

The day had grown darker by the time they had reached the northern gate. Za feared they would be hours getting any closer, though. The crowd of people had grown, packing in closer and closer.

"Elmas," Kintansa shouted and drew the woman's attention. "Bring out the colors."

Zaron hadn't realized the woman carried the banner. Now

she unfurled the cloth and lifted the pole so that the Lightning symbol rose up above the crowd. People shouted, and many of them scrambled to move out of the way. That was a power he'd only seen in the royalty before -- and that made him think there might have been a reason for the demons to come after the Company that had nothing to do with his being in the building.

Zaron had feared those deaths had been his fault because the demons had sensed him there. What did any of them know about how demons worked? However, the demon hadn't seemed much interested in him, even when he had come close enough to kill it.

He'd always heard about the Lightning Company at the palace. The guards talked about them sometimes, and never said anything good. Endris had not taken part in those conversations.

They began to move closer --

"Damn them to the deepest hells," Mai snarled. She was looking back over her shoulder.

Zaron glanced back and felt a wave of new panic take him. The banner of the Palace Guard stood up above the crowd, and people moved aside for the soldiers. Worse than that, though, he could hear the shout of one of the men.

"Close the gate by order of the Queen!"

"The gate guards haven't heard him yet above the noise of the crowd," Kintansa said. "We better make certain that they don't get close enough to be heard. Kisi do your best to keep the others moving. Just do it. Get them out so that if Mai and I need to move quickly, we don't have to worry about the rest of you!"

"And what about him?" Kisi asked with a nod to Zaron.

"He better come with us," Mai said.

Zaron wondered if it was to keep him safe from the rest of the people in the Company or because she thought he might be a good distraction for the Palace Guards. Za didn't ask, and he didn't argue. They began to work their way back against the crowd which was far more difficult than going with it. Zaron pushed people aside as he tried to stay close to Mai and Kintansa. Maybe they wanted to lose him here. Perhaps he should ask --

Mai glanced back and looked glad to find he was still at her back. They were within a couple yards of the Palace Guard. Captain Gar stood at the lead beside the banner boy and continued to shout his orders. Za wished the crowd to get much louder -- and they did just then. Chance, he knew, but he felt a strange chill go through him and for a moment, he almost heard Endris whispering his last orders again --

He had no time to consider what had already happened. Mai leapt forward, grabbed Gar by the arm and pushed a knife up to the man's side, though she didn't use it.

"Mai," he snarled. "This is treason --"

"This is keeping you and your people from being killed by a rioting, angry mob," Kintansa corrected. People hurried past, worried at what they saw and moving faster to get away. Zaron counted only ten of the Palace Guards, all of them in uniform, and all but Gar looking worried. "What kind of an idiot are you? Do you really think that the people here are going to quietly let you trap them in the city after what happened? Do you want to start that kind of trouble on top of everything else?"

"The Queen ordered," he said, and Za saw unexpected panic in his face. "We must obey the queen or be charged with treason and supporting the prince and his demons."

"The prince didn't --" Mai began.

Zaron put a hand on her arm, and she stopped.

"We've no choice," the banner boy said. He couldn't have been more than fourteen. His voice was barely loud enough to be heard. "She gave us no choice."

None of them had recognized the prince, standing right there by Kintansa. Zaron stopped himself from pushing the strands of hair from his face, and kept his head slightly bowed. He did nothing. This was neither in his hands nor was it his decision.

"Do any of you want a choice?" Kintansa asked leaning closer to Gar. More of the crowd went around them, rushing now before the gate closed. "If so, then move on with us. If we work together, we can all get out of the city alive. Try to close that gate, and people are going to get very angry and very scared."

The boy, wiser than some of the others, nodded. "I'd fight for the queen, but I don't want to die for nothing."

"We need to trap the prince," Gar protested.

"If the prince called demons, do you really think locking a gate is going to stop him?" Mai asked.

Others nodded. Still more people surged past them, and the line never seemed to end.

"My father -- he seen something different," one of the soldiers said. "He seen the princesses on the demons. He's deaf, you see. Didn't hear the sounds like others did, wot drove them all crazy. But they scared him, and he ran to tell me. No one wants to listen, though. But -- but I hoped to go out if I got near the gate."

"Treason," Captain Gar said, though not so loudly.

"We need to go now," Kintansa said. "Any who want to come with us are welcome to take the same chances that we are taking. What you do outside the gate is your own business. Gar, just keep moving along."

Mai cast one glance at Zaron, but he only nodded and wisely said nothing. He moved in behind Mai in case any of the others thought to kill her, save their captain, and gain the approval of the Queen. He didn't think any of these people would be that stupid, though. The Queen always found fault.

Gar didn't argue as they moved forward, still under the banner of the Palace Guard. Zaron found it funny that people moved aside, but not with the same swiftness when they retreated before the mercenary's banner. He could see that banner already going out the gate and felt a wave of relief, even if he still stood on the wrong side and with a group of people he most certainly didn't trust.

Kintansa had moved back to be with the soldiers. She spoke quietly to them, and he didn't hear enough to know what was said. They were moving faster and getting quite close to the gate.

"If you say one word, Captain Gar, you will not live to see what happens afterward," Mai warned. "Once we are through the gate, you can say and do as you please."

"I'm not a fool," he replied with a sullen growl.

"You haven't proven that yet."

He grunted and said no more. Mai shifted slightly behind him, the knife still in hand, and now poised behind his kidney. Kintansa got the other soldiers to spread out around them. There might be trouble with any one of them, but it was Gar whom Za really mistrusted. Besides, spread out they could not mass an attack.

Za thought again about all the time Gar spent with the Queen, and he knew the man was not about to betray her now. He could say nothing, but he probably didn't need to. Mai wasn't going to be careless. Za stayed at her back and found it strange that the woman clearly trusted him there.

Closer and closer to the gate. People stepped aside, but with less speed as the path narrowed near the gate. Kintansa moved closer to Mai who was the one most likely to have trouble. They were only a few yards away and some of the Palace Guards had already gone through the gate. Some of the Company lingered on the other side and were clearly watching those soldiers, as well as waiting for Kintansa and Mai.

Closer.

Gar likely realized he had no chance of survival, or at least of having his old position back, if he let them all escape. He still didn't know that the prince stood within reach of him. Za would have found that amusing at another time, but not here and now, with swords drawn all around them, the commoners ready to riot, and the mercenaries prepared for treachery.

This could not go well.

Predictably, it was Gar who lifted his head and shouted. "I order you in the name of the Queen --"

He grunted and fell.

A heartbeat later and they stood amid a riot. Gar's shout had started people panicking. Some guards might have been heading to close the gate, but the rioters went crazy, and the noise grew louder. Someone hit Za in the back, and he almost went down, tripping over Gar who might not be alive.

Mai caught his arm and pulled him to the side and away from the worst of the trouble. They no longer moved toward the gate, instead skirting along the outer edges of the trouble. Kintansa kept with them.

"Damned fool!" the Commander hissed. Za looked around and saw the Palace Guard banner trampled in the mud. He hoped the boy had gotten away.

"He was dead if he didn't," Za said softly. "He was the Queen's pet, you know. She only kept him because he obeyed her every wish. Spent a great deal of time with her --"

People began to press in around them again, so he didn't dare say more, but he had the feeling they both realized what he had meant. Gar might have known about the demons. A few of the Palace Guards stood with the City Guards who were holding the gate. Za knew they would get the gate closed soon, even if that meant they would have to kill people to do so. Gar was going to win and trap them inside, though at least all the others had apparently made it out.

"Never make it," Mai growled. "Kintansa --"

"You're right. We need to get clear of this mess. We'll go out another way, now that it's just the two -- three -- of us."

They turned and retreated from the mass of people, moving out along the edges of buildings -- a long way from the gate which Za could no longer see. He felt relief that they were not going to try to press through, but he wasn't happier about being trapped in Willoway.

"What are we going to do?" Za asked.

"Back to the inn," Mai said. Tansa gave a reluctant nod of agreement. "Then we find another way out. You have to trust us, Za."

The prince gave a nod of agreement and followed them into the shadows of the desperate city.

No choice for any of them.

CHAPTER NINE

The Lost Way Inn sat more than halfway back across the city and perhaps too close to the Summer Cloud Palace to be safe, though I hadn't thought that way for many years. I couldn't think of anywhere else to go. We dared not go near the Lightning headquarters. I hoped that they wouldn't destroy the building with the hope that they would lure Kintansa back. Not all of Gar's people had been on our side so they'd be quick to report that she hadn't gotten out -- or at least they hadn't seen her do so. The longer the three of us stayed out of sight, the more certain the Queen's people would be that we had escaped.

They would not know about Prince Zaron, though. I had to hope that our own people would not give up that secret.

The three of us circled around a bit. I would not make a straight run at the only place that might be safe. I knew all the paths that would lead there, and away again. I had expected trouble for years. I had never thought it would be something this terrible.

We had a graphic view of how horrible the world had turned as we tried to make our way through the city. The dead that had been killed by demons lay scattered across the main road, as far as we could see. We darted across the usually busy street, leaping over bodies, the faces that were not trampled grotesque with the fear that had killed them.

We found other signs of the terror and those no better. Not everyone affected by the demons had died. Many wandered around, lost to the world, crying out in fear, though most could do no more than make a whisper of sound now. A few people led afflicted friends or family away, watching us with worried, furtive stares as though we might be trouble.

The city had died. The Queen and her darling daughters had killed it, this place that had been called a haven of peace and prosperity. Oh, it had never been a perfect city. I was not going to pretend to such foolishness, even now. Whatever we'd had was gone, though. Willoway would never be the same again.

When we spotted others on the streets, Kintansa moved aside and farther into the shadows, so we were less obviously together. She'd gotten a cloak from one of the dead, covering her odd hair and shadowing her face, though she didn't obviously try to hide. Zaron stayed with me, and a couple times he even played at being afflicted, with me leading him toward home. He did an excellent job of it so that the City Guards who rode past didn't even glance our way. I could see despair in their faces. They didn't know what to do with a city that seemed half dead and half filled with madmen.

We reached the narrow street that curved around to my inn. I saw no dead here, but the feeling of dread hung in the air as it had all the rest of the way. I waited for Kintansa to catch up with us as we knelt between two buildings, our goal in sight.

"We don't dare go in together. I don't even know what we're going to find," I said. "Go to the back door and hide near there. I'll see what I can learn, and if it is safe, I'll let you in. If not, you might have to climb up to the room. You know the way, Tansa."

She nodded. I had noted how she had begun limping, and so was Za who also appeared to have some wounds bleeding. I looked at Tansa's hand, but she just gave me another nod and a nudge.

"Go," she said.

I wanted to stay and give them more orders and instructions. Then I reminded myself that Za was the heir to the throne and maybe giving constant orders was not a good plan. I had started to see the first hints of rebellion in his eyes and wondered what had held him back so long. Injury and shock, I supposed.

Despite Za's status, I also reminded myself that Tansa was my commanding officer. We didn't always stand on rank between the two of us, but I could see that look in her face as well.

I gave a bow of my head and walked away. I didn't look back, though my hands trembled, and I felt ill for fear that I would never see the two again. I didn't like the reaction, and I did my best to hide it as I went around the curve of the road and hurried toward the building.

The street and the inn looked deceptively calm and untouched by the madness. A few people, no more than six, moved along the edges of the buildings or hurried past doors and into buildings. We did not acknowledge each other. I noted them, but I kept my eyes on the doorway to the Lost Way Inn. The door stood open, the interior dark. I could not see into it, and I felt a cold wave of dread pass through me as I drew closer.

I had my hand on the knife at my belt as I moved up the steps. I thought about going cautiously and moving to the side, trying to see what was within the building before I charged in.

I wouldn't see anything more than I saw now. I walked in.

It looked as though the inn had been the scene of the mother of all brawl fights. I didn't think more than a single table remained intact and perhaps a couple benches. Broken pottery littered the floor, and the stink of liquor rose as I entered. I found myself counting coins lost with each stinking step.

Danisin sat at the only intact table.

"There you are," he said, his voice a little husky. "I wondered if you'd survived."

"Barely," I admitted. "What a mess -- and I don't mean the inn."

He nodded. I could see that he had bruises on his face and cloth wrapped around one hand. "You might find another cup somewhere," he said with a nod towards the back of the room. "I managed to save half a dozen bottles of our best. They went crazy, Mai. Just went insane, and not like those poor souls who saw the demons."

"You know about that part," I said and went to scavenge something, so I could join in him a drink -- or ten. I found a cup by the kitchen door and returned. I needed a little more information before I brought in the other two.

"Heard about it," he said. "Heard the distant screams but didn't run off to look like some of the fools."

"I saw," I said and shuddered. "I really don't know how I survived. The demons and the princesses riding --"

"Careful," he said softly. "The Queen has already said that anyone claiming such things about the princesses will be hung for treason before the day is out."

"Has she? Not a surprise there," I said. I didn't mention the demons and princesses again, but I could tell he believed me.

Danisin poured from a bottle of fine old wine, and I sipped. He filled his cup, lifted it and looked at me.

"Who are you really?" he asked. "It's a game I've played for years, you know -- trying to piece together little hints and clues. This is not a time to play games. Can I trust you?"

"I served King Yasidin," I said. That won a nod and no sign of surprise. "I was a Captain in his guard, but I happened to be elsewhere in the city when they took him." A slight show of surprise this time, probably about the rank.

"And whom do you serve now?" he asked.

"Commander Kintansa."

"Ah. Mercenary," he said and gave a quick nod. "I had wondered. There were a few times when you disappeared, and you were rather bad-tempered the times they left town without you."

"I imagine so," I said, thinking back to those days. "And now let's hear your story."

"Not nearly as interesting as yours," Danisin admitted and smiled, though he winced and touched the corner of his lip. "I was with the City Guard until I caught my commander demanding protection money from shopkeepers. He went to the labor camps. I couldn't find another commander who would have me."

"Amazing how doing the right thing can get you into so much trouble," I mumbled. I sipped the fine southern wine and wondered if I could get drunk. If I dared to. "And that brings us to a choice you must make, Danisin. I am going to go bring two people in the back door. You can go out the front and close it behind you, or you can close the door and come back to the table. You don't have much time to make the decision."

I stood and headed for the kitchen. It was a mess as well, and I had to kick things out of the way to get to the door. I wondered if we could salvage enough food to make a stew. We would need to eat soon.

Kintansa and Za hurried through the door.

"People wandering around too close," Tansa whispered. She saw my face and frowned. "What problems now?"

"Danisin," I said. "I told you about him. We've had a

moment of honesty, and he knows about me. He was with the city guard until he proved too honest for them."

"Not an uncommon tale," she said.

I closed the door and put the bar back into place. I thought about shoving the table over as well, but I just wasn't that ambitious.

"He doesn't know whom I am bringing in, but I gave him the option to leave. Let's see what he decided."

I was not surprised to find the door closed and bared, and Danisin back at the table.

"Commander Kintansa. And honor to meet you," he said and with hardly a glance at the boy.

This was no time to keep secrets. I sat down. Kintansa sat beside Danisin and gave me a nod as Za settled beside me.

"And this is Prince Zaron," I said with a nod to our other companion. Best just to get it out.

Danisin started to smile at the joke, then shook his head, and then put both his hands on the table and stared.

"By the Gods, known, unknown and forgotten, what the hell is going on?"

I told the story, though Za filled in some of the things about the palace and what had happened there. Danisin looked startled every time the prince spoke; there was no way to hide his education or the anger and distrust when he spoke about his mother and sisters.

We had downed a good amount of the wine by then which probably wasn't wise since I couldn't remember the last time we'd had a meal. Danisin found some bread and cheese. We shared it around.

"I'll stand guard," Danisin said as he pushed his cup aside. "I have done that every night so far. The rest of you get some sleep."

I nodded and stood -- and did not give way to worries about his loyalty, though I saw the fear in Za's face. For a moment I thought the prince might finally try to assert his control, but he shook his head as though in an argument with himself and went quietly with Kintansa and me to the stairs.

We put Za in my bedroom despite his protests. Then I dragged a bed from across the hall, tilting it so that it went through the door, and dropped it between the door and the desk, leaving just barely enough room to get the door open.

Kintansa sat down on the mattress and made a show of straightening out the blankets. "What the hell are we going to do now?" Tansa finally asked.

"Sleep," I said. The door to the other room stood open in case there was trouble. Za had stretched out on the bed, still fully clothed, and either asleep or unconscious. I thought I ought to check on him. I sat down instead. "Sleep while we can, Tansa. There are not going to be a lot of chances."

"Trust Danisin," she said. It was not a question. She all but threw herself on the bed, cursed at a pain in her hand or leg -- or both -- and was asleep before I could get the covers up over the two of us.

Safe here, I thought. Not for long, but safe for the moment. I curled up with Tansa. Tomorrow I would start looking for a way out. What we did after we got out of the city, I didn't know. Tomorrow --

We didn't get to sleep that long.

Danisin pounded on the door to the room. I'd already gotten up, having heard him on the stairs.

"What's wrong?" I asked, pulling clothing into place. Tansa did the same, though she looked half asleep still.

"City Guards out on the street and checking every building," he said. "You better get the two of them in hiding."

I cursed under my breath. Prince Zaron stood at the door to the other room, and he looked awake. Tansa was up and moving as well.

"Both of you get --"

"No time to take out the other bed," Za pointed out, which was an excellent observation. "Get the commander into hiding. I can be your nephew, Mai. They are more likely to recognize her than me."

"Yes. Tansa, go. Just do it!"

Kintansa snarled a curse and darted to my desk, slid it aside, pulled up the floor, and headed into the small cubby hole there. It would have been difficult for two people to hide within there. She worked the lever herself, and the desk slid back into place.

"Back to bed," I told Za. "Danisin, did you hear about Za?"

"Yes."

"Just let them in. If they knew about us already, they wouldn't be checking every building."

"Be careful," he warned and gave a worried look toward the prince. He hadn't spent time with Za out on the street. I knew he could handle himself.

I heard Danisin hurrying away before I could say more to him.

I did what I could to make the bed look like only one person had been there, but I found spots of blood, and there was no time to clean up or change sheets. I could hear the guard downstairs at the door.

"Za, this bed. Wounds," I said softly as I hurried into the room where he was in bed.

He nodded, slipped quietly from the bed, and moved like a ghost across the floor. The boy had talents that were not what I expected in the heir --

The Art of Ata. I didn't know much about the eastern discipline, and I was starting to believe I needed to find out more. Endris used to mention the philosophy to me --

I laid down as quietly as possible. We didn't have long to wait. I hoped Tansa was alright. I hoped no one recognized the prince. I wished I had never gotten involved. I could have sent the boy on his way --

On his way to die, and what good would that have done? The princesses and their demon pets would still have been out there. The prince had helped, and he was still providing us with information --

I heard them coming up the stairs and opening doors.

"End of the hall," Danisin said with a bit of a growl. "I told you --"

"We have to check every room," a woman said. She sounded steady and professional. Good.

Za and I couldn't have slept through the noise, even if we had been dead drunk. I sat up. Za was on his feet when the door opened.

"See," Danisin said with a bit of a smirk. "I told you, Villat."

He knew the woman. Knew her well enough to be a bit snide and to maybe joke with her. I took that as a good sign, though I didn't relax. I was coming out into the room when the woman signaled Za away from the bed. She frowned looking at him, and for a moment I feared that even with the scraggly hair and peasant clothing, he was going to be recognized.

"What is the problem?"

"How were you wounded, boy?" she asked.

He kept his head bowed like a good little peasant in the face of authority. Our prince had a love of theater, I suspected.

"Riots," he mumbled, looked up just briefly and then down again. "Trying to get out the gate."

"Which one?"

"South," he said. Wise, not saying the north gate where the mercenaries had gone. "Tryin' ta get home. Came to stay with Aunt Mai instead."

That was more than the woman had asked, and a peasant

usually wouldn't have offered so much without more questions. However, Za looked unsteady, and I didn't think that was an act, either. I crossed and took hold of his arm. The older guards had started to move in on me, but Villat waved them off.

"Check the other room," she said.

"What is going on?" Danisin asked.

"Damned if I know," she mumbled. "We're just told to get out and look for anyone in hiding. By all the hells, anyone with half a brain would be in hiding by now."

Wise woman. I gave a little nod. "We had to close down to save what little is left after the damned rioters went through. I wish I could say I thought things would get better soon."

She nodded again.

"No one hiding in there," one of the men said. He scowled, and I had the feeling he didn't like how she talked to potential enemies.

"Continue searching the building," Villat said with a grim nod. "We dare not be lax."

That suited the man better. He and the other five left the room. Villat shook her head with a little disgust as they left, but she soon lost that look when she turned back to us.

"We've searched these rooms. Please remain here until we leave. Danisin, come with me."

I didn't want to see him go with her, but I thought we could trust her. Danisin gave me a nod of his head as he went out, the door closing behind him.

I got Za to sit back down on the bed.

"You did well, Za. It's all right. Go back to sleep now."

Kindly words from an aunt in case someone lingered nearby -- and I had the feeling someone did. Praise the Goddess of Truth that they hadn't questioned us too closely on our relationship or that none of them had a truth charm. It was also apparent that no one had seen the three of us together or that I'd let them in the back door. This was simply a check of all places. Having passed it, we might have fewer problems if we stayed here. Two days, no more. I walked back to my bed and sat down, working my way through ideas of how to get away from the city when the time came.

I heard the soldiers leave, but Danisin didn't come back upstairs, and I didn't let Tansa out, despite how she must feel by now. I waited and waited, and worried --

The door opened and closed again.

Not long afterward, Danisin came up the stairs. I was already at the door and letting him in. Za rose on an elbow but didn't get out of the bed. He looked pale and feverish again.

"I gave her some good wine and asked Vil for all the rumors," he confessed. "I worked with her back before I left the City Guard. When she made Captain, she even asked me to come back -- but I'd been free of it for too long, and I liked working here." He stopped and shook his head, no doubt thinking about how unlikely it would be that the Lost Inn ever opened again. "I can tell you straight out that there are many people out there who are questioning the story the Queen's put out about Prince Zaron and the demons. However, that doesn't mean they wouldn't hand him over to gain her good favor. Also, Queen Taranis is claiming that the mercenaries are in the employ of the enemy -- I'm not certain if she said which one -- and that they must be destroyed. Oddly, she has not linked the mercenaries to the prince."

"Oh, she wouldn't," Za said. I saw an odd smile for a moment. "The idea that any of the royal house, even one dealing with demons, would become allied with such a group is beyond her comprehension."

"And yours?" I asked as I crossed to the desk and began to carefully pull it back and open the door.

"Endris told me more than once that the only force I could trust in this city was the mercenaries, precisely because they did not rely on the Queen for their survival. I didn't realize he was one of you, but even so, he made sense."

I nodded and helped pull Tansa up. She didn't seem any worse for wear.

"I heard it all," she said and dropped into the chair by my desk, stretching out her legs. "We got lucky there. If it had been someone that Danisin didn't know, the person might have asked a few more questions, and something would have fallen apart."

"True," I agreed and felt a touch of a chill. "We'll work on it, just in case. But not now. Sleep yet. We need more sleep."

Neither of them argued. Za stayed in the bed in the outer room. Tansa and I curled up in my bed, and she was soon asleep. I thought the prince might be as well.

But I stayed awake for a long, long time still.

CHAPTER TEN

Prince Zaron had never hurt as much as he did when he awoke to find the light of day coming through the shuttered window at the Inn. He moved little at first, trying to find some part of his body that did not ache. How could his life have changed so quickly? He didn't know what to expect.

That thought stopped him. When was the last time he did not know what was going to happen? Change had been the way of each day since he'd left the palace, but all his life before that had been controlled by ritual and schedules -- and nothing dared ever be out of place.

Za hadn't realized the true enormity of the change in his life until now. He was awake before the others. There had always been someone awake before him in the palace, and while Danisin might still be downstairs, guarding, Za was virtually alone here. He did not move much, savoring a moment to himself before the Commander and the Captain awoke.

Savoring even a painful moment like this just for the sense of privacy.

Endris had sent him here. That had not been his decision. Everything they'd done since had been in the hands of others -- except two. He had severed the hair that tied him to the rule of the Empire. Za had never believed he would rule anyway, so it hadn't mattered.

And second ... he had not been told to leap forward and drive the sword into the head of the demon.

That had been *him* and his decision, perhaps the first real decision he'd ever made in his life. He wondered if that made him brave or a fool -- or both.

The moment came to him with an odd clarity while everything else since this madness began to fade. He had followed Kintansa down the stairs. She'd given him one look of worry, but they had no time for anything else. The demon had been as horrible as he remembered them from the first encounter. Za had wondered if the demon had come for him as it crowded into the lower level, tearing out walls, killing everyone in its reach.

When he and Kintansa reached the last steps of the stairs, the demon leapt forward at the commander and grabbed her by the leg. Za had desperately wished he had a sword --

And one appeared in his hand. He killed the demon with one strike through the top of the skull.

No one ever asked him where he had gotten the sword.

Magic. He knew that was what had happened and denied it at the same time. He could almost touch something Endris had given him at that moment before his friend died. A terrible gift; mages were evil, dark creatures --

Only Endris had not been so.

Mai was up; he had no more time to consider who or what he was now. They'd be doing something today. He would follow along as he had been already; they had kept him alive so far, and until Za learned more about the art of survival in the common world, he was not stupid enough to try to command himself, let alone them.

He followed them downstairs like an obedient puppy and used the outhouse while the others waited. Why was he starting to get annoyed?

Za needed a few moments to practice *Ata* and regain his calm. With *Ata*, he could look at what he had done and decide if he needed to adjust for future circumstances. Za couldn't follow the others forever. Their way was not his path; he must find his own way.

"How are you today, Za?" Tansa asked as sat at the single table. Danisin had gotten food together. He must have been sleeping by the door since there were still blankets piled up there.

"Sore," Za said and offered a bit of a smile. "As I imagine you and Mai are sore."

She nodded and made no more of it.

Let him pretend to be one of them. Surely, they knew he was not used to this kind of life. And yet, and yet...

It didn't bother him to sit at the table with them, and to eat coarse bread and cheese, and sip weak cider. He did not mind his wounds -- except that they slowed him. He'd won them honorably.

Though the pain in his side, where the demon had taken part of the bone, slowed him more than he liked. He knew it would be a longtime healing. He'd broken his leg once --

Best not to think about that, falling down the stairs, his mother watching --

"Za?"

"There are things I do not wish to remember from life at court," he admitted and sat down the cider which he had barely sipped. "But they come to me sometimes. I will try not to make any of it a problem."

"It hasn't been so far," Mai said, which he took as a compliment. "We've been moving pretty fast, and you have not been any trouble. However, I was thinking -- what is it you expect to do now?"

"I expect -- that I have a lot left to learn," he admitted to what he'd been thinking earlier. It was not easy to say, but Mai looked startled and pleased by the answer. "I don't want to make a mistake that gets others killed."

"Or you killed," Kintansa added. She frowned. "I am grateful that you leapt in and saved me from the demon, but I want you to stay safe as well."

"Why?" he asked. They both started to protest, but he lifted a hand, and they quieted -- the power of being royalty he supposed. Amusing how little it had meant at the palace. "I mean that in a very general way. What do you expect of me? Why are you worried about my survival?"

"You have always been the chosen heir," Kintansa said with a tilt of her head. "And now more so than before."

"Or maybe it is time for a new ruling house," Za replied; treason to say those words, but they'd done worse than talk about a needed change in the last few days. "I've read enough history to know that things change. The Grandfathers are old. No one talks about such things, but there is a reason why my mother acted now. If she waited until one or the other died, then someone stronger might have stepped in, and she would lose her chance."

"Well damn," Mai said. "I hadn't looked at the larger picture. You're right. Do you want to be the stronger person?"

"I am *not* the stronger," he said. He sipped the cider and saw how all three of them watched, waiting for more. He put the cup aside and nodded. "I might become stronger, maybe even in time to stop this from getting worse. What I really want, though, is *to learn what is needed* to stop this from getting worse. I can't do that if my true goal is to make certain that I win. They are not the same thing."

"They might be -- but you are right, they aren't at this moment," Mai agreed. Once she said those words, the other two didn't argue. "You are the only person we have, Prince Zaron, who knows anything about what the Queen and

Princesses might have been doing that led to this disaster. You are also right to point out that the two Emperors are getting too old to take up this kind of battle. We haven't seen either of them for a long time."

"It keeps them young in our minds," Danisin replied with a slight nod. "We still envision them as men in their prime. They're wise to stay away."

"I haven't seen either since my naming ceremony when I was five." There had been a week-long festival, food distributed, music played -- but he'd not enjoyed it much, made to wear perfect clothing and stand in perfect attendance. There had been a lot of gold, he remembered.

"Za?"

"I think there might be something in my memory that I need to recall," he admitted with a shake of his head. "It is the *Art of Ata*, you know. The mind begins to sort through matters, looking for a piece of information, but it does so in the background. Sometimes a piece of the answer is clear and will take my attention. If I were better trained, I wouldn't do that -- lose track of where I am and what I'm doing."

He supposed he sounded frustrated. He realized that was how he felt. Strange. He wasn't used to letting his emotions show and that unsettled him even more.

"Anything that might help would be good." Mai pushed another piece of bread his way. "My idea is that we hold up here for the day. Tonight, I'll study the city, and if I find a way out that I think is safe, we'll leave before dawn. The sooner we get clear of Willoway, the less chance of someone checking in on us again and recognizing Tansa. It's less likely they'll recognize you. And you should come with us, my friend. It's not safe here, and it's going to be worse if anyone figures out that I am with the mercenaries."

"But the inn --" Danisin said, his eyes darting around the place.

"Not safe," she replied. Za could see the loss in her face, too. "I'm sorry."

Danisin sighed and nodded. "I hadn't realized how much I enjoyed working here until just now," he admitted. "And mostly because you trusted me at it."

"There will be another inn," she said.

Za agreed though he said nothing aloud. He would not make promises he might not be able to fulfil. Za put that promise into a special place in his memory, though. He didn't need to say the words aloud.

They spoke for a little while longer, Mai explaining about some of the places she would check -- over the walls, under the walls, etc. Za found the explanations fascinating. He'd never thought a city known for being impregnable would have so many possible openings --

Someone tapped on the door. An odd pattern that unsettled the other three.

"City Guard," Danisin said softly. "Kintansa, in the kitchen. Don't try to go up the stairs -- they'd hear you. Go."

She didn't argue. Mai and Za remained at the table. Mai quickly spread the food around in a new pattern, so there was no visible sign there had been four of them, even tossing one of the cups to Kintansa as she started past.

Danisin went to the door and carefully opened the peephole.

"Villat," he said, both as a greeting and to let the others know.

"Let me in," she said. Za could barely hear her voice. "Fast."

Mai nodded, and Danisin pulled the bar up, opening the door only enough to let her slide through. Once she had come inside, he pushed the door shut and dropped the bar back into place.

"What are you doing here?" Danisin asked, waving her to

the table. She went and sat down, looking both weary and worried.

"It's crazy out there," she said and looked at Mai. "And the Queen has sent out orders that -- I just don't like the orders, Danis. You're the only one I can talk to about it."

She gave a worried glance to the other two, but Danisin nodded. "They're fine. What's happened?"

"The Queen called the City Guard to the palace -- all of us, with no exceptions. Anyone who did not attend was to be considered a traitor and turned over to the Palace Guard immediately. Wounds, no matter how severe, were not an excuse. We lost three people moving them. It was unreasonable. It was tyrannical!"

Her voice had risen, and her face went dark with rage. The unnecessary loss of the guards had severely affected her. She put her hands on the table. Danisin pushed his cider over to her, and she nodded and took a sip. Once she put the cup down, she looked steadier but no less pleased.

"There is more, isn't there?" Mai asked.

She nodded. "The announcement itself. Until further notice, we are to immediately kill anyone found on the streets after the ninth bell. And we are not to tell anyone about this new order."

Za had never felt such a sudden surge of revulsion and rage. Mai took hold of his arm. Za wasn't sure what he had been about to do or say, but he went silent and bowed his head again. Power had started to grow inside him, he feared. He might have done something he would regret afterward. The magic that he denied and ignored grew stronger with emotions.

The *Art of Ata* -- Endris had been teaching him how to control his emotions for years.

"Why?" Villat finally asked as though they would have an answer. "Why do any of this? She is killing people with indifference, either way. If we can't warn them --"

"Terror," Za said softly. He glanced at Mai.

"Go on," Mai said. Villat looked at him as though she thought he might have some sort of answer.

"Everything she is doing is to create a sense of terror," he said. "And if you cannot give warnings, that means that you are the only ones the rest of the people will hold accountable."

"They'll turn on us," Villat whispered, only now seeing that worse answer. "And if we are loyal to the crown, we dare not say why we are killing people. And if we do say, then we will be committing treason --"

"Calm, Villat," Danisin said softly. "Calm. You've already done better than you can know."

She took several deep breathes. "It's not like me to get emotional over *anything*," she admitted. "But I had already known this was untenable. I can't go back. I can't kill people that I took an oath to protect, even if the Queen orders it. I just --"

"You can stay with us," Mai said. "Unless Danisin has a reason that you shouldn't."

"She's more than trustworthy," he said and only briefly glanced at Za. "And she has already helped."

Should they believe this tale she wove for them? If he had not known his mother so well, he would have distrusted Villat. However, having seen the Queen growing more callous and crueler over the last few years, Za found that he could believe far worse of her.

That said very dire things.

"... She loves gold too much," the Wolf of the West warned. *"She wants power, Prince Yasidin. She is my own daughter, but I would not trust her much without a tight leash...."*

Za realized that he had never trusted his mother from that day onward -- his naming day. He'd been precocious in some ways, and even at the age of five, he'd had a good grasp of politics. He also knew how to survive in a court filled with hostile and influential people. He had never asked for help from his mother or his sisters.

The others had kept talking; Za supposed he should have paid attention, but it was a sign of how much he trusted these people. Mai got up and went to the kitchen. She came back with Kintansa who gave the newcomer a nod of welcome.

"Commander," Villat said with a nod of surprise. "Then there is more going on here. We didn't realize. You did well."

"We have to find a way to get out of the city," Kintansa said. The woman frowned and shook her head. "Not just for my sake, Villat. Or even for Mai's -- she's well known enough in the mercenaries, and someone will finally realize that this place is a link to us. But there is another reason."

Kintansa looked to Za. He supposed there was no use trying to keep quiet about his own identity. Besides, it would hardly have been fair to Villat.

Villat looked where Kintansa did and frowned still until Za looked up and she stared into his face.

Paled. Tried to speak and could not.

"Let us tell you a tale, Villat," Za said. He brushed the hair back annoyed with it again. "There is much you need to know before you decide what to do next."

CHAPTER ELEVEN

Prince Zaron told the tale very well. I only filled in a few spots and Kintansa a couple others. Villat listened with a kind of numb look on her face through most of it, but by the end, I could see color coming back to her cheeks and the intelligence returning to her eyes.

There had been no doubt about the demons and who had called them into the world. She never showed any surprise at that revelation. Villat stared at the table after the tale, silent -- but not for long.

"How can we deal with the Queen and Princesses if they have demons as their allies?"

"I don't know yet," Kintansa said, taking up this part of the story. "I do know that if we stay in Willoway, we aren't going to survive long enough to do anything."

"She wants the prince dead," Villat said with a sideways glance at Zaron. "That's why she wants everyone moving at night killed."

"That could be one reason," Za agreed. "However, she also wants to create panic and fear."

"Where will you go if you leave?" she asked.

I worried about how she said that statement. Unconsciously, at least, Villat did not consider herself one of us. I didn't want to mistrust her, but unless she came entirely to our side ... I didn't look at Danisin who must have some feelings for her. This was getting complicated.

"I don't know where we'll go yet," Kintansa admitted. She looked at the barred door with a frown. "We have no knowledge of how things are outside the city. The word of this trouble must have spread beyond the walls by now. Tales of demons will be dismissed, at least for a while -- but the sooner we get away, the better chance we'll have of getting far enough that we can outrun the news. I don't know --"

"We should go to the Tiger," the prince said.

Silence for a moment. I looked at him, a little surprised and distrustful. "Go to your grandfather? Why?"

"Because he'll believe us," Za said. He sat up straighter. "And he's the only person with enough power -- and power he can lend us -- to make a difference. He's not come near her since she had my father killed. There is a reason, you know."

"We expected him to attack," Mai admitted. "It was the fear that swept through the city."

"He wouldn't so long as I was alive -- and I was safe as long as she was less powerful than the Tiger of the East. Now she's made her move."

"We're a long way from his capital," Kintansa reminded him. "We'd have to either make our way to the coast and sail north or cross the mountains. Neither of those ways is safe for various reasons. Pirates in the seas, dragons in the mountains -- and more."

I hadn't really thought about the mountain dragons. They were capricious creatures from all that I'd heard. I'd never been to the mountains. I'd never been to the coast either. I wasn't certain Kintansa realized that I'd never been more than a few miles beyond the walls of Willoway. I'd been born here, served in the City Guard and then the Royal Guard for the king. Then here. The mercenaries sometimes took jobs that took them a good distance away, but I had never gone with them.

I said nothing.

"Are there other options?" Za asked. I didn't think of him as Prince Zaron. "Really, I want to know if there are. My knowledge of the world is limited, you know. I think we need to go to the Tiger, but that doesn't mean I'm right."

Villat still stared at Za as though she didn't know what he said and wouldn't have trusted it much anyway. I suppose I understood. After all, he was the son of a Queen who wasn't precisely well-loved. Villat might even believe that his father had been a traitor. Then, of course, the Queen had already spread the word that Prince Za had called the demons.

I saw in Villat a problem for the future, though. While she didn't seem to trust the prince, she didn't appear to be ready to turn us in, either. We would watch her, of course. We would also have to leave the city today. I had hoped for another day but found myself shaking my head.

"What's wrong?" Danisin asked.

"Start packing up what we need. We'll have to go during the daylight since they'll shoot people after dark. There is nowhere we could get before midnight," I said. Kintansa sighed, but since she didn't argue, I knew I was right. "They'll be looking for people to try going over the walls at night."

"But they'll see us during the daylight," Danisin protested.

"Only if we go *over* the walls. We're going to go out *under* them."

"But --" Kintansa began. Then she stopped. "Yes. The tunnel isn't entirely safe, but we can get this end open and hope for the best at the far end."

"Tunnel?" Villat asked. Then she frowned. "There was a tunnel about five years ago, used by smugglers, but I thought it was brought down."

"Part of it was," Kintansa said. She already looked anxious

to get moving and began prodding at the bandages on her hand. I took that as a good sign. "My people cleared some of it out; we thought we might want a quiet way out of the city. Things were already looking worrisome. We gave it up, though. It didn't look viable."

"Not for several hundred people," I agreed. "But a small group should be able to get through. I am open to other ideas, though."

"I'll consider other possibilities," Kintansa agreed, but I could tell that she didn't think there was any other answer. "Or we could stay. Not here, but there are other places."

"I need to get to the Tiger," Za said. He sounded as assured as I had heard him since this trouble began. I hadn't heard that tone -- one that I remembered so well from his father. It gave me a chill. "If one of you will show me this tunnel, I'll go out and do my best to get to my grandfather. You'll be safer here without me."

"No, I'll go with you," I said. "The others can make up their own minds -- though Villat, we'll have to be careful of you."

"Yes," she said and didn't seem at all upset. "Under the circumstances, I couldn't expect anything else. Why do you need to go to your grandfather, Prince Zaron? Do you think he's the only one who can keep you safe?"

I heard a touch of condescension in her words. I'm sure Zaron heard it as well, but he didn't give any sign of annoyance. I was about to protest. However, Zaron leaned forward, pushed back his hair again, and gave the woman a serious look. "The Tiger of the East is the only person with the power to fight my mother and her pet demons. I hope she does not have more such allies yet, and that the Tiger has answers that we can't see. I cannot think of anyone else we might turn to, and I don't think we can fight this problem on our own."

"What about your other grandfather?"

"My mother's father?" he said with a slight wave of his hand. "He didn't trust her the last time I saw him, it's true. However, he's gotten old and, from what I've heard at court, he is not able to lead as he once had."

"Oh." She took that news like a blow. I suspected it might be more startling to her than the demons themselves. We had lived all our lives under the shadows of those two giants.

"I have a question," Zaron said. "When the Queen spoke to you today, were the princesses with her?"

"No. There was no sign of them anywhere."

"That's unfortunate. I wonder if the death of one of the demons might not have affected the one who rode it. Was there anything else you noticed that was unusual?"

"The Queen met us outside the Summer Cloud Gate, not within. The gate remained closed, even with her outside the grounds. The Palace Guard stood on the wall and with weapons ready. I feared she intended to kill us all, to be honest. She never met us outside the gate before."

"And now we have to wonder what she has hidden inside," I said. "Do we try to find out?"

"No," Zaron said, which surprised me. "If wouldn't matter, would it? If she has taken in stray cats or has an entire army of demon -- what could we do? Nothing. Better that we get out of the city as soon as we can. This can only get worse."

I agreed, though I desperately wanted to know what the Queen might be hiding. Probably just the demons, I thought. After all, she'd never shown any liking for cats.

We went through the building and collected some things we thought might be useful on the journey. Blankets, food, and several knives. Danisin surprised me by bringing out a very nice bow.

"I've used to go hunting," he admitted. "I came from a small village to the east, and we had some hunting grounds. I always kept it in good shape since I told myself I was going to go back, but I haven't made it yet. I haven't practiced in a while, but I used to be good."

I found this a good sign. I was not a hunter, and the fewer supplies we had to buy outside the city, the better. He even had a quiver of arrows.

I had never imagined Danisin anywhere but in the city. Odd how easy it was not to imagine people beyond my own limited focus. I had pegged him as a City Guard and never looked for anything else.

And Prince Zaron? I had begun to see unexpected depths to him. I also saw that stubborn streak for which his father had been well known. For that matter, his mother had been just as bad. I supposed I was lucky not to have slammed up against that wall of his personality yet.

I wished Endris had spoken more often about him. I didn't know what part of his moods I should trust. Za had been too quiet so far, and he'd been far too good at taking orders.

I thought about those traits as I packed some of my own supplies and showed him how best to manage his own pack. He listened, and he learned from what I said. There was no doubt he was wise enough to pay attention, at least.

The *Art of Ata?* I had known Endris followed those teachings. What I had taken to be Endris's calm personality now seemed something different. I saw the same patience in Za that had always been present in Endris, even before an important battle. Others had chided him for it. I'd joked with him about his disinterest. He'd always been open to humor, even at his own expense.

Did I see those qualities transferred to the young prince? Was that part of the practice of *Ata?* Or was he only mimicking the man who must have offered him companionship? Friendship. Za couldn't have had many friends, being his father's son and heir in a world where the Queen ruled and didn't want him to take her throne or any other.

Maybe we'd have time to talk about it on this journey.

"We'll be going out the back," I said as we gathered in the room downstairs again. "The shadows will be in our favor now. Make sure you are wearing the cloaks, and you have anything that might glint covered." I had given those orders a half dozen times already. Even Kintansa looked ready to chide me about it. "Say nothing once we are out that door. Tansa or I will let you know when it is safe to speak again."

The others all nodded. I worried most about Za, who was the only one who had never been with the military. I had the impression that up until now he'd been suffering from both his wounds and the shock of the situation and that had made him cooperative to a fault. That could change at any time.

His insistence that he go to his grandfather was likely just the first sign of rebellion --

No. I had to stop looking for trouble where there was none. This was not rebellion; Prince Zaron had given good reasons why he needed to go to the Eastern Court. The others agreed as well. Za hadn't caused us any trouble. He would be careful and wise as we left the building and tried to escape the city. He had been so the last time we secretly left the Lost Way Inn, and he'd been in far worse shape.

I went to the door and looked back at Kintansa. She bowed her head, putting this in my hands. Kintansa was a great strategist, and she could direct whole companies of mercenaries without a problem. I was better at the smaller details, like sneaking through the city. I'd done it often enough before, slipping back and forth from the Lightning Headquarters and the Lost Way Inn.

As I stepped out, I looked back at the kitchen. This time I truly could see no way I'd ever return. I had lived here in relative calm, pretending to work at first -- and then enjoying it more as time went on. If I survived this madness -- and there was some reasonable doubt to that happening -- then I might open another inn. Not in Willoway, though. I would not be able to walk these streets without seeing the demons and the dead.

I found it amusing that we hadn't decided how we would get to the Court of the Tiger. By sea? We had enough funds to buy our way onto a ship. Actually, we had enough funds to buy a craft of our own.

First, we must get out of the city, and I turned my attention back to that problem. This was where I would do the most good. I knew the paths, and I knew the sounds.

We went through the fence and moved along the shadowed side, as silent as a group of people could manage. Villat was with Danisin at the end of the line. I would rather she wasn't in a location where we might have trouble stopping her, but the only other choice was to put her with Tansa and Za -- and I didn't like that much either.

Did we need Za?

I dropped that thought as quickly as it formed as I moved from one shadow to another. The day was bright, and the shadows stark. People walked around on the streets, and we had to wait often for a clear moment. At least that meant we all had time to recover our breath and rest. As much as I wanted to rush into the tunnel, I knew that was not wise. We did not want to be seen. Move carefully.

We took hours moving through Willoway. No one spoke unless I asked a question. Odd, but they were better behaved than a lot of military groups I had led. Such a strange mixed group, with a plethora of unique backgrounds: Innkeepers, mercenaries, concubine, City Guard, Prince Heir.

The alleys I chose were some of the worst in the city, filled with debris and infested with rats. I had to kill some of the more persistent animals but leaving those dead behind kept some of the other rats busy.

Other things lurked there, too. Mangy dogs, cats who looked no better than the rats, and even a couple humans. I considered killing the people, but I couldn't see that they would do us any harm since none of them did more than lift their heads for a moment when we passed too close. I just made sure that we were far from that area as fast as possible.

Tansa limped badly after a few hours. Za walked with a hand to his side. I was doing my best to ignore any of my own wounds. It was good that this was not an escape that counted on speed.

I glanced at Villat. She had made no sign of trouble so far. I had sometimes even forgotten her presence or that I might not fully trust her. We finally neared the edge of the ruined building where we'd find the tunnel. Someone had tried to build over it, but part of the house had collapsed when the tunnel gave way again. Since then, nothing more had been built on the site.

The collapse had been on purpose. In fact, the mercenaries had funded the house building and purposely brought it down, just to discourage others. We were sneaky sometimes, though I could never have seen this reason for having kept the place in such a state.

I shoved at a bit of fallen wall and it slid almost silently aside. I waved the others in rather than check it out first, and then followed. I thought I saw shadows moving along the street heading our way, just as I slipped in and closed the opening again.

We sat there in the near darkness, silent and still. A bit of light came through the broken debris over the top of us, and I could hear voices, though I couldn't make out the muffled words.

Someone pounded on the wall. I leaned against the

hidden door with my knife in hand, though I doubted that they'd find the spring. We waited. And waited.

The light shifted. We needed to get going before true darkness fell.

"We made it this far," I finally whispered. Even those words sounded too loud. "Let's see if the tunnel is usable. Otherwise, we're going to have to go wandering back out on the streets."

"I will dig it through with my bare hands," Tansa replied.

I suspected she would. We were going to leave the city.

CHAPTER TWELVE

Za felt so exhausted that he could have slept sitting there in the dirt. He did nod off a couple times but awoke again whenever Villat handed him more stone and wood to pass on to Danisin.

They might have been days down in this hole while trying to get through the tunnel. Za couldn't be sure. They had drunk tepid cider and ate some cheese a few times. They had candles that lit the little stretch of the cave, and he had once wished them to give more light -- and they did. The light lasted longer than he thought usual, but the others didn't notice. The air became thick and hot. He didn't care. He just wanted to sleep. Let the city go to the demons. Let the world go to them. It didn't matter if --

Villat nudged him. He took a huge piece of rock and handed it on. He thought he could see a hint of dislike in the woman's face, as though by being so tired, he proved himself to be nothing more than a pampered prince.

His side ached. Every time he passed something heavy on, it felt as though it pulled a bit worse. He wished Sirma was here with them. He trusted the man to take care of the wound.

Did it matter? If the demons won, it might be best to die here in the dark.

He took the next stone without being prompted. None of them spoke much now.

Just keep working.

Then he felt something odd. Like a little breath of air.

The candle had wobbled.

Mai and Tansa crawled backward and joined them in the slightly larger area where the other three had worked.

"We have an opening," Mai whispered. Tansa only nodded. Za hadn't considered how much harder the work had been for them.

"There might be another collapse farther on," Villat said with a shake of her head. "We might have to --"

Za lifted his hand. "Fresh air."

"Right," Tansa said. Her voice sounded rough, and she took a sip of water before passing the canteen around. "There might be more debris, but there must be some sort of opening that leads out. We're beyond the city walls, and we should be coming out in a stand of trees."

Villat had scowled at Za. Apparently, she hadn't liked the idea that the Prince had figured something out so quickly and she hadn't. Za began to see problems there -- but from the way Mai looked at the woman, he was not the only one who had taken note of her attitude. He would say nothing. He could only make matters worse if he provoked Villat.

Za glanced at Danisin. He scowled, but at nothing in general. Za trusted him. Danisin seemed to trust Villat, so he was willing to give the woman the benefit of the doubt for now. They were all under pressure.

"I will go first," Tansa said and shook her head when Mai started to speak. "Me first this time. Remember, I was through here before the collapse, so I know a little of what to expect. Mai next, Za, Villat, and Danisin. Each of you grab your packs. You'll have to push them ahead of you."

Za hadn't liked the thought of having Villat at his back --

well, at his feet, at least. The pack between them would help, though. And no one argued.

They ate a little and then started the last part of the journey through the earth. Za had been tired before, but he started to feel far more awake as they moved into the narrow opening. The dirt, he noticed, was not as dry and crumbling as it had been when they first entered the tunnel. Here it held the scent and feel of dampness. He couldn't see much. Mai had put out the candles except one that she moved ahead of her somehow. The little flashes of light showed uneven stones shoved into the wall. The people who had built this tunnel had worked very hard on it. Industrious smugglers.

The tunnel was old, though, and bits of dirt and rock began to drop down around them. Tansa tried to move faster, and he wasn't sure that would help. Villat made soft sounds of distress, especially when the dirt above them began to shift --

"No," he whispered and wished for it to stay. He felt an odd chill again, and this time a headache grew with sudden intensity -- but by the Forgotten Gods, the dirt stayed in place. He kept moving.

Forward, forward. Za's legs hurt from pushing him onward. His arm cramped, and he almost cursed. He kept moving. Villat sometimes shoved her pack into his feet. He thought she might be doing it on purpose, which only reinforced the belief that he was no longer heir to the throne. His mother had made certain of that already by claiming he had brought the demons, and he suspected more than a few people cursed his name today.

Did Villat believe he was going to his grandfather so he would get his status back? There was nothing that could be done about the lies. There would always be those who now believed that he had brought the demons, and even if he proved that it was his mother and sisters, some would think that a trick -- or simply that he was born of the same man and woman and I could not be any better.

Did he care if he never ruled here?

The tunnel turned, dipped, turned again -- would it never end? Then the land began to tilt upward, but he didn't trust they headed for the surface until Mai pulled him up out of the dirt and into the early morning light and the tall shadows of trees. They'd been all night in the tunnel.

Villat came out and sat down on the ground. Za wanted to stand for a while, but he wasn't confident that his legs would hold him for long. Danisin didn't come out right away, though -- he started to worry when the pack arrived and Danisin not far after it. The man was larger than the rest of them, and Za only now thought about how much worse crawling through there must have been for him.

"I pulled down the debris again and made certain we didn't leave any noticeable tracks. If someone does go into the tunnel, he'll find it much the way it had been. I did my best to spread the stuff we dug out into different areas."

"Damned good work, Danisin," Mai praised. She sat on a log beside Kintansa. Za sat on the ground and took several deep breaths, trying to call back the calm and power of *Ata*. They were far from safe yet, and he would not slow them down.

Ata had limitations, though. Or rather the body did. *Ata* could train you to go farther than some might think possible, but the body still had to find the strength from somewhere within. Looking at the others, he could tell that they, too, were moving on the last of their strength. They'd have to find a safer place to rest soon.

Za could see the high walls of the city through the scattered trunks of tall trees. They must have gone at least a mile underground and probably more. Out of the town, out into the trees. He'd ridden the road that couldn't be too far away, but he had never been out into the wilds before.

Everything around him looked dangerous. Were the plants poisonous? Were dangerous creatures lurking in the shadows? How far would they have to go before they could find safety?

All the way to his grandfather's court?

He must have been insane to think this would work -- but he quickly buried that feeling of fear and distrust before the others saw it. On one level, he knew that heading for the Tiger was the wisest thing he could do. On the other hand, he knew that he could not get there on his own. He hoped the others did not expect --

Oh, they would not expect much from him at all. Za had seen how pleased Mai had been even at the simple things he could do, and Za wanted to be annoyed that she thought so little of him. However, Mai had served at the palace, and she knew how little training he'd had in anything practical.

Except for the training he got from Endris, who had introduced him to the *Art of Ata*, and in that subtle way showed him how to deal with any problems.

No one is born knowing answers. A wise person seeks knowledge from those who have gone ahead.

Za took a deeper breath and turned to Mai -- and found something he had not expected. She looked around the area with the same sort of narrow-eyed worry that he'd felt. She was part of the mercenaries. She must have been in places like this before --

Hadn't she?

Kintansa, Danisin, and Villat all looked more assured. He listened to what they said about getting out of the vicinity of Willoway by staying in the woods and moving slowly for the first few days.

"The longer we can stay in the woods, the better," Kintansa explained. She looked around with a different sort of frown. "The military is bound to be watching for Prince Za especially, and probably for me, too. They can't afford to trust we're still in the city. The farther we go, the fewer people will be looking for us."

"But we go slowly?" Villat asked. She looked confused.

"None of us are used to wandering through the woods," Kintansa replied with a quick look around. "I've been out on campaigns, but that meant my people, who were trained scouts, were keeping an eye open for trouble. Have you spent much time in the wilderness?"

"One short campaign, but that was to the south and mostly in the grasslands," Villat admitted and gave a nod of understanding.

"Mai hasn't often gone out on a campaign with us and we never fought in this kind of terrain anyway," Kintansa said. "She is our city expert."

"And I've never been very far from the city," Mai admitted. "This is a foreign land to me."

"Za --" Kintansa began.

Za laughed softly. "No, I have not wandered around in the woods before, Commander. There is much I will need to learn."

"I spent time in the woods," Danisin said. "But that was a couple decades ago when I was young. I've spent a little time in the wilds since I went to the city, but not nearly enough."

"You still rate as an expert compared to the rest of us."

"The Gods save us all," he mumbled with a shake of his head.

Oddly, Za found himself feeling more confident. They had all admitted to their lack of ability as far as the woods were concerned -- but wasn't that better than the sort of thing he would have seen at court? At the palace, people would have claimed expertise just to impress others. He would much rather deal with people who were cautious and careful rather than with some of the boasting lords and ladies who were likely to get others killed, and still wouldn't admit to their lack of knowledge.

Nor were they willing to learn. Za had never wanted to be like those people. This was his chance to study things that no one else at court knew. That appealed to him, even while the idea of being out here in the wilds and hunted by guards made him think he could not possibly survive.

"Za?" Kintansa said.

He focused on her and sighed. "I am out of my element. So far out of my element that I might as well be on another world. The best I can do is to apply *Ata* to the situation and learn all I can."

"Wise," Kintansa said and gave a bow of her head. At that moment, he remembered her as his father's favorite; she had been a lovely young woman with a feel of wildness to her. He had never imagined that the wildness came from having been free to roam the world.

As he was free now?

Would he go back to the palace? He suspected that there might not be anything left of that place by the time the demons finished their work in the city. The thought did not bother him. Part of that was because he had never expected to live long enough to take the throne anyway. He'd known that when they took his father away. He'd seen the way his mother looked at him as she gathered her daughters to her.

So, if he never went back, what would he do?

Za paid attention to what Danisin said as they walked along a narrow path that had been made by deer, the man explained. They frightened a few away, and each time Danisin made them stop and wait while he listened to see if the startled deer had brought any other attention.

Then they would creep on.

If they'd all been healthy and uninjured, he imagined they would have made much better time. The day passed too quickly, especially since they had to rest often. It didn't bother Za so much that he didn't know where they were going, but he also feared none of the others did as well.

They stopped late in the day and prepared for the night by a little brook. He did what he could to help, but when he pulled something in his side again, Mai directed him to sit down with Kintansa.

"Just rest. We are not going to have many chances like this."

The others made food in a pot, heated over a small fire. Danisin killed a rabbit and prepared to roast it as well. Mai still looked startled at every odd sound.

As the sun went down, they gathered around the little fire, wrapped in blankets and none of them comfortable from the looks on their faces.

"We have to decide which way to go," Kintansa said. Odd how out of the city, she seemed to have taken command rather than Mai. "Getting as far away from the city as possible was the best we could do today, but if we are not going to cross the mountains, then we had better start heading east rather than north."

"Dragons in the mountains," Mai said with a shake of her head.

"Pirates in the sea," Kintansa countered. "And storms this time of year."

"Not to mention the difficulty of the group of us getting on a ship, money or not," Danisin added.

"But *dragons*," Mai still said with a wave of her hand. "How many people do you know who have crossed the mountains this time of year and survived both the storms and the dragons? They make legends of those people, they're so rare."

"True," Kintansa agreed. She chewed at a rabbit leg. "I don't like the idea of pirates -- or all the people we'll have to deal with between here and the ocean -- but it is probably the safer way to go. What do the rest of you think? Danisin?"

"I don't like either. I'd hide out in the woods if it were just me -- but it's not." He stopped and looked at Za, and then shook his head. "Even if Prince Zaron weren't with us, we'd still be heading somewhere to try and get help against the demons, wouldn't we? Za has given us a good destination, but do you really think you can reach your grandfather once we get to the east?"

"Yes," Za said. He held up his left hand and touched an unpretentious metal ring on his middle finger. "This will get me to him. If anything happens to me, be certain that you get the ring. Present it at the gate to his palace."

The others nodded. Za found himself frowning. "Why do you take me at my word? At court --"

"At court, no one believes anyone, especially if they are offering something that might help," Kintansa replied and tossed the gnawed bone into the fire. "I've lived long enough outside Summer Cloud to have accepted that the world is different out here. I hope that you will get the chance to learn the same."

"You were at court?" Villat asked. From the frown on her face, Za thought she must suspect something she could not quite name.

"Oh yes," Kintansa said and gave a perfect little flutter of her fingers across her face -- a sign in the court. "I was even well known --"

"Goddesses," Villat yelped. "The Favorite?"

Kintansa laughed. "I'm afraid so, though it was never a role I had willingly taken."

"So, you went to her --" Villat said, looking at Za.

"Not exactly. I was as surprised as you to realize the truth about Commander Kintansa. I had a friend at court. He died saving me and sent me to the Lost Way Inn where I found

Mai. She had been a Captain in my father's guard. She took me to Commander Kintansa."

"Did you know?" she asked, looking at Danisin. A touch of distrust had come back to her face again. She apparently did not trust people from the court.

"No," Danisin said and stared at Kintansa this time. "I knew Mai had some military background, but I thought she'd been with the mercenaries and still was with them. I had never met the Commander of Lightning Company, and even if I had, I wouldn't have known about her past."

"And you still worked for her?"

"There are far worse than mercenaries in Willoway, Villat."

"Yes. Yes, you're right," Villat agreed. "I haven't had time to adjust, that's all. And every time I think I know what's going on, something else odd comes along."

"Here is what you need to remember," Mai said and leaned forward, her face lighted from below, casting shadows so that her eyes glittered in a sea of darkness. "The demons are real. The Queen and her daughters are the ones who called them forth, but you don't know that for certain. I understand. Kintansa and I have seen things that make us believe Za is telling the truth. The two of us will do our best to get him to his grandfather. The prince is right in that part -- there is no one else who has power enough to go up against Queen Taranis and her pets."

"Others will take the Tiger the news, won't they?" Villat asked and looked at Za.

Looked to him for an answer for the first time.

"Rumors will reach him before we do," Za agreed. "But the only official news he might get will be from the Queen herself. You can bet that none of his own people at court have survived. I had always thought Endris served the Tiger --"

"I believe he did," Mai said. "We never outwardly spoke

our loyalties, but his loyalties were not to the queen. To you, beyond a doubt, and probably to the Tiger."

Za nodded. He looked back at Villat. She still tended to do a quick bow of her head. He could not imagine why. He had never been less of a prince.

"If we can reach him with some haste, then we can give him the true news, and he will be able to move more quickly and with the kind of power he needs to take on this battle. I can't tell what my mother might tell him. I suspect she'll say she had heard odd rumors about demons in the city, but so far there is no sign of them. He won't know any difference at first. By the time he does learn, I suspect she'll be moving on him with an army he might not be able to fight."

"An army of demons?" Danisin asked, clearly unsettled by the idea.

"If you can call three, why not a thousand?" Mai asked.

"Why hasn't she?" Villat asked.

"It takes power," Kintansa replied. She pulled her cloak up around her as though chilled by the thought. "And besides, she will want to know she can control them before she calls so many."

"And there is the other question," Mai said as she looked again at Za. "How did she learn to call up demons to begin with?"

"I'm not sure," Za admitted. "It's not as though I have been close to any of them. It must have been done in extreme secrecy, though. Even Endris didn't know, or else he would have given me a warning."

"True," Mai agreed. "They were cautious --"

"Or else it happened quite suddenly," Villat suggested. "The queen has always been quick to take advantage of something that might help her."

"Sudden," Za said and gave a nod of agreement. "Maybe so. Word of unusual behavior always spreads through the servants. I had neither seen nor heard anything lately. Nothing that stands out anyway."

"We need to rest," Kintansa advised. "We're going to have a long day tomorrow."

And many more days after that one, Za thought with some worry though that disappeared as he curled up on the hard ground and fell asleep soon afterward.

CHAPTER THIRTEEN

I had never imagined there could be so many trees in the world.

We had kept to the woods for several days, but we couldn't for much longer. Danisin had led us eastward over the damned hills, across stone fords in streams, through more trees and more trees and more trees. We had bypassed villages, though Danisin had gone in and stolen from gardens and a smokehouse. It was enough to keep us going for several more days.

We had no idea who might be a friend or foe around here. If the Queen had sent orders to capture the prince, then our excellent mannered companion might give himself away, even if no one recognized him. I had even tried to teach him to be rude, but he seemed incapable to even *acting* rude. We had to be very careful and avoid everyone.

I never thought I would oversee keeping a member of the Royal House safe again. I didn't mean to fail this time, either. Having given myself a purpose in this insanity helped. It also helped that Za was so damned cooperative. I didn't trust his attitude because at times he sounded and looked too much like his father who had never cooperated with anyone as far as I could remember.

"You'll never survive as a ruler if you don't start commanding rather than accepting," I said as I handed him a bowl of stew.

"Oh, is that what you want of me?" he said with a sudden laugh. I hadn't heard him laugh before. The conversation had drawn all the others, too. "I wouldn't think so, Captain Mai. You don't want me to suddenly become royal, do you?"

"Getting bored, are you, Mai?" Tansa asked with a shake of her head. "Trying to make trouble for us?"

"No," I said and hid my own smile. Za had taken the words better than I had expected. I can't say why I poked at him. "It's just that --"

"I'll never rule, you know," he said.

The words came without any hint of regret or other emotion unless that was a touch of relief that I heard in his words. I looked at Za with a bit of surprise.

"Just because we've left the city --" I began.

He put aside the soup and shook his head. "My mother never intended for me to rule. We all know that truth. The Grandfathers sometimes made threats to take me -- but if one took me to his court, the other would be up in arms. Literally, up in arms. I remained where I was and I stayed as quiet as I could, but I'm lucky I got out of there with my life. I never expected to be king, and you can't tell me that anyone in Willoway expected me to survive long enough to take the throne."

"He's right," Villat said with a snarl. I had the idea that she didn't much like the prince under any circumstances. "Besides, do you think any of us are going to survive?"

"We've managed to so far," Kintansa reminded the woman. Her faced hardened. "And I wouldn't be here if Za hadn't leapt in and killed the demon."

"Yes, of course," Villat said with a nod of her head and went back to her soup. She'd learned not to make a fuss, at least, but she did still scowl.

Even Danisin gave the woman a look of distaste this time. I wondered if we could trust Villat if we left her behind in some village along the way. If we were sufficiently far enough to the east, then she wouldn't be able to get word back to the Willoway very fast. We'd have to trust that she wouldn't run straight to the Queen with news about the wayward prince. I wasn't certain I trusted her that much.

Something might happen to Villat.

I glanced at Za, not Villat, when I thought those words. I had come to realize that our prince had a high standard of ethics. It was another reason he wouldn't last long on the throne.

He was right about never surviving long enough to get there, not under his mother. I had thought the Tiger had intended for Za to take the throne. And yet he left the boy at Summer Clouds Palace with no --

My breath caught, and I had to pretend I coughed. In the names of all the Forgotten Gods -- why had I not seen it? The boy had not been left there, unprotected. He'd had Endris at his side, probably even when he didn't realize it.

Then, when Endris knew he would die, he had sent the Prince to *me*. I had done the right thing without realizing the implications. I had kept the prince alive. I would continue to do so, but I didn't think I liked the idea that Endris had shoved him into my hands.

It was easy to be angry at someone already dead.

The anger I had carried for the last few days wanted a place to go, and it would be easy to transfer my rage to Prince Zaron. I kept that urge in control as well. I was dealing with frustration more than anything else. We had spent five days in the woods. Nothing had changed. We knew no more than when we started, and the trees went on forever.

And then, in the early afternoon, it all changed.

The trees lessened to brush, and the brush slowly gave way to grass. Waves of green spread out so far ahead of us that I couldn't see the end of this grassland. Clouds dotted the sky, white and fleecy near us, but I thought those in the far distance looked darker and menacing.

I had thought the land empty of life, but as I stared in shock, I could see the bounding bodies of deer and elk that moved through the grass, springing upward as they raced at an angle away from us.

"Must be a predator out there," Tansa said as she watched. "Either a big cat, wolves, or humans. There will be nomads in the area hunting food for winter."

"This is your land," I said, surprised that I hadn't considered such a possibility.

"It was," she agreed and gave a shrug. "I've been away a long time."

"I'll yield the point to you, Tansa," Danisin said and stepped aside to let her take the lead. "I am a forest man. I don't want to make a mistake now."

Tansa showed no uncertainty as she started out on a narrow path. I knew from experience that didn't mean she knew what she was doing. I stayed behind her and slightly to the left where I could see over her shoulder in case we ran into trouble.

I soon realized one good point about having spent so much time in the woods. We had all started healing and feeling better. We'd never pushed too hard on that long walk.

Zaron surprised me, though. I had buried the memory of the pretentious child who had been his father's favorite, of course. I didn't know how he had turned out so well --

Endris. Endris again -- and the *Art of Ata*, I supposed

Once I had stopped thinking about survival at every moment, memories of other things returned, like why we were out here in this forsaken grassland. I had disliked the forest, and I really couldn't see why I would like the grasslands any better. It was unnatural to see so far in all directions. The sky seemed too bright, and I could spot no cover, except to huddle down in the grass like rabbits. I purposely didn't ask how far we would go in this land, but I saw days ahead of us traveling along these deer paths. Maybe years.

We took a little break not far from the edge of the trees. Villat scowled at us all as she usually did. She was not making the journey any better. I began to think more of ways to be rid of her without killing the woman, though she pushed me a bit more in that direction each time I had to deal with her. Even Danisin was growing weary of her attitude.

"I have not been to the grasslands for a long time," Tansa said, but she smiled as she looked out into that green world. "We won't meet any of the tribes this close to the woods, and the tribe of my people will be far to the east still. We'll have to move carefully here."

"How does one move at all through such lands?" Za asked. He chewed on sweet grass and looked for all the world like some country boy. Only his speech and accent gave him away now, and if we came close to anyone, I'd have to remind him to keep silent.

"We follow the paths left by the larger animals, just like in the woods," Tansa replied. I looked where she did and could see such paths not far away. "There to the right, you can see where one leads to a stand of berries. We will follow it and try to stay in a generally eastward direction. The paths will lead us to water holes. Those are the most dangerous spots because we're likely to find predators and people there."

"Can we make it across without being spotted?" Danisin asked. He looked doubtful.

"I doubt it. I hope to get far enough east to meet up with allied tribes. Allied to my people, that is. While all these tribes are nominally under the control of the throne, that doesn't mean we'd be safe with them for that reason."

Villat looked at Za as though she expected him to make some protest. Was she ever going to realize that he wasn't that stupid? Maybe not.

We soon started the trek through the damned grasslands. I had only thought I hated the forest; now I was beginning to realize what true hate meant. The grassy path was a pitfall of small holes that twisted ankles, while the grass itself, so soft and pretty at a distance, turned out to be sharp enough to cut faces and hands if it struck at the right angle. At the first opening, we stopped and cut cloth to make coverings for our faces. Burrs had begun to stick to pant legs and dig needles into our skin. No one complained, but even Kintansa looked unhappy when we started out again.

I thought I would be happy to be out of the hills, away from the endless hiking up and down, crossing brooks and streams, and then climbing up and down again. I soon realized that walking the grasslands was far worse. There was no way to judge distance. The plants often blocked out the view of everything but more grass.

We startled birds, and sometimes something more substantial moved through the grass nearby. I kept my hand on my knife, but I didn't think it would do much good since whatever was out there sounded huge.

That feeling multiplied when the largest snake I'd ever seen crossed our path, pausing to measure us for prey, and moving on. Kintansa had drawn her blade as well when faced with that monster, which must have been at least twelve feet long. The snake slid off into the grass to our left, and it was a long time before my heart started beating slowly again.

By then I began to hear sounds ahead of us -- the call of birds and the huffing of larger animals. Splashes in water -- so I knew we had reached a large waterhole before Kintansa lifted a hand for silence and the two of us crept forward while the others waited.

I had never seen so many animals in my life. The pond was no more than 100 feet across at the widest spot. All around it stood clusters of deer, elk, birds, a couple snakes in the water, rabbits -- I stared in absolute disbelief until Kintansa touched my arm and signaled me back again.

"It's not safe to go near the water," Kintansa said as soon as we were all gathered in a little group. "Our appearance would send everything running, and that would draw attention we don't want."

"Wouldn't someone just assume it's a predator?" Danisin asked.

"Oh yes, absolutely. The problem is that hunting big cats is a sign of power in the grasslands. Finding us instead means they'd just take us captive and sell us as slaves."

"Oh." Danisin looked around with new worry. "I hadn't thought of that part. Do we backtrack to the last path we found?"

"Yes," Tansa said. "Head north for a little distance and then start heading east again. We'll have to decide where to camp soon."

"We've been leaving a trail where we passed," I said and pointed down at our footprints.

"Yes, but so far we haven't crossed the paths of anyone else. I've been watching," Tansa said. "That means we are not within walking distance of any village or else they would have been here getting water and hunting. Most villages should be to the south, but I can't guarantee it. Heading north, I think, is our best bet. We need to get farther into the grasslands where I might have a chance at finding someone we can trust."

"And you think you can," Villat said. She didn't sound pleased, but then she never did.

"I hope so," Kintansa replied. She met the woman's stare, and Villat looked away first. "Let's find a spot to camp."

I watched Villat. She turned and moved away again as though nothing were wrong. Our prince was finally showing signs of fatigue, though. Danisin had moved up to walk beside him which I appreciated. I didn't want Za to be only in my hands -- or to feel like I was the only one he could turn to. It had started bothering me before we left the forest, but out here --

We walked another few miles before Kintansa decided that this path leading north (rather than the half dozen we had passed) was suitable. I understood what she was saying about the tracks of animals and being too close to the watering hole, but northward was not better than eastward. It would not get us closer to the Tiger.

As the sun began going down, and sounds seemed louder in the growing dusk.

"We have a choice," Kintansa said finally. We were crowded as close as we could be, assaulted by the grass that started to move erratically in the growing breeze. "We can try to work our way into the grass to get off the path, or we can camp down here --"

"Here," Danisin said before she continued. "If we go off the path, we'll just leave a trail anyway, right? It's not like we can hide. Let's not make more work for ourselves."

Kintansa frowned for a moment but then nodded. "Yes, I agree. We simply don't have the resources to do something tricky. I should have considered -- but where could we have gotten machetes?"

I didn't like to see Kintansa so unsettled, which I suspected came from exhaustion. No doubt she worried about our circumstances, but I also suspected her memories of this place were coming back and she had come to realize the amount of danger we faced.

Better this than dragons, though.

We found a spot that was somewhat wider than the rest

of the area and cleared it of stones, burrs, and dung. Kintansa made a fire with dried grass, but only a small one.

"You don't want the grass around us to catch fire," she said.

I looked around with a shudder.

We didn't have much left in the supplies, but I didn't think any of us were particularly hungry anyway. I was going to take the midnight watch, so I pulled a blanket around me, mostly in hopes of discouraging insects, and tried to sleep.

I awoke to a growl and a scream.

I grabbed both of my swords from the pack and leapt to my feet. The gibbous moon lit the area enough that I could see shapes, if not details. Villat was on her feet, her screams becoming breathless as she backed away from a massive cat -- cheetah, I thought. We'd all made it to our feet. Danisin grabbed at Villat, but she lost her footing and went down --

I surged forward, but Za, on the other side of the Villat, moved faster. He lifted his hands and swung a glowing sword that had not been in his hold a heartbeat before.

With one move, he decapitated the cat.

The sword was no longer in his hands.

The cat was dead. Villat still gasped. Za went to his knees.

Silence then, except for a sharp breeze I had not felt before this. Villat, finally, was the one to move. She had her knife in hand and leapt forward -- and straight at Za.

"What are you! *What the hell are you!*"

The knife slashed at his upraised hand and cut into his arm before I could grab the fool and drag her away. Kintansa and Danisin took hold of Za who looked stunned, though I didn't think it was from the cut. It bled, but I left Tansa to take care of him.

I had to throw Villat to the ground by the body of the dead cat. "What kind of an idiot are you?" I demanded.

"It's not right! I don't care if he is a prince -- what he did isn't right --"

"What he did, you fool, was *save your life* -- but there's another aspect to it. He brought a sword out of nowhere and then beheaded the cat with one swing. Then you attacked *him*. He didn't attack you."

She had been about to yell and stopped. Her eyes went to the dead cat, then back to me.

"It's not right. He -- he --"

"Maybe so. That still doesn't make you any less of an idiot. Get up and get your things. We have to get away from here now."

"Yes," Kintansa agreed as she tied off a bandage on Za's arm. "He'll be okay, at least from the cut. Za?"

"I -- " He stopped and bowed his head for a moment. "Leave, yes."

Za went to gather his belongings while a rather stunned Danisin helped the prince. Tansa took Villat in hand since she had started to look annoyed at me. Some people cannot handle the truth very well, especially when the truth says how stupid they are.

Besides, it wasn't as though I hadn't reacted badly to what our Prince had done. I wanted answers from him but looking at Za made me realize that he felt as shocked by what had happened as Villat. He had not expected to do whatever he had done, and it had left him shaky and pale.

"We'll head north," Tansa said. "If we need to, we can get back into the woods for a while."

"I apologize," Za whispered. "I --"

"You saved Villat and probably the rest of us since we would have been trying to fight it. You did nothing wrong, though how --"

"I don't know," he said. His voice rose a little as we started away, taking his pack from Danisin with a nod of thanks. "I think -- it must have been something Endris did when he sent me to Captain Mai. He gave the path to me in my mind. I think he gave other things as well."

"Damn," I said, and he looked back, worried. "No, I'm not upset with you, Za. I just hadn't thought of it. Has anything else --"

"Fighting the demon at Lightning Headquarters," he said. "The sword came to me then, too. Now I think it was the magic of the weapon that killed the demon, not just the stab through the head, though that seemed the best way to attack it."

"I never considered where you got the sword," Tansa said and put a hand on his arm. "It's alright. Anything else?"

"One other thing, maybe. Or it might have been chance," he said. He sounded calmer. "In the crowd, when Captain Gar arrived -- I wished for the people to get much louder so that the guards at the gate did not hear him."

"Oh, that is interesting," Tansa said and sounded pleased this time. "I remember having the urge to suddenly yell at the top of my voice, and I had to stop myself, though I noticed that several others did yell. Mai? What do you know about Endris?"

"Not nearly enough," I admitted. "And I counted Edris one of my best friends. He was teaching you the *Art of Ata*, right?"

"He and Master Drital," Za replied, and I heard the loss in his voice this time. The prince from the royal court was usually much better at hiding his emotions. "But they told me they had taken me as far as they could, and I would find my own path now."

"I've read ancient books where the *Art of Ata* was linked with magic," Tansa said with a glance at him.

"Oh yes, old myths -- ah." He stopped talking and I could see that he considered the possibility. "I need time to meditate and to remember the nuances of Master Drital's teachings. My mind is too jumbled right now. And my head aches."

"There is one part of this you might not have considered," I said and saw him glance back at me. "You, Prince Zaron, have given me far more hope that we can survive. Despite how Villat might feel, you did save her life from something the rest of us might not have been able to fight."

"I don't know if I can do it again," he said. "I don't even know how or why --"

"Times of need," Tansa said. "It might be an emotional state. The three times you have used this power, there has been a danger."

"And not just danger to him," I added as I moved up by Tansa. This path was wider at least, though I didn't like to see the moving grass in the dark. "He could have escaped from the demon or the cat. He could have abandoned the crowd at the gate. You've done the right thing, Za."

He looked back at me, and as the moonlight struck his face, I saw a smile.

We would do fine, if Villat wasn't a fool again. I wished I could count on that much wisdom from her.

CHAPTER FOURTEEN

Za couldn't decide what had happened. He tried to replay the event in his mind, but one moment he had been standing to get away from the cheetah, and the next he had the sword in hand and killed it.

Then the sword disappeared, and a lot of his strength went with it. He'd been barely aware of Villat's reaction. He couldn't say he thought her a fool like the others did. Magic was not a part of the world either of them knew and not something easily trusted.

They had walked until they reached morning. They'd walked miles. Za could see the line of trees in the distance where the grass parted somewhat, and he wasn't sure he wanted to go back there. He felt as though they lost ground with every step.

He would not second-guess Kintansa or Mai. Or Danisin, for that matter. He would not leave Villat at his back, though. Every time he happened to look her way, her face held growing rage and distrust.

They stopped once the sun had come up. Kintansa found a small opening where a trail headed off to the east again, and she looked that way with a nod as they sat down and passed around the bits of food.

"We'll be heading east now," she said after a sip of water. "The path might be longer than one in the center of the grasslands, but I think we want to be closer to the trees. I should have considered that before."

"The forest is no safer though," Danisin protested.

"Dangerous in other ways," she agreed. "However, we won't have much trouble from the grassland tribes if we head into the woods. They considered such areas to be filled with magical creatures and a place where no human walks safely. I remember when I was taken to Willoway. I hid under a blanket the entire trip. They thought it was some sort of ritual for marriage or something."

Mai gave a little laugh. "Well, at least you got over it."

"I'd feel safer in the woods than the grass," she admitted. "But the trees continue to diminish to the north as the grasslands spread out. If we tried to get to the ocean by following along the trees, we would add months to our journey, and not arrive at anywhere helpful. We need to get to Evisto, I think. It's the only port of any size that I know of along the coast."

"Have you been to the ocean?" Za asked. He found himself curious this time.

"Only once. My father negotiated the trade routes through the grasslands with the traders who came from the coast or the west with whatever had come in by ship. I took the journey with him the last time, just four moons before I went to Willoway. The city smelled of fish and the sea, and everything was constantly drenched. Fogs came each morning we were there, and rains almost every day. We went to the docks and met in a wooden building there; a strange, wondrous place for someone who had only lived in huts and tents. The walls were decorated with murals of seas, sea monsters, and ships. Twisted limbs of trees, washed ashore I was told, had been worked into fantastic furniture. Shells everywhere -- but even as wondrous as it was, it couldn't block out the constant beat of the ocean or the cold wind that blew through every crack."

"But you saw the ocean itself," Za said. He felt an unexpected bit of excitement. "I've only ever heard of it, you know. Until now, I've only ever seen the land a little beyond Willoway, and then only along the trails with guards blocking most of the view."

Kintansa smiled. Za remembered that smile, suddenly, in a woman with long hair and a perfect face. His mother had despised her as a *grasslander*. Uncivilized, she'd said with a snarl and would not have Kintansa in her presence. Za had known, even as a child, that jealousy sparked that reaction. *The Favorite* was far prettier than the Queen.

"The ocean was a daunting mass of gray and blue that stretched on forever," Tansa replied and blinked at the memory. "Ships that you could see on the far horizon would take a day or two before they reached the port. Water rose in swells -- waves -- that crashed against the shell-covered beach. If the weather turned stormy -- and it did many times in the twenty days that we were there -- then the waves would rush up taller than the buildings and crash far inland. The ships were in dire danger of such storms, and one broke loose of the dock and was pummel against the land until only pieces of wood were left. All the crew who had still been aboard were killed."

Za nodded, still entranced despite the dangers of her tale. All his life had been filled with man-made hazards. Those of nature sounded more exciting. They were heading toward this place. Za wasn't confident he would like it better in real life. Something to think about, though.

And not think about the sword.

Za fought not to shudder at the thought of what he had done. He needed time for meditation, but he would not get it yet. They were already gathering up their supplies and starting to stand. Za had trouble getting to his feet, but Danisin helped him up. His side ached, still. He wondered if it would ever heal.

Villat kept her distance still. Good.

They walked for the entire day, down one trail and another, going past a few that crossed where they walked and often heading on ones that appeared less used. Tansa found some wild berries; tart fruit but a nice change from the dried meat and old cheese. They'd have to locate more food soon, he supposed.

Though Tansa knew what was edible here and that helped.

They heard people somewhere around midday. Tansa hissed and pulled aside stands of grass, shoving each of them into place along the trail, kneeling, and silent. She took her place with Za, a hand on her knife.

Za could barely see the party through the grass. They were not, praise the gods and goddesses, looking at the ground as they headed past in the opposite direction Za and his friends had been moving. They were not quiet, either. Two carried a large deer, already dead and hanging by its legs from a pole they rested on their shoulders. Their hunt was done. They were heading home.

They wore loose clothing, mostly as green as the grass around them. Long hair hung in braids decorated with ribbons and carved stones and reached down past their shoulders. They carried bows, quivers, swords, knives -- they could have been going to war instead of hunting.

The women were dressed just like the men, too, and looked just as dangerous -- but then he had expected as much, knowing Kintansa. They were not looking into the grass, but Za didn't think it hurt to hope that they were not noticed.

He couldn't say that the hope accomplished anything,

though the grasslanders went on without a problem. They waited, and Tansa finally came out of the grass and signaled the others to follow her. They moved at a trot now, heading away from the hunters.

At least they'd had a little rest.

The next couple of days went much the same, though they had no more trouble with wild animals. They had to stop at a watering hole, startling far too many creatures, but Tansa found the spring at the edge where the water came clear and fresh from the ground. They filled canteens and moved away as quickly as possible.

They slept in pairs with three always on guard duty. Villat had calmed enough to take her place with Danisin and Mai, but they worked it so that she was never on duty with Za. That was probably for the best, but he thought that Villat didn't appreciate having special treatment any more than he did.

Zaron could not trust her, though. There were times, still, when he caught her staring at him with a look that marked them as enemies. The others didn't trust Villat, and that made the journey even more uncomfortable.

Za also thought they were never going to walk beyond the grasslands. As the days passed, Tansa began to take them farther south again and away from the distant line of trees so that there was nothing left by which he could mark the distance they traveled except for one step after another.

He did notice, though, when Kintansa began to look less worried and perhaps even hopeful. Having been raised at court, though, Za continued to be distrustful. This daughter had been a long time from home. Many things may have changed. He could not make himself feel any hope, even in the face of her growing smiles.

He thought Mai harbored many of his same worries, though she never put anything into words. In fact, none of them said much at all, fearing they might be heard as they traveled east, south, and then east again. Then, by one of the waterholes, Kintansa pointed out a large round boulder.

"The sign of my father's clan," she said with a decisive nod. "We are in safe territory now."

"Are you certain?" Mai asked, then lifted a hand when Tansa pointed to the boulder. "Oh, not that we're inside your clan's land. I only wonder if it is really safe."

"I can see no reason why it shouldn't be," she said with a frown.

"You were given to the king," Mai said. "Granted that he's long dead, may the gods accept his soul. But they might not want you to come back --"

"Oh, the wise woman always said I would return," she replied with a wave of her hand. She started to lead them around the pool of water, uncaring about the animals that ran and the birds that took to the air. Za couldn't recognize many of them, adding to the alien look of this land. "We knew I was going to Willoway long before Yasidin happened along. He was coming back from his father's court, you know. I was waiting for him to notice me."

Mai looked bothered by the statement, but Tansa had already turned away and started following a trail that led southward again. If the Captain had wanted to discuss Tansa's statements, there was no time. Villat did not look happy, probably because those statements had hinted at unworldly power. The woman still didn't seem to appreciate being alive --

Za looked down at his ragged clothing and saw the dirt on his hands. He couldn't say he blamed her for being unhappy with where they were, at least. Would going to this tribe help? Tansa expected something better. Za had not yet questioned anything that the others had decided; he had gone into an *Ata* stance, at least in his mind. *Take in everything you see and everything others do. Learn from them.* He was, he could tell, reaching the end of that learning period. He knew how to better take care of himself and how not to be a burden to those who were taking him to the destination he had named.

Then something struck him as odd.

His father had been *here.*

Za had only ever seen his father at Summer Cloud Palace and in his mind, that was where he had always been, despite knowing that he'd brought Kintansa back from one of his journeys. What had his father thought of these lands? He'd have been mounted, of course. Not walking in the mud (and worse) that Za had gotten so used to over the days since they left Willoway. What was going on back at the capital now? Za's mind began to bounce between too many things. He had to take several deep breaths and force his concentration on the problem at hand.

Villat. She was a problem for him. She might also become be a problem for the others, though he doubted that Mai would let her do anything rash. Danisin? He'd been showing more annoyance with Villat of late. Za wondered if it was just the journey wearing on all of them.

Had he accepted the magic for himself?

Za wasn't certain, though it had helped them survive. He had something that contributed to this journey that none of the others could do. Time to accept how he could help and turn his attention to other things.

Like the sounds of a village which they were nearing.

CHAPTER FIFTEEN

Tansa pushed ahead of me. I almost reached out to stop her, but this was her place, and I had to trust her here as much as I trusted her in the city. Though, when it came to danger, I had never trusted her much at all. Was this danger? Yes -- but this was still her place.

Two guards, both women, appeared on the trail with spears in hand and moving towards Tansa and the rest of us. I automatically glanced at Za to mark where he stood and prepared to pull Tansa back to help protect him.

Tansa said something I didn't catch, though over the years she had taught me to speak the grasslanders' language with some proficiency. She moved her hand, and the two with the spears took a step backward and looked shocked, though that quickly gave way to amazement. As the rest of us came closer, the taller woman turned and bounded away towards the village I could barely see, a place of huts, tents, and sheep in an enclosure. Children darted everywhere, and dogs barked. I could smell spices and the type of cooking that Tansa liked best.

She waved the rest of us to catch up with her and took my arm. I don't think I'd ever seen her smile so brightly.

"Let us make our grand entrance," she said with a bit of a

laugh.

"We cannot possibly be grand, the way we look," I protested.

She still smiled, kept hold of my arm, and looked back at the others. Za stood behind the two of us and Villat and Danisin remained at the rear. Villat did not, of course, look happy.

Tansa did, though, which made me happier. I did my best not to let my free hand go to my belt knife, even when I saw others gathering in a line near the sheep. They worried me, except that I saw looks of surprise and not distrust. We had really found Kintansa's people. I can't say that made me anymore trusting, but I did enjoy seeing how pleased they were at her return.

A larger man stepped forward, his long-legged stride bringing him right to us so quickly that I could barely yelp. Tansa let go of me just as the man grabbed her --

And held her close. I don't think he ever saw the rest of us. I had a moment to study him; his long hair hung with foxtails, his clothing well made, rings glittering on his fingers. He mumbled something I couldn't hear. Kintansa laughed, said something, and gave a wave of her hand to the rest of us.

"Ah," the man said. He stepped back. Despite a few lines of age and some sprinkling of silver in his hair, he looked robust. "Welcome to Fox Clan, friends of my daughter."

"Sir," Za said with a bow of his head, all very proper.

Had the man ever been to court? He gave the prince a long look and then bowed to him. Then he turned and smiled at me.

"And you our Tansa's Mai. I am pleased to finally meet you in person. Now come, all of you. To my tent. I see that we must talk."

He shouted orders, and people laughed and hurried off to their work. Kintansa gave me a nod which said that all was going well. Good.

The village seemed a strange combination of huts that appeared to have been there for a long, long time with walls of baked brick and doors made of colorful cloth. However, at the far end of the dozen huts sat even more tents, a corral with many sheep -- and to the right a larger enclosure with horses.

Horses were rare creatures in Willoway. I'd only seen a handful in my entire life, and they'd belonged to the royal house. Here she found a couple dozen or more belonging to this Fox Clan. I remembered how, when we had first met, Kintansa had talked about riding, but for some reason, I had never thought about the horses themselves. Now they took my breath away, and I was glad Tansa still had hold of my arm to keep me moving.

We went to the largest of the tents. Tansa was swarmed by a dozen women and then two younger men who came at a rush. Family, I realized.

I had the oddest sensation, to realize that Kintansa had this life apart from me. She'd let go of my arm for a moment, I think because I ran the risk of being trampled, and she babbled to all of them, laughed, and took my arm once more.

Tansa did not abandon me here. I don't know why I would fear such a thing suddenly. I smiled for Tansa as we were taken to a low table and pillows all around.

"Sit down," she said to the rest of our party. "We'll have food and cold tea. We'll tell my father about what has happened."

"Everything?" Villat asked with a dark glance at Za.

"Oh yes, everything," Tansa said and lost a little of her smile. I wanted to kick Villat for upsetting her, even a little.

We settled where Tansa directed us, with Villat between Danisin and me. Tansa sat to my right and Za across from her and beside Danisin.

I wished we'd had time to clean up a little -- but

apparently, that was already a consideration. Tansa's father came into the tent while others followed with towels and bowls of water. We all cleaned up as best we could, and even Villat looked happier for it.

"My father is Tanisk, leader of the Fox Clan," Tansa introduced him as he sat between Tansa and Za. "Father, this is Mai, Villat, Danisin, and Za."

"Welcome to the holdings of my people," he said with a bow of his head. Tansa's father spoke the language well, but then so had Tansa when she first arrived at Summer Clouds Palace. He nodded to each of us, but then turned back to Tansa. "You look well, daughter, but I have to say that I expected you years ago when the king died."

"There was still work to do, and you know it," she said with a moment of seriousness. "I have no idea how many of the mercenaries survived to get out of the city, though. Have you heard anything from the West?"

"You have outraced the rumors," he said, curious now.

"Race is not a word I would use," Tansa replied. "We've already had a long, perilous journey."

People brought in some food and drink. Tansa thanked them. More than a few stopped to put a hand on her shoulder and said words of welcome.

Once we were settled once more, Tansa told the tale of what had brought us here. She left nothing out, including the identity of the prince and what he had done. She did not add how Villat had reacted, but I thought that might only be because she didn't want the woman to create a scene. I had no doubt that her father would learn of that problem before long -- if he hadn't already figured it out. Villat had scowled through most of the tale, even though she was shown as someone who had done the right thing by coming to Danisin.

"Demons," Tanisk said after the tale was done. "The Wise Woman had said there was something unnatural in the world, and she said we would know when the time was right, but it's such a bother, waiting for the signs."

"Has she said anything else?" Tansa asked.

"Enough to make us all uneasy," Tanisk admitted. "Dangers, changes, and that we should not go to the West to trade."

"Wise," I said. I was starting to feel more at ease here. "There is going to be chaos in the borderlands as the truth about Willoway spreads. And it will spread -- enough people saw the demons to know the real danger."

"But not who brought them," Villat said. She looked at Za. "So far, I've only seen one person with magic."

I sighed, but Za was the one who looked past Danisin to her. "You're right, I am the only one you saw. Mai saw something different. Tansa saw something else."

"And you saved my life from the demon," Tansa added.

"We don't know --"

"For all we know, *you* brought the demons, Villat," I said, annoyed with her continuing attack. "You've had your say. Za, do you have anything to add?"

He did, in fact. He told the tale of the demons in the palace and spoke the words with much the same flare that Kintansa had told her tale. Tanisk listened and nodded and shook his head at the death of Endris and what had apparently been the passing of power, though Za hadn't realized it at the time.

"Hardly a fair thing to do without permission or warning," Tanisk replied with a look of commiseration. "However, I think, this was the best the brave man could do to keep you safe, Prince Zaron --"

"Za. I cannot see that being a prince is ever going to matter again. Whatever I do, there will be others like Villat who believe the Queen, no matter how she acts, rather than me."

"I do not believe --" Villat began, but then she stopped as though she realized the contradictory nature of her feelings for the first time. She picked up a piece of bread and dipped it in honey and stayed silent.

There was an improvement at last.

"We know of the *Art of Ata*," Tanisk said as he leaned back on his pillows. I could see the same look of contemplation on his face as I had sometimes seen in Tansa. "And the ancient tales of magic that had been part of the stories. Such tales often have a whisper of truth in them. I think, Za, that you must spend some time with the Wise Woman. I'll talk to her. She doesn't like outsiders much, but I think you will intrigue her. Are you willing?"

"I am happy to learn anything I can about what has happened to me," Za replied with a bow of his head. "And I wish to know how I can help in the future."

"Good. You'll be with us for a few days, at least. I'll send riders west to see if there is any sign of trouble. We'll prepare you for the journey to the sea, though I cannot say it is safe to sail, but I see no other way for you to get to the Court of the Tiger. Going overland and through the northern mountains -- no, especially this time of year. Once the rumors of what happened in Willoway reach the east, they'll spread quickly. Sailing will be safer and faster."

That night the tribe held a homecoming feast for Tansa. She apparently had not expected it. We'd napped -- gods and goddesses, it was good to sleep and let others worry about guarding us. We'd been exhausted, but at sunset we awoke to the sounds of drums and flutes and spent the rest of the night in joyous celebration.

Za stayed with Tanisk, and I counted him safe enough that I didn't spend all my time trying to watch him. For a few hours as the moon rose over us, we listened to tales, translated by Tanisk or Tansa, about the gods, the animals -- and once even about the *Art of Ata*, which I saw Za listen to with rapt attention.

Tansa and I danced together. She taught me the simple steps and though I felt clumsy at first, I soon began to enjoy myself. Men and women danced with us in various pairs, so we were not the only two women together, and there were two sets of men as well.

We ate more. We drank sweet cider, and I wondered how far these people had to go for the apples. We danced and sang.

And I realized, suddenly, that Tanisk and the Fox Clan had given us back our joy in life. Not everything in the world had gone wrong since the moment the prince arrived at my inn. There were still places untouched by the evil, and by the gods, I hoped it never came here.

They gave me a new reason to fight.

We slept in a tent, Villat, Tansa and me. Danisin and Za took another one, and I did make certain he felt safe there. He waved me away with a laugh. One of Tansa's brothers stood guard between the two tents that night.

Out of my hands for a little while.

I curled up in Tansa's arms and slept well.

CHAPTER SIXTEEN

Za had never known such a place or people. He felt unexpectedly safe with them, though. He woke early to the sounds of the village and walked to the latrine and back to the tent before the sun even fully rose. Danisin had gotten up as well, stretching and looking more at ease than he had since they met.

Za stood outside the tent, taking in the scents and the sights. These were not wealthy people, at least in the way that would have counted in Willoway, let alone in the Summer Clouds Palace. They were happier, though. He could see that in all the faces that passed him.

Time, he thought, to meditate on what he had learned.

Za sat down on the ground to the right of the tent's opening, pulled his legs up to cross them, clasped his hands, and bowed his head. He had feared that calling back the calm of *Ata* would be difficult, but he fell into a trance far easier today than he ever had in the past.

His mind ran through all the things he'd learned, especially since he had come to this village. The tales from the night before had held so much wisdom that he'd had to grab at everything he could, keep it in his mind, and wait for this moment to look more closely at the tales. He knew he wouldn't be able to untangle it all in one sitting, but Za started the work of sorting what he'd heard. He knew to accept knowledge where anyone offered him help.

Later, he lifted his head, knowing someone had come to see him. He gave Tanisk a nod of greeting and rose to his feet, aching far less than he had for many days, though his side still bothered him.

An older woman stood with Tanisk. He'd seen her at the gathering and knew she was the Wise Woman of the village. He gave her a proper bow of his head.

"Polite, at least," she mumbled in her own language.

"I try to be," he answered in the same language and saw one eyebrow lift in the wrinkled face. "I was raised as a Prince Heir. My teachers thought it wise if I knew the words of as many of the people as possible so that I did not have to depend on the translations of those who might not want me to know the truth."

"Wise not to be so trusting," she admitted and tilted her head, scraggly gray hair flying in the breeze. "And now you speak the languages of the people you rule --"

"I rule no one. I cannot see that I ever will. Everything changed when the demons came back to our world."

"Yes," she agreed with such an emphatic nod that set her hair bouncing this time, shells clapping against each other. How far did this clan trade that she casually wore such gifts from the sea? Za appeared to have passed a test because even Tanisk relaxed. "Come with me. You alone. She cannot always guard you."

Za looked back to see that Mai had, indeed, stepped forward as though she meant to go with him. Za shook his head. She would have argued, but Tanisk and Kintansa took her in hand.

Za went with the old woman, out along the edges of the village and finally to a hut that stood apart from the others.

Birds flew off from the roof as they approached, a swarm of them circling up into the sky in a spiral before they settled down again.

"Good sign," the woman grunted and led him inside the little building.

The place was so fragrant with herbs and dried flowers that Za had to stifle a sneeze fearing that it would be an insult. The woman tied the cloth covering back from the door, so he had a little light. A good thing since the single room was littered with baskets woven from grass and filled with supplies.

She waved him toward a pile of pillows, and he sat down quickly, glad to be still. It wasn't that he felt weak today. However, in the dark, close room he had feared that he might kick things over at any moment.

Movement at the woman's feet drew his startled attention. A fox had come out of the darker shadows and watched Za for a moment. Then the creature sat on the pillow beside him.

"Ah, like that is it?" the old woman said with a nod. "Good then. I don't have to guess."

She left the two of them, crossing the room and pulling out items he could not clearly see. She poured something into a bottle and from the faint scent he picked out from the others, it was not water. Other things went in as well, and she swirled the bottle in her hand, round and round while she chanted. They were not the words of the Fox Clan, he realized. The Wise Woman held the keys to a far older, different culture.

She came back, kicked a pillow away from him and sat on it so that they faced one another. The fox remained.

"We shall journey together," she said and handed him a small clay cup encircled with intricate designs. She filled it with a sweet-smelling liquid. "I do not know where we will go, but if we are lucky, there will be answers."

She poured some of the same liquid into a cup of her own

and put the bottle aside. Then she drank it down in one gulp.

He did the same.

"Good," she mumbled. She grabbed Za's hand, her gnarled, warm fingers wrapping tight around his. "Hold to me."

Za nodded and wondered what --

Chaos.

A portion of Za's mind held to the fact that he remained in the hut. He knew that to be true, and he would not lose that link to reality. The more significant portion of his mind believed they were no longer even in the world, he and the Wise Woman he held to so tightly. He almost panicked, but he called *Ata* too him, forced calm, and looked around for some way out.

"Not yet," Wise Woman said.

She stood beside him, more shape or shadow than real, but he recognized her, nonetheless. The fox stood at her feet, that animal fully formed and as real as the one on the pillow back in the hut. The creature gave a little bark and bounded off into a swirl of green and black.

"That way," she said.

Za followed the fox. As long as he could hold to *Ata*, he felt remarkably calm and curious. Za could not tell if the Wise Woman and Fox were indeed with him or if he conjured them from his own mind, but it hardly mattered. Either way, they led him toward something.

The green and black chaos swept in curls around him, so thick and dark that he could not see the fox itself, but only the swirl of where he passed. They went on, not far, though he knew that it wasn't a safe journey.

The fox stopped. For a moment Za didn't know --

The miasma of the clouds took shapes now. We looked down at streets -- Willoway, Za realized when he spotted the palace grounds overlooking the city from the north.

The city seemed a dark place, even in the light of day. Shadows hung over every building and street. The great gates leading in and out of Willoway remained locked at all four quarters, and no one stood there now, demanding to leave.

Za saw few people, though he sensed others hiding in their homes. No business had opened, but some brave souls scurried from door to door and apparently made quiet trades.

Draw no attention.

Something watched.

Za turned to the towering Summer Clouds Palace, knowing he would find trouble there, hidden in the golden walls and silken pavilions. Even this place appeared as empty of life as everywhere else. Nothing stirred --

Except two huge, dark shadows that rose above the gardens -- or the grounds at least, since none of the plants and statues had survived.

Wise Woman made a little hiss of worry and held his arm, stopping him. Fox darted to stand behind them. They had found the demons, and the demons sensed that they were near. Za saw the shapes he remembered too well, but they appeared to be far more extensive now, as though they were bloated with power. Their eyes glowed with a sickly yellow, and the claws that lifted into the air dripped with poisons as did their teeth. One and then the other let out shrill yells of defiance. He shuddered, and so did Wise Woman. Fox retreated in haste. He thought they should follow, but then he realized that although the demons sensed them, they didn't seem to know where they were. The two had stood to show their strength -- but they stared at the ground where any other human would be.

He, Wise Woman and the fox were not truly at Willoway. They looked on from some other plane, and one that kept them a little apart from the demons. Za found this frustrating in some ways, because though he could watch, he could do nothing. Za accepted that this was not a drug-inspired dream, and that the single cup of liquid would not keep him here for long. He needed to learn something.

Za moved slightly to the right. The demons screamed again, but they still had no clear idea of where the intruders were or -- Za hoped -- who they might be.

Something glowed near the ground. Za wanted a closer look, but Wise Woman held him back, which was indeed wise, he realized. The demons still looked at the ground for them. Best not to go near where they were expected.

He maneuvered in a wide circle instead, hoping to see better. The glow came from something flat and swirling with green, yellow, and red light. A portal of some sort?

Za didn't ask; if he could hear the world, then those of the world would hear him. The demons growled, a low snarl that promised destruction to the enemy. Za could almost hear words in those sounds. Did demons have a language? Was it one that could be taught, like learning Ristan or the language of the Grassland clans? *Ata* taught that words were powerful, and that sometimes individual words had a power of their own, and one must be careful not to be ensnared by them.

A worrisome thought as the demons growled their words.

Queen Taranis arrived at the garden gate, the three princesses following. Aia, he noted, had to be held to her feet by her two sisters, neither of whom looked happy at the job. No guards here. No servants.

"Oh, great ones, what troubles you?" his mother yelled.

She was brave to stand here before the unsettled demons -- and more willfully stupid than he had believed, as well. The demons were not in the mood to talk to humans, and even he could see so. Both snapped at her, mouths so close that he thought she would be killed. The queen backed away in haste but did not leave.

"Is it time to hunt again?" she shouted above their

growing growls. "There are still people enough in the city for you. They are trapped like pigs in a pen."

Za snarled, a little sound, but it drew attention again. He held his breath. The demons looked back at his mother, huge mouths moving towards her, eyes of yellow showing such hatred that she must see their intentions.

A murmur of growls again.

"Then it shall be so," the Queen said. The Queen understood the language of the demons? "You shall have that strength. Let us begin. Give them Aia, my sweets."

Aia gave a weak scream of protest. Her two sisters, though, happily dragged her forward and threw her at the feet of the demons.

First one and then the other demon hooked their clawed feet into her arms. Her screams grew louder, but neither mother nor sisters showed any compassion. Za, who had never liked his sisters at all, still felt the compulsion to rush to her aid. Only Wise Woman's tight hold held him in place.

They tore her apart. She had died long before they were finished, and one kicked her head into the swirling portal where it disappeared.

They were stronger.

Time to go.

Za and his two companions retreated from the palace in haste, back along the roofs of the city buildings, watching the poor people who had heard the demons if not the screams of the princess. Several of the buildings they passed this time had been torn apart, and Za had no doubt the demons had done the work, prying out humans to eat.

Nowhere safe in Willoway.

Fox nudged at his legs, and he turned and followed the creature back into the green and black cloud. He let Wise Woman lead him back while he considered --

They did not go back to her hut.

Za looked around in shock as they glided over water that spread out everywhere. Ocean, he realized with a start. He could not see land in any direction which made him shiver despite himself. This was where he and his friends intended to go? How could they hope to cross such an expanse of nothing? No. There had to be another --

"Look there," Wise Woman said and pointed.

He saw land off to the left. They turned that way; Za was at least curious about what they would find and wondered if it really meant anything helpful.

An island. Volcanic, he realized. He'd read of such things in his studies, but it was odd to see the smoke belching upward from the depths of the earth, a faint foul smell to the air. The ground itself trembled and trees perched precariously on the edges of the cone swayed. A few fell and tumbled towards the lower lands.

An extensive settlement stood on the edge of the sea. Za never would have expected to see a place filled with people in such an inhospitable location. The bay seemed deep and secluded, though, and several ships sat at anchor. He noted how people in the town's narrow streets, and even crews on the ships, stood still and watched the tip of the volcano. The trembling of the trees stopped, and the smoke became a mere trickle of white into the sky. He felt as much as saw the relief of the others.

"Remember this place," Wise Woman whispered.

And they were moving away before he had any idea of why they'd come to the island. He felt a little surge of frustration. He could not act when they saw the demons and he could not understand what the island could mean to him.

Better, though, to have some warning rather than be ignorant of everything. Za hoped to find out what the ocean and island meant. He must meditate on all he learned --

Back into the cloud, Fox leading the way. Back through

the chaos that seemed worse than it had been when they first entered.

Then, for a moment, he saw something odd off to the right -- golden lighted-flowers, the skull of an antelope, antlers glowing with light as well. Something ancient and reaching toward Za. Hadn't that been the old symbol of the Goddess Aia, who was the goddess of hope for the new spring --

Wise Woman grabbed and yanked him along.

Back to the hut.

"Ah," he said. He put both of his hands to the ground. Everything still moved, and he feared he would be very ill. He could not even think of what words to say.

"Lie down. Rest until the feeling passes," Wise Woman said. "Think on what we saw, both in Willoway and the island. I cannot see the link, but it will be there, somewhere. That business with your sister - that was more than it seemed, I think."

Za laid back and shivered, both at the illness and at a reality he had not fully accepted until Wise Woman confirmed what they had both seen. Za had known the liquid held drugs -- but he had thought, deep in his subconscious, that he'd imagined his two companions. To have Wise Woman say those words about the city and the island put that convenient lie for his sanity aside. They had taken that journey together, and that meant everything he had seen was probably the literal truth.

Should he be sorry for Aia's death?

Why did he wonder such a thing now? He felt anger at what his mother and sisters were doing to Willoway and knew they would spread such evils far beyond the city. Why should he care about Aia at a time like this?

Maybe because it made him more human. Perhaps because it made him better than his mother and sisters, who had thrown Aia away.

Za stayed still for a long time. Wise Woman went about her business as though the journey had been nothing more than a walk through the village for her. He thought to be angry or embarrassed, but neither emotion would help.

Eventually, he sat up. Wise Woman crossed and handed him another clay cup which he stared at with some consternation.

She laughed with a cackle of sound, but still enough to bring a smile even to him.

"Oh wise, prince -- to be careful, even if one cup too late," she said at last. "This one is only water, though. Drink. You will feel better. Then I will return you to your friends before Mai comes demanding you back and we have to face off against each other." She laughed again and took back the empty cup. "She is brave and loyal. Yes. Like a fox. All of you are like foxes, moving carefully and quietly through the land. All except the one who works against you, even though she doesn't realize the harm. Yes."

She nodded several times and went back across the room to putter around with herbs and baskets.

Za did feel better, and when he stood, she came to him and nodded, leading him back out. The day was all but gone, and he was glad for the softer shades of sunset rather than the bright light of afternoon. His head ached. He wanted to sit and truly meditate on what he'd seen. He couldn't even decide if he should tell the others, though he suspected Kintansa would believe in the journey, and Mai would accept for her sake. Danisin? Maybe. Villat -- no, he would not share this with her. She was not one of them.

An odd realization, but it was true.

Mai came away from her tent when they neared. She looked worried and shook her head. "You don't look well, Za." She dared a worried glance at the woman who had brought him.

"Headache is all," Za replied with a wave of his hand. "I need to sit and think on all I've experienced today."

Kintansa, as he had expected, gave a nod of agreement. "Let him rest a while," Tansa said with a look of commiseration. "Spirit journeys are hard on those of us who prepare years for them. I can't imagine what it was like to just suddenly take such a perilous trip through the edges of reality without any preparation. Dangerous and difficult, I would guess."

He gave a nod of agreement and settled by his tent. "I just need to think. Thank you, Wise Woman. And Fox."

Fox was there at the woman's feet. The little creature gave what looked like a proper bow of his head which amused Za but seemed to worry Mai.

"I must talk to Tanisk," Wise Woman said. She turned and walked away with her odd companion, and Za had the feeling there was far more on her mind than the few things he'd seen.

Mai knelt by him, still looking worried. Kintansa, Danisin, and Villat stood close by. He would say nothing important before that woman, though. She still glared.

"I need to think," he said softly to Mai. "I'm fine. I believe I have learned things, but I cannot parse them yet."

Villat scoffed and turned away, though she didn't go far enough. He gave a last nod to Mai, bowed his head and sought if not enlightenment, at least a bit of peace.

CHAPTER SEVENTEEN

Za appeared to be better when Tanisk called for the evening meal just after the sun had gone down. The day had been more difficult for me than I had expected. I couldn't say that I trusted Prince Zaron out of my sight, which was going to make life difficult if I didn't get over that obsession. Even Tansa had barely kept me occupied and entertained, though I appreciated that she did her best to try.

I had spent most of the day with Tansa while she wandered through the village and greeted old friends and relatives. I'd been uneasy at first, the outsider who had laid some claim to *their* Kintansa. The greetings and friendliness of the others soon put that worry aside, though. They made me feel as though I belonged here with them just as much as Tansa.

That was an odd feeling for a woman who had never belonged anywhere except for a few years in Prince Yasidin's Guard. I'd had a family once, but they'd been poor farmers working just outside the city walls. The chance came to join the army when I was twelve, and I'd gone off without much thought about my family again. I'd been one of a dozen children, and we'd worked as hard as our parents. I'd hated farming.

I knew they'd all moved off to another village when I was sixteen and finally old enough to take the patrols in the city. I'd never seen any of them again.

How odd. I had not thought about that life in a lot of years. Maybe it was the fields of wheat and barley that they grew near the village that had reawakened those memories. It was not, I thought, Tansa's relationship with her relatives which was like nothing like I'd ever known.

I studied Za for a moment as he watched Tansa -- and I realized he had even less understanding of family relationships than I did. Not a surprise there since Za's father, though he'd cared about the boy, had never developed any kind of lasting relationship with the child. I'd been under the impression that would have come when the boy came of age and could have shared his father's life. King Yasidin had liked to hunt, to race ... to do any number of things that a young child could not.

And his mother never cared for the prince at all.

Za stood by me. He still seemed distant a day after whatever had happened with the Wise Woman, but I thought that distance came from thought, not whatever drugs she'd used. I still felt a flare of rage at what had happened, but I kept that anger buried as best I could. I did not trust the Wise Woman alone with Za again, though, and I could tell she knew my intentions and found them amusing if nothing else.

"We dare not stay much longer," Za said with a solemn shake of his head.

"Why do you say that?" I asked.

"For the same reason that you spend so much time at the edge of the village looking toward the west. If anyone is following us, I don't want my war to catch them as well."

"Your war?" I asked, shocked by the words. "What makes you think this is your war alone?"

"If it had not been for me, the rest of you would all be back in the city still --"

"And dead by now. We would have been fighting against something we could not win against, not even if we had joined forces with others. You, Za, have given us a reason to escape and learn what we need to win. This is not your war alone. You have not told me what happened with the Wise Woman."

"Tansa didn't tell you?" he asked, surprised.

"You told Tansa because you knew she would understand and believe. She didn't feel she had the right to tell the rest of us since this is your spirit journey. She said that such journeys are sometimes too personal to share."

"That's not the case this time. We went back to Willoway, Wise Woman, Fox and I."

Za told me the tale, of everything he saw, and I did my best to keep the skepticism from my face. It wasn't until he spoke about being back in the hut and the Wise Woman saying the things she had about where they'd been that I felt one of those unpleasant moments when I feared it had all been true.

"Well damn," I mumbled.

He laughed. "I felt much the same way. I wanted it all to have been a dream -- a nightmare, really -- with some esoteric meaning that it might take me years to parse. I did not want it to be now and real."

"But you think it is."

"I fear so."

I didn't argue. I looked to the west again, as though I could see all the way back to Willoway. Demons and dead princesses notwithstanding, I still feared an army coming after us the most.

Tansa found us standing there. She put a hand on my shoulder and offered a smile. "Don't worry. We'll be leaving in the morning," she said softly.

"No, Tansa, I didn't mean to --"

She caught my arm and lead me aside. Za, being a well-mannered young man, headed towards his tent. I had stopped panicking every time he walked away by himself, but I still didn't like it.

"We are leaving in the morning," Tansa said again and more forcefully. "I've already made all the arrangements."

"All?" I asked softly. We walked back amongst people again.

"Yes."

That brought a surge of relief on many counts. I was glad to have everything in Tansa's hands this time. I think my standing aside might have helped her in some ways. She had proven herself the leader of our group and no longer the young woman who had been stolen away --

I rethought that one.

"You went willingly with King Yasidin," I said.

She gave me a bright smile. "Father noticed his attention was more on me than on him. We let him think that I could be bought. If he'd been half as observant as his son, he never would have fallen for the trick. I was to go to Willoway and the palace for a few years and then make my way back home as best I could."

"You never told me that," I said and tried not to sound hurt

"I feared you would think I was stupid for having chosen to come there. I couldn't bear the thought that you'd think badly of me," she admitted, her head bowed.

I placed my fingers under her chin and lifted her face to look into mine. "I understand. I never told you I was the child of farmer for fear you'd think less of me. So, there we are, secret traded for secret. Could you have escaped that day without me?" I asked.

"No," she replied with a frown, and I thought she meant that word. We paused by the sheep pen and the creatures crowded around. Tansa liked sheep but she hardly noticed them at all this time. "I was taken completely unprepared, and the good Queen would have moved in on me before I had the word that he'd been taken. There had always been dangers. I'd been sending messages home with traders when I could, but even that had gotten difficult."

"Why didn't you leave after I got you free?" I asked.

She pulled me into an embrace, her lips close to my ear. "I could not leave you behind, my love," she whispered. Then she pulled back and smiled. "And you were not ready to go. We were right to create the Lightning Mercenaries. For a few years, they helped to hold the line, you know. We kept the Queen from moving too soon."

"Maybe we pushed her toward contact with the demons," I suggested.

She frowned. "Maybe so. But would it have been better to slip away in the shadows and do nothing? We could not know she would do something so drastic, so we fought her in human ways, mostly by the sides we took in other battles when she wasn't paying enough attention. No, we did the right thing, Mai. I am not going to regret doing our best to keep her from killing others, including the prince."

I glanced over at the prince's tent. As I had expected, I found him sitting cross-legged on the ground beside it, his head bowed and his ragged dark hair falling like a veil over his face. He looked like someone different than the person we had gathered up in the city and herded along with us. It wasn't just the hair. He'd grown up.

And oddly, he no longer looked so much like his father. That made me wonder if King Yasidin had ever grown up. I suspected that he had naively never believed his wife would dare move against him, the son of the Tiger of the East. The queen had dared many things, testing the water, over the years. We all should have seen his death coming. I had feared Yasidin would be poisoned. The public execution had been shocking -- so much so, that it stopped all of us from reacting in any reasonable way.

I shook my head and went with Tansa into our tent. We spoke softly and alone for a little while. We had a short time to ourselves. I pulled her into my arms, and we put the time to good use.

We had another feast that night. Word had spread that we would be leaving in the morning. Supplies were already being gathered, and we were all showered with personal gifts -- necklaces, rings, clothing. They seemed genuinely reluctant to have us leave, though I could not imagine why. Everyone had to know the trouble that we could draw by now.

"You have been most kind and generous to your wayward daughter and her friends," Tansa announced after the last dance. "You have both reminded me of what I am and made me proud to be Fox Clan. I wish that matters were not so dire that we must go on already, but we will leave at first light. Villat, you will not be going with us."

The woman looked up, her perpetual glare replaced by shock and worry. "You can't --"

"You will stay here as the guest of Fox Clan for a full turning of the seasons. You will be treated as a guest unless you try to escape; then you will be a prisoner and denied the freedoms you already have. At the end of the seasons, you will be given supplies and taken back to the main road that goes to Willoway --"

"Let me go now!" she cried out, starting to get to her feet. Danisin held her down. He looked troubled, but he did not argue.

"We cannot trust you, Villat," I said and met her glare full on this time, though without the anger I had expected to find in myself. "I'm sorry, but we simply cannot trust you with everything you know of our plans and about Prince Zaron. You'll be fine here. I think, once you accept that you are a guest and treated well, you might even enjoy it. You would not enjoy what we are going to do."

She stared for a moment, and I saw unexpected intelligence as she took in those words. Villat didn't like the idea of staying among strangers -- neither would I -- for the entire next year, but she knew I told the truth about our journey to come. None of us would like it, and I wondered if Danisin might want to remain as well.

He looked to me and shook his head. There was no question about leaving Za behind, and Tansa wouldn't remain, even though she loved her people.

Did I want to go?

No, but I would. Duty and honor, as well as love of Tansa, would not allow me to step aside at this point. So, the prince would have three guards. I hoped we were enough to get him all the way to the Court of the Tiger.

I slept as best I could that night, awakening at the odd sounds of the little village which I had already come to recognize and accept. Soon we would leave the grasslands behind, but there were the farmers of the highlands and then the fishing folk along the shore. Tansa hadn't traveled this way in a while, but she remembered the trails. Besides, all you really had to do was head east until you reached the ocean. You couldn't miss it unless you didn't know enough to follow the rising sun.

That sun rose too early the next day. We packed up our supplies. Tansa and I were out first, but Za and Danisin arrived only a moment later. Villat had taken up residence with Tansa's widowed aunt, a kind but strict and observant woman. I had the feeling that Villat would do well there.

Tansa's father and four others met us. They were dressed for travel.

"Father --" Kintansa began to protest.

"I am only going a few weeks early to the coast for the regular trade," Tanisk said before she could start. "There have been rumors of trouble to the west, you see. I want to know if it is more widespread, and to get to the coast ahead of any trouble that might be heading our way."

"This is the truth," I found myself saying with a nod.

"Yes," he agreed. "That my daughter and her friends are with us is of no matter right now. Come. The horses are ready."

"Horses," I said, startled.

"You don't think I'd make you walk, did you?" He flashed a bright smile. "Tansa says you have ridden, you and Za."

"Not for many years," Za replied, though he looked pleased. I nodded agreement. "Danisin?"

"I'm a city boy. I've never been near a horse or on one. Maybe I should --"

"Learn to ride," Tanisk said with a slap on his shoulder. "Don't worry. We will go slowly. To ride off in a rush now would only draw attention."

Danisin gave a reluctant nod of agreement. He spotted Villat off to the left and went that way to say goodbye. I considered the same but gave her only a nod that she returned without a glare.

I had only walked past the horses before this, always thinking that I would have nothing to do with the long-legged creatures. Now we each had a mount plus they brought three more horses to carry extra supplies. The saddles were not the same as I had seen back at court, but then those had been mostly for show anyway.

The Wise Woman waited by the horses. She crossed straight to Za. "Be wise boy. Remember what you've seen."

"I could hardly forget it," he replied, which was more straightforward than he usually spoke. Wise Woman grinned agreement. The fox barked and Za bowed his head to the creature. I didn't even ask if he understood what the creature had said. I didn't want to consider any more strangeness this morning.

We mounted the horses, Danisin so uneasy that I almost laughed.

We headed out into the rising sun.

CHAPTER EIGHTEEN

Za didn't worry about leaving Villat behind. She would be treated well, and for the first time since this insane journey began, he didn't worry about having her out of his sight. He also didn't worry about who rode behind him. He knew the four who came with Tanisk; they'd been friendly from the first day, and he suspected they'd been preparing him for this addition to his usual traveling companions. Linta and Pala were a little older than Tansa and looked a great deal like their cousin. Was that done on purpose, so that Kintansa did not stand out?

Kintansa no longer wore her hair in spikes, he'd noticed. Her hair wasn't as long as that of her Fox Clan cousins, but it wasn't unusually short, either.

Nysin and Yotsky were introduced as trusted friends of her father. Hunting companions, they'd said as they rode off, but from the way they talked about the trails to the coast, it was clear they'd both made that journey more than once.

A good group. Za was glad to have them along, but mostly because it allowed Mai and Tansa to relax just a little. Za always made certain he remained near one of his original companions as they rode along the narrow, grass-lined trails. He didn't mistrust any of the others, but he wanted to keep

Mai happy.

Za liked to ride beside Danisin, giving him pointers on how to sit and control the horse. Though Za was no expert rider, he could at least help in this way.

"We'll all be sore for the first few days," Za admitted and shifted slightly. From the horse, he could see over the tall grass, which he thought Mai especially appreciated. "It can't be helped. But this will significantly shorten the journey. And the company is good."

He smiled at Nysin as he said those words. Nysin had moved up beside them in an area where the trail widened. After half a day of riding, the grasslands were already less dense than they had been near the village.

"We'll be in the borderlands before sunset," Nysin explained with a wave of his hand to the world before them. "Yot is going to ride ahead and see if there is any reason to avoid the town. Sometimes we do if it looks too boisterous, so if we camp off in the wilds, it won't look entirely too strange. We aren't going to do anything too out of the ordinary, but then we've always made certain we weren't too set in our ways, either."

"And we'll be speaking trade-talk, which is really just the language of the realm," Tansa added, looking back over her shoulder. The horse rode on without her guidance, following the others. Mai still looked like she didn't trust her animal, and she kept a close hold on her own mount.

"I don't look much like you," Danisin said with a touch of worry.

"Fox is a border clan," Nysin replied. "Yotsky was born to the farmers. We have a couple people who came all the way from the fishing villages. We are not one people."

"I noticed that," Za said and found himself smiling. "You seemed to be everything that the empire should embrace instead of fragmenting into each little group, each little territory."

Nysin smiled. "Yes. And you sounded more like a prince just then than you have since you came to be with us."

"My apologies," he said with a laugh. "But I am glad to know there are such places."

Nysin gave a bow of his head and rode on. Danisin went back to trying to understand his horse, and Za let his body relax as he thought about the last few days with Fox Clan, though not the time with Wise Woman; that was something apart from the rest. Instead, he considered how willing to accept even him the people had been. They had been welcomed for Tansa's sake, at least at first, but as the villagers had learned about what had happened, they'd been more willing to help, even if it meant they might one day face the Queen's wrath.

They had done what was right, as had Za's companions. Was he doing the same? Had he drawn them into this journey for his own sake, or for the sake of the empire?

Why go to the Tiger of the East? Why not stay and fight? Could they build an army before the Queen moved against them? No, he really didn't think they could have done that work, even with the mercenaries at the core. Better to go someplace that had an army fully trained. Why not to the Wolf of the West? The journey through the river valleys and over the mountain pass would not have been any longer -- but less safe, too. The Wolf had started to lose his hold. Bandits ruled in some villages. His mother had not been willing to send help to such places, and he knew it was because she wanted the Wolf weakened. Za had begun to wonder if she hadn't sent the bandits out herself.

The Queen (he had never in his life called her mother) had made an irreparable rift when she had the Tiger of the East's son killed for treason. Za hated politics, but it had been the whole basis of his life and still drove him to his grandfather's court. He knew that if they did not find someone to stand against Queen Taranis, then they might as well sail across the vast ocean to other lands.

Za even played with that idea for a while as they rode along. His grandfather was no fool; as soon as the rumors of what was happening at Willoway reached him, he would consider the matter. He might dismiss the talk of demons the first time, but before long he would hear of the demons more often and know something odd must be happening. He would send someone --

A long time for a spy's travel, back and forth. Would he employ magic instead? Try to spy on Queen Taranis through some spell? The Eastern Court did deal more in magic than the Willoway or the Western Court. If they had such spells, wouldn't they be watching over her already? Wouldn't they already know?

Couldn't he sail away across the ocean to some new life? Maybe that was what the sight of that volcanic island had meant. Perhaps he should go there -- though it had not looked so safe in the visions.

"You look troubled," Danisin said as he shifted again and winced.

"I dare not swerve from the right path," he replied with a sigh of regret. Danisin looked surprised. "I've spent all my life at court and under the Queen's careful watch. Having a little freedom, even under these circumstances, makes me wish I were a different person."

"You had a good life at Summer Cloud Palace," Danisin protested.

"I had a life of pretense," he corrected with a courtly wave of his hand. Servants would have leapt at that signal. "Not a bad life, but one in which everyone bowed to me, but ran to my mother with anything out of the ordinary. I don't know how Endris convinced her that the *Art of Ata* was something that would be good for me. I suspect, since I was getting older, he told her it was a way to keep me busy and out of the eyes of others, since so much of the *Art* is done in quiet corners, sitting still and meditating. Her acceptance of that training is also a sign that she never intended for me to rule, you know. *Ata* is still considered a peasant practice."

"Do you want to go back to Willoway and rule?"

"No," he said. He couldn't lie about it.

"But you will," Danisin said with a nod of understanding.

"I will if that is how the days unfold. The times are odd, my friend. None of us may make it to the Eastern Court, and even if we do, my grandfather may not agree to even see me." He brushed his hair back and shook his head. "I would like to think that something as insubstantial as a braid would not stop him from doing the right thing. I've heard, though, that he's grown even more stubborn in his old age. I've only met him once in my life. I can't say what we'll find."

"But he is the best chance we have for stopping the Queen and her pet demons."

"I think so. If some of the rest of you have other ideas --"

"We would have voiced them long before now, my friend." Danisin shook his head. "I shouldn't call you by that term."

"Ah," Za said and bowed his head.

"Oh, not because I don't think you are my friend," Danisin said and daringly reached over and touched his arm, drawing Za's attention. "You, though, are the Prince Heir. You could well be my king before we're done --"

"It is unlikely I'll hold that title," Za replied. "Yes, I'd be willing to rule, but they won't have me, you know. She spread the lies about me, and those lies will grow, especially since I won't be there to counter them. That I won't rule doesn't bother me. I never expected to since I was never in her favor. She was only waiting for the right time and situation to be rid of me."

"Well, that's true enough," Danisin agreed, not in the least surprised. "We speculated daily on your chances of surviving until sunset. Festivals, when you rode out with the guard, were days of great bets on whether or not you would get back to the palace alive."

"Were they truly?" he asked and then laughed at the nod. "The servants used to do the same. They didn't even try to hide it from me. When I was younger, they frightened me with the game, but as I grew older, I used to toss in a coin or two myself."

Danisin laughed. "And how did you choose?"

"I based it on the Queen's last interview with me. If she had been at all kind, I figured I was not meant to survive long."

"You never call her your mother."

"No, I do not. Neither do the Queen's daughters. She is The Queen, and we were never allowed to forget her place."

Danisin said nothing more. Za had the impression he still tried to understand what had happened. Za could have told him the single, most important answer: *The Queen is ambitious.* However, he thought Danisin should figure it all out on his own. The Queen's constant grabbing at power was no secret outside the court, but the degree to which it reached had come as a surprise even to Za.

Not long before the sun went down, Yot rode back to talk to Tanisk. Za hoped only that they would stop, get off the horses, and walk the rest of the way to The Court of the Tiger.

Unfortunately, they rode on. Tanisk spoke to Kintansa and Mai. Mai pulled back to talk to Danisin and him.

"We're going to the village," she said, but with a frown. "Yotsky says rumors from the west have reached it, but nothing about demons that he heard. We'll want to know what they're saying."

"How did rumors get here ahead of us?" Danisin asked.

"Traders came through the grasslands and the rumors passed from clan to clan," Mai said. "That's what Tansa told me. We stayed off the main trails, and we moved on foot. People on horseback had plenty of time."

"Are they looking for me?" Za asked.

"We don't think so," Mai replied with a shake of her head, though she looked back as though she expected someone to suddenly appear. "But we'll be careful, all of us. Yotsky arranged for us to stop at the inn where members of the Fox Clan always stay. By the time we get there, people will be ready for us with food, drink -- and gossip."

"And I should stay silent and listen," Za said with a nod.

"Not too quiet. You speak the language of the clans better than the rest of us, you know. However, do listen. I suspect that you have a good knack for hearing things that mean something we don't catch."

"The only way to survive at court," Za replied, and she nodded agreement. She had, after all, spent time at court as a guard.

As they came over the next small rise, he finally saw the village in the distance, setting at the bottom of a hill and nestled by a wide river. This was the largest settlement they'd visited since they left Willoway. They'd avoided towns and villages all the way to the Fox Clan settlement. Za's worry about going back among strangers almost made him slow and pull back, but he kept control, loosened his hold on the reins, and made no show of himself as they rode down the widening road through well-kept farmlands.

"What is this place?" he asked when Pala moved past.

"Dell Crossing," she explained as she slowed to ride with them. "The river is the Dell. It's low right now so we'll wade the horses across rather than taking the ferry. That will be tomorrow morning."

He nodded, though the thought of riding horses through that water did not appeal to him.

They rode past the small homes of farmers and twice had to slow for sheep and goats to cross the roads. Farmers with wagons rode past, all of them coming from town, and all the carts empty. It must have been market day. A shame they had not arrived earlier and had a chance at picking up more supplies.

Dell Crossing had a rampart and moat around it, but both were in bad repair so that the villagers must not have worried about attacks any longer. Grass and even small bushes had grown up the rampart and dotted the top. The moat had separated into small ponds, and Za could see a dozen ducks in the nearest one. The place had the feel of somewhere safe and long past its old wars.

Za hoped he didn't bring a new one with him.

CHAPTER NINETEEN

I had gotten twitchy again as soon as we entered the town. I wanted to ride back and place myself beside Prince Zaron as his guard. That was my duty, right? Better not to draw any attention to him. I had to believe that no one would expect the Prince Heir to be riding with a band from a grassland clan.

Besides, Tanisk's arrival was drawing all the attention to him. The leader of the Fox Clan had taken us through the dilapidated and unguarded gates and into the dusty streets of Dell Crossing. He greeted many friends by name, traded friendly insults with many, and took us straight through the untidy maze of paths.

This was not Willoway. The buildings here were small, many of them in need of repair. Chickens, cats, and dogs darted in and out of the path around us. The dogs tended to bark at the horses, and I worried that those of us with less experience (like Za and me) might lose our hold on the beasts.

Then, at the second rush of a dog, the animal suddenly seemed to lose interest in us, as did a couple more who had been following us. I glanced back and saw Za with his head slightly bowed.

"Za's work?" Kintansa asked softly.

"I expect so," I replied and allowed myself a sigh of relief. "I don't like Za using that magic, but it will help if none of us fall off the horses."

"True."

"It's not much like Willoway," I said softly.

"No, it isn't."

Chickens and cats still tended to stand in the way and only move at the last moment. I wondered how any of them survived, although I had started to find them amusing. I realized there was something else different about Dell's Crossing. People here did not stare at us as though measuring how much trouble we were going to be.

If this had been Willoway, we would have had trouble getting through the gate, let alone riding along the main road without being stopped by the local guards. Here, though, people laughed, called greetings, wished us all a pleasant stay.

"I want to live here," I suddenly said, surprising even myself.

Kintansa gave a bright smile and reached over to pat my arm. "It is a wonderful place, isn't it? We could raise chickens and cats. I've always loved cats, but the mercenary's headquarters was no place for them. Maybe a couple dogs, too. And sheep."

"I never realized you liked animals so well," I said with a smile of my own, thinking about such a future, away from wars, palaces, and even princes. "Though I do seem to remember the court peacocks trailing you wherever you went."

"Yes, until she had them killed for being nuisances," Tansa said with a sigh. I had forgotten that or wouldn't have brought it up. "Do you think we could get a couple here, too?"

"I'll get you peacocks," I promised.

She smiled brightly. By all the Forgotten Gods, I would give her that life.

We were nearing the river when we finally stopped by the

massive building that had a fenced yard and stalls for the horses. The owner and his helpers had been standing outside the yard's gate, apparently waiting for us since the news of our arrival must have gotten there ahead of us. Here, I realized, was a true friend. The woman was lean, tall, and with a head of such pure gray hair that it looked more like a spray of silver threads. Tanisk greeted her by dropping off his horse and giving her an embrace that took the woman's breath away.

Her face belayed the older age I had first thought because of her silver hair. There were few lines on her tan skin, and her eyes showed none of the dullness I was used to seeing in older people. She and Tanisk spoke while the rest of us rode into the yard.

"I will be glad to be down," I mumbled to Tansa. "But I fear I might not be able to walk to the building."

"I feel the same way," Tansa admitted and looked around. "I think all of us except for father probably do, you know. We don't ride that much in the grasslands, after all. Just slide down and let the girl take the horse."

I did what she said. My legs felt wobbly. Gods help us if anyone attacked right now. We'd all just fall over.

We were not attacked as we headed for the main building, Za moving in beside me and looking a little pale, I thought. That might have been from his work with the dogs. He was on his feet and walking, though as we went into the building where the scents of a dozen spices filled the air.

"Oh yes, she's been getting ready for us," Tansa said with a bright smile again.

A few other patrons sat at tables and drinking a bitter ale that I could smell as we went past the first group. Strong ale -- I didn't think that would be a good idea. I'd speak to Danisin and suggest the two of us forgo it, if possible. As much as I liked this place, I still couldn't feel entirely safe.

We sat down at a long table with benches on both sides. I

would have preferred a chair so that I could lean back, but the bench was far better than standing. Food appeared almost immediately and along with it came pitchers of sweet cider, which, though still fermented, was not nearly as strong as the ale.

"Eat a little," I urged Za who had not made a move towards the food like the rest of us. "You don't know when you'll get such a good meal again."

"I used to like horses," he mumbled. "I have never ridden one for any length of time, though."

"We'll get used to it," I said, repeating what Tansa had told me, though I had started finding the words annoying. "And we have a little break now. Eat."

He obeyed me, though I could tell that food did not appeal to him. I also noticed how his hand rested on his side where the demon had cut into the bone. I would have thought that should have been less trouble by now, and it worried me that maybe such a wound might not heal well.

Or might not heal at all? The wound had been made by something magical, and there had been old myths --

I tried to bury that thought. It had been easy to forget the demons for a little while as we stayed with Fox Clan. I didn't want to bring them to this gathering tonight, either. Whatever time we could spend without their shadows falling over us was welcome. To live in constant dread would only blind me to what we fought for in this odd war. I would not let the demons be more important than the people.

We didn't hear much during the meal, but afterward, the Fox Clan people spread out a bit, joining in local games of chance or talking with old acquaintances. Even Tansa went to join them, leaving me with Za and Danisin who looked worried that someone might realize he was not local. We abandoned the big table and settled at a small one in the corner, murmuring below the roar of sound as the place became even more crowded. Obviously, Tanisk and his people were quite a draw.

"We're safe enough," I said. "No one will hear us back here."

"Not that we have much to talk about," Danisin added and even gave a little smile. "It seems odd to have everything placed in other hands, even if Kintansa is one of them."

"Very odd," I agreed. "Za? How are you."

His smile was a little more frayed, but he gave me a nod. "I'll be glad to sleep, but I fear that will not be for quite a while. I understand that we will be sleeping in the common room, which means we'll have to wait until the crowd clears out. It is going to be a long night."

I nodded agreement. "I am tired enough, though, that I might just sleep anyway. The voices have already become a dull roar and background noise."

"But -- people," he said with a slight wave of his hand. "I don't mind the noise. This many people -- "

"I hadn't thought of that part. We've been throwing you into a lot of crowds lately. You might get used to it. How is your side?"

The last took him by surprise, and his hand went to the wound and drew back again with a frown. "I am --"

"Tell me the truth," I ordered. I didn't often use that tone with him. "It is important that we know. We need you, Za."

He frowned at those words and then sighed. "The wound is still tender. The bone aches. I don't know that it is healing anymore."

"I feared as much. Damn, I wish we had Sirma with us," I admitted.

"It hasn't stopped me," Za added with a bit more defiance. Voices rose and quieted again. "Or even slowed me, but only because we aren't rushing anywhere. I hope matters stay that way. I hope to get help at my grandfather's court."

"Ah. Yes." I hoped he would be better before then because we had a long distance to go, but that at least gave me some hope.

Tansa crossed and dragged a chair over to sit with us. I dropped the subject, though I would tell her later. There was no reason to embarrass the prince now, though. He'd been a remarkably cooperative traveling companion. He'd even been helpful more than a few times. I would try not to do anything that might change his attitude towards us. His father had tended to become sullen whenever something embarrassed him.

Za was not his father. I could not even imagine what a journey like this would have been like with King Yasidin. I still regretted his death, but the difference between father and son was --

Was the difference Endris had made? Endris and the *Art of Ata*.

"There are some rumors about the west," Tansa said finally when she thought the others stopped watching her and us. "Rumors of the evil done by Prince Zaron and how he's fled from what he put in place and left his poor mothers and sisters to try and deal with it."

I had to clamp my mouth shut to keep from snarling at those words. Not that they weren't unexpected, only that I had hoped the worst of it hadn't gotten this far. In fact --

"Magic," I said softly. Tansa looked at me, startled. "She's using magic to spread these lies as quickly as possible so that Za can find no refuge anywhere."

"Ah," Danisin replied and gave a nod before he sipped more of his drink. "But if she has that much magic, why can't she attack him wherever he happens to be?"

"She can't find me," Za replied. He looked more contemplative rather than angry. His mother's actions did not surprise him. "I have been under the shield of the *Art of Ata* since the first attack. She could not find me in the city with whatever magic she was able to use, and neither could the demons find me. I suspect she's sent these rumors out like one might throw seeds across a field. She hopes that one seed will sprout in a fertile land and draw me into her trap. I dare not be recognized."

I nodded agreement and forced myself to take up my mug and even smile as I sipped. "How far are we from the ocean? Perhaps being on a ship really is going to be safer."

"Maybe so. A week or more, depending on the weather."

"What about other trouble we might encounter?" I asked.

"There is always a chance of bandits, but they'd be hard-pressed to attack a large group of grasslanders. I think we'll be all right in that respect. Za, the only real possible trouble I see is that as we head into the more settled lands, there are going to be those who have journeyed to Willoway and may have seen you. I don't think you'll be recognized as you are now, but just be aware that it could happen."

"You are more likely to be recognized than me," Za said. "You are rather more famous than I am, at least as the mercenary commander."

My heart thumped.

I had not considered the possibility. I turned to Kintansa with a start -- and then felt a welling of relief.

"You've let your hair down. You are wearing Fox Clan clothing. And no sword."

"Not a noticeable blade of any kind. Za is right though. I might still be recognized, though I hope that they won't be looking for me without the rest of the mercenaries."

"I should not be with you," I replied, feeling a surge of new worry.

"Not a lot of people knew you were a mercenary Mai, and even outside of the mercenaries, no one knew we are lovers. I *need* you with me. No one who thinks of me as the commander of the Lightning Company would ever imagine me in the arms of someone I love. People tend to be blind that way. They have many sides, but they'll only see one characteristic in others."

I was still having trouble with the beating of my heart and the fear of something happening to Tansa. She was right, though. I had to hope that, like the prince, we did not run into anyone who knew either of us.

I wanted everyone at this inn to go home so we could sleep. I already missed the tent we'd shared back with the rest of the Fox Clan. A week to reach the ocean wasn't so bad, but after that -- oh, I wish I knew what was going to happen once we were there. How did one take a journey on a ship? What would Tanisk do? Wouldn't going back without us look unusual?

The crowd eventually began to thin out. I looked forward to some sleep. Tomorrow we would be back on the horses and that thought kept me awake -- but not for long.

I awoke with a hand on my mouth and another holding down my right arm. I started to throw the attacker off, but words whispered in my ear stopped me.

"Something here, Mai. Not natural."

Za. I blinked at his face, hardly more than a shadow in the flickering light of the waning candles. He took his hands away but otherwise stayed still.

I mumbled as though still asleep and turned slightly.

The Fox Clan party were not the only ones in the common room. We'd taken our blankets and staked out a corner for ourselves, far from the door and windows, nestling Za into the middle. My eyes had cleared of sleep, and I could hear nothing but the thunderous snoring of many drunk people. He'd had a nightmare, and I tried to curb my annoyance.

Something moved.

Not natural. The shape drifted like a black cloud over the people by the door, and though they didn't awake, I heard some sounds of protest. I turned and did to Kintansa what Za had done to me. Now we were all three awake, tracking the unholy creature as it passed from one to another.

The sounds of snoring remained loud enough that Za could press close to me on one side and Tansa on the other and we could all three whisper.

"Searching?" Tansa asked.

"And spreading tales," Za replied. "Good place, an inn. I can almost hear the whispers as it passes over others. Might be one of these creatures in every major town, making the rounds at night. Looking for me and making it harder for me to make this journey without trouble."

"Yes," Tansa agreed. "What do we do?"

The creature came closer.

"Wake up," Za said. "Wake everyone up. It does not want to be seen."

Tansa and I both nodded. "You stay down. Stay behind us. Do not draw attention."

He said nothing. We had no time to discuss the matter. The black ghost had almost reached our party.

I leapt to my feet and drew my belt knife. "Begone, you hellish creature!"

That brought an odd reaction from some of the others: first, a spattering of laughter interspersed with the word *drunk* and more than a few curses. The Fox Clan people reacted as I had hoped, though. Danisin spotted the thing and gave out a bellow of rage that brought everyone else stumbling to their feet.

The front half of the blackness turned as though looking left and right and then back to where Tansa and I stood. The others of our party pressed in closer and Za rose to his feet behind us, though he said nothing. I hoped he had enough control to know that he should not draw that magical sword again.

The other people in the room started to panic. Several rushed out the door, and the cold wind passed over the cloud and brought an unpleasant stench, like an animal left dead in the rain.

The shadow came closer. In the dull light, I could see a shape within the darkness. Human-like, though stretched out and thin, and almost as black as the cloud itself. I chose the thin shoulder on the right and threw my knife.

The creature gave an agitated snarl, a shudder of movement, and the blade dropped to the floor. I had hit it; the blade glistened with something that might have been blood.

"What is it!" someone yelled. The creature's head moved in that direction. It could hear us.

"Another of the prince's vile creatures," someone else snarled. He'd been near the door and had already heard the whispers of this thing, so I didn't take him too seriously.

The creature turned his attention back to me. I wouldn't have minded so much if I still had my knife, but I held my ground. Tansa cursed and pushed a blade into my hand. I worried, but Tanisk had moved up beside his daughter, and I suspected the Fox Clan leader had weapons to spare.

The creature suddenly swept at me. I swung the blade toward the face, but where there had been darkness, I suddenly encountered fire as one of the arms reached out and dragged needle-sharp claws across my hand. I started to drop to my knees, but Za stood behind me --

No, he was moving. He had a knife and slashed at the side of the cloud. It turned on him, and I grabbed him back out of way, though maybe I was precipitous in my actions. He wasn't without abilities of his own.

Tansa moved in, and that was no better to my mind. I pushed Za behind me and leapt to help Tansa. The others were getting the idea as well. I would have thought the creature would have retreated by now, but the thing seemed intent on us. I had to do something that would take that attention away from our prince. Za gave me the opportunity. He saw the thing coming at me again and moved to sweep the blade into the black.

I shoved him back, dangerous though it was for both of us.

"Stop being a damned fool, my son! This is not the time to prove your manhood!"

That brought a moment's shock to everyone in my group -- except for Za.

"Stop treating me like a child!" he screamed in perfect grassland words.

The creature hesitated a moment, but by then all the rest of the Fox Clan had moved in, along with more than a few of the locals, including the innkeeper with a massive cleaver in her hand. It dripped blood (or something like it) on the floor and retreated an arm's length, rose higher towards the ceiling -- and then spun and rushed out the door past startled and frightened people.

By the time Za, Tansa, and I had reached the doorway, it was lost in the darkness of the night. It might have been a yard away or a mile away. I couldn't tell.

"Gone," Za whispered. He had a cut on his arm that I had not noticed. My hand felt as though it was on fire. "I sensed it come in. *Ata*. I would know if it lingered near here."

I nodded. We went back in and back to our corner. The innkeeper delivered cider all around. Many of the locals had left, and I felt sorry for her -- but she appeared not to be too worried.

Thinking about it from the view of someone had run the Lost Way Inn for so many years, I could understand. We had made her inn famous. She might lose some business for a day or two, but they'd come back in droves once they realized the place was safe.

I stopped worrying about stupid things. Tansa had treated my hand with medicinal herbs and wrapped it in bandages. She did the same with Za's cut. By then the dawn was almost upon us. We prepared to leave.

I would have liked a little more sleep.

Tanisk made the farewells to Arli and even promised to stay there on the way back. I knew he'd keep his word, though some of us would not be with him then.

"How is he going to explain the four of us being gone?" I asked as we rode away. I needed a distraction. It hurt to sit in the saddle today.

"Sending his daughter and guards on to Tiger Court," Za said softly as he rode beside me. "Find out about the trouble in the west, and now this as well."

"I will talk to father," Tansa said.

We waded across the Dell River at dawn. The water was treacherously cold, the rocks slick beneath our feet, and the horses no happier than we were. The river was shallow, though, even the middle hardly rising no higher than my knees. I went down twice but always managed to keep my head above water. Za went down three times, and on the last, his head did go beneath the cold rush of water. He came back up before I could move to help him and sputtered such language that I didn't think a prince of Summer Cloud Palace should know.

We reached the muddy bank on the other side, inadvertently coated ourselves in the muck, and then mounted the horses again. The clear sky and light breeze made the day comfortable, even if we were wet and muddy.

Another, smaller version of the village sat on this side. We passed through, Tanisk and his people greeting people they knew. Then we were beyond the buildings and into farmlands.

People herded sheep and even cattle along the road, and we made way for them. I didn't mind. I had a chance to study the land behind us every time we stopped. Nothing unusual seemed to be moving in our direction.

"We should be safe," Za said at last. He even gave me a bright smile, which I had not expected. "No one would dare to talk to the Prince Heir the way you did last night. You fooled it, and that confirms where that black cloud originated."

"Good point," I said. "Thank you for reacting so well to my ploy."

"I am remarkably adept at saving my own life," he replied and laughed. He patted the horse on the neck. "We have been blessed with help on this journey."

Every odd sound made me uneasy, though. I wasn't surprised to see Za react in the same way, despite the facade of calm that he managed most of the time. The day went well. We camped in the open, kept a guard rotating, and I think most of us slept better than we had the night before.

In this way we passed the next several days. We did not stay at any of the small villages we passed through, though Tanisk was well known here, too. We did pick up supplies and gifts of fresh bread and preserves. We were in a land of orchards by the third day and vineyards the next. I had become more accustomed to the horse, and I was more than grateful for the time and trouble the creatures saved us, but we did have our moments of disagreement. My mount was apt to stop at any moment and not go on no matter how I coaxed or threatened. For that reason, one of the others stayed with me. We even traded horses sometimes, but it didn't help.

"You certainly have a way with horses," Tansa said with a laugh. She patted the horse on the rump and got it moving again. "I think they're just toying with you, my friend."

"Huh." I stared at the horse's head for a moment, then glanced back, always mindful that someone or something might be after us. Nothing this time. "Your father may be the one who has saved the Empire, you know," I said. Tansa and I rode side by side at the back of the crowd. It was our turn to keep watch for anything coming our way. There hadn't been so much as a stray dog for the last two days, and we were all more at ease. "Tanisk has gotten us through this part of the journey far faster and with little notice."

"True," she said, pleased at my observation. "He's always worked for peace, and to make certain the grasslands are not harmed by battles between other people. That's why I went to Willoway. Even secluded as I was at court, I still learned more of what was going on than we would have known otherwise."

"How did you get messages back?" I asked.

"Endris, of course. I gave messages to him, and he sent them on. Sometimes he delivered the few messages my father dared to send back to me."

"You never asked me to take a note out for you," I said and felt a pang of pain I had not expected.

"No, I did not," she said. Tansa reached over and caught my arm so that we both stopped. "Look at me, Mai. I would never have compromised you. Endris had his job -- a job he had *before* he came to the palace. I now realize he had many positions. He was working with my father, but the more I think about it, the more I suspect he was really in the employ of The Tiger."

"I realized it as well. Too late, but I thought it must have been Endris's true job. He watched over Prince Zaron. I wonder if The Tiger of the East ever understood the full extent of what Endris had been doing, though. I wish I'd had a chance to speak to Endris about it. I wonder how The Tiger will react to the *Art of Ata*, in all its ancient magical glory."

Tansa looked ahead to where the prince rode beside Danisin. "What have we gotten ourselves into, Mai?"

"The sort of thing we have trained for all our lives -- you, me, and Za."

Tansa gave a quick nod and sighed. "I wonder where the rest of Lightning Company have gone. I worry about them every day. I created the group, trained them -- and then abandoned them when --"

"No, you did not abandon them. You sent them off to do what work they could. There had always been a chance you wouldn't be with them for some battles, and you trained us for that possibility. I can't say they are in battle now, but you made certain they knew how to take care of themselves without either of us."

"If they were with us --"

"We'd have been fighting the enemy at every turn. They would have drawn trouble. You could have been with them or with us."

"You wouldn't choose to come with me?" she asked, her eyes narrowed as she looked my way.

"I would have wanted to go with you -- but Endris sent the boy to *me*. I had to do my duty, Tansa. Isn't that why you are here, rather than following Lightning Company? You know they don't need you as much as we do."

"You don't need --"

"I never would have gone to Fox Clan."

She glanced my way and gave a nod of agreement. "I know, I know. I need to focus on here. We still have a long way to go."

"We've done better than I had hoped," I admitted and watched the group ahead of us. My horse stopped and took interest in a rock in the middle of the road. Tansa got it moving again and I only gave one frustrated sigh. "Za has done everything right, from coming to me to start with and then cutting off his hair -- and waking me when that creature arrived at the inn. I no longer have any fear that he will do something stupid."

She gave another nod, and I saw her shoulders relax. "We saw the demons. There are not a lot of people who did. We are witnesses to the truth."

There was another part of the tale that I had not fully considered. I knew that people would not believe Prince Zaron, and the farther we went from Willoway, the less likely it would be that people would accept the tale about the queen, the princesses, and the demons. They equally might not believe the lie the queen put out about the prince and the demons, though, either.

A problem for the future. The Queen still hunted for her wayward son, and we still had too far to go before we *might* be safe from her.

I shaded my eyes and looked ahead. Though we couldn't see as far as we had in the grasslands, the distant line of clouds appeared dark through the stands of trees. We'd have bad weather before too long. I wondered if there was a village nearby where we would dare to take cover.

We'd entered a vast apple orchard that stretched out on both sides of the road. Signs had warned against picking from the trees, but apples in the ditches or on the road itself were free to be taken. Nysin and Pala had already gotten down, picking up windfalls for both humans and horses. Though others had been through, they'd left a few for later travelers.

I'd been nervous watching every stranger even though there'd been no more trouble since the shadowy visitor at the inn. I hoped that we'd managed to hide Prince Zaron in that attack.

My horse stopped.

So, though, did the others. We stood alone on the road just where it dipped down by a small stream, the edges of the water mostly obscured by wild bushes with long gray-green leaves.

The leaves, I realized, moved when there was no breeze.

The bandits swarmed out of hiding and up the incline towards us. It was a stupid move on their part, but they must have thought we had seen them before we went down the incline. They were right -- but if they'd melted away into hiding, we would have gone past, and they would have survived.

Tanisk gave a shout of anger and challenge as he rode straight down at them, his long knife in hand. The rest of the Fox Clan followed, including my darling Kintansa screaming like a wild thing. I charged after her. Za was already moving to help Yotsky who had two burly men coming at him. Danisin had moved off to the right, and I saw him draw his bow, string it, place the arrow, and fire -- all in the time it took me to get back to Kintansa's side.

One bandit went down.

Tansa had veered from following her father and headed toward Za. Good -- although Za and Yot were not having much trouble as far as I could tell. In fact, I pulled back, so I didn't get in the way.

More bandits surged out of the muck and mud. We had plenty of others to fight.

"Off the horses," Tansa ordered.

I threw myself down though I found myself reluctant to let go of the reins. As much as I disliked riding the horse, I hated the idea of walking, and without supplies, the rest of the way to the coast.

The press of the bandits, who still outnumbered us two to one, forced me to abandon the horse to stay alive. Tansa and I fought side-by-side. There was nothing romantic about it, but we did have trust and understanding. Za joined us but knew enough to fight to the left side, staying clear of what we did. I kept an eye on him. The bandits were not trained, but they had a purpose. Four got past us, already dragging hoses along, and moving to grab others. They could ride off and leave us rather than fight to the death.

The Fox Clan horses were not ready to go off with new owners. They fought the thieves with kicks, bites, and knocking people down. In the end, only two bandits remained on their feet, and they fled back down into the cover of the stream.

"Let's go," Tanisk ordered. He grabbed his horse and mounted. "I think that's the lot of them. However, they usually don't come in this large a group, so we can't know if there are others or not."

Za, I noted, didn't seem to have taken a dangerous wound. He had a small cut on his hand, but he wrapped that as he walked. Pala had a worse cut on her side, but Nysin bandaged that one. The others all appeared to have come through without more than scratches. I had a cut on my arm, but it was more an annoyance than a danger. Tansa quickly dealt with it. She didn't appear to have been wounded at all.

The bandits were either dead or too badly wounded to get back to their feet.

"What about them?" Za asked with a wave toward the downed enemy.

"We'll send guards back from the next village," Tanisk said. "It's no more than five miles away."

Za accepted that answer with a nod of his head.

I was the last to mount. I leaned forward and patted the horse on the neck. "Good work," I said to it. "Thank you for not running off without me."

The horse seemed to give me a startled look over the shoulder. Then she moved off with the others, and without anyone else having to urge her on. I thought we must have finally come to an understanding.

Linta stayed some distance ahead of us while Yotsky rode behind. We did not race to the village, and when Tanisk rode back to be with Za, Tansa, and me, I knew there was something more going on.

"Nysin, Linta, and Pala are going on to the village. We are going to cut down a small side trail just ahead and get off this road."

"Do you think they were after Za?" Tansa asked.

"No. I think the bandits were after the trade goods and coin the Fox Clan carries to the coast each year. This is not the first time we've been attacked. I had hoped that going early would perhaps get us through, but news of our journey has managed to get ahead of us."

I nodded. We were not going to argue with Tanisk's reasoning, though I saw him give Za a quick glance. I suspected that like me, he thought the Prince Heir would have some say in matters. I was beginning to think that Za was far too reasonable. That sounded odd, even in my mind, but I worried about what sort of ruler he would make --

Oh, but he would not rule I reminded myself yet again. His mother had been paving the way for her daughters long before she blamed Zaron for the arrival of the demons. There would always be that whisper of doubt about him, especially if others learned that he was adept at the *Art of Ata*.

His purpose was only to get to the Court of the Tiger and tell the truth about his mother's work to someone who could stop her. To that end, he certainly was not going to argue with anyone who continued to do an excellent job of getting him there.

We took the side trail. It had not been much used and wound in and out among stands of trees and scraggly bushes. Squirrels and rabbits ran from our path. Birds shouted protests as we passed.

"No problem," Nysin told us when the three caught up with us again. "There had been news of a large group traveling through the woods and orchards, and everyone expected one of the villages to be attacked. They were more than happy to have us take care of at least part of the problem. The town elder regretted not seeing you this year, Tanisk."

"I'll make certain we pass through on the way back," he said. "We'll be on this rode most of the day and camp near the crossroads that will head east again. This won't put us too much out of the way."

"Thank you," I said. That had been an explanation for the three of us who were not Fox Clan. The others obviously knew the way.

I didn't like riding in this area of rolling hills and overgrown wilds. We were all quiet and careful along this way, and each open glade felt like a chance to breathe again. We were well past noon when we reached our campsite, a small meadow surrounded by tall trees. Deer reluctantly gave way to our horses. I was glad to sit on the ground again, and we had a pleasant meal that evening. Guards took their places all through the darkness. I had the feel of being watched, but it might have been an owl as likely as a person. Nothing came for us that night except for the annoying insects, but we survived them and rode on the next morning.

We reached the next road no more than an hour after we left camp. I gave a sigh of relief at the site of the long, straight path, at least until I saw where we were heading.

"That's a city," I said with some dismay.

"Springway," Tanisk explained. "I had hoped to avoid any large settlements, but we had to get clear of the bandits. Don't worry. Unless we are invited in, we'll skirt along the edge of the walls."

"I have met the Lord and Lady of Springway," Za warned.

"I don't think that will be a problem, Za," Tanisk replied. "It's not likely that we'll be invited to court."

"True. Still, they always arrived at Willoway with a full contingent of guards, any one of whom could have seen me as well, not to mention servants."

"Ah. Good point. Let us hope you are changed enough, then."

"Ride with Danisin," Tansa ordered. "We'll ride behind you. Commander Kintansa might be recognized sooner than you would be, so let me draw the attention."

Za nodded and moved up by Danisin. I stayed back with Tansa, but at least I could keep him in sight.

Springway didn't look anything like Willoway, I realized. The walls stood higher and were made of dark gray or black stone. Oddly, though, the gates themselves seemed without any sort of covering to move into place. Did they no longer worry about invaders?

I saw Za studying the walls and gates as well. We were both city people and given to worrying about how to defend things. Tansa probably thought much the same way as the two of us, but she'd been past this city before. She'd probably even been inside.

"How do they close the gates?"

"They don't. They let attackers inside, where they find a series of buildings built in a maze. Those buildings happen to be the guard's barracks. Past those buildings is a second wall, with a gate closed. They're trapped. No attacker has ever survived."

"Oh, now that's a lovely plan," I said with appreciation. "I assume some know the trap, though."

"Yes. Attackers generally try to go through or over the walls. It's not a good plan. Springway has never been taken, even when the city sat on the southern and eastern borders. Now they only have to worry about bandit armies."

"Or an invasion from the coast," I said.

"That's been a worry since the beginning of time," she said with a nod, her eyes still studying the city before us. "But an army would take days to get from the coast to here -- and it is unlikely that such a group would know the trick. If the locals pretend to have a gate in place that goes down after a short battle, they can trap a thousand in the maze. More if they were anxious to be the first to loot the city."

"Ingenious," I admitted.

"And ancient," she added with a glance up at the opening that led inside. "They were wise people in those days, and not so set in their ways."

"Before the Empire?" I said with a glance at the prince who represented that entity.

"Well before the empire. This is the heart of the East before there was even a Court of the Tiger. I think we've lost something when we melded everything -- damn."

She stopped and stared at the gate. Someone rode out with a flag. I felt my heart begin to beat harder as Tanisk rode forward to meet the half-dozen riders.

After a short talk and a nod, he turned back and rode to us. The guards waited.

"We're going in, but only to talk to the commander of the guards," Tanisk explained. "We shouldn't have to go all the way into the city."

"What should I do?" Tansa asked.

"Wait to be asked. Someone might recognize you, and if they do, pretend that you have been deferring to your father. I'll show some exasperation that they'd turn to my *daughter* for information. They don't have as much contact with the Fox Clan here or any of the grasslanders. They also tend to be more inclined to patriarchal hierarchy, so we can play the part. Even if you are known for your role as a mercenary, they aren't likely to think much of it."

"What should I tell them?" Tansa asked.

"That you came home half a year ago. I doubt anyone will know better."

She nodded agreement. The rest of us did the same, as though Tanisk had been lecturing us on how to behave in company. I almost smiled.

Would they recognize Za or Tansa? Danisin stayed with Za still, and we followed Tanisk and Nysin towards the city.

I shouldn't have shown so much interest in the place. The Gods might think they were doing me a favor.

CHAPTER TWENTY

Za wanted to bow his head and hide beneath the fall of his ragged hair as they rode through the gate. That, though, would only draw attention. He had to sit up straight like the rest of the Fox Clan, though he was careful about where he looked.

He'd heard Tansa explain about the gate and the walls, so he wasn't surprised to find the road turn a bit past some tall barracks, and then take another curve back the other way. By then, anyone invading might have noticed the second wall, but they would likely expect it to be the edge of the older city and not have a closed gate when the other opened so easily.

Za wanted to know how often this ploy had worked for the city. News would likely spread during a war -- ah, but he'd not known of it, who had studied the empire...

This city had been built before the empire formed. Tansa had pointed that out. He had never considered how things might have been different before then.

The commander of the guard met them outside his headquarters. He was a short man, well-dressed, and faintly familiar to Za, so the man had likely gone to court with the Lord and Lady at some time. Za dismounted and gave his horse over to the locals as all the others did. Danisin kept with him. Mai and Kintansa moved in ahead of Za, the others behind him -- and they went into the building.

Tanisk and Commander Arteg discussed the problem with the bandits.

"My guards reported that a few of you were injured," Arteg said. "I assumed you'd had a run in with one of the bands of bandits. Anything you can tell me --"

Tanisk, in fact, told him so much that the man seemed to forget any thought about questioning the others. Linta added the information that she'd gathered from the village when they went to report the trouble. Arteg was so happy with all the information that he immediately sent out soldiers into the woods and to the village.

Then he asked Tanisk to dine with him and for the entire group to be his guests for the night.

"It's late already," the commander pointed out. "There is no reason for you to camp out in the wilds."

"We are grasslanders," Tanisk said with a laugh, but it was clear he had to accept.

Za and the others ate with the rest of the troops. The food lacked spices but was filling. They were given a corner of the barracks to themselves as well. What had looked like courting disaster now became a time of quiet and repose. Even Mai looked happier.

Za even found the hard, wood-framed bed very comfortable after so long sleeping on the ground. He thought he might have trouble getting to sleep in such a strange place, but he'd been in far stranger, and far more dangerous, locations of late.

He slept well. Za thought the others must have as well because they all looked happier when the group gathered outside the next morning after a quick breakfast. Tansa accepted back their horses (and even the animals looked better) and waited for Tanisk to join them.

He came out of the building with Commander Arteg and Lord Saiden.

Za had already taken hold of his horse. He took a step backward. Danisin moved closer, partially blocking the view.

"Should I worry about such outlandish rumors?" Tanisk asked. "Oh, I'm not saying there are not strange things afoot. We saw strangeness enough at Dell Crossing. But if the Prince had demons at his call, I don't think he'd be worrying too much about his mother being upset."

Za had not expected Lord Saiden to laugh agreement. "Well, that's true enough. Not that she would admit worrying anyway. Besides, from what I saw of the Prince Heir, she had nothing to fear. I'd have been more worried about her daughters, to be honest. They were far too ambitious."

"Ah. Well, that falls outside my little realm, your lordship. Thank you for a pleasant visit."

"On your way then," the man said with a laugh. "I'm sure you've had enough of the city."

Tanisk mounted. The others did as well, Za neither the first nor the last. They turned the horses back the way they had come and headed out of the city without any trouble.

Before long they'd crossed the fields of grain that stretched out beyond the city. Lines of people were out harvesting the crop and watched the group ride by with a bit of worry. Soon Tanisk had taken them back into the wilds. The city disappeared behind trees and hills before Tanisk called a stop.

"No trouble back there," he said, as though they hadn't figured that out yet. "Lord Saiden had a few rumors about the demons and you, Za -- but there's been no rumor that you are anywhere but in Willoway, as far as I can tell. That doesn't mean we can relax, though."

Za nodded. "I think, at another time, I would like to talk to Lord Saiden about my sisters. I've never had outside impressions of them before."

"And you thought your own impressions of them were skewed," Mai added as her horse moved up beside his. She seemed to be having less trouble. "Trust me, they were not."

That helped.

Za had an odd revelation over the next few days as they rode closer and closer to the vast ocean that marked the edge of the empire. He realized that he had never understood anything about the lands and people at all.

Oh, he had known numbers of population and lists of items that those people grew or made. He had never considered the work that went into such labor, though. Now, as they rode through tiny hamlets and larger villages, or past farmers and shepherds, Za felt as though he saw the world in a way few others ever experienced. People rarely wandered more than a few miles from their places of residence. Traders -- they'd crossed paths with a few of those -- might go in larger circles, but even so, they tended to stay in one area.

This was more than just seeing the individual areas. The *Art of Ata* and the inner kernel of training allowed him to look at each feature and create a whole. His father had traveled widely. However, he'd been with grandfather during the wars for most of those travels, and such occasions would not be times to contemplate how the land and people worked. He wouldn't have brought Kintansa back with him if he'd had even the slightest understanding of Fox Clan.

Or maybe he did his father a disservice, Za thought. Maybe his father had known exactly what he did by bringing Tansa into the palace and putting her up against the Queen. She'd survived it, after all, even when he hadn't.

A cool breeze blew against his face. He looked up, startled at the sudden change.

Clouds swept in over the top of hills no more than ten miles away. They were dark clouds pushing winds before them that swept up dust and obscured the view of the land.

"Oh, that doesn't look good," Yotsky said as they all pulled to a stop. The horses suddenly seemed uneasy. "I can't say if it is natural or not, either."

Tanisk gave a nod of agreement and looked to Za.

"I don't know," Za admitted. "There is magic in all of nature. Every storm carries some of it, for good or bad."

"True," Tanisk agreed. "This one looks on the bad side, no matter what the cause. And it is moving too fast. We don't want to run straight into it. To the north. We want the higher country if we can reach it."

Za looked that way through the bushes and scraggly apple trees that grew haphazardly over the hills. The ground had a gentle slope upwards, putting distant trees higher than the ones beside them. It was not much of a rise, but it might help.

He knew about floods which happened to Willoway some springs. Summer Cloud Palace stood high above the city and such problems, but he had seen the devastation roll through the town below and take buildings down and drag people to their deaths.

He did not want to be caught out in such a deluge, but the highest ground here would have meant heading straight into the heart of the storm, and he doubted they'd make anywhere safe fast enough.

They headed north. The wind soon grew worse, and the trees bowed, and some broke. The horses protested and wanted to run away from the storm instead of at an angle to it. Before long, the humans were all on foot, holding tight to the reins to coax the animals forward, and moving slowly onward.

Unnatural dark swept over them, and Za looked up. Lightning flashed deep within the dark clouds, so obscured that it didn't truly light the world. He thought he heard the distant crash of thunder, but the winds grew louder, and the rains came.

Or worse than rain. Hail fell in a torrent that stripped leaves and fruit from the trees and hit both man and horse with bruising force.

"Up against the trees and under the limbs!" Nysin shouted. "Protect the horses!"

They obeyed, spread out, each as close against the wider limbs of as large of a tree as each could manage. Za looked at Nysin and saw the way he pulled the horses head down to his chest and protected it as best he could. Za did the same, grateful that the horse he rode this day was one of the calmer ones.

Hail still found them, pounding against his back, and then stopping almost as suddenly as it had begun. He lifted his head and looked around, appalled at how much damage had been done so quickly.

Not done yet. The wind had picked up again, howling like some wild creature. The rain came like a veil to part them from the world. The group headed northward still with the wind and rain which came from the right, trying to push them aside as it destroyed trees.

Za couldn't say they really found refuge. They got higher, but the ground still ran with mud and sometimes limbs. The rain began to ease, though. He wasn't certain how long they'd fought against it, but the clouds rolled back, the sun came again, and they all stopped. The air felt warmer and more humid on this side of the storm; a sign, he suspected, that the weather was far from settled.

Around them, rain had carved channels into the ground and water still rushed down through them and into larger masses where the tumultuous rush pulled along branches and occasionally whole trees.

"Camp here or head northward still?" Tansa asked when her father came to stand by her.

"Higher. North," Tanisk said and looked to the sky. "This

isn't over."

Za looked upward as well. Another set of clouds, these seeming to rise to the sun itself, stood over the hills. He looked northward and couldn't say the direction looked any better, except that the ground did still rise. Looking at the new-made streams that cut them off from the road they'd been on, he decided that higher would be the better choice.

He couldn't imagine the loss of income this storm had cost the owner of the orchard as well as those who lived nearby and who counted on working the harvest. There had been disasters nearly every year in various parts of the land. People applied to both the Wolf and the Tiger for help, and sometimes even asked the Queen, who was supposed to be the middle ground between the two great courts.

Her answers had always been the same. *It is the work of the Gods and not her job to change what they have decreed. Correct your evil ways so that the Gods will not find a reason to strike at you again.*

No one ever came twice to her. The Queen wouldn't part with a single coin to help those in need. When he was younger, fool that he had been, Za had thought her proclamation about the Gods was true and this was no matter for human rulers to change.

"Za?" Mai said as she moved up by him.

"I don't much like the weather," he said, burying away the thoughts of his own weaknesses, and accepting too easily the path his mother had taken. "Before this journey, I have never been out in so much as a sprinkle for more than a moment or two."

"We are helping you expand your understanding of the world," Mai said, though with a snarl that showed she wasn't thrilled with the lesson either.

He did laugh. "I will have such a deep understanding of the world that I will be a high master of *Ata* before too much longer."

"You aren't already there?" Mai asked. She sounded serious, which surprised him.

"No," he said and fought to pull his foot, with the boot still attached, from another puddle that was more mud than water. "I had only just started down my own path when this madness began. I have a long, long way to go before I can even begin to touch mastery of *Ata*. I doubt that I'll go much farther than I am now. I cannot see a future where I might have the time to contemplate the world and open myself to the full understanding of all I see. Gods and Goddesses," he said with a sudden laugh. "I remember Master Drital saying the same thing to me when I asked him that question."

"And yet he was a Master of *Ata*," Mai pointed out.

"There are levels," he said and frowned.

Mai asked no more. At least the conversation had taken his attention away from the storm for a short while. They'd reached the highest point, finally, though this was far from safe. The worried horses complained and tried to break free, but the Fox Clan people kept them in hand. The wind blew cold and more clouds rose high above them, blotting out the sun. He feared magic at work, but Nysin grumbled about bad luck to run into such a storm.

"Lightning is what we must fear now," Tanisk explained. "We'll move to the lee side of the hill when the storm is a little closer. Lay flat. Hold to the horse's rein, though if the animal gets too wild, let go. Better to walk than to have broken bones."

Za eyed his mount, which already looked ready to bolt.

"Should we take down our supplies?" Za asked.

Tanisk looked at him and at the horses. "Yes. Yes, that is a good idea. Take whatever you need from the horse, just in case."

Za didn't think they needed much. He took down supplies and the coins and gems Mai and Tansa had given over to him.

He had another change in clothing from the Fox Clan. He stuffed everything into one saddlebag and draped it over his shoulder. The horse was already starting to fight him.

Lightning flashed across the sky and thunder roared so loud that even he jumped. Hail began to fall again, but not as hard as the last time. They moved to the side of the hill, Mai maneuvering to where she could settle beside him.

The winds grew louder, rushing up over the hill and grabbing at them. Horses yelled in protest. Linta and Yotsky came to take their mounts, fighting against the wind.

"Down lower for them," Linta shouted. "Faces away from the wind. Stay here!"

Za wanted to go help the others, but Tanisk, Mai, and Kintansa were all staying. Danisin, who was large and steady, helped with the recalcitrant horses, and it didn't look as though they were going very far.

The clouds that had been towering up now seemed to spread outward in a line of gray and white that pushed forward to roll over them.

A swirl of cloud reached down and grabbed at the ground.

"Damn," Tanisk growled. "A finger of the forgotten gods, stirring things up. It's going to pass south of us, but not by far. I hope it misses any holdings and villages."

Za had heard the term, but he had never imagined the dread and wonder of such a thing. The cloud moved along the ground, tearing up trees, dirt, rocks -- he hoped there were no buildings and people in the path. Leaves from the destroyed trees began to rain down around them, a mile or more from the destruction.

And then the cloud thinned and seemed more a rope tied to the ground -- but even that disappeared a moment later. Almost as suddenly, the clouds all around them began to break apart, the sun bright, and the air humid. The winds had died down and now a swarm of gnats and flies swept up to torment them.

Za looked back over his shoulder and found that the others had held to the horses. Good.

"We'll wait for the flood waters to go down," Tanisk said he moved to look down the hillside. "Take a meal now. Feed the horses and calm them."

The turbid flow of muddy water appeared to almost encircle the hill. Za was in no hurry to try to wade through it. If the day had been later, they might have stayed here, he thought.

He needed time to think.

Instead, he helped the others. Maybe that was the better way to learn.

CHAPTER TWENTY-ONE

I had never been as frightened as I had been the midst of that storm from hell. Afterward, I moved with the others and did what needed to be done, but every stray breeze startled me, and I looked too often to the sky.

I didn't think even Tansa had noticed how troubled I was by what had happened.

And why? Why did it --

No control and no choices. Unlike in the city, there had been no one to order to make things better, and no way to take a different path to avoid the fury of nature that struck in a way I had never seen before. I had never been so aware of being a city person before in my life. We'd had bad weather in Willoway, and I'd seen floods take down buildings -- but I had never stood uncovered -- unprotected -- in the path of such unreasoning power before.

By the time we'd mounted the uneasy horses, I had at least managed to get my outward emotions in hand. Za, though, was too perceptive. I knew he could see I was troubled, and I suspected he knew why, probably because he was also a city person and had never faced such weather before.

I watched him. He glanced at the sky too often.

I felt better for not being alone in my unreasoning fears.

Soon slogging through the mud took more attention than the pretty clouds. We rescued three deer and killed a fourth that had broken two legs. Nysin packed it onto one of the supply mounts. The horse didn't much like having a dead animal to carry, but like the humans, he was too weary to make much of a protest.

When we finally reached a little village of no more than twenty buildings, we found it ravaged by winds, rain, and flooding. We spent the rest of the day there, helping as best we could. Four people had died -- a large number for such a small population.

We also donated the deer and shared in a communal meal as the sun went down. I had lost track of Za at some point, a sign of how tired I had become after such an overpowering day. I found him with Danisin, though, when the food was parsed out.

Tansa came and dropped down beside the wall where I sat, both of us leaning back and content to be still. She glanced around, found Za, and looked relieved as well. I wasn't confident either of us had enough energy to eat, though.

"We'll ride on at dawn," she told me. "Three more days to the ocean. Maybe two if we push harder."

I could tell that she was as tired of this land as I had become, but I wasn't sure that meant we'd be happier on the next part of the journey. She looked restless and I felt annoyed. This was not, I thought, that we were sorry to help others, but that we were slowed on our larger mission, which would be challenging enough.

I started to despair that we would never really achieve anything. The Court of the Tiger still sat a long way from here.

Give up and do what instead?

I ate the food, which was a better meal than we would have had if we hadn't stopped to help. The horses were well fed and cared for as well. We slept in a barn at the edge of Applegate, and though we kept our own watch that night, I didn't fear attack as much as I had out on the open road. No shadows creatures showed up, either.

The next sunrise arrived with a dull, gray fog that obscured everything around us. The locals were in a worst state than the night before, having not yet come to terms with their losses. The hopelessness of their loss washed over all of us and even the horses hung their heads as we rode away.

The fog clung to the land well into late morning, and I couldn't say I really cared what might be lurking out there watching us, waiting to attack. I rode with my hand on my weapon and all but dared anything to come at me.

Tansa recognized the mood and perhaps even mirrored it. She knew enough to say little to me. I noted, after a while, that we were all uncommonly quiet today. Worn out, maybe.

We stopped at midday and had some food. The fog had lessened, and I found myself relaxing as I leaned back on the grass and let the sun brush over my face.

"This is better," Linta said. She looked around as though she had just come awake. "I don't know what the problem was this morning. The fog wasn't that bad."

I mumbled agreement, still looking at the strands of fog that swirled through the trees in the valley below. I was more than glad to be out of the dank, wet, miserable --

But it hadn't been that bad. Linta was right.

I turned to Za. He sat cross-legged and meditating beside me. Some change in his breathing had drawn my attention, and he lifted his head now and looked down at the fog with much the same attitude as I'd had a moment before.

Then his look changed. He lifted his hand and spread his fingers, brushing them through the air.

"There is magic in the fog," he said. Everyone stopped and turned to him. "A very odd, pure magic. I've never felt or heard of anything like this before."

"What is it doing?" Kintansa asked.

"It's like a blanket of hopelessness," he replied. I felt a shudder at the remembrance of that feel. He was right.

"To stop you?" Danisin asked.

"I don't think so." Za lowered his hand and looked out over the valley, his eyes narrowing. "If my mother knew I was anywhere in the area, she wouldn't waste power on something that would do no more than inconvenience me for a while. I don't feel anything of her in this fog."

"What then?" Tanisk asked.

"Something to have to do with the demons being in the world?" I asked.

"Yes, that might be the reason," he agreed and relaxed more at that idea. "I don't know enough about the demons to guess what they might do -- let alone what influence they might have. This might be the world reacting to their presence."

"Which might mean they are close." Tanisk stood, plainly intending that they move on immediately.

"I don't know. I don't think so, but it is probably best that we don't wait to find out."

The rest in the sun was over. I suppressed a sigh of frustration and went to get my horse. At least I'd stopped being quite so sore. Horse and I were coming to an understanding, too.

Once we mounted, Tanisk looked around and chose a way that was not the path straight down into the next fog-shrouded valley.

"We'll stick to the highlands as much as we can," he told us. "If we must ride through a fog, we'll do it at a run and get back out again. I hope that the fog will still burn off, but I suspect we'll have it through the rest of the day and maybe longer."

Tanisk didn't sound any happier about the problems with this journey than the rest of us. We did alright, though, riding up along the fog line where we could, and then cutting through narrow draws and up again. We headed more southward that way, but no one minded. It turned out to be a smooth ride except for the mad rushes through the fog.

We'd gone off the main road, and we found animals standing around as though blind and deaf to the world around them. We managed to send a few running to the upper, lighted areas. I feared that if the fog stayed on for many days, some of the creatures would be too weak to save themselves.

We camped that night on a hilltop, all of us exhausted again. Tansa and I shared a blanket in the colder night, and I slept better for having her close and safe.

Woke up in the late night to a kick at my foot.

"Up," Tanisk said. His voice sounded gruff from sleep. "The fog is moving in on us. I don't think we dare stay still or we might end up like those poor animals."

Tansa and I were both getting up. The others did as well. Za got our horses, and we packed away our supplies while the tendrils of fog advanced up the hillside. The horses stomped as though they didn't like the touch of those small fingers of mist.

"There," Tanisk said when we were mounted. He pointed to the east. "See that hill? Higher than ours, and with luck it will stay above the thicker fog. Ride straight for it. We dare not ride as fast as we could during the day, though, since we won't see much around us. Just keep moving."

We started out. I wrapped my cloak tighter around me and rode with Tansa and Za ahead where I could watch them both.

The fog seemed thicker in the dark. We were not on a trail, so trees appeared in the path as though they sprang suddenly out of the ground. Before long, we were on our feet and leading the horses who didn't like moving into this strange, dark world. And, of course, the feeling of loss and despair kept trying to take me.

It was a long, long walk until the ground began to tilt upward again, and we climbed over ferns, rocks, and trickles of water until we reached the high ground. Better here, but we still had fog. We rested a bit and then headed down into the next chasm.

The night went on with us wearily moving from one hill after another. I had to fight against the feeling of hopelessness and the belief that we would never really be free of the fog again. It held to me, clinging to my clothing and my hair.

The morning light cleared the fog away from all but the deepest valleys. We rode for a while and then found a place to camp in the daylight, on a hill where the fog slid away from the light.

"We won't be able to sleep at night," Tanisk warned.

No one cared as long as they could sleep now.

The next day was much like the last -- until we realized we had lost Pala somewhere in the fog between one hill and the next.

"She was with us at our last rest," Nysin said with a worried stare into the fog. "We shared some cheese. She can't be far away."

He'd yelled a few times and gotten no reply.

"Leave the horses," Za said as he stood, apparently intending to go down into the fog again.

"Za, you shouldn't --" I began.

He lifted his hand, a sign for silence that I obeyed from an old habit. There in the near dark, he looked very much like his father again. If there is a problem other than she lost her way or succumbed to the fog, then you might need my help," he said. "I am the only one with magic."

"Za, Tansa, and I," I said, then looked at Tanisk with a

bow of my head. "My apologies. I'm just used to taking charge when there's trouble."

"Go," he said. "Be quick. If you do not come back out, we'll wait here until morning and then see if we can find you. Be careful!"

I nodded. My two companions didn't argue, though I wondered why Tansa let me have my way -- and I wondered why I intended to drag her back into the fog. Za and I could --

When I turned her way, Tansa shook her head and started out with Za so that I had to rush to keep up with them. It had been easier to move through the fog before when I could see the horse in front of me and knew others walked behind me. Pala had been at the end of the line this time, but she shouldn't have had any trouble keeping track of the horses in front of her. We were not moving quickly.

Going down that treacherous hill of ferns and rocks proved more difficult than climbing up the same surface. I slid part of the way. Za tumbled, got up with a quiet curse, and limped on.

"Pala!" Tansa suddenly yelled, startling both of us.

I didn't like the idea of making loud noises here in the fog. It was not natural. We'd never find her in this muck --

No, that was the fog talking to me again.

"Do you feel this hopelessness like the rest of us, Za?" I finally asked.

"I think so," he admitted. "But --"

"Your magic helps?"

"No, not that," he said. I could barely see the shape of him in the darkness. The fog seemed to catch what little light there was and spread it softly around us, though. The moon had risen high overhead by now. It helped.

"What helps you then?" Tansa finally asked.

"I lived most of my life with the whisper of hopelessness, you know. I wasn't stupid. I knew my mother never intended for me to live, and the slightest thing might give her reason to kill me. I never understood how Endris got around her to teach me the *Art of Ata*. I suspect magic now."

"Probably so," I agreed. I thought about the young prince whom I had known well enough that he trusted me, even still. "I'm sorry I didn't get you away with Tansa."

"You couldn't have, not that day. She kept me very close." He stopped and waved his hand. "Let's find Pala."

We had little trouble tracing the path where the horses had upset the ground, rocks, and plants. Tansa even found where Pala had gone right around a tree when we had gone left. I looked around. The fog had gone thicker here, and a few steps could have left her completely lost. But why hadn't she called out?

"Pa--" Tansa began but fell silent when Za grabbed her arm and shook his head.

He led us onward.

I heard voices.

We moved carefully forward, spread out slightly, with Za in the middle. The voices sounded odd, but that might only have been the night and the unnatural fog. I had drawn my knife, but I didn't hear anything that sounded angry.

"I don't understand," Pala said, her voice clear.

We inched closer.

A moment later we viewed a myth.

A circle of pixies moved before us, the small bodies fluttering around on colorful, glowing wings. Pala and her horse stood in the middle of them, the horse looking about with what could only be surprised.

There was no fog here, I realized.

If I had not already seen demons, I might have had a harder time accepting this odd scene. As it was, I found ... I found a strange sense of hope here within the light of those little beings that had been consigned to children's tales.

They were speaking to Pala. She looked bemused.

"I don't know," she said. "None of us do."

Za tapped my arm and nodded. I agreed, as did Tansa.

We walked closer.

The fairies were upset for a moment, but they settled back into their circle rather quickly, including us in the middle with Pala and the horse. I had put away my knife. I could draw it fast enough if they turned on us.

"What brings the fog!" one said, fluttering near my ear. "Why has it come to hurt the land?"

Ah. I looked at Za.

"We think it might have been brought by demons who are in a city far away. We go to try and find help to end this evil," Za said.

The fairies moved closer to Za, but they still didn't seem dangerous. They had always been considered helpful in the children's tales, but maybe I shouldn't let that affect my view. I wondered what else might be out there in the world that had only been stories to me before now.

"We are inside their shield," Za said to Tansa and me. "Protected from the fog. I feel as though I can think clearly for the first time in days."

"I wasn't certain what I should say," Pala admitted. "I just waited for someone to find me."

"Faith that we'd come back, even for you?" Tansa said with a bright smile.

Pala laughed. When had any of us last laughed?

The fairies seemed to be having a conference, most of them compacted into a glowing ball. None were larger than my hand. I wondered what had drawn them to show themselves to us. We could have wandered on without ever seeing them, after all.

They at least provided some protection from the fog. The relief made me worry about how poorly the others were still doing. I had thought I was fighting off the effects of hopelessness well until the fairies protected me from the magic and I realized how truly overpowering the hopelessness had been.

I was going to be sorry to go back into the fog.

Only it turned out that we didn't have to. The fairies swarmed around us again, and one who might have been the leader landed on Za's shoulder.

"The Earth Mother sorrows for her daughter," the little voice proclaimed. "The evil of the demons must be stopped. We will see you away from here. Come."

We moved with the fairies swarming around us and traveled back up the hillside. I could hear the others sounding worried when the lights came their way, but Tansa shouted that it was safe, and soon we were with the rest of the group. They were glad to have Pala back, but less assured about our guides, at least until they realized how much better they felt.

We made good time that night.

The next morning the fairies were gone.

CHAPTER TWENTY-TWO

Za wasn't sure if he was glad to have the odd little creatures gone or not. He wasn't unappreciative of what they'd done during the long night, but at first, he didn't understand why they were gone.

"I think we're lucky that the demons didn't locate us," Tanisk admitted as they packed up and prepared to go on. "I feared just being with them would draw attention."

"That's why they aren't here now," Za said and applied the things he knew that others did not. Odd how well he understood the fairies when he looked at them through the *Art of Ata.* "There is far less fog today, and their magic would be apparent to anyone who happened to search in this direction. I realize now that the fog masked their magic. They could not risk being so obvious today."

"Ah. Well, that makes sense," Tanisk said. He looked back down the hillside into the woods. "The world is stranger than I thought."

Za nodded agreement.

They crossed only small bands of fog that morning and by noon the landscape and the weather had both changed. Za thought there was a strange scent to the air --

They cleared one rise and before him stood nothing but

blue. Blue sky with a distant row of white clouds. Blue land that rolled and moved. When he looked downward and closer to him, he saw the way the water crashed against the sand and rocks, sending up sprays of water.

This was the Eastern Ocean. The three companions who had come with him from Willoway seemed to be equally entranced with the view, though Kintansa must have seen this wondrous sight before.

"I had not imagined the largeness of it," Mai admitted. "How can the world hold so much water in one place?"

"I often feel the same way," Tanisk answered as he stared as well. "I'll never understand the wonder of it."

A road curved downward less than a mile away, the path trailing along the edge of the cliffs and then downhill toward the sea and shore. Something moved out on the water and Za saw a ship skimming along the water with the sails full, just as he had seen in drawings back at court. That would be the next part of the journey.

Like Mai, he had never visualized the vastness of the ocean. Now that he had, he thought this next step was not a good idea. How could they get on a craft and end up at the Court of the Tiger?

Well, how did anyone else? People sailed there from far more distant places than down the coast. Just the same, couldn't they ride north instead? Za asked.

"You'd have to go over the mountains, which stretch out even into the ocean itself," Tanisk explained. "They're wickedly dangerous near the ocean, too."

"Dragons?" Mai asked with a hint of worry.

"They seem to stay back in the high country and the snow lands. Here, the land has been eroded so badly by the constant assault of sea and storm that huge blocks will give way at the slightest pressure. The last I heard, there had been no one in living memory who had made it across."

"And the earthquakes don't help," Nysin added.

"You have convinced me," Za replied, though he wondered if all they said was true -- or was it a convenient set of tales to keep people from finding an easy way to the Court of the Tiger? Such tales might be helpful.

"Evisto Port sits at the edge of the sea cliffs. The ships sail out near one hundred miles to get around the outliers of jagged rock that rise in the sea, but even so, it's far faster than trying to go overland. Crossing the mountains means going a long way inland to a pass."

Za nodded again. He'd stopped looking down at the sea and the ship -- which, to give it credit, did move quickly past them and on towards a line of black where the mountains reached all the way down into the sea. If he could see those peaks at this distance -- and not yet spot the city -- that meant they must be formidable indeed.

In fact, they did not reach Evisto Port that night. They took refuge in a caravansary still a few hours out from the city and apparently a favorite spot to stop.

"Oh yes," a woman trader said at a table nearby. "We ran into the fog, too. Damned uncanny stuff. I feared we would never get free of it, but once we reached the coast, all was well."

There were similar tales from up and down the coast. The city had been spared, at least. There were no tales about trouble far to the west. Za counted both as excellent signs. They had ridden far and fast the last few days and must have mostly gotten ahead of the rumors.

The closer inland storms were part of the discussion, though. Apparently, the fingers of the gods had touched the world in many places over the last few days, though the storms appeared to have cleared up -- only to be replaced by the fog.

"Unnatural," a woman said. She had the kind of voice that carried across the room and drew attention. "All of it unnatural, and I fear we are in for worse."

Za realized the depth of how much the royal family affected the empire, for both good and bad. His grandfathers had been the worst disasters to have stuck either half of the lands. He'd read about the battles, and he'd known about the destruction, but until this journey, he had not put a human face on the very people they had fought over. And now those people would look to the Grandfathers for help to recover and rebuild.

Za didn't sleep that night. He sat in a dark corner and contemplated all the people around him, both those who had helped to get him this far and the strangers who slept in the same room with them. Before this journey, he never would have been safe with strangers. He'd been someone different then.

No shadows invaded the room during the long night. The next morning, they gathered their horses and rode on down the foggy path -- a natural fog, it seemed, that came in off the ocean almost every day. It blocked away the view, and when it finally burnt away, Za looked in shock and surprise at the city that rose up along the shore and back onto the slightly higher ground stretching inland. From where they rode, he could see the series of canals that led ships of various shapes and sizes up along the docks. People, distant dots of continual movement, swarmed everywhere. He was glad the horse he rode followed the others without his attention because he found the place fascinating.

"Looks busy," Mai said and didn't sound nearly as enthralled as Za felt.

"Evisto Port is the largest, busiest city in the land," Za said, calling that information up from some depth of childhood learning. He cast a quick look around and found they were, as usual, some distance from any other group. "This was a contested prize between the grandfathers. They had to agree to let the city rule itself, even more so than Willoway. Trade won out in this case. They both swore oaths not to interfere as long as the city did not take a side either."

"And they actually stuck to *that* oath, at least," Kintansa said.

Za nodded agreement.

More people crowded the roads as they neared the city, though they did make way for horses when possible. Wagons moved along the road, and Za's group snaked their way around those. Guards from the city, also on horseback, patrolled the line and kept things moving. Za had trouble understanding their words, but Tanisk spoke to a few and came back to tell Za and his companions the news.

"There is some anxiety in the city," he explained. "Mostly spread by people who came through inland fogs. Some of them panicked as soon as the sea fog began to roll in. I told them that we'd faced the same things, and he asked that we not add to the tales."

"He fears that if the stories come from grasslanders, then people will take them more seriously and panic all the more," Mai said.

"Yes, I suspect so. We'll keep that part of the news to ourselves. In fact, I suggest we say as little as possible about the journey."

Za nodded agreement along with the others.

"Where will we stay tonight?" Za asked.

"An inn near the docks. Not the best place in town, but palatial compared to where we've been lately," Tanisk said with a laugh. "I always stay there so that I can deal easily with captains as they come in."

The road led slightly uphill to the gate; not as fancy a place as Springway, but it did look solid and the city guard appeared ready for trouble. The port town had always been a jewel beckoning to the foolhardy to try and take her. Za had read the reports on several attacks in his lifetime, but the city had always held out.

It wouldn't stand against demons.

He shook that thought off and turned his attention to soaking up all the information about Evisto that he could manage as they rode through the gate. The buildings nearest the gate were small and haphazard, thrown together with bits of stone and wood. The road was lined with rock, but that had worn down to muddy holes in places. It must have been a constant problem since workers -- apparently prisoners with guards -- worked even now on one of the larger spots so that everyone had to circle around them.

The squalor of the outer area soon gave way to better buildings, all of stone. He supposed anything less durable wouldn't stand up to the wet weather so near the ocean. With the mountains so close, they would have a steady supply of quarried stone, too.

The buildings all seemed to be rather dull, though. The stone was almost all the same gray granite, cut into neat blocks and stacked up. Doorways were square, the lintels of flat stone across the top. Doors seemed mostly to be made of wood, but without design or paint.

A few windows showed colored cloth hanging over them, and he thought some of the interior walls might have stucco or wood coverings from the few things he'd managed to see.

Overall, though, this seemed a very dull, drab city. He would have expected better from somewhere so rich.

Looking away from the buildings he found the colors and richness he had expected. The people dressed in such a myriad of styles that he suddenly felt as though he rode through a moving tapestry of flowers. Fox Clan, which was in no way sedate compared to the people of Willoway, looked as though they dressed conservatively.

Za wondered if there were any rules about how one

dressed in the city. He supposed the finer clothing marked status as it would any place, but he also noted that ladies dressed primarily in shades of blue tended to gather together, as did those in yellows.

Some of the styles were quite preposterous. Za fought very hard not to laugh at a man mincing along in tiny steps so that he didn't lose the elaborate wrap of cloth and flowers atop his head.

Mai, he saw, had to bow her head and look away.

They rode through a pretty temple square. Statues lined the road, pillars and carvings decorated the buildings, and Za could hear the distant chant of prayers from the open doors of some. None of the temples stood as large as their brethren in Willoway, but he thought they had a more refined look. The Willoway temples had all moved to the Summer Cloud Palace lands and became ostentatious as well as cut off from most of the population.

He liked these temples better, though one had suffered some damage, which couldn't have happened long ago. People worked at piling up the stones and clearing the debris. Not prisoners, either -- he could tell that most of them were locals, both rich and poor.

They rode by, and he glanced back, wondering what god the people of Evisto worked so hard to bring back to them.

"We're heading into Ambassador Row," Tanisk warned as he pulled back to ride by Za. "I hadn't considered it, but there is an Ambassador from the Summer Cloud palace here."

"Oh yes," Za said and looked ahead at the buildings with banners flying on each side of the street. He could easily pick out the Summer Cloud colors about halfway up the path. How odd to find that touch of home in this strange place. "Ambassador Wytimi. She was the closest my mother ever had to a friend."

"She is not well-liked here, but she's not been called

home."

"No surprise. I happened to hear the last orders the queen gave to her: *Do as you please.* Wytimi wasn't a person to be discreet in her wants."

"She knows you," he said and sounded worried.

"Not like this," Za replied and found himself smiling. "I am a new person. But I will avoid going to the door and asking to talk to her."

Tanisk, who had never seen Prince Zaron at court, probably had no idea the amount of change that had taken place. Mai did though and nodded agreement.

Being someone else had given Za an odd freedom he had never imagined. He tried to help each night at camp, though he was little trained for anything. They had been patient with him, though. Za had begun to learn how to take care of himself.

Endris had taught him how to learn by observation. He'd applied those lessons to the entire journey so far, and he thought himself a wiser person for it.

Mai had moved up to ride between him and the building.

"You knew Wytimi," Za said. "She might recognize you faster than she would me."

"Recognize a mere guard?" Mai said with a snort of amusement. "Not likely, Za. And especially not one who served your father. She -- damn, that must be her coming home."

A fancy carriage came down the road toward them, the Summer Cloud pennant flying high and the guards riding with her ordering everyone to clear the way. Oh yes, that would be Wytimi; she always loved to be on show.

The person who sat on the seat behind the driver, though, bore little resemblance to the woman he'd last seen. She'd put on enough weight to make two of her, and besides she had swathed her body in enough multicolored cloths to make a tent or two. Za bowed his head, as did the others, but he watched her under the fall of hair. He'd gotten used to the shorter hair and found it somewhat useful. Wytimi still had a haughty stare that she directed at everyone, in turn, making sure they paid her homage in that bow. Then the carriage turned slightly and maneuvered past the gate and into the ambassador's home. Servants ran to meet her needs.

"Not a happy woman," Mai said as they rode on.

"True," Za agreed. He did not look back at the place, having already studied all he needed to. "I wonder how much she knows about what the Queen does."

"Not much, I would guess," Kintansa said softly as she slipped back to ride with them. "The Queen would not have let her out of sight otherwise."

"Oh, true," Mai agreed and looked relieved. "And here's an odd bit of trivia about palace life that I only now remembered. There were rumors that your mother would give *secrets* to various people and see which of her tidbits became knowledge to others. If she found she couldn't trust Wytimi, she might have decided to ship her off before she learned anything dangerous."

Za remembered those rumors whispered by servants. A few of those servants had disappeared, and they had not run away. The Queen would have had them killed if she felt she could not trust them. Her old friend, though, and one from a prestigious family, needed better care. Send her clear across the land and don't call her back home. Wytimi would not know about the demons, but that did not mean she could be trusted.

None of the other ambassadors appeared to have been out and about. He wondered what had drawn her to the streets. Maybe just for a ride in the sunlight.

The street turned again, dipped down off a slight hill, and emptied into an area of warehouses and inns. Yotsky rode on ahead to a building not far away, and by the time the rest of them arrived, stable hands were already there to take the horses and help with their bags. The four boys and three girls all shouted greetings at Tanisk and Linta, both of whom must have been here often.

The innkeepers appeared in the yard before they were dismounted, a happy couple of advancing age who greeted Tanisk like a long-lost brother come home again. Za still didn't understand half of what was said; some because the words were foreign, but the rest were spoken with an accent so thick that it sometimes obscured the words he should understand.

Za had not expected such a thing to bother him. He didn't like not understanding what the others said, and if he'd had an ounce more of his families' paranoia, it might have made him dangerous.

Mai had much the same problem, he realized, but the others kept clustered around them and mumbled anything they needed to know. Kintansa understood most of what was said, and that helped. They were able to get all the way into the main room and sit down for food without any undue notice.

"This is as far as my part of the journey takes me," Tanisk said with a worried look across at his daughter. "We'll find a ship for the four of you to take. What reason --"

"We should still use the rumors of trouble in the west," Za said. "You are sending your trusted daughter to find out if there is anything you should prepare for in the grasslands."

Tanisk nodded but still with a frown. "Will she be safe with you?"

"Father!" she said in a tone more of a warning than worry. "You are not --"

"She will be no safer than she has been since this journey started," Za interrupted. "I don't know what reaction my grandfather will have to find me at his gate. If I had my way, I would go on alone."

"No, you would not," Mai replied. "You will not deny me my duty."

"I won't argue it," Za said. He looked at Kintansa and then Mai. "I am grateful for the help you've provided so far. I would not have made it here."

"And I am being unreasonable," Tanisk admitted. "I missed my daughter, though. I don't want to see harm come to her, but I suspect she's managed far worse than a journey to the Court of the Tiger."

"We all have," Kintansa replied softly. "I'll see this all the way to the court. I couldn't step away now."

"I understand." Tanisk sipped some wine. Imported, and strong enough that the staff brought water to cut it for those who wanted to cut it. Za did -- he needed to be clearheaded still. "Well, we'll have a few days together here before you go. I hope to see you again on the way back."

Kintansa nodded and smiled. Za was glad to see that problem settled so quickly. He would have left Tansa behind, but that wouldn't have been fair to Mai. Mai would not let him go with only Danisin, providing even he felt an obligation to go on.

"I never asked any of you if you wanted to make this journey with me," he said softly.

"True," Mai said. "But you also had no way of making us go with you. We are here by our own choice, Za."

That was also true. Za let that useless worry go. The group went back to their meal, and Za tried not to worry about their safety. He had never heard that The Tiger was needlessly cruel. However, the Court of the Tiger had been far away, and there would be many things he'd never heard about his grandfather.

He should have been asking before this. Now was not the time with others listening. The next part of the journey was about to begin, and they would soon be walking into the

Court, prepared or not.

CHAPTER TWENTY-THREE

I appreciated the few days in Evisto, and especially since Tansa and I had a room of our own. Za stayed with Tanisk and Danisin, and after the first night, I stopped worrying about what would happen to him. Tansa had been very good at lecturing me about not thinking the prince was only my concern. We all watched over him -- and besides, Prince Zaron turned out to be far more capable of taking care of himself than I would have expected.

Endris's work, of course. I silently thanked his spirit, but I still wasn't done with my protest to Tansa. I had my best knife in hand, trying to decide the best place to put it tonight. We might need it quickly.

"What if another of those black cloud figures comes after him?" I asked as I sat on the edge of our bed. Kintansa was already lying down, looking remarkably relaxed. And seductive.

"They're in the room next door. We'll hear any trouble," Tansa said with a snarl that was a sure sign her temper was about to give way.

"But --"

She grabbed me by the shoulder and pulled me down. Tansa was not some weak little plaything. She held me there, her head close to my face.

"Put your damned knife under the pillow before one of us is wounded."

I obeyed.

Oh yes, having the room to ourselves helped my temper a great deal, as did passing the first night without any trouble. When we came down to breakfast the next day, I felt as though things were going to go better. That was a new experience for me.

"I checked at the docks," Tanisk said and smiled. "No ships heading north just yet, so you'll have a few days here, at least. I've already spread the word that the four of you will go on to the Court of the Tiger and see what information you might get there. You won't be the only ones heading north, though I'll try not to get you on a ship with anyone important. Locals are getting uneasy as well."

"The fog," Za said quietly. His accent still marked him as not really one of the Fox Clan, so he didn't talk much in public. Not that he had ever talked much at all, in fact. I had picked up more of the accent from my years with Tansa, but I was careful, too. "That is enough to have made everyone worried. Too many people, too many different places, talking about the same trouble."

"Yes," Tanisk agreed. Then he started eating as others came to sit near us. I wanted to snarl and chase them away, but that would only draw more attention.

We ate, discussed the journey -- except for the trouble spots which limited our discussion quite a bit. Tanisk changed the conversation to trade and began talking about what ships were already in the dock. He seemed to know most of the captains, and I could tell from his tone which ones he trusted.

I hadn't thought about what the Fox Clan -- and the grasslanders in general -- would trade. They were not unprepared, though. The clans rented a warehouse in the area, set their own guards and clerks to it, and brought in material over the year: furs, cloth, pottery. They mostly traded for grain, wine, and a small number of gems that they could use for additional trade elsewhere.

"And iron when we can get it," Tanisk added. "That's more expensive, and there are some years when we're lucky to get a few ingots, but it's better quality than we can get from trading to the south."

Za showed considerable interest in trade. I supposed it was part of his training, I knew --but he seemed to take a real delight in finding out how things worked. Tanisk also lost the last bit of reserve he'd had when dealing with the prince. They'd found common ground. The rest of us just followed them around, and I suspected I was not the only one bored.

But it was good to be bored. Pleasant. Za never went looking for trouble, though he was happy when we went exploring a bit of the city. We stayed clear of places where the elite might be gathered which gave Za more freedom. He remained careful nonetheless, but I had never seen anyone so enthralled with anything as simple and noisy as a market square. If anyone noticed him at all, they probably took him to be a grasslander who had come to the city for the first time.

On the fourth day, Tanisk had news.

"I've found your ship," he told us at the dinner that night. Everyone looked up in shock, even though we had known the news would come soon enough. "She's the *Vagabond* and out of a small port to the south. A simple trader and more than happy to take on five passengers for a price. You'll be staying on deck beneath a canopy. I trust that won't be a problem."

We all agreed that it would not. We'd lived in the wilds and traveled with the Fox Clan.

Tanisk nodded. He didn't look happy, but I knew that was because he was going to lose his daughter again. If I could have convinced her to stay, I would have. I thought Za might have felt the same way, but neither of us was stupid enough to say so.

"When do we go?" I finally asked.

"The morning tide," he said and sat up straighter. "You will be well supplied, of course. And I've gotten papers from the local council that will get you at least to the court -- but it will be up to you from there."

Za nodded and reached over to lay his fingers on the man's arm. He didn't do that often, and the touch startled Tanisk. "Thank you. I will do my best to see her, and the others, safely home again. I give you my word."

Tanisk gave him an odd look and then a nod. "It's easy to forget who you really are, you know."

"I am no one," he said and smiled. "My only power is in my friends."

"And a rather strange sword," Kintansa added.

He smiled. Za did not smile often enough, and for a moment I was glad that I hadn't seen that look before. Prince Zaron looked far too much like his father right before the man had done something daring. I glanced at Kintansa. She had a startled look that meant she'd seen the father in the son as well.

Za did not, like his father, go looking for trouble, though. Just the same, he found it that evening when we were out for a quick walk. I had been thinking about being trapped on a small ship for the next week or more -- depending on the weather and if the Shala, the Goddess of the Sea, was with us in this crazy endeavor.

I'd never prayed to Shala before, but I did that evening as we walked along, and that was how I missed the trouble that came hurtling towards us out of one of the cloth shops. A line of men carried away bundles of cloth. Za had been the closest and shoved the rest of us back while he scrambled out of the way. Unfortunately, he bumped into the rotund woman coming out the door behind the others.

Ambassador Wytimi, of course.

She screamed in such protest that you might have thought Za had pulled a knife on her. A guard coming just behind her reached over and shoved him to the ground and kicked.

"Vermin!" she yelled. "How dare you touch me! Vermin!"

Za, wisely, covered his face and kept down so that she did not get a good look at him. Danisin waded in and got between the guard and the prince while I was left to deal with the Ambassador. That suited me fine at that moment, though a wise voice inside my head said not to make this worse.

She'd run out of breath to yell, at least, but her gray eyes glared at me as I gave her a very proper bow. "How unfortunate that your servants are so silent, lady!" I said in my best grasslander accent. "But the boy did his best to avoid knocking any of those fine clothes onto the ground."

"He touched me! Do you know who I am?"

"Of course," I answered with another bow. "You are Ambassador Wytimi."

"Huh." I had almost pleased her with that one. "I want the boy beaten."

"No," I said.

I don't think anyone had dared say no to her in a long, long time. This time she grew enraged beyond even the ability to speak. I took advantage of it and turned to the others. "Get the boy out of here," I ordered.

"No!" Za rose to his feet and moved to stand beside me. I had feared he would, and I wanted to curse. The ambassador's guards had finally moved to trap us, too. I had hoped the others would --

"Beat them all," the woman said. "And if they dare to try and stop you, kill them."

"There are laws in Evisto," I replied and was having a hard time holding to the accent.

"They do not apply to me, vermin," she said and started

to turn away.

"You have lost your gods," Za said.

I was ready to turn and beat him myself at this point, especially when I saw him looking directly into the woman's face.

When I turned back to the Ambassador, though, I fell silent. She'd gone white and took a step away from all of us. Did she recognize him? I didn't think so. Did he have some knowledge of her that made that statement so powerful? Maybe.

It worked. The woman fled back to her carriage, and after only a heartbeat of uncertainty, the others followed her. I saw curious glances turned our way, but in a moment the carriage rushed down the street and her people trotted along behind it.

"Back to the inn," Za whispered. He put a hand on Danisin's shoulder and grimaced. "Kicked me in the side."

"Damn." I had not considered the wound where the demon had gouged the bone. "What did you do to her?"

"Told her the truth," he said as we hurried away and probably at a faster pace than we should have, at least for his sake. "I can't say how ... how I knew. Just that she had lost all link to even her own humanity."

"And it may have helped that she might have felt as though she recognized you," Danisin added.

"Let's just hope she doesn't put it all together," I added. I slowed when we'd gone around one corner.

"We will be gone with the dawn," Za reminded me. "Even if she realized the truth within the hour, she'd have a hard time tracking us down. She won't have any hope of remembering that soon, you know. She's too upset."

"True," I agreed. For the first time, though, I was glad we were going to leave soon.

I was going to miss our room at the inn.

Kintansa had spent the last day with her father while the

rest of us had been out. We told the others the tale of our encounter, and I could tell from Tanisk's face that he was just as suddenly glad to see us gone.

"You'll be careful of her," I said to him as we sat at the table.

"Yes," he said and took the warning seriously. I hoped, as well, that someone as unpleasant as Wytimi would have a hard time gaining any real help from others.

Kintansa sighed at my restlessness that night, but she was no better. We were up before anyone else the next day, taking our packs down to the main room. The others wandered in a couple at a time.

One more nice meal and then we were on our way to the docks. The morning fog curled around the buildings but didn't hold any of the magic we'd felt away from the sea. Gulls screamed in protest as we made our way down the dock to the ship.

The *Vagabond* was not as large as the ships we'd passed, and she sat out at the far end of the dock -- I took that as a good sign that we'd have no trouble getting away. Tanisk introduced us to Captain Magar, an older man with neat gray hair. He did not smile, but he didn't look unfriendly, either.

"We go, ten days, maybe another and another," he said, betraying the fact he spoke little of the language. "Up, up coast. One night at sea, one night at small port, sea, port, sea, port -- slow but safe."

I liked that idea.

We went up the small plank of wood that stretched from the dock to ship. The movement of the craft in the water made me feel as though I couldn't get my footing at all. Za didn't look any happier than I did. Danisin frowned but braced his legs, and I thought he would defy the ocean itself. I just sent another silent prayer to Shala to keep us safe.

Kintansa stayed to give a last farewell to her father,

nodded several times at things he said, and then came up to the ship.

"Here and here," Captain Magar said with a wave to the railing. "Out of way."

We took places where he indicated. Kintansa watched her father walk away, but the rest of us showed more interested in what the ship's crew did as they prepared to sail. I didn't understand a single word that the Captain and others shouted back and forth as they made efficient work of getting clear of the dock. Ropes came free, sails began to climb up the masts, and the ship began to move outward.

The ship also moved up and down. I was sorry I had eaten so well. I refused to be ill, though. Danisin was, but then he seemed to recover quickly. Tansa looked a bit green, but she must have taken the same tack as me and just refused to admit or allow it. We were too much alike.

And Za? He looked as though he'd been born to sail. He moved steadily across the deck while the rest of us walked as though we were three days drunk.

The ship sailed out into the fog and soon we could see nothing at all but the ocean water beneath the hull. I could see no land anywhere and even the cries of the gulls grew distant enough to be in another world.

I had to trust the sailors knew which way they were going. Unfortunately, of late I was not a very trusting person.

"Let's go rest," Tansa said softly, her hand resting atop mine on the railing. "I think we'll both feel better if we can just get used to this damned movement."

I wanted to stay and stare -- but there was nothing but gray fog, and I couldn't stand here the entire trip. I let Tansa take me to a little canvas-covered area, though I made sure I knew where Za was before we settled beneath the covering. I wondered why they bothered with such cover since everything was damp with the fog.

Za and Danisin talked with the captain. I wanted to tell the boy to stay where I could see him, but that would only draw attention to him. Besides, there wasn't far he could go.

By noon the fog had burnt off, and I was glad for the canvas that blocked out the bright rays of the sun. I felt well enough to stand at the rail again and was rewarded with a view of magnificent rock peaks rising high over the ocean. I could not see the end of them in either direction.

They did, however, provide a landmark, so to speak, that I could watch. I had not liked the dull gray of the fog-shrouded morning. We were also moving at a reasonable speed, the crew working the sails in some arcane way that meant we bounced along about two miles off the barren, rocky land.

Except for the bouncing part, it was not bad. If I trusted the crew -- and that might take me a few days -- I thought this might be a pleasant journey.

I had not counted on the pirates.

CHAPTER TWENTY-FOUR

They spent the first night at sea anchored in a shallow bay near rocky peaks that reached upward into the dark sky. Za had slept well -- better than he had in quite a while. Not that he believed they were safe. By now the Queen had to wonder where he had gone. Her black ghosts had not found him (he assumed). Had she given up looking and believed that he couldn't have survived this long on his own?

Za was not alone, though. He didn't like to think that he would have been helpless without the others, but he did admit that Mai and Kintansa had been instrumental in getting him this far. Now they had only a few day's sailing to reach the Court of the Tiger.

The Queen might have realized where he would head and try to set a trap there. They did not a lot of choices.

Za used this time on the ship as a chance to calm and to think about what he would do once he reached his grandfather. He also learned what he could about how the ship functioned, but that was only because learning things pleased him and kept him busy.

Mai was not happy when Za learned how to climb up amongst the sails, though. Za found it amusing to see her want to tell him not to do such things but at the same time to realize she had no right to order him at all. This was a good lesson for her because they were going to the place where he would be Prince Zaron again.

Not a role Za wanted to play anymore, but he had to do what would be best for others, even if he knew he would never rule them nor wanted to.

Odd feelings.

Small groups of people lived along the edges of the protruding rocks, and some higher up on the craggy peaks. Ascetics, Captain Magar had told him in his broken words. Holy people, mostly people devoted to the Goddess Shala and the sea. If any of them flew a white banner, that meant they needed help, and a ship might put a rowboat out to see if they could do anything. It depended, the Captain explained, on how devoted to Shala the crew might be, and what they would fear if they did not help.

There were a handful of tiny villages as well. On the second evening of the journey, they put into the bay by one. The place had been built entirely of wood from shipwrecks -- not a pleasant sight, Za thought as they watched from afar. When the Captain lowered a rowboat, he almost asked to go with the crew to see this strange place -- but he stopped himself when he caught sight of Mai. She would likely throw herself in the water and follow, whether she could swim or not.

"Freshwater," the Captain said to Kintansa when she asked. "Some fruit. Help through the longer days ahead. Safe bay. Rest, all of us."

He walked away looking happy. Za realized the usually dour man loved the sea voyages and had not much liked being stuck a port like Evisto.

"They're not going to get much in supplies here," Kintansa observed as the four of them watched the rowboat head for the shore. "Considering all the ships that must come by here --"

"The bay is too shallow for anything heavier than a craft like this," Za said with a pat on the railing. "They wouldn't want to anchor out in the open sea and wait the long time it took for a rowboat to get to shore and back, at least not unless they were really desperate. Besides, larger ships have more room for supplies and don't need to restock so often."

"You were quick to pick up that information," Kintansa said with an approving nod.

"I am interested in learning everything," he replied and hoped that he didn't sound too childish.

They all nodded as though this were a perfectly normal behavior for a royal prince. He didn't think even Mai considered how little opportunity he'd had to learn much about the world. Oh, he could read and write, even in more than one language -- but if his mother had caught him studying ships, she would have accused him of joining forces with some foreign land. She had loved the word *treason* and used it far more widely than most people outside of Summer Cloud realized. The word promised the same fate as his father had received. The word had frightened him as a child.

He would not go back. He likely would not survive anyway -- he knew that truth as well. However, in the days of his brief freedom, he would store up a lifetime of knowledge, and if he was fortunate, he might have time to relive this amazing gathering of experience in his mind.

"Za?" Mai said with a tap on his arm.

He had been staring at the little village. "It must be like a prison living there, you know," he said. "They have so few opportunities to go anywhere."

"A desperate person might try hiking along the mountains," Danisin said looking up and down the coast. "They're lower here than they were back near the mainland. I imagine you could get quite some distance, but the land looked treacherous and the peaks grew higher nearer to Evisto. If you didn't know what you might find out there, the village might seem less horrible. They get visitors, too -- like this crew. I suspect some sign on to ships now and then."

They ate from their own supplies that night, though the captain brought them fresh oranges and shared with delight.

Not a bad life, really.

The next morning, they sailed eastward again. The day after, they came to a wide break in the mountains; the peaks had seemed to go on forever to the east and west, one set attached to the land and the eastern range seeming to stretch out forever into the sea.

"We cross here," Captain Magar explained. "Stay mostly middle, watch for reefs, rocks. Most ships too large. Sail another three days around the far end."

Za stayed with the Captain, watching for the sharp spikes that could tear into the hull. There were, in fact, a few old wrecks with the masts still rising or the shell turned on the side and pushed up against the rocky shore where it became a home for birds and seals. The twenty-mile passage took them well into the late afternoon, and Za felt a wave of relief as they crossed between two tall pillars that seemed to mark the entry into another world. He could see endless sea there, and perhaps a distant land, but the mountains that had blocked most of the view now lay behind them.

The pirate ship had been waiting. The other crew must have had someone on the upper land, though Za knew the crew of the *Vagabond* had been watching for any sign of trouble. Captain Magar only cursed once and started yelling orders.

"Get to cover, you, your companions. Stay out of way!"

Za didn't think that the wisest order the man had given, but Za also didn't want to worry him. Mai had come running his way, but he snagged her arm and started back toward the stern of the ship. It hardly mattered. The new craft moved fast across the ocean. The *Vagabond* hadn't a chance, even if she could discard cargo and move faster.

The pirates moved in very fast.

"Weapons!" Captain Magar shouted as the crew of the other ship threw weighted ropes, the twine thicker than an arm, across from their ship. The ends dug into the deck and held, even while crew tried to tear them out and toss them back.

For a moment both crews stared across the abyss as the pirate ship moved closer, huge men turning the winches that pulled the rope back and dragged the *Vagabond* closer. There was no challenge shouted on either side nor any look of pleasure in the eyes of the pirates. One man stepped in front of that crew; he was probably the epitome of what a pirate should look like, from his wind-blown dark hair to the velvet vest and lace cuffs.

"Friends," he shouted, and Captain Magar snarled at the word. "Give up. We are the crew of the *Blue Rose* and you know I have a reputation for not killing where I do not need to. You will be put ashore to sail again. Otherwise, we will fight. We outnumber you. Be wise! But also, be quick."

"You would be wise to do as he says, Captain Magar," Kintansa said. "There is no need to make this worse --"

"I dare no do it," the captain replied with a frantic shake of his head. "*I promised*. I cannot. Your father say I must get you to the capital!"

"Oh hell," Kintansa cursed. She grabbed the man's arm. "Listen to me, Captain! My father was clearly not considering all the problems we might face. We cannot fight the others --"

"Better to die fighting than risk the curse of the Grasslanders!" he said and pulled free, striding away from her. None of the crew wore more than long knives, but he drew his now. "We fight!"

The pirate looked shocked and dismayed, but he gave a reluctant nod and then signaled his own people.

"No," Za whispered. Mai looked at him, truly worried for the first time. "Mai -- stop them!"

"What in the name of the Gods can I --"

Za hadn't waited to discuss the situation with her. He ran straight toward the spot where one of the three spiked ropes held to the ship. He still didn't know how he drew the sword into his hand, but it was there, and the pure magic of it cut straight through the first rope.

No one noticed at first. The rope snapped away and fell off the *Vagabond*. Pirates had started across on a wide board, but with the one cord cut loose, the board proved far less steady than they had expected. The pirate captain looked startled, but he was almost to the deck already.

Za cut the next rope, and that was noticed on all sides. Then he was going for the last, but it was on the other side of the boarding pirates. He did not want to use the sword on them, especially since the captain of that other craft was already shouting for his men to retreat.

Za noted that the pirate captain also didn't shove or push to make certain he would get safely to his ship, although his men started to panic. Za held back for a moment, thinking to give the man a chance to get to safety --

One of the *Vagabond* crew rushed forward with his knife in hand and stabbed the man --

"No!" Za shouted. The pirate captain was going to fall.

Za cut the last rope -- grabbed it with one hand as he let go of the sword and leapt toward the board and the pirate.

The board pitched and fell, but he had grabbed the man and tightened his other hand around the rope. Not a good hold, and he feared they would hit the far ship with too much force, and both would end up in the water between the two craft.

Mai yelled something. He couldn't quite make out the words, but he suspected it was something a guard should not be saying to a prince.

They hit the other ship. Za slid downward, the weight of the pirate captain dragging them both toward the sea.

"Grab hold!" Za shouted. "Grab the rope, or we'll both be caught between the ships!"

The man moved, lifted both arms and caught hold, though not well. At least it lessened some of the weight, but they could not stay here. He didn't think the captain could move upward, though. He was having trouble just holding on. The wound bled severely -- Za could see the stain running down his back. Water from the ocean splashed up over them and crews yelled from both sides, but the ships moved apart. They wouldn't be crushed between the hulls, though there was still a good chance they would slip and fall into the turbulent ocean between the two craft and drown.

A net fell over them, and a moment later someone climbed down and grabbed the captain. "You make it up on your own?" he asked.

"Yes."

"Good. Careful."

Za followed the man upward. The net was rough and tore at his hands as he climbed. He wondered what sort of mess he'd thrown himself into --

The net moved. He thought they might be pulling him up, but then he realized the pull came from below. He looked down and saw not just Mai, but Kintansa and Danisin as well, climbing up after him.

"Fools!" he said, but not too loudly.

He reached the railing, and someone pulled him up. One held to his arm, but it was not a tight grasp. The pirate captain remained, on his feet and lifted a hand to wave at Za and the others who scrambled up behind him.

"Friends," the man said. "Treat well."

"Yes, Captain," another man said. Za took him to be the second in command.

They carried the captain away. Za hoped he survived because he suspected their future depended on the man's goodwill.

He got little information out of the crewmen who took them to a nice cabin -- a bit small for the four of them, but he supposed there wasn't much room on the ship.

"The ship is the *Blue Rose*," Za told the others after the door had closed. Not locked, but he could hear a guard outside. "The Captain's name is Ardeth Gamba. Even I know that name."

"Well *damn*," Mai said. She squeezed seawater out of her clothing, but the movement looked more like nervousness rather than anything helpful. "We are in the company of very famous pirates."

Danisin grunted agreement. Kintansa had gone to the porthole and stared out, though.

"The *Vagabond* is getting away without a problem as far as I can tell," she finally said. "I had not expected Captain Magar to be such a fool. I'll have to talk to father about how he deals with these people."

"There have been a lot of fools involved in this mess," Mai said and settled on a chair bolted to the floor. She stared at Za.

"You should not have followed me," Za replied. Mai might not have expected that answer from the way she scowled. "But that doesn't mean I'm not glad to have you here."

She made a sound of agreement.

Za had no idea where they were going.

CHAPTER TWENTY-FIVE

We sailed farther and farther out to sea with no land in sight for the next six days. I didn't like all that water everywhere and not a bit of land that we could spot from the cabin. We'd been out on the deck for a few minutes each day, but that had not helped. I wanted to believe that the pirates knew where they were going, but all I saw was worry in their faces.

The worry must be for their captain, though. He had not shown himself since we came aboard, and when any of us asked, we got the same mute shake of the head and mumbled words about fever.

They fed us twice a day. I was impressed with the quality of the food, in fact, after a few days on the *Vagabond*. Long days passed, though. We managed not to go at each other's throats even though none of us were happy. I had the hardest time. I even had moments when I considered how the four of us could take over the ship, despite that none of us had a clue of what to do with such a craft.

Slept, ate, walked the deck. Repeat. How long would this go on?

Even Za began to show signs of stress. By the sixth day, he had taken to spending most of his time on the single bed, sitting cross-legged and meditating. I started to get annoyed even at that because I thought it unfair that he had an escape and the rest of us did not.

A soft knock and the door opened. The usual woman put a platter of food on the table, glanced around --

Shock came to her face.

"*Ata!*" she said with a bit of a squeak. "*Ata!*"

She spun and hurried out of the room.

Za looked up with a frown. "I had not expected that reaction."

I had expected trouble to come back through the door and I didn't know what we could do this time. We had our knives, but those wouldn't be much use against the whole crew. Besides, they could just lock us in and starve us out. I'd already thought of many ways they could kill us.

I heard sounds outside the door, but nothing like I had expected. The people sounded excited. I thought they might even be hopeful. I put the blade away. Za still sat on the bed, his legs crossed, but now he had his head tilted as he watched for the entrance.

A soft knock and the door opened. Captain Ardeth came into the little room, leaning on the arm of the woman had left in such haste. He appeared pale, feverish, and barely able to stay to his feet.

"Sit down!" I ordered and quickly gave way from the seat I had claimed.

He gave a weary smile and settled where I said, leaning forward slightly so he put no pressure on the back wound. Za grabbed the pillow from the bed and brought it over, arranging it so Captain Ardeth -- as I'd heard the crew call him -- could sit comfortably. Captain Ardeth watched the prince with open speculation this time.

I noted that Captain Ardeth was slightly more exotic than I had first realized. The empire had become a blend of east and west, much like Prince Za. That had been happening for hundreds of years before the Tiger and the Wolf held their epic battles. Ardeth had the look of the old east, with coal black hair that hung in ringlets down his shoulders, a thin mustache, and tan skin. The fall of his hair didn't obscure the pain in his dark eyes.

It also couldn't hide the surprise he showed.

"You, Za," he said and stopped to catch his breath. He must have learned our names from his crew, who had asked. "You know the *Art of Ata*."

"Yes," Za said with a nod of his head. Then he dropped down on his heels so that the Captain didn't have to look upward at him. "You do as well."

"Yes. You called the *Sword of Glory* to you, and that's how you cut the ropes."

"The *Sword of Glory*? I didn't know the name."

"But -- but --" He gasped and waved a hand as though to say something he could not even articulate.

Za took the Captain's hand. "Be calm. I have had odd training with a man named Endris and later the Master Drital --"

"Ah," he nodded and took a small breath. I could tell he should not be up and visiting. "I know this name."

"He said he had taught me all that he could, and I must find my own path. Endris taught me more, but it was in a rush as he died."

"Goddess of the Sea," Ardeth said with a shake of his head. "That could have as soon killed you or driven you mad."

"The situation was perilous," Za said.

"And you are not a Grasslander. Are any of you?"

"I was born one," Kintansa said. I had noted that the conversation didn't worry her even though she must have suspected where it would go. Za would not lie. "But I've gone far since then and done ... other things."

She looked to Za.

He smiled.

"I was born Prince Zaron, heir to the Tiger and the Wolf -- but matters have changed rather drastically of late. My mother and her daughters have called up demons, and I am going to the Court of the Tiger to get what help I can to defeat them. You must take us back, my friend."

I wasn't surprised when Ardeth shook his head in denial at the tale, but I was surprised by his words. "I dare not. If the *Blue Rose* sailed into port, they'd have hanged us all before you could get your tale told. We're only a day from Peace Port, and I can find you a ship from there. I believe there might be something at Peace Port that you'll want to see anyway, Prince Zaron."

"Za," he said. The prince reached back and ruffled his ragged hair. "I've given up my pursuit of the throne. Now, let me see if I might help you."

Captain Ardeth started to argue and changed his mind. Za moved to the side and gently put a hand on the area of the wound at his back. The Captain bit back a sound of pain and the woman and two other crew at the door started to move --

But they stopped almost immediately. Captain Ardeth already looked better, blinking in surprise as he sat up straighter. Za remained where he was for a little longer, his brow furrowed as he concentrated on something no one else could see or do. When he stepped back, he put a hand on the table and took a ragged breath of his own.

I didn't chastise him, though. I suspected he had just saved the Captain's life and probably ours as well.

"I have not done that before," he said and looked at the rest of us as though in apology. "I might have made our journey easier if I had tried at other times."

"Sit down," I said.

"What did you do?" Danisin asked. He looked pleased,

and I suspected that until now he hadn't thought the Captain or any of the rest of us would survive.

"I burnt away most of the fever and sealed the lung," Za said with a bit of a frown. "Not a strong patch, Captain. Do not strain it and the wound should heal well."

"I am grateful," Captain Ardeth said with a bow of his head.

I could hear word spreading out into the hall and up onto the deck. Ardeth gave a smile at the shouts of pleasure we heard everywhere. This was a well-liked captain.

I settled on the bed where Za had been, and Tansa sat beside me. "We need information Captain Ardeth," I said and hoped that I would not annoy him. "Peace Port where we're going -- that's your home? Will we be safe there?"

"No one is safe there, but it has little to do with those who live on the island." His eyes narrowed for a moment but quickly cleared before he continued. He did glance at Za with a bit of curiosity, though. I was sure he had more questions, but he applied himself to mine first. "The people of the island are only a remnant of the people we once were, and we lived along the southern coast of the mainland in fishing villages. Others came from north and west, and they wanted our fine villages. There was a war."

"There is always a war," Za said with a sigh.

Ardeth nodded unhappy agreement. "We lost, of course. Two centuries ago, now. They piled us into our fishing boats, took our sails and dragged the little craft out into the sea and to the mercy of Shala. We had little in food and only a few other things we had managed to save. We did our best to keep together, tying the ships within a line with the ropes from the ruined sails and praying to Shala for help. The goddess was kind and brought us to Peace Port. Less than five hundred had survived out of several thousand, but it was enough for us to settle there. Then, about a hundred years ago, we were found again. This time, though, the new people did not want our island, but only to have a place to take on supplies. We played that game and still do, but when the chance came, some of us sailed with crews and learned the craft. Then, when the time was right, we acquired a ship of your own."

"And not with gold," Tansa said with a slight smile.

He bowed his head in agreement. "Ships still come to this port. They know enough to ignore The *Blue Rose* when we are there as well. And we are not often in port -- just long enough to bring in the supplies we have acquired elsewhere and that we cannot buy with the paltry payments the ships give us for fruit and water."

Za nodded as though he totally agreed with this form of piracy. I wasn't so confident Ardeth was telling us the truth, but Za did believe ... and I was starting to think that Za could genuinely tell a spoken truth.

Could Captain Ardeth, another practitioner of *Ata*, also tell the spoken truth? Was that why he didn't question Za's odd tale about being a prince?

"We will be at the port by sunset tomorrow," Ardeth said. He carefully stood but waved away the woman's arm. "I can walk to my cabin, though thank you, Osana. Rest well, my friends."

He left before we could ask more questions and I thought I saw a look of contemplation on his face.

"Well," I said.

Za leaned back on the chair now, clearly worn. "He would have died. The crew might have still dealt well with us, but in their sorrow, they might have done something unfortunate."

"Yes," I agreed. "And it seems as though our pirate captain might be a good ally. You need to sleep for a while, Za."

He started to argue and changed his mind.

The food still sat on the table. We ate and saved some for

Za who slept soundly. I was glad to see him resting so well, but the rest of us felt obliged to keep quiet. That was annoying because I wanted to talk about what we might do once we get to this pirate port.

Useless talk, I supposed. I took my spot by the porthole and listened to the sea and the crew. They were happy, and that helped me relax for the first time. I'd heard them speak before and there had always been a darker edge to their words, even when I could only hear a few words. The word dead had been a good part of those conversations, and being too damned egotistical, I had always applied those words to us. Now I realized they had spoken about what they would do once their captain died.

We all rested better that night. Osana brought us breakfast with a bright smile, too.

"He's doing very well, the Captain," she said. She looked years younger, I thought. "We will keep him from doing too much, but the crew must see him and know it is true, he is better. You are a blessing to us."

Those words startled me to silence, but Tansa was quick to take it up. "If we hadn't been on the *Vagabond*, this might not have happened --"

"We had set our eyes on her some months ago," Osana said. "*Vagabond* is a good ship, small and easy to take, we thought. Shala brought you along. The one who stabbed Captain Ardeth in the back -- he would have done so anyway at the first chance. There is a bounty for my Captain, you know."

"Ah," Tansa said and nodded. I couldn't tell if she believed it less our fault or not, but her words did make some sense.

The crew remained exceedingly busy over the next few hours. We stayed in the cabin and out of the way. Food came rather hurriedly, and it wasn't Osana this time. We didn't ask the young man anything -- he seemed far too nervous already.

"Coming into port," Danisin said. "They don't know what they'll find."

As the sun began to decline, we were told the Captain would like to see us on the deck. We found him at the rail staring at an island that trailed smoke up into the sky. Volcano. I didn't like --

"Ah, there it is," Za said with a nod. "I suspected as much. It is the island I saw in the vision with the Fox Clan Wise woman."

"And that's good?" Captain Ardeth asked.

"I don't know," Za replied with a bright grin. "I never saw what happens here. I will trust in the gods -- and you."

"Ha!" Captain Ardeth gave a short laugh. "Well, first the bad news. The volcano is not always active, and I do not like to see the smoke now."

I watched the volcano which seemed to glow with a sullen red as we sailed closer to the bay. More trouble, I supposed. I was not surprised.

CHAPTER TWENTY-SIX

Za stayed close to Captain Ardeth as they left the ship. He worried that the man was not ready for any trouble --

Ardeth would not find trouble here. People shouted his name and came running to see him. The man was well-liked, that was certain.

"My people will say nothing of who you are," the Captain assured him. Za believed it true since they were oddly trustworthy people despite their chosen profession. "You and your people are safe to wander the streets, too. It is an interesting village. Come back to sleep on the ship, though. With those other four ships at the dock, the little inn is going to be packed and boisterous. I wouldn't want anything to happen to you now."

Za looked at Mai, and she gave a nod of agreement. "What are you doing to do?" she dared ask.

"There is someone I must see before I can make any more decisions," he replied and shook his head as though stopping himself from saying more. "I'll tell you about it when I get back."

They had reached the end of the dock. Ardeth gave a bow and then headed down the sandy beach. Za watched him but did not try to follow, though he hoped Ardeth didn't go far.

The injury was still dangerous.

Others who had come to greet the captain still shouted and waved, but they didn't go after him either.

"Bad stuff, eh?" someone said. "Bad stuff, send him rushing to the temple."

The crew of the ship had disembarked behind Za and his companions, some of them carrying bags of grain. More shouts of pleasure rose, and Za decided they had better get out of the way.

The village turned out to be a fascinating place. The buildings were all single floor huts made of palm trees, from the limbs in the walls to the leaves on the roofs. Sand seemed to be the common flooring, and cooking was done outside, filling the winding street with uncommon scents. The food appeared to include exotic fruits, fish, and birds. Za saw a lot of flatbreads as well, but he didn't think they were made of the usual grains.

These were people who had learned to survive against the odds. The goddess of the sea had seemed to smile on them with this island, though twice while the four of them walked the streets, the ground shifted slightly in a small tremor.

The locals always paused and gave a glance toward the volcano that rose up at the far end of the island, but in clear view of the village. There were no other mountains, and the ground rose slowly towards that glowing top.

The village turned out to be rather large. People from the other ships roamed around, a bit rowdier than they should have been, Za thought. Local guards watched for trouble, though, and the more belligerent people were escorted straight back to their ships.

Za found everything remarkably well-handled. He found studying the island civilization, clearly outside the rule of the Empire, a captivating pastime, but he suspected his companions were getting bored since he stopped to examine every little thing, including how walls were built. Everything fascinated him, but he took pity on the three and started back toward the bay.

Osana met them about halfway.

"Are you coming back?" she asked and smiled at their nods. "Good. The captain would like to speak with you. He says he'll sleep afterward."

Which, Za realized, was Osana's way of trying to hurry them along. He imagined that the captain had walked too far today and wore himself down.

A cool breeze blew in off the ocean, and a distant storm spawned lightning across the sky and sea.

"I am so glad to be on land right now," Mai said. "Even land that does not always stand as still as it should."

Osana nodded agreement with a glance at the volcano and perhaps a small prayer in words Za didn't understand.

The wind blew sharp across the bay, the *Blue Rose* making small leaps, even secured by the ropes. Za helped to balance Mai on the way up the gangplank and was glad to see that Ardeth was, in fact, on the deck and seated in a chair. Two others sat with him, strangers with long hair and beards, dark eyes, and serenity that Za immediately recognized.

"Brothers," he said with a proper *Ata* bow, his hands folded against his chest.

"Sit down, all of you," Ardeth said with a wave of his hand to the other chairs. The arm did tremble, and he looked pale, but Za could tell breathed easily still.

Za thought he might be about to learn why the gods had sent him so far out of the way on his journey to help the others. He didn't think this had been chance -- Za had stopped believing in chance at all during this journey.

"You are a follower of *Ata*," the man across from him said. He had a book in his lap, something ancient and bound in leather and gold. Jewels sparkled on the cover. "Ardeth says that you were taught both by Brother Drital and by Endris. Did you ever wonder where such a wondrous gift of *Ata* came from, Za?"

"I assumed it came from the gods," he answered and won a quick nod and a hint of humor. "But I had also studied enough to know that it had once been powerful in the southeast -- ah. The *Art of Ata* left the land when your people were forced away."

"Yes. You are quick to see connections. Good. Your lack of full training may be a danger, though -- to you mostly, but also to others."

Ardeth moved slightly as though he didn't like the way this conversation had gone. Za noted it without looking his way.

"I would be grateful for any teachings you can give me, but such work must be done quickly. I don't have time to remain here for long."

The second one leaned forward. "*Ata* is not something to be taught in the morning and set free in the afternoon."

"I have had years of training, sir," Za assured them. "And other, less normal learning."

"I have heard that you say so," the man said. "This Endris would have had to be a master to impart any true knowledge that way. We do not know this man. He is not of the true *Art of Ata*."

Za tilted his head, wondering what this man wanted from him. "So be it, then. I am not traditionally trained. I cannot change what has happened to me. We will not linger here for long."

Both men shook their heads, but the one holding the book seemed to have become their speaker. "No, that cannot be allowed, that you go out into the world so badly trained --"

Za lifted a hand when his people began to move. Mai made a soft growling sound, but they all settled back into their chairs while the two older men watched with narrowed eyes. Za didn't want to think about what might have happened. He needed to settle the trouble.

"I have a duty to perform. If I survive, I will do my best to come back. I want the training you can give me," Za admitted. "I just cannot take that time for *myself* right now."

"That is not acceptable."

"Much in the world is not acceptable," Za replied. Were they trying to make him angry? He could not imagine why. It was not the path of *Ata*, and he refused to be blinded by the rush of such a useless emotion.

"To turn you free on the world would be a dangerous game we are not willing to play. You will stay with us until we think you wise enough to leave again."

"You really can't think to keep me here." Za looked from one to the other, and even at the impassive Ardeth. "No, you don't."

They relaxed, all three of them. His people did not yet, but they had not seen what he did. Testing him, were they? He still didn't understand the reason.

"Ardeth has told us that you have the gift of perception. And, also, that you can call the *Sword of Glory*, though you didn't know the name," the man said. He'd sat back. His voice had calmed, and all pretense disappeared. "Perception is the basis of all *Ata*. To know the true thoughts of any, you deal with is the only way to follow the path without a useless waste of energy. We are not your enemies, and you not only refused to let us make you angry, you saw past my own false face. This is excellent. However, you truly are lacking in the full *Art of Ata*, Za."

"I know. I want to come back."

"You feel this mission is important to the world. I can see so in your eyes."

"If any should know, I think it ought to be you," Za

admitted. He didn't look at his companions. Instead, he told the tale about his mother, his sisters, the demons -- his bloodline and where he went.

"Armies create a wasteful loss of life, but sometimes there are no other ways. Yes, you must go -- but this might help," he held up the book, and Za took it carefully, stunned by the feel of age and power in the barest touch of the cover. "This is the *Book of Voyaging*, one of the ten books of *Ata* that we took with us from the mainland to our island. I brought it because I had a sense that you would need it. So, we lend it to you, Prince Zaron, and hope that you can return this to us in good time."

Stunned, he ran his fingers over the cover and then dared to open and turn the first few pages, entranced by the gilded writing and the colorful drawings. However, when he looked up, he shook his head.

"I cannot accept this, even for a time. I fear I cannot read more than one or two letters. This is a language and script I don't recognize at all."

"Ah," the man said but didn't look bothered. "Then you must take Ardeth as well to translate for you."

Ardeth made a little sound of surprise, but then nodded agreement. "I'll finally put The *Blue Rose* into dry dock for some needed repairs and tell Osana and the rest of the crew to go on without me if I am not back before she's done."

"Good then. Take care, all of you. Be at peace with *Ata*, Za. We will meet again."

The two got up and walked away, heading off the ship. Za looked at the book again and felt a thrill to think there might be secrets here, learning that would help him in the world the way *Ata* had already.

"My apologies Captain Ardeth," Za said. "I hadn't meant to drag you into this mess with the rest of us. I am sure we can work out a way, so you need not come along."

"I'm going," Ardeth replied, though he looked around the

ship with a touch of loss. Then he shook his head. "The ship needs repairs. I might as well take that time to do something useful in the world."

"We were told that there is a bounty on your head," Tansa pointed out. "It isn't safe for you to take this journey."

"And it is safe for the rest of you? I think not. But don't worry. The farther inland we go, the less likely it is that I'll be recognized. I'll be careful at the capital, but I don't foresee any trouble."

"You seem to have no question that my grandfather will give us an army," Za replied.

"I think the Tiger is wise," Ardeth replied and stood. The storm in the distance had moved closer, and he stared at it for a moment. "The storm will not come close. We'll sail with the morning tide on the *Lighttracker*. She's headed straight for the home port at the capital. She's also a ship I've never raided, so with a bit of a change, I should not be recognized at all. Does that suit you?"

"This is your place, and we are grateful for your help," Mai said. She sounded more assured again, as though everything had fallen into place.

Za had that feeling as well, but he thought some of it came from the book he held -- a precious gift they'd loaned him, and Za realized he must do everything he could to protect those pages and learn from them.

And to save the world.

CHAPTER TWENTY-SEVEN

We boarded the ship the next day, Ardeth's crew having provided us with new clothing, food, and even coin to replace what we'd lost on the **Vagabond**. I enjoyed the journey from Peace Port to Tigris, the capital. We had eight days of calm. Za and Ardeth spent most of their time going over the book with Ardeth translating things that made no sense at all to me -- and I suspected to the rest of us -- but sometimes Za would make such a sound of pleasure and understanding that I had to smile.

They meditated a lot, too.

Ardeth wore his hair braided, had given up his fancy clothing, and shaved his mustache. He looked almost as young as Za. They might have been cousins, in fact, with that same hint of old eastern blood. That helped both, who as individuals were each famous in their own way.

Quiet days. Peaceful days. We'd paid well for this voyage, and the crew appreciated the extra coin. They had not heard that we'd sailed in on *The Blue Rose* and might not have cared if we continued to behave. It was easy enough to concoct a tale of having come to Peace Port on a ship that was heading southward now, and how we caught a different craft heading north to the capital, which was not unknown. Ardeth had no trouble supplying the name of our previous ship, and if the two craft ever crossed paths in the future, it would be long past when we did what we must.

I did not look forward to going back to Willoway and facing the demons -- but we were pointed that way now. We had gone as far east as we would, and every step we took from the moment we reached the port would take us back to the danger we had escaped.

Oh, we'd always known we were going back, of course. Za never intended to run away, only to go where he would find help. The Court of the Tiger had always been our intended end point as well as starting point for the next actions.

I accepted the peace of the few days at sea knowing things would get crazy after this. Tansa didn't say anything, but I could see the look she always had before she went off to battle. Tension showed along the edges of her lovely eyes where the lines deepened, and her mouth rarely curled into a smile. As much as I didn't like to see the change, I knew it meant she was prepared for whatever trouble we would face once we were back on land.

I had come up to the deck on the dawn of the eighth day and looked across the last of the sea to the city which showed as a spray of lights across the land. Huge, I realized even before the sun rose behind me and began to outline the buildings that stretched across the horizon. The bay came into view, crowded with ships.

And high on the promontory stood a castle that rose in a dozen spires to catch the first light: The Court of the Tiger.

"Impressive, isn't it?" Ardeth asked as he leaned against the railing beside me. "I've only seen it once when I sailed here before I took on other work."

"I'd only seen drawings," I admitted. "And they didn't do it justice. I can't imagine how Za thinks he can get to his grandfather. Yes, the ring -- but will that be enough? And if not, what else can we do."

"We'll have to wait and see," Ardeth replied.

I had come to realize that those who followed the *Art of Ata* did not tend to get upset or worried about maybes and what ifs. I wondered if I should emulate them or admit that they just annoyed me. Now was probably not the time to make such a decision.

We were well past noon by the time we had taken a spot along the docks and the guards allowed us to leave the ship to go to the city. The noise and the stink of the place were nearly overwhelming, and we had crossed well into the city before I felt as though we'd left the smell of gutted fish behind. Danisin took up the job of finding us a proper inn for the night since it was clear we wouldn't get near the castle before the next day. We would have one more day of relative peace, I thought.

"Besides, we can listen for rumors about the west," Za said quietly as he walked between Ardeth and me. "We will want to know as much as we can about what he's already been told."

"If they bother to give him rumors at all," Ardeth said. "From all I've heard, the Tiger only deals in facts."

"I don't know him well enough," Za admitted with a touch of mistrust in his voice. I hadn't expected to hear that sound. We sidestepped a cart pulled by a man who snarled and cursed, but apparently at life and not at us. "I only met them both once when I was very young."

Ardeth nodded but with a sidelong glance that meant he had only just remembered that he walked beside Prince Zaron. I knew that look because I still felt it sometimes.

Tansa walked behind us, keeping guard though we tried not to make it obvious. Danisin appeared now and then, shook his head, and went off again. I wondered what the problem with the inns was that he found so many of them wanting.

We'd lost our belongings on the *Vagabond*. I missed my two swords, even though I'd had little reason to use them on this journey, despite all the dangers we'd faced. Walking the streets of the capital, though, felt too much like Willoway. I wanted Danisin to find us a place away from the crowds of people and wondered what the problem could be.

Passing a couple of such places, though, I heard the din of noise. No, not there. And the next one smelled of a bad fish stew -- not that one either. Danisin knew about inns, of course. He had worked at The Lost Way for a long time.

I suppressed a sigh as I thought about that more comfortable life.

We found an inn, at last, a pricey place, but quieter. The food smelled good. We were dressed well enough to fit in, too, which helped. This was not a place where crewmen off a ship would rush to for a wild night.

Good. I thought I understood part of Danisin's care then, as well. We were very close to the sea, and we didn't want Ardeth recognized, not only for his sake but for our own as well. If we were caught in the company of a notorious pirate, it would not help our cause.

Even so, I found I was glad to have him along. He'd recovered well from his injury, and I could tell from the way he moved that the man knew how to fight, both with and without weapons. His willingness not to fight when he tried to take the *Vagabond* had stayed with me as well. This was a man who would try to find ways not to go into battle. Good. I was not looking for someone who looked for trouble.

Presenting ourselves as traders from the grasslands won instant acceptance, which shocked me. Kintansa, though, knew the right words and she now became our leader. I could play along with her, knowing enough of the grasslander language to take the part. The men, we said, were partners from the south. Our trade goods were in storage -- a standard action -- until we were ready to head back south and then west.

The mention of our destination broke out a flood of rumors. It seemed everyone in the dining hall had heard something. Only a couple had come from the west, and those not as far as Willoway, but they still had interesting news.

"One dead princess," the man mumbled. He wasn't used to talking in public and didn't much like the attention when everyone focused on him. "They say the prince killed her and will kill the others as soon as he can. Only..."

"Yes?" Tansa asked softly.

"Well, if he has called the demons, why would he have trouble killing them?" He gave an expansive shrug. "I don't say nothing is going on in Willoway and the lands nearby, but I don't think it is as simple as we've heard."

No one argued with that pronouncement, and I took the reaction as something of a good sign, even if it didn't help us right now. The rest of the rumors had been what we expected; demons, prince, power. We listened with an avid interest that had nothing to do with trade, though the others didn't realize.

Za and Ardeth said nothing. I had the feeling they were masking out other sounds, listening to the words of people who were not talking to us. I had seen Za do so before.

The *Art of Ata* looked more and more useful.

By the time we retired to our rooms -- side-by-side on the third floor --my head was spinning, and it wasn't from the excellent wine that we'd had with dinner. With a nod from Tansa, we all went into one room and gathered quietly to talk.

"The Tiger is already uneasy," Za said quickly. "He's called in army officers. They have not yet started to gather more than the usual troops, but there are rumors the order will not be long in coming. Merchants are worried because they'll be expected to contribute anything that is needed."

"Where will the troops go?" Kansa asked.

"West is all we heard," Ardeth replied. "I think this might be good, that things are already on the move. The question is if Za really needs to show himself and risk the danger that involves."

I looked to Za though I knew what his answer was going to be already.

Za shook his head. "The Tiger is still working only with rumors. He's not moving yet. I still need to give him information."

"Others --" Ardeth began.

"Others may come with the truth. The Queen will have sent her own people."

"You think he'll listen to you."

"I hope he will." Za looked around. "The rest of you should not go with me."

"I think we've discussed this before," Tansa replied with a tone that clearly meant no argument. "We are going to do our best to get you to your grandfather. Ardeth, you weren't --"

"But I am now," he said. "I think we better sleep for a few hours. We'll want to be at the gate at dawn."

And it wasn't going to be pleasant.

The men took the other room. Tansa and I went to bed. I didn't sleep much, though I tried. Tomorrow we headed into a danger I could not even begin to imagine. The Court of the Tiger was a perilous place and as terrible as any battlefield, in fact. People died there of stupidity or too much daring. We'd all heard tales about assassins who thought they could kill the Tiger, who was one of the two most powerful men in the empire.

Or was he the most powerful? If the Wolf had grown old and lost his way, then the Tiger was the one true ruler of the Empire. Queen Taranis had always been a player there at the edge of the divide, but she'd not had the power that the Wolf or the Tiger held.

She had demons now. I remembered my own encounter with them and about how I had raced to the building to find the demon dead. I shivered, and Tansa pulled me closer saying nothing.

A long night for so few short hours.

The others met us out in the hall. We'd dressed in the best clothing we could from the fine supplies Ardeth's crew had given us. The people running the inn looked surprised to see us up and leaving so early, but they managed to get us a little breakfast. I wasn't sure eating was a good idea -- but then I thought about how we might be standing around for hours. Yes, food would help.

And then we started through the city.

Some of Tigris reminded me so much of Willoway that I wished we were still back there before the trouble started. I would have liked to have known Za under other circumstances, though that was a silly thing to think. If his mother and sisters' actions had not sent him to me, I would never have seen him except at a distance -- or at his funeral.

Za took the lead now. We all knew that this part of the journey would rest in his hands. Za headed along the roads that winded upward, leading toward the distant citadel and the palace. The darkness was broken only by the scattered lights of others who were at work already -- bakers, guards, a gaggle of children being shepherded towards a school.

The streets themselves were well-paved and cared for, which did mark a difference with Willoway. The Queen had not been too keen on spending money on anything that she did not use. The Royal Road there remained in excellent condition, but many of the side streets and alleys had fallen into disrepair. I hadn't considered it much until now.

People moved around us and cleaned up the trash that had been thrown out on the street. Well organized, with a wagon for the debris and packs for anything that these industrious workers thought might be usable.

Nearly everyone here had an Eastern look to them, too. Considering that this had been the lynchpin to the Eastern world -- this city built in the crags of mountains so hard to reach except by sea -- I wasn't surprised to see fewer of the Westerners, despite the linked empires. Za, Ardeth and I fit the local type well enough, but there were just enough people from the west that Kintansa and Danisin didn't stand out.

We kept going upward, and the walls of the citadel rose higher over us. The sun would rise to our right soon. The buildings were more widely spaced here and more elaborate, and I knew that when the morning light spread through their vast grounds, I would be able to clearly see the ocean again. I wanted to see it today. We'd survived that strange journey.

We reached the gate just before the dawn. People already stood before us, most of them with scrolled messages. Our group drew worried stares, and I wondered if we shouldn't have thought about trying to act like others come before the court.

Za seemed to think otherwise, and I had to leave this in his hands.

The line quickly grew longer behind us. We didn't speak much. Some of the people had apparently come from far, but we didn't want questions or speculation about why we were here.

The light rose and a breeze blew in off the sea. I could still see the ocean which pleased me. I noted how Ardeth had moved so that he could watch the waves and fog along the shore. The pirate captain looked steady.

The *Art of Ata*? He had the book in the pouch he carried close to his side. He and Za had gone over it at practically every free moment they had found on the ship. I wondered if it helped Za. Had he learned something more?

Did it matter?

The line began to move. One of the first was sent away without getting in. The man looked angered as he headed back down the hill.

I moved up by Za. This was my place.

We eventually stepped up to the guard and the gate, and I knew that things would change here, one way or another.

CHAPTER TWENTY-EIGHT

Za nodded to the guard and leaned close to him, though with both his hands clearly in sight. He did not make any sudden move.

He pulled the plain ring from his finger and held it out. "The inside has an inscription: The claw must be unsheathed for the honor of the world," Za said softly.

The guard pulled back with a start and then looked to the side and gave a whistle. The sound startled everyone inside and outside the wall. Za dared one glance at Mai who stood steady beside him and then at the others. Ardeth looked amused.

Two more guards came at a run; one of them was a man of rank. The guard at the gate gave a sign and said nothing. The others looked at Za and his group with misgivings.

"You know why I am here," Za dared to say as he handed the ring over to the man in charge. He stood straighter now. Regal; a role he must play once more. They didn't know whom he might be, but he gave the right impression.

"Inside. You and you --"

"All of my party," Za said. He looked at the captain of the royal guard. "Surely you do not fear to let the five of us go inside. Take our weapons. Do what you think wise, but we must go to the Court of the Tiger."

People outside the gate heard those words. The Captain gave a little snarl. He didn't like being manipulated, but he signaled them all in. Za waited just within the gate until all four of his companions had gotten inside.

"If this is some game, I'll have all your heads hanging from the wall by noon."

Za nodded agreement. That settled well with the Captain, in fact.

They were divested of their belongings and weapons -- all except for the book which Za convinced them was too important to be abandoned. Ardeth still carried the tome. A glance within the cover showed that it was not hiding a weapon and that the text did, indeed, look ancient. People here in the east appreciated old books.

All of this was done between one wall and the next, while they hurried along a corridor that held several hundred soldiers, all of them ready for trouble. They were not let past this hall, though. Soldiers guarded them, and they stood in a line against the wall as though they were about to be executed. The Captain talked with another soldier and another. The sun went higher, and others came and went through the two gates, barely seen to the left of where they stood.

"This way," the Captain finally said.

A hundred guards went with them and the Captain past a second open gate and into a vast stone-paved courtyard that held not horses and carriages, but rather dozens of small buildings, open on one side and with a desk and someone working behind it, often with a line of others before them.

Clerks, ready to see the people as they came in, Za realized. Well-organized so that business could be dealt with quickly. Za could tell from the way the clerks and the others acted that having a group escorted straight past this area had to be rare.

Za considered the layout as they moved, wondering how

well it worked. How many people ever did get all the way to the Court of the Tiger? He doubted it happened often.

His grandfather had been a proud, demanding man the last time he'd seen him -- the day he'd given him the ring with the code to get through the gate.

The next wall was inlaid with mosaics of animals, both common and uncommon. Two dragons flanked the golden gate which stood twice as high as mere mortals and wide enough for twenty soldiers to march through at once. It opened slightly as they neared, and two men came out. Not the Tiger, of course, but they were closer to their goal. Za knew one of the men.

"General Gedquin," Za greeted him with a polite nod, though not a bow. The others with him did bow though -- wise people, his friends. Gedquin's name was very well known.

"I don't know you," the general said, though the narrowing of his eyes betrayed interest mixed with the mistrust. "How did you learn that code? Where --"

Za lifted his hand, palm down, and showed the ring. He did not wear any other jewels today. Back at his mother's court, he had always hidden the ring among other jewels once he had grown old enough to wear it without it dropping off. He'd buried it beneath emeralds, rubies, and diamonds.

Gedquin knew that the ring meant, but he shook his head in denial. "You cannot be --"

Za pushed back his hair, a nervous gesture because he was going to have to deal with that problem now, too. "You were there with the two of us, just before you rode away. We stood behind the Temple of Mercy. I'd slipped away as he asked me to, no easy job at my age --"

"Damn," Gedquin said, then seemed to catch himself and bowed his head. "Prince Zaron. We had not expected you."

"I wouldn't think so. I have news. Shall I give it to you or to him?"

"Both of us. This way. Yes, all of you, this way."

Za heard sounds of surprise as the group went through that inner golden gate and into the true place of power. He tried not to gawk. Full-sized golden tigers lined the path to the next building, those walls gilded in gold, with banners of silk flying in the morning breeze.

Gedquin sent several people on ahead, but he did not hurry. Za was grateful because he needed to compose himself. He pulled the *Art of Ata* to him with each step up the stairs to the ornate building. His mother would have wept that this place was not hers, but he only admired the grace and beauty of the lines. They passed more people here than he had expected, and all of them apparently rushing to see this meeting. Lords and Ladies, mostly, he thought. Some guards and a few minor officials. Za had the feeling of people hurrying to something that rarely occurred, and some of them were still pulling their intricate clothing into place.

They would have an audience. Za couldn't decide if that was good or not.

Up the stairs, into the shadowed building. A large building, with stairs that lead upward at the right and left, and a long hall of blood red walls light by a hundred torches. The floors were black stone polished to such a shine, and Za was glad they were not rushing down them.

Sounds ahead.

Almost there.

Za took a deeper breath and stood up straighter. Mai still walked at his side, Kintansa and Ardeth behind him, Danisin the last, a guard at the rear. None of them had dressed as well as the audience, but he thought they looked better than most.

The golden doors came open ahead of them. A few people still rushed in, but he could see the room was crowded already. They were not loud, these people, but they did make a sound like the buzz of an angry nest of wasps, the whispers of people who looked at them as they entered and wondered how these strangers dared to come into *their* place.

The Tiger Throne stood at the far wall. No one sat there yet, but Za had the feeling that they would not have long to wait. His group walked all the way to the front of the room, General Gedquin leading the way with a purposeful stride that had opened a corridor in this mass of people. This was not a man one could be rude to and they quickly moved aside. Besides, they were ready for the show.

Gedquin gave a sign and Za, and his companions stopped. Gedquin went on a few steps farther to the foot of the stairs and waited.

Drums.

The room fell silent. People began to bow down to their knees already as did his companions -- but Gedquin and Za did not. He was still the Heir, though that was not going to last for long, he knew. The ragged hair that fell over his face was just one reminder of all that had changed.

The fact that he had not bowed did not go unnoticed. The soldiers started to move towards him. Gedquin signaled them back. That didn't go unnoticed as well.

Za saw the Tiger of the East enter the room from a door beside the throne. The older man looked him over as he went to his throne. The Tiger moved like a young man still and the extended stare he gave Za, barely seen through his bowed head and hair, was not a look he would have courted at any other time.

A signal of his hand. The drumming stopped. People began to rise to their feet, and Za lifted his head to look straight at his grandfather.

Silver hair now -- it had been graying when last they met. Oh yes, The Tiger of the East kept his hair back in a long, whip-like braid, bands of gold and jewels embedded in the hair. His face had lines of age, but they were not deep. The dark eyes were the same.

"Where did you get the code and the ring," The Tiger demanded.

"From you," Za replied. That won a bit of whispering again, quickly silenced by a glance from his grandfather.

"And if you are who you claim, what happened to your hair?"

"I cut off the braid," he said. That would tell everyone who he claimed to be. "It was necessary so that I could go unnoticed to get out of Willoway and bring the news to you."

"I have heard the news," he said with a dismissive wave of his hand.

"But you don't believe it," Za replied. He took one step closer, slipping away from all the others, his loyal companions. "If you did, you would have an army halfway to Willoway by now."

"You're right. I never believed that you brought demons to the world, boy."

"I didn't. But my mother and sisters have done so."

There. He had said it.

The Tiger looked at him, blinking. "Where is Endris?"

"Dead," he replied and could not hide the moment of loss that brought. "Killed in the first battle with the demons, but he is not the only one dead. The danger is real, grandfather. I've already taken too long to reach you. I can't say what has been happening back at the city since then."

"So, you cut off your hair and came to me," he said with a touch of a scowl.

Za caught a bit of his hair in his fist. "I thought a braid of hair a little price to pay for the hope that I might reach you and that you could save the land."

"Ah!" The Tiger stood up suddenly, his smile so radiant that Za felt surprised. "There! There is the power of my blood in your veins! To do what must be done, no matter the cost.

You knew that if you cut off the braid, you could not be heir to the throne."

"Yes, of course. It doesn't matter," Za said. "There can be other heirs."

"I worried that you might have too much of your mother's treacherous blood in you," he admitted and took a step closer.

Had he ever said anything about Za's mother before? Za didn't think so -- and it marked a moment when he felt he had a chance to make the Tiger understand why he had come here. Why he had done all he had so far, and what he hoped, still, to gain.

"You are the only one who can stand up to her and her new allies," Za said. "But the time it took me to reach here --"

"Why didn't you go to The Wolf instead?"

"I should trust my mother's father?" I asked. "And besides, I have heard other things about the Wolf of late. He is not --"

Movement came from the right and slightly behind him, amongst the crowd that had been utterly still so far. Someone moved who should not have moved, and Za heard another shoved aside. Za did not look to the right, though he sensed his own people already moving.

He leapt at the Tiger and brought him down. Soldiers leapt at them, dragged Za back with a blade cutting at his side --

But the assassin had been caught as well, and before either he or his grandfather could speak, the man killed himself.

The panic had been enough to create other problems, but Mai had been fast to move to help protect him, or else there would have been worse than just a cut.

Gedquin had taken command, and with his orders, everyone stopped moving to rush out of the room. When he told them to sit, they sat -- including Za's people.

"Well, at least now we know we were right," Gedquin said as he came to stand by the Tiger. "She had sent assassins. And false rumors."

Za didn't have to ask who *she* might be, either. He had a hand to his side, but the wound was not severe. Mai was looking belligerent, though she had no weapon. He could not see Kintansa from where he sat and thought it best not to turn and try to find her or the others. He was not going to do anything that might unsettle the situation.

The assassin, he realized, must have been waiting for Za and his people to arrive. If they had killed the Tiger now, it would have looked as though the prince had come for that reason. The Tiger killed, the prince heir implicated -- even now they might suspect him, though his people had done what they could to save the man.

He could see some of that reasoning in Gedquin's face when he moved closer to Za.

"You just came close to having the throne," he said with a frown.

Za brushed his free hand over his hair. "I have already given up that place in the world."

"You will be taken to a suite, you and your companions. Guarded," General Gedquin said. "Do not attempt to leave. Your needs will be seen to."

"Thank you," Za replied with a bow of his head.

The Tiger looked around at the crowd with a hint of mistrust. How many others were here to kill him? With the Tiger dead, there would have been such chaos that Queen Taranis could have done anything in the west and still had time to take the east as well.

When the Tiger looked at him, his eyes narrowed, but not in distrust and anger. Za had brought him a challenge, and now it was up to the Tiger to decide if he wanted to take on such trouble.

CHAPTER TWENTY-NINE

We had survived meeting the Tiger.

The closer we had gotten to The Court of the Tiger over the last few days, the more I had considered the possibility that we would not live through the meeting, even if the man believed us. He had a reputation for quick action, and not for doing things in the best interest of others.

I had started to feel safer, though, when we saw all the clerks in the courtyard. This was not a place of sudden, irredeemable actions. Whatever the Tiger had been in his youth, he had learned to rule wisely.

I had known this in many ways, of course. The Empire had remained oddly peaceful, despite having two great conquerors poised facing each other over the land. Ah, but maybe that was part of it. Even if the Wolf had lost his bite, his court could be riled and send out troops. It had happened even five years ago, along the border where barbarians had raided villages. The army had been decisive in putting an end to that trouble, and the Tiger was no less diligent in keeping the eastern half of the empire safe.

The Tiger was still a tall, strong man despite his white hair. I saw no slowness in his mind, either. I could also see that learning the truth about the rumors of demons in

Willoway truly bothered him. He did not trust Queen Taranis, and I thought that meant he would side with his grandson.

Then I reconsidered such a simple answer. Prince Zaron had been raised at court: The Queen's court. The Tiger had no real way of knowing if the Prince worked at the command of his mother or not. Even the tale that Za had called the demons might be a ruse to help insinuate him with the king once the boy denied such charges.

I didn't complain when we were escorted out of the Appearance Hall and up to another floor. Dour guards kept by us all the way and servants led the path and followed behind. From the orders given along the way, I could tell that we would not want for anything.

Wise, I supposed. The Tiger believed this was Prince Zaron, and despite the trouble with his hair, the servants would be wise to treat his grandson and companions well until told otherwise.

The suite had a central room, two bathing rooms, and four sleeping quarters. The central room was already laden with baskets of fruit and pitchers of drink. We were not going to starve. Should I worry about poison? Only if Za said so.

Servants moved in a whirlwind of activity and then just as suddenly disappeared out the door. Two guards still stood slightly inside the room. They bowed, stepped outside, and closed the door behind them. They would not be moving from that post until they were relieved.

"Well," Kintansa said with a glance around their rather ornate prison. "We survived."

"So far," Ardeth agreed. He settled on one of the long lounges and looked more at home than I thought he ought to.

Za gave a distracted nod of agreement. I did wonder what he was thinking, and if I should be prepared for trouble. I crossed the room and pushed open intricately carved doors (tigers) that led to a balcony -- and a drop of several hundred feet to the stone-paved courtyard. The stonework on the balcony and above it did look promising for a climb, but the person would be out in the open. Guards walked the walls straight ahead. Not a good way to try to escape if we found a reason to make an attempt.

I looked at Kintansa when I came back in and shook my head. She'd been into the bedrooms and gave me the same sign.

So, if we needed to get away, it would have to be through the building itself.

Danisin had gotten into the supplies and cleaned and bandaged the cut on Za's side. The prince looked more at ease now. Good. We should, I knew, take advantage of some peace and quiet here in a place where others had the job of keeping trouble out.

Not that we wouldn't post our own guards.

The morning passed quietly. We heard voices out in the courtyard once, but it appeared to be people leaving the building. They sounded unsettled, but I didn't see any sign that they were angry. I took that as a good sign.

The day dragged on, though. Food came by way of silent servants, and none of us tried to question them. That would admit to weakness and worry. We all took our turns at bathing which at least helped pass the time. Ardeth and Za went back to the book. The rest of us ... waited.

Sunset came. Servants lighted scented candles and brought more food. We ate. The plates went away.

And then the Tiger and General Gedquin arrived.

They came without ceremony. The guards at the door bowed as they passed. No one followed them in.

We had all gotten to our feet and bowed, but the Tiger waved that away. "Sit. We don't have much time to talk before someone comes looking for me. We must make a plan of what to do."

"Then you do believe me," Za said with a bow of his head and an unmistakable look of relief.

"You were wise to come to me," the emperor replied. He took the chair where I had been sitting, and Gedquin stood behind him. The rest of us settled on the lounges at a wave of his hand. "When the rumors began about you and the demons, I already knew they were not true. Endris was my man. He'd kept a close watch on you. I am sorry that we lost such a noble man." He stopped and shook his head. "But we have to deal with the world without him. You are Captain Mai. Endris said that he would send the prince to you if there were a reason for the boy to escape."

"Just Mai, sir," I said. "I left the palace guard when your son died."

"Yes," he said as his eyes narrowed, a flicker of true anger there, but not aimed at me. He turned slightly. "And you are Commander Kintansa, the famous leader of the mercenaries."

Kintansa made a sound of protest. "Not famous --"

"You are with us," Gedquin said, surprising them all. "The Wolf no longer is powerful enough to protect his borders and the bitch queen stopped following her duties long before now. We know who has been keeping the barbarians at bay."

Tansa didn't deny those words. I had never fully considered the battles she'd fought until now -- blind, I suppose. My only concern had always been that she might not come back. I never thought much about why she fought.

"My people, the ones who escaped the demons, got out of the city," Tansa said. She hadn't talked much about them on the journey, though I had hoped they would catch up with us. "We had to go another route rather than the way I sent them. I cannot say if I can get them regrouped, or if there are even enough of them left to fight the demons."

"You were wise to come here," Gedquin said, and the Tiger nodded. "But we must be careful. If Queen Taranis and her new companions learn that we're marching against them, they'll be prepared."

"They'll learn anyway," Tansa replied. "It's apparent she has people at court. The moment you march, someone will head for her."

"That is why we must be discreet," the Tiger said. His dark eyes flashed. He'd been the leader of armies, and I suspected he missed the old glories. Just the same, I didn't see any carelessness in his attitude. He would not throw people into battle without preparation. "Gedquin and I have discussed the matter. The weather is changeable this time of year. A storm should strike within the next few days. We rarely go more than three or four without something blowing in off the ocean."

"We need a storm that stretches into the night," Gedquin added. "When that happens, Prince Zaron and the rest of you will slip out, along with a third of the standing army. I dare not go with you or the ruse will be too obvious. You will oversee the forces, Commander Kintansa."

"I -- but -- I --" She sputtered, and I put a hand on Tansa's arm. She quieted and calmed, finally giving one quick nod before she spoke. "Yes. That makes sense. I know Willoway and the area around it, and I have had one battle with the demons."

"She's bound to hear we are marching toward her," Za said. "We'll have to prepare --"

"She may miss you," Gedquin said. "I'll be bringing the bulk of the army through the lowlands where she's bound to hear of our very slow passage. In the meantime, the rest of you will be going through the mountains."

"Won't that take too long?" Kintansa dared ask. "I thought there was no easy passage --"

"We have kept some paths secret," Gedquin admitted. "You'll go mostly to the north of the mountains and then through the paths that cross the high mountains north of Willoway."

"But -- but *dragons*," I said with a wave of my hand.

"We have to believe that the dragons don't want demons in the world any more than we do," Gedquin replied but did not sound as assured as I would have liked. "If they let you through, then you will come down from the north while we draw the attention from the east."

"We might surprise the Queen. Confuse her people," Kintansa said and seemed to think this was a good idea, despite dragons. "Unfortunately, I can't say numbers or surprise will destroy them --"

"Ardeth and I are studying to find that answer," Za said with a wave of his hand toward the book on the table. "There is a reason the book came into my hands."

Gedquin and Kintansa both gave the book the same sort of look of disbelief. They were warriors and finding answers in an ancient text was not likely to appeal to them.

I, though, had started to believe more strongly in the power of *Ata*. Besides, this wasn't an ordinary war, and the battle wouldn't be like any the army had faced in the past.

We spoke for a little longer as they gave Kintansa some general numbers about the troops she would have, their weapons, and their supplies.

"We'll talk again," the Tiger said and stood. "I regret that I cannot show you true hospitality, but where I go, people look. We don't want more attention on you than we need. When the time comes, I'll say that you are going to the Wolf. I'll kick you out into the storm."

Za smiled --

The balcony doors flew open, and six gray-clad figures leapt into the room. Ardeth had been the closest to balcony and moved quickly as he pushed up from the chair and kicked. One of the men went down and rolled away. Another swept a dagger across Ardeth's uplifted hand, and he stepped back with a hiss of pain --

By then the rest of us had moved. Danisin made a prodigious leap over furniture and tried to tackle two of the attackers. General Gedquin moved to protect the Tiger, and I rushed toward Za. Za had moved to defend his grandfather as well, throwing himself in front of the Tiger and calling the sword into his hand. I did not collide with him, having expected the move.

Tansa had rushed to attack the other two assassins. I knew that she would throw herself into the battle and I had faith she would do so wisely. I would be doing the same as two rushed toward the group of us: Tiger, General, Za, and me.

Danisin went down, blood running from a dangerous wound across his chest. Ardeth had dropped to his knees, holding the wrist of his wounded hand, gasping. Such a little injury. I had thought he was stronger --

Was stronger. I knew it. *Something wrong.*

"Careful!" Ardeth warned without looking at the rest of us. "Poison!"

I looked at Danisin. He twitched and gasped.

Fear and rage merged as I attacked the one who swung a sword at Za. I tackled the assassin at the knees, and he went down on his back and under my weight. Za let go of the sword which would have been dangerous with all of us moving in so close to him. He kicked the assassin hard in the throat, and the man's weapon fell from his hands as his eyes bulged. Kintansa and the guards had taken down two more. The last of the assassins fell under the swords of the guards as they rushed in. The last one alive -- the one Za had kicked -- still gasped for breath. He rolled to the side, grabbed the blade he had dropped, and drove it into his own heart.

Za darted forward and dropped to his knees beside Danisin. He put a hand to the man's chest and then looked back at me and shook his head.

"Go peacefully, my friend," Za said in the sudden silence. Danisin twitched still -- but then his face grew calm and his eyes closed. All movement in his body stopped. Za bowed his head for a moment and then looked up. "The poison had reached his heart. I could do nothing but let him go quickly."

I knew Danisin had died, but I hadn't had a chance to accept the reality. The confirmation came as a blow.

Za rose instantly back to his feet and rushed to Ardeth who still knelt, one hand holding the wrist of the other, his eyes unfocused, and his breathing labored. Za knelt and gently laid his fingers against Ardeth's chest. The pirate showed no sign of noticing.

We were going to lose him as well.

More soldiers arrived. The Tiger and General Gedquin directed them to take the bodies and beware of any weapons. I moved to Kintansa, and we stood over Ardeth and Za, making sure they were not disturbed. I would have stood up even to the Tiger if he'd decided to try and take his grandson away.

Guards moved out to the balcony. Guards climbed the roof. General Gedquin spoke to the men and gave quiet, angry orders. The Tiger had retaken his seat and glared at them all -- I saw that only briefly as I looked his way.

How did the assassins get this far? Granted that the dark would have helped them, and they were professionals. I wanted to demand answers, but just then Ardeth made a sound of pain, and I swept back to see blood suddenly flowing far too hard from his hand.

"Get something -- we have to stop --" Tansa said, tearing at her tunic.

"Cleansing poison," Za said and took a ragged breath. "Got most. He'll survive -- but he will be ill and weak."

The bleeding slowed and stopped. Ardeth started to fall backward, but Za caught hold of him. Tansa wrapped her cloth around the hand, and she and I got him off the floor and into a chair. He was pale white, cold, and damp -- but he opened his eyes and gave us a nod of thanks.

Quiet again after that moment.

"I would suggest we move to a smaller room," Tansa said with a look at the balcony. "We're going to want to stay close together as long as we're here."

"Yes," Gedquin agreed and went to order the servants. They'd have quite a mess to clean up here, with dead bodies and blood everywhere. Ah, but maybe they were used to assassins here. I was glad they were not so common in Willoway.

Tansa, who was too used to losing people in battle, went to Danisin, knelt and said a prayer, and then searched through his clothing. She found a few coins and put them back to help him in the afterlife. He had nothing else. So little for what had seemed to me to be a life well-lived.

Perhaps that was a sign that he had not needed more. Damn, I'd miss him. I knew we all would, but I thought back to the days at the Lost Way Inn and working in the kitchen -- and for a moment I resented Za and all the trouble he'd brought me.

Unfair. I managed not to glare his way as I pulled that anger back and sent it where it belonged -- winging its way back to the Queen. We'd be heading back to see her soon, and I'd be able to deliver that anger in person.

"The body of your friend --" the Tiger began.

"Give him honors," Tansa replied. "May the Goddesses treat him well."

"This way," General Gedquin said at the door. "We have your room ready."

We left Danisin as we took our things and moved to a room with a single sleeping chamber and bathing area -- but no less elegant. No balcony and the window had iron shutters and a thick iron bar to secure them.

Za had helped Ardeth while Tansa and I guarded. Now he took the pirate to the bedchamber and forced him to rest despite Ardeth's weak protests. I was glad to hear the pirate sound strong enough to argue.

"Prince Zaron used a magic sword," the Tiger said as he looked to the bedroom where Za had pulled a chair to the side of the bed and put a hand on Ardeth's chest again. "The Prince knows magic."

"The *Art of Ata*," I said. There was no use in denying or staying quiet. "Endris taught him what he could, and Ardeth is helping him learn more."

"I thought as much," the Tiger said. "Endris would not teach me."

Gedquin and the Tiger left us. With Za in the bedchamber that left Tansa and me alone in the outer room.

She took me silently into her arms. For a moment we both wept, though quietly. How could we have managed to get so far, only to lose one of our own now? We should have been safe here.

There was no safety in the world.

CHAPTER THIRTY

Three days later, Za and his companions slipped out of the palace and into the pouring rain. Za looked back at the building from the courtyard and shook his head. If things had gone differently, he would have ruled from this place of elegance, beauty -- and power.

Za found that he truly didn't care. Even the few days inside had felt as though he had returned to the prison his mother had made for him in Willoway. Unfortunately, he didn't fit into the rest of the world. He'd realized how little he knew at every step of the journey while the others took everything for granted. He'd never been to the outer world. He'd never realized how difficult it was to get food and water or a warm place to sleep.

Za wasn't sure having even two thousand soldiers with them was going to make this journey any easier, either. Tansa and Mai had both told him that the soldiers would be a real danger for him.

"Anyone can work their way into the army if they're careful," Tansa explained. "All they need do is bide their time and if the person is a true fanatic, then that person will not care if he or she survives. Those are the worst. You are too easy of a target right now. Be very careful, Za."

Za had agreed, though he really didn't know what he could do unless he huddled close to his protectors and hope they didn't get killed as well. He didn't like that idea. Instead of worrying over it, he kept close to Ardeth and made certain their friend didn't get too worn. The two of them had used *Ata* to help Ardeth recover faster, but that had drawbacks as well since it drew on the strength of the body to heal. Ardeth had lost several pounds in the last few days and his body trembled with any long exertion. He also didn't want to slow down or rest when he needed to.

The rain would not help Ardeth. However, it would help to keep most people off the road. The Tiger had stopped opening the gates to anyone since the assassination attempt, too, so no one stood in the outer courtyard, either.

They had gotten the help they needed from the Tiger and now instead of running away, they had turned and would return to the battle. The loss of Danisin wore heavily on him, though. He feared to see the others killed, both his close companions and the soldiers who would travel with them. War was not a pastime he had ever thought to pursue.

No choice.

They left by a postern gate that had rarely been opened, they were told. The four hurried out and moved along an old stone trail until they were nearly to the edge of the city. They slid between two storage sheds, both running with water so there was nowhere to shield from the storm. From there they were back on the main road through town and had gone all the way down the hill when a figure to the right gave a short soft whistle. Mai caught hold of Ardeth's arm, and they hurried into a dark doorway. At the same time, another group of four, wearing the same long cloaks as they wore, rushed out and continued down the road.

Za kept hold of Ardeth though he wasn't really shivering any more than the rest of them. They remained still and silent.

It paid off. Someone had followed them, of course, but in the downpour, the enemy had missed the switch and kept going after the group that headed down the road.

The soldier who had signaled them to the side stayed still for some time longer.

"This way," he finally said, startling them all. They began to turn their cloaks inside out -- no longer dark coverings, but a variety of colors, Za's a light blue. Their number had grown to five and the soldier was not in uniform. "The others will lead the spy down to the bay and a ship going out with the tide and heading south. It is unlikely that anyone will realize it's not your group that went aboard."

"Well done," Kintansa said.

The soldier gave a quick smile of thanks. "We better hurry. General Gedquin will be waiting."

They moved back out of the building, retraced their steps partly up the hill, and took a side road between two large estates. It was a hard, long hike out past the towering buildings of The Court of the Tiger and finally to an inconspicuous gate with a guard of six. No one said anything; the gate opened into a passage within the walls where torches lit the way. They had gone a hundred yards to the right when another small door opened. They were let out of the city once more. Za tried not to sigh at the thought of all the walking they would have to do again, though not toward the bay this time.

They followed along the wall and out another small gate. While most of the roads to any large settlement they'd seen had been littered with small villages for miles, and then inns and stables for the last mile to the city, here it appeared as though they had stepped from civilization and into the wilderness. The impression was not much helped by the strong winds and incessant rain. They moved through a stand of trees, the limbs waving madly. The trail, which looked little more than a deer path, led uphill. They slogged against the mud and wind, and Mai helped him with Ardeth.

Ardeth had quietly suggested they leave him behind, but Za hadn't thought that a wise decision on many levels. First, Za still wasn't entirely comfortable with the language that their precious book had been written in, and there were too many passages about demons to think it might not matter. Second, the longer Ardeth stayed so close to the sea, the greater the chance that someone might recognize him, and that would be a poor payment for the help he'd given so far.

Za started to realize how difficult this trip would be, though. They would not have a pleasant walk through the grasslands this time. They would head into the snowy peaks and beyond to the lands of the dragons. Mai had reasons to be worried about trying to cross their lands. The dragons did not see the world in the same way as humans. They might not think demons in Willoway were any of their concern, while humans trespassing across their lands could be a significant problem.

Should he send Ardeth back? Send him somewhere else? What about the others? Mai and Kintansa were not going to give up this battle. He suspected Ardeth felt the same way but did not want to slow them.

The trail led up and away from the city. They paused at one point among the trees where the view was probably breathtaking on a better day with the sea laid out far below them. Then they went on.

The soldiers and General Gedquin waited in a hollow by a fast-flowing stream that had almost topped its banks already. Horses and donkeys were gathered in groups. A portable bridge stood over the creek to where the troops waited on the other side. Mai, reaching it first, rushed across, probably to make sure it was safe before the rest of them crossed.

Gedquin at least had a tent. The soldier hurried them inside and then disappeared into the ranks of the others before

Za could even say anything.

"Well, this is worse weather than we anticipated," Gedquin admitted as he stood from his camp desk. "Sit down by the brazier and get warm. We might have to move quickly if that stream goes over the bank, though."

"I have the feeling the entire journey is going to be like this," Tansa said.

The four settled on the chairs already in place for them. Ardeth, Za thought, didn't look any worse for the hike, though he didn't look any better, either. Ardeth lifted shaking hands toward the warmth and frowned, but Za could see more determination in his face, too.

Za had the feeling that if they'd left Ardeth behind, he might not have had a reason to survive. The poison was painful and dangerous. It took both to keep the effects at bay sometimes, and though they had worn the poison down, it was still dangerous.

Gedquin finished up some writing, caught hold of his chair, and came to sit with them. The sounds outside the tent seemed muted and calm. No trouble had followed them this far.

"If the weather clears, you'll leave about midday. If not, you'll wait until morning. There would be no use going off too soon in this storm. You saw the stream out there. There are far worse ahead of you, and it would not be a place to go wandering in the rain and dark."

"Yes, I agree," Kintansa said. She sounded assured, the Commander back in charge. No one, Za realized, had recognized her as *The Favorite* from his father's court. He'd not even thought to mention it the few times he'd talked to the Tiger. Irrelevant to the rest of this trouble.

Gedquin must have accepted her. He nodded. "Lt. Ebru will have the overall charge of making certain the troops are moving and ready for trouble. You, Commander, will be the one who chooses how and when they go into battle. Since we hope that you will be a surprise after we have drawn Taranis's attention toward the larger force, I hope that you will act judiciously. We will not have a second chance."

"Yes sir," she said. Kintansa did not look upset by what was clearly an unnecessary reminder. Gedquin was the one who looked uncertain, but they were already in motion and Za could tell he would not call them back now.

The rains did not let up until late afternoon. Gedquin went out at sunset, said farewell to the troops, and left. They had his tent to sleep in. They had his supplies, which included a lovely dinner prepared by the General's aide who was also going with them. Alit was a jolly man, older by a few years than the rest of them.

"Yes, yes," he said when he faced them the first time. "There's no need to say it. I am a spy to watch over you in case you do something dangerous that will get the army destroyed out of hand. You're not going to do that, are you? No? Good. Then I'm also an excellent cook, even of camp food. The Tiger made mention that you were all worn too thin already and you have a hard hike ahead. Be prepared to be shocked and amazed by my culinary abilities."

A couple guards had set up a table. They laughed at Alit's last words, and Za couldn't tell if they were going to be more shocked than amazed --

The food he provided proved to be excellent and as good as anything they'd gotten in the court. Even Ardeth ate with some pleasure -- another good sign that coming with them had been the right decision.

Lt. Ebru had been in and out, declined dinner with them, and gave reports. The tall, lean woman seemed uncertain in their presence with glances more at Za than at Commander Kintansa. Getting her to trust them would take time, he supposed.

At Ebru's suggestion, Kintansa went out to talk with the troops. Mai went with her, a visible guard. Ebru gave a nod of appreciation at that sight and seemed to realize that they were not fools.

If only Danisin had still been here. Za wasn't sure he was a good guard for Ardeth. If the soldiers turned on them --

"Don't look for trouble," Ardeth said softly. Za had brought out the book and put it on the cleared table. "We need not make this worse."

"Yes," Za agreed. He took a deep breath and drew calm back to him again. "And we have our own work to do."

They studied the book. Tansa and Mai never asked what they found there. Ebru and Alit, both passing through sometimes, gave the book curious glances. They were both soldiers, though. They weren't likely to think a book would be much help.

Za only hoped he could learn enough to make it count when the time came to face the demons.

They left camp at dawn. Alit took care of directing the men who took down the tent and packed away the supplies. He had made sure they had warm bread and fruit for breakfast, though. Ebru brought them four horses, but Za shook his head.

"Ardeth will ride with me for the next few days," he said.

And being still a prince, his word was law. The extra horse went back with the supply train.

The soldiers would hike on foot. Za wouldn't have minded being on foot as well, but the horse would help Ardeth marshal his strength for later. The path they took narrowed as they left the camp and soon the soldiers stretched out only two or three abreast. The horses could only go one abreast, with Kintansa in the lead, Za and Ardeth after her, and Mai behind them. Lt. Ebru rode up and down the line for the first few hours and then finally settled in with them on a stretch where the path widened, and she could report to Kintansa.

"We've seen no sign that anyone is following us, Commander," she reported. Za thought Ebru sounded almost cheery. "The weather looks as though it will hold as well."

"Praise all the gods and goddesses for that," Tansa said. "We don't need more mud."

"True. I'd like permission to send out a party to hunt deer for tonight's meal. We'll want to save our packed supplies for going through the snow lands."

"Yes, very wise, thank you," Kintansa said. She reached over and patted Ebru on the arm, startling the woman. "I give you the right to do whatever you think is best from here until we come down the other side of the mountains, into lands that I actually know and where we might run into trouble I might predict. Do keep me informed, though. I want to learn how to survive here."

"Yes. Thank you." Ebru said. Za could tell the difference in her attitude. Kintansa had played that well. By the time they reached Willoway, they would be working well together.

Ebru still gave him a worried glance when she pulled back again and headed to look after her people. Za intended to do nothing that would upset the balance between the lieutenant and the commander, though. He had no intention of giving orders of his own unless they were needed for something specific.

The tent went up that night. They dined well on venison. Kintansa and Mai dealt with military matters as they spoke with Ebru and her own top people. Za and Ardeth studied the book.

And so, by quiet steps, they made their way through the deep valleys on the far side of the mountains. When the trail turned upward to the steeper, more difficult trails, they sent the horses back and they turned upwards with only the high peaks between them and the lands around Willoway.

CHAPTER THIRTY-ONE

The farther we went into the mountains, the twitchier I became.

Every odd breeze made me stare into the sky with dread, expecting dragons to soar down and attack us. I wouldn't see them until they drew close since we had moved out of the rainy lowlands ... and into the snowy mountains.

It wasn't a pleasant change.

We were wrapped in layers of wool. Ardeth walked with Za at his side, and I had to remind myself that he was not exactly helpless, nor would he lack in guards if anything happened. The bulk of the soldiers trudged along behind him, most draped in their woolen blankets and none of them happy -- though it turned out that most were from mountainous areas. The Tiger had chosen wisely. The donkeys, more sure-footed than the horses would have been, came at the end of the line. We'd found one supply depot hidden away in some caves. The Tiger had been prepared to come this way at some time.

The sun started to go down. The scouts found a place, slightly out of the wind, to put up the tent and where the others could camp around us. I looked forward to being inside even that flimsy cover and felt sorry for the others, though they were quick to find little hollows and depressions out of the wind as well. Guards went out at Ebru's orders. Cook fires started.

Ebru had started taking dinner with us the last four days after Kintansa pointed out that they needed to spend more time with each other, so the troops accepted Tansa as well. If anything happened to Ebru, we might have had trouble, though I liked to think that the soldiers were professional enough to get over it. Eventually.

We might not have that much time.

Tonight, though, Tansa said something over dinner that we'd been discussing throughout the day. I was ready for the statement, and I knew she was right, as much as I disliked some of the aspects of this plan.

"You need to spend time with the rest of the soldiers, Za. We need them to be used to you," she said after a sip of tea. "You are, as far as they are concerned, nothing more than a prince and heir. They don't realize that you will be with us in this battle, not just a statue to watch over the trouble."

"I am not an heir," he said and fluffed at his hair. I hadn't thought much about that since the time he'd cut it off.

"The Tiger did not say so," I said.

Za looked at me with a start. "I had assumed that truth was understood. The Emperors of the East never cut their hair. *Never.*"

Ebru gave the prince a long look. She had never done so before. Had she even looked at him for that long until this moment?

"He did not say," Ebru repeated what I had said. "And the soldiers call you nothing but prince, you know. I hadn't even considered it."

"So, I should spend time with them," Za said with a nod and no show of reluctance. "I don't mind. I'd like to know more about who they are, why they are here, and what they expect."

"You want to know everything about everything," Ardeth said with a smile.

"I've led a rather secluded life until lately," Za reminded us. He tilted his head and looked intrigued even by the weave of the tent. "There is a lot to learn."

Ebru gave him an odd look this time. I hoped that meant a change in her attitude toward Za and without any of us having to say something directly. She would need to work with him as well, and to accept that he asked questions for a reason, but that reason might be nothing more than curiosity.

I wondered what he would do after the battles were fought -- and won. I didn't doubt we'd win. If we didn't, I was fairly certain none of us would survive, so there was no need to think about a future where the demons won.

However, when we won, I realized that Za would not be in a much better situation than he was now -- and he had seen that future all along. People would have heard that he brought the demons, and some would believe it, no matter what happened. He had, as he pointed out, given up the right to be heir -- which meant he had given up that safety as well as the power. Ebru might have figured that part out during dinner. I wasn't sure what his status meant to her.

Ardeth, at least, looked better than he had at the start of the journey, though still pale. He tended to weaken too easily, but our pirate had a deep well of determination. He did his best not to slow us, even on those days when he could barely cross from one side of the tent to the other on his own. He hoarded his strength and slept longer than the rest of us.

Za watched over him which gave Za a special purpose.

Alit continued to delight us with his meals. The man would have made a fortune at the right inn. Maybe after the war, I could hire him.

Pretending that everything would go back to normal.

Pretending that Alit could take Danisin's place, and the prince would disappear.

The wind shook the tent. I held my breath.

"You are going to be too paranoid to be of any help soon, Mai," Tansa said with a slap against my arm. "You had better start relaxing, or we'll have to sedate you."

"Relax?" I said. I waved my hand toward the door. "Dragons!"

"I hope that we don't run into any," Ebru admitted and gave her own worried look to the door.

"You haven't been with us for long," Za said. I wasn't sure he'd ever spoken directly to her before. "You might as well get used to the idea of dragons. If something is out there that we don't want to run into, then it's going to happen. "

The rest of us nodded. Ebru looked as though she couldn't decide between being worried and amused.

The conversation about dragon myths did not help me with my worry about running into them. When I went with Kintansa on our nightly walk around the camp, I had to stop looking up or else I would fall, and she would laugh at me. Tansa was right; I had to get my fear of dragons under control, especially before any encounter. I didn't doubt Za was right in that respect: if there were anything out there that we didn't want to meet, it would find us.

We had passed over the snow line two days earlier. Tomorrow we'd climb out of the tree line and enter a world of snowfields and sheets of ice. We would find no trail across that covering -- at least not one the humans had made. As Kintansa talked to a few of the soldiers, I looked up the expanse of mountain and saw deer darting up what must have been their own path. That gave me hope.

Also, nothing huge sailed through the sky and obscured the rising moon. Even better.

The travel to get this far so quickly had worn me out.

Despite my worries, I did sleep well enough that night, only twitching at the worst of the winds. Tansa growled at my movement and went back to sleep, but I always stayed silent and still for a minute or two as I listened. The guards would have called out, of course. I had to remind myself of those people keeping the watch. Then I'd go back to sleep for a while again.

I have always found mornings annoying and they seemed worse on this trip. I hated to see the tent go down and watch everything that meant any comfort get packed away. We were soon on the move, and we climbed higher into an area colder than the morning before. The soldiers complained of the cold. The donkeys complained of the cold. I think the four of us were the only ones who kept the complaints to ourselves, though I could see the dislike even in Za's face as he broke away the ice that had formed on the edge of his cloak.

By mid-morning we walked single file across the ice at the edge of the snow. I suspected we were going to walk for a long way.

I looked back at Ardeth who moved with Za at his side, the prince putting a hand to the other's arm. How much power did Za use to keep Ardeth on his feet? I'd have to convince them both that everyday human aid, without the *Art of Ata*, might be a better choice soon. We were going to be a long time in the snow, and there was no telling what trouble we would find.

Except for dragons.

The journey became a series of ups and downs over ice, snow, and treacherous rocks. We'd climb for days to reach a pass -- often on no more than an animal path -- and then head down the other side before we'd start up the next, higher mountain. By the fourth day, we no longer left the snowfields at all, and the mountains before us looked more daunting. A river path led through a pass, the track beside it narrow and treacherous. The donkeys with our supplies did not want to cross certain sections. Za used his magic to keep them going and prevented the animals from falling. I decided I didn't mind the snow so much after all and I was glad when we climbed the path back out, all of us wet and icy. We camped early that night.

Za and I walked through the camp, and he made certain everyone had a fire that would last the night. The soldiers were quick to accept the bit of magical help that he placed on the wood and flame. We would not lose any of them to ice and fevers.

Za barely made it back to the tent, though, before he collapsed to his knees. Ebru and I got him to the chair by the table where the others had been eating.

"I won't say you did wrong," I told him as I sat across from him and by Kintansa. "But you need to be careful, Za."

He gave a distracted nod and huddled closer to the warmth. I hoped it would help. Ardeth frowned at the prince, but he did not look worried, so I let it go as well.

Ice clinked against the canvas the next morning. Lt. Ebru arrived at dawn and shook her head. "Not today. The world is covered in ice. If the sun burns it off before midmorning, we might move on. I don't think it will. So, we rest a day and see how tomorrow looks."

Kintansa nodded. "It's not as though the soldiers don't deserve a day of rest. Are they comfortable?"

"Oh yes," Ebru said as she turned to Za. "Is there any way to take that magic fire with us when we go? Or do you need to restart it -- that doesn't seem like a wise idea."

"Ah," Za said and tilted his head. "Maybe Ardeth and I can find an answer today. That would be helpful."

"Maybe a torch of some sort?" I suggested.

The two went to work on that idea which clearly intrigued them both. Kintansa and I spoke with Ebru about the land on the other side of the mountains. Even after we made it through the mountain passes there would be long rolling hills to cross before we reached Willoway. Kintansa knew the roads and villages on that side and placed the marks of even small family holdings on the map. She and Ebru were two of a kind when it came to battle. They wanted to know the placement of each stick on the field before they committed to the fight.

So Ebru listened to the tales about the demons as well. Za turned out to be an excellent artist and was able to differentiate between one demon and the other in his drawings. He was the only one of us who had seen them back at the Summer Cloud Palace.

"*Ata*," he said with a little wave of his hand and the ink quill he held. "Observance is the first truth."

"First truth?" I asked.

He smiled, and so did Ardeth. I suppose people didn't ask often enough about *Ata*, which was odd since we saw the use of it quite often lately.

"The First Truth is that you cannot know the world until you truly observe it and can lock any moment in your mind to examine again when the moment is gone," Ardeth explained softly. He really didn't talk much, and I suspected that was more worry about giving away his secrets rather than any weakness. "We must be able to not only see, but feel, smell, and hear that moment when we call it back. It is the hardest, and most essential, first step in the *Art of Ata*."

I supposed such an idea made sense. I would have asked more, but Alit arrived with food, and we were all too happy about the morning feast to discuss anything else. I feared we were getting spoiled, in fact.

We had a leisurely day. I thought the gods smiled on us, in fact. The ice did not melt at all. The next morning began slightly warmer, but it was not safe to head out with the animals yet. Ebru and Tansa agreed that one more day of rest would be helpful for all of us. Some of the scouts went to check the trail ahead and came back with deer and rabbit. A few others went hunting as well so that they didn't strain the supplies by our more extended stay. I even decided it was pretty in the ice and snow. Willoway might get a day or two of snow in the winter, but this was a land of forever winter, and I marveled at how everything had adapted.

Even so, I was glad to see the weather change the next morning and we packed up and prepared to move on.

The soldiers had dozens of torches that held a spark of magic to start the next night's fire without any help from Za. He and Ardeth had both gone out and worked with the devices. Since we could ride for the first part of the day, I didn't think it had done Ardeth any lasting harm. I had hoped that he would be better by now, but it seemed his lungs and heart continued to labor against the poison. I hoped he still recovered.

We'd dropped down into the trees on the third day. They were small stands of pines, some of them twisted and bent by the relentless winds. We found a spot behind a windbreak behind a long line of pines for the night's rest. I feared the wind blew too hard from the mountain down at us, but the fires stayed lit. We didn't bother with the tent, though. Sleeping by the fires wasn't so bad -- the magic spread warmth better than I had hoped. By the next morning the wind had calmed somewhat.

For the next two days, Ardeth rode on a donkey with the book balanced before him while he and Za discussed whatever it was that Ardeth read there. The words made no sense to me, even when they were spoken in a language that we all shared.

I guess I wasn't ready for that much truth.

We passed two frozen waterfalls, trapped in this snow world. They had been beautiful as well as a reminder of how perilous this land could be, where even water could be stopped by the cold. I felt as though we dared not stop at all, and even that night's camp left me afraid to sleep, though I napped off and on, warm in Tansa's arms.

"We're nearing the highest pass," Ebru announced the next morning. I hadn't realized we were so close since the clouds seemed to cling to the land here, obscuring the view. I had been aware that we were climbing quite high again, though. The air was thin and some of the soldiers were suffering from headaches and sickness, but they had help from their comrades and we all kept moving. "There are still more mountains to climb beyond this one, but there are fewer than we had to cross to get here, and they will be progressively lower as we continue west and southward."

"Praise all the gods, known and unknown," Kintansa said. "I have seen my fill of snow."

No one argued.

By midday, we had climbed up to another pass that lifted us back out of the trees once more. The fragrant scent of pine followed us for a while until the sharp, cold wind drove it back down to the lower lands again. The air up here tasted of nothing more than snow and ice, so cold it seemed to burn the skin and lungs. I'd gotten somewhat used to these high passes, but this one -- the highest of all -- seemed a place where no human should tread. I would have thought no creatures at all would come this way except that we sometimes saw enormous deer-like animals racing off across the snow plain to our left. I could not imagine what they found to eat up here.

The path rose into a plain of solid rock, the edge carved away by the forces of nature. The wind blew so hard that we had to walk and hold tight to ropes. Even the pack animals each had a soldier to hold on to it. Za and Ardeth moved back and forth along the line, helping where they could. I wanted to go with them, but Za waved me away this time, and I didn't argue. I knew he wouldn't risk Ardeth, which meant he would be careful of his own life as well.

The wind blew straight through the pass and tried to press us back. Ebru and Tansa had a hard time keeping any forward movement. Ardeth had come forward and helped somehow -- I was beginning to better appreciate such subtle magics -- and then headed back to help Za. He looked steady. I could not see Za in the long twist of the trail and the lines of men and donkeys.

I didn't like having him out of sight -- and I knew I had to get over that feeling. I was his guard, it was true. Endris had given me that job, and I had accepted without any regrets so far -- but I knew those regrets would come before too long. We were going into battle. This was Za's war, and I knew we would both face dangers. If I tried too hard to protect him, I would only make more dangers for us both. Besides, he was not helpless.

We would survive the mountains. The storms had not stopped us yet. Once we traversed this pass, we would --

We would face dragons.

A dozen of them stood gathered on the mountainside as we came through the pass.

CHAPTER THIRTY-TWO

Something had gone wrong.

Za wasn't sure what the problem might be; the people in front had stopped moving, even though he could see that the front of the line had gone beyond the uphill climb and had started to descend. Was there no path beyond the pass? Would they have to turn back?

Ardeth caught up with Za as he started past the others to reach the front of the line. The soldiers looked worried but waited for word. They had their fire sticks still and even carried wood for fires. They had made it this far without any loss of life, though there were four back with the medical group recovering from falls and frostbite.

Za had been proud of how much he'd helped so far. He hoped that whatever trouble stood on the other side of the rise, it wouldn't be so much that they might have to retreat.

"Can't see," Ardeth yelled above the incessant wind. Za could still barely hear him. He caught hold of his friend's arm, and they anchored each other against the blast. An excellent heavy horse to hold on to would have been helpful as they moved on past soldiers who were starting to look worried.

Za suddenly had the feeling he knew what they were about to find, even before they reached the heights and started down the far side.

The wind grew less within a few yards of the top.

The dragons were impressive, their wings spread so wide that he could not take one of the creatures in with a single glance. The sudden flapping of wings sent snow flying and people dropping to the ground lest they got blown away as half the creatures took to the sky and circled.

Za studied the one that stepped forward toward them. The dragon's neck was lined with sharp, protective spikes, and long claws glittered like ice. His teeth looked longer than a forearm and as sharp as a glass dagger.

The others circled twice, remaining low in the sky and drifted down to the land again like geese on a pond. The ground shook and plumes of snow swept upward into the sky.

The rest of the soldiers still tried to press through the passage to the calmer side of the pass. However, those who had seen the dragons wanted to retreat into the cover of the high granite stone that capped the mountain. Chaos spread on both sides, but the press of those behind was still stronger than the worries of those at the lead. They came through the pass in a surge, nearly trampling their own people. Even the pack animals pushed forward into the small snowfield --

Then the animals panicked worse than humans had at the sight of the dragons. Some turned, tore free of the human hold, and rushed back into the pass, the wind at their backs now. The soldiers tried to hold them back, even cutting the ropes that tied some of them together in case one slipped over a cliff and took others as well. They lost two along with precious supplies.

Dragons began to sweep down at them, and Za saw one soldier grabbed and dropped again, though not so far it would have done serious harm and apparently the claw had not gone through more than the heavy winter clothing. The soldier stood and rushed back to join the others who had crowded together at the edge of the pass -- but dragons had circled into that area as well and drove all the soldiers to this side. At least there was less wind here.

Za made a quick study of the problems while the dragons landed, blocking the path forward and backward. Even if they could climb down the cliffs, they could not go all the way back to the lowlands and try a different way. The Tiger's army would already be on the move and counting on them.

Ebru, Kintansa, and Mai stood in the front of the line facing down a dozen massive, silver and white creatures. Dragon heads moved on long sinewy necks, weaving back and forth in unison, which proved to be frighteningly hypnotic. The heads were more massive than a horse, the body the size of a building and the tail like a tree brought to ground. One of them would have been frightening. Twelve made such a show of power that Za found he could not call up the true emotions it brought to him. He stared. The others stared. The dragons weaved back and forth. A couple unfurled their wings and then dropped them back again, scattering more snow.

Za and Ardeth moved forward. Soldiers continued to back away, but they stopped as the two went past, as though they gave the soldiers strength. Maybe after the gift of lasting fire, they thought the prince and his companion might have even better magic.

Za would like to think so, but as he stopped by Mai, he couldn't do more than stare in horrified wonder.

Mai looked at him. "Dragons," she said.

He suspected there was nothing else she could say.

The dragons abruptly stopped weaving their necks back and forth. The foremost of the group lowered his head and stared at them, no more than a hundred feet away. His hot breath melted the snow around them and brought up a fog that disappeared into the still strong wind.

"Payment," the creature said, a rumble of sound but

clearly a word. "Payment for us or you do not survive."

Za had the feeling they did not expect to get whatever they wanted in payment. Bright eyes glittered everywhere as they stared, ready for the answer.

"We will attempt to pay anything reasonable," Za offered. He would not, under any circumstances, promise something to dragons.

Ardeth moved beside him, but they tried to signal the others to back away. He wanted Mai, Kintansa, and Ebru to prepare to get the soldiers away however they could. Za couldn't believe that he'd have much luck in talking with these creatures.

"We want humans," the dragon said. A long, slit tongue danced out of the mouth and back. "A hundred humans. Sacrifice those few from your numbers. You have plenty to spare."

"No," Za replied

The dragon drew back in surprise. Za didn't think that came from the answer but rather from the quickness of his reply. He supposed that others would have tried to bargain before they said no.

Za, though, knew that the dragons wouldn't believe any suggestion that they might make a deal. He could see it in their inhuman faces and feel it in their emotions, so strong in this place.

The heads stopped weaving. Wings fluttered. He had taken them by surprise.

"You condemn far more than the hundred to be our meals," the dragon said, the eyes narrowing as he stared at Za. He probably had not really looked before.

"If you attack, then we will fight. We have swords."

"We'll take to the sky."

"We have bows and arrows."

"We have scales to protect us."

"Not on your wings."

Silence for a moment. The dragons went still. Za had begun to suspect they communicated in some way in those moments of silence. Za waited. He had, if nothing else, surprised them. The others might be able to escape. He knew they looked for such a retreat. He didn't know what else they could do at this point.

"I had thought you would want us to get through," Za said to the dragon. "I didn't think you would want the demons in the world."

"They are far away, and they are not interested in a place of ice and winter."

"They want to rule all the world -- and they cannot if you are here," Za replied. He knew that much truth about demons. "They will bring fire to your lands and make them like their own."

"And we will fight them."

"Wouldn't you rather that the humans fight them?"

"You have no power against such creatures. Numbers mean nothing," the dragon replied with a sound of disgust. "Why should we forgo our pleasure for your useless campaign? We will take what we want."

The head moved quickly, mouth open, tongue reaching toward Ardeth.

Za moved faster, the sword suddenly in hand. The dragon hissed in surprise and pulled back so quickly it reared up on hind legs. Za had a clear swipe at the underbelly and noted that the scales did not spread under the limbs. He suspected that with the Sword of Glory that he would have had an easy kill.

He pulled back instead.

The dragon came back down, the vast legs sending up puffs of snow and ice. Murmurs of sound came from all the other dragons now, and a couple even backed away. That was not as reassuring as it could have been. Za realized that they now saw him as a far more dangerous enemy. Za let go of the sword through Ardeth made a sound of worry.

"We only want to go through the pass and down to the lowlands," Za said to the dragons. He didn't think they were interested in listening to him, though the heads turned his way. "We will go and fight the demons. If you do not let us through, then we will probably be too late, and you will be faced with handling the demons."

"You think you can win a battle against them," the dragon dropping his head down again to look him in the face. "You, such a puny little mortal --"

"I have some help."

The dragon's eyes narrowed. "What will you pay us?"

"The honor that you deserve for being wise and letting us pass to handle this trouble."

A rumble of sound came from all the dragons. He thought it a growl at first, and then realized it was laughter. Ardeth put a hand on his arm; his friend trembled, and this was probably more excitement than he should have experienced.

"If we win against the demons, my fine dragon friends, I will send you five hundred fat cattle," Za said. Oh, he did have their attention. "I give you my word this will be done, even if I do not survive. The others have heard -- the cattle will come to you as soon as is possible."

"And we should trust your word."

"Yes."

"Because you are a follower of the *Art of Ata*," the dragon said.

The dragon realized the full significance of the sword. He bowed his head in agreement. "Both Ardeth and I are followers. However, even if we don't survive, the others will see that the cattle are brought to you."

"You could fight us and maybe get a few skinny humans,"

Ardeth added. "Or you can let us pass and have five hundred fat cattle."

"And will you also pay us what The Wolf promised when he came this way, wolfling cub? Should we trust you any better after being tricked by him?"

"Well damn," Za mumbled. He looked into the eye of the dragon. "I do not know what my grandfather promised you, but if I can, I will get it for you."

"He knows the promise, a secret between us," the dragon said. The head moved closer to Za, and he held his place though his heart began to beat harder. "He never brought it back."

"He has it? What?" Za asked.

"I will not say. I trusted him. He betrayed us."

"If I promise to go to him and get this thing --"

"And the five hundred cattle."

"And the five hundred cattle," Za agreed. "Will you let us through?"

"Get that which was promised by him first and bring it back to us."

"I cannot get there and back in time for this passage to make a difference in our own battle. Besides, the people here will freeze and starve -- so what good would that do us? We must find a better answer, friend dragon."

The dragon made a little growl of noise and backed away, apparently to discuss the matter with his companions. Za stood his ground and looked to Ardeth who remained on his left. Mai stood to his right and Kintansa beside her. Lt. Ebru had wisely left this in their hands and gone back to deal with the soldiers. He hated to think how many pack animals and how much of their supplies they'd already lost. He hoped none of the humans had gone down the cliffs as well.

"Za --" Mai began, her voice trembling slightly.

"I don't know," he said before she could ask any

questions. He honestly had no answers to anything now. "I don't want this journey to be for nothing -- but there are some prices we simply will not pay."

Mai nodded agreement. Kintansa took the moment to go help Ebru.

"I don't know what else to do," Za admitted. "I never knew the Wolf came this way. I can't imagine what he promised the dragons. If he had made a deal with them, why has he never claimed the deed?"

"Probably because he never completed his part," Ardeth said. "I suspect it would be unwise to tell how you fooled dragons. They might get ... unpleasant about it. They are not tied to these mountains, you know."

"They haven't gone after him, though," Mai said and sounded steadier, though her eyes never left the dragons. "There's something odd going on here."

"Odd," Za agreed and looked at her with a shake of his head. "We're trying to make a deal with dragons, Mai. Odd does not begin to cover what is going on here."

The dragon turned back their way and took one lumbering step in their direction before he lowered his massive head and looked straight into Za's face, this time so close that Za could only look into one eye.

"I will take you to the Court of the Wolf. We will fly."

"Ah --" Za looked upward. "I -- honored -- but --"

"You go and get that which was promised. Then we come back, and your people go through the pass."

"But -- I --" He stopped himself from babbling anything else and looked at Mai for help.

"He is not going alone," Mai said.

That was not the answer he'd expected.

"Not alone. I will carry two. If we do not return in three days, my companions will deal with the humans here."

"Five days," Za said. "My grandfather is old. If you won't

tell me what he promised, it may not be easy to get the answer from him."

"Old," the dragon said and sounded annoyed at the idea. "Why would old matter? We grow old and wise."

"Alas, humans grow old and sometimes they no longer remember their own past," Za explained. "They lose all sense of who they are. I have heard it is so with the Wolf. I have not seen him in many years."

"I will take you," the dragon said. "Five days. You will get that which was promised."

So, it was probably the best they could do. "Mai, you don't have to --"

"I am your guard."

"Mai --"

"When do we leave?" she asked the dragon.

"Immediately."

"A moment to say goodbye," Za said, grabbed Ardeth by the arm before he said anything, and headed back to the others. "You are not going with me, Ardeth. They're going to need you to get out of this mess if what we do doesn't work."

"I --"

"Don't argue with me. Let me think that there is some hope and it isn't all in my hands. My grandfather is senile, Ardeth. I doubt he has any idea what he promised to the dragons."

"Damn. You shouldn't go --"

"No choice. Be wise here. You have five days to come up with a plan."

Za nodded to Kintansa, and she started the people to make a camp. The dragons backed away which helped.

"Do the best you can," Za said to Ardeth while Mai crossed and made a quick goodbye to Kintansa. "I will do my best not to make this worse but have plans just in case."

"Za." He said and put a hand on his arm but said no

more.

The dragon watched him, perhaps as curious about humans as Za found himself about dragons. This was going to be a dangerous journey. Could he trust the dragon to take them there and bring them back?

He thought so. He thought they were beings of honor.

"How do we ride?" he dared ask.

"On my neck," he answered. "Beware my spikes. They are sharp."

That meant they couldn't use rope. Did he have an *Ata* ability that would keep them both secured somehow? Could he leave Mai behind if he moved quickly --

Should have thought of that before now. Mai had already returned to his side. For someone who had worried about the remote idea of even seeing dragons when they had even headed into the mountains, she seemed amazingly calm now.

"Climb up on my neck, there at the base," the dragon said and laid his neck on the ground. "My magic will keep you there. Be careful of the spikes."

Za looked at Mai. She shook her head -- but she climbed up before he did. The base of the neck met at the dragon's shoulders, and the scales made it easy to find footing to climb and to hold on once he reached a spot, though he couldn't say it felt safe. He took a spot in front of Mai with a spike between them. The razor-sharp spikes, which doubtless kept the neck safe from attackers, looked like a quick death if they were not very careful.

Other attackers? What would go after a dragon? Maybe other dragons, Za supposed. Perhaps they were territorial. Perhaps they were going to run into dozens of dragon clans --

Magic swept up around and over him like a protective bubble, cutting out the icy wind and muting the sounds. Though not particularly comfortable, he didn't feel as though he would fall or be cut to shreds on the spikes before and behind him.

Za hoped Mai remained safe. He had to believe.

The dragon rose back to his feet, rushed toward the pass and leapt out over the cliff beyond. The winds they had fought climbing upward now caught the unfolded wings, and they soared effortlessly -- gracefully -- out into the sky.

Za watched the camp disappear into the cold wastes of winter. Ardeth and Kintansa had been standing side-by-side, which he took to be a good sign since they were both strong and wise. The dragons had all watched as well, and he had sensed a whisper of trepidation there. Distrust.

The dragons didn't trust the humans who flew away with the one that Za thought might be their leader. The humans didn't trust the dragon who flew away with the two humans. This was the natural order of things, of course, but right now it might be the start of destruction on either side.

Kintansa would be wise and keep the humans in line. Ardeth would deal with the dragons as best he could. Za trusted them both.

There, finally, was something Za had not realized until he sat on the neck of a dragon, flying across the endless land of mountains and snow, heading for another grandfather's fabled lands.

He trusted very few people.

Za trusted Mai. He thought she must be crazy to climb up and fly away with him -- but he trusted her more than he had anyone except for Endris. Endris had sent him to her. And now --

Some might think they had all gone on an adventure, given all they'd faced during this journey. Such tales were always more exciting in the telling rather than the living. He might later tell others about the horrible cold of the snow-capped mountains, and the wind that felt as though it would tear your skin from your body. He could tell people about drawing the Sword of Honor and decapitating the big cat in one swing, saving the life of someone who did not appreciate the gesture, though she dearly loved her life.

He could tell many things.

However, how could he explain the utter dread that came with each new step they took? Could he describe how painful the death of Danisin had been? How much he feared to lose any of the others, even those he did not know, and how that drove him to do such dangerous things so that others would not? The fear of his own death was nothing compared to the fear he felt for others.

He shouldn't have brought Mai with him.

Of course, that implied that he could have left her behind. She remained his guard, and that was not a part-time occupation in her mind. Za wondered how he had won over her loyalty. Sometimes, though, he suspected she might not actually serve him, but rather his father. Even as a boy, he had noted how devoted she had been to keeping his reckless father safe.

He'd sworn he would never be so reckless.

And now he rode on the neck of a dragon.

The *Art of Ata* had not prepared him for this much insanity.

Hold to the calm, Master Drital had told him so often that the words were always there in his mind at any moment of stress. *Hold to the calm and be yourself.*

But who was he? The man had taught *Prince Zaron*, who had already known for years that he would not survive his mother's treachery any more than his father had survived.

And yet...

Oh, he had not yet survived, but he had already done the one thing his father had never thought to do: he had moved to work against her and found allies in the cause. Powerful ones. Why had King Yasidin never gone to his own father for help?

Why had he stayed at Willoway and believed in his own safety in a nest of vipers?

Why had he left his son unprotected?

He hadn't. Endris had always been there. Endris who had been powerful in the *Art of Ata*. So much so, in fact, that he never drew the attention of the Queen. Queen Taranis had sent away any servant who showed interest or kindness to the prince, and yet Endris held on. More than that, he brought in Master Drital, and no one made any show of it.

The two men had prepared Za for this.

He would not fail them.

The view of the troops and the dragons had disappeared far behind them. Below he could see only white and white, with clouds moving in swirls that promised yet more snow. The wind blew past, but the warmth of the dragon and his magic enveloped them and kept them in place.

Odd, Za thought, but this was probably as safe as he had been since Endris had died. Za doubted Mai appreciated such safety, though to give her credit, she would still be more worried about the ones they left behind than about herself. Leaving Kintansa behind could not have been easy for her, especially knowing the danger they faced at the mountainous camp.

Her ties made her human.

A strange thought, but he had come to realize, suddenly, that while he was flesh and blood of a human, he had never learned how to be counted as one of them in actions and soul. It was a surprisingly bitter revelation.

If he was not one of them, why did he care what happened? It couldn't be simple revenge against his mother. The idea of revenge was anathema to the *Art of Ata* -- and at that moment he realized he was a true practitioner, and not merely someone going through the motions, memorizing the adages, and pretending to the meditations.

Za had given up being a prince. He had given up what he had been born to do and took the path he was trained for instead.

If he was not to rule, what good did this state do for him?

Observe. That was the *Art of Ata* at its finest because observation brought clarity of thought that might be obscured by emotion, though to observe without empathy was as bad as to act only on emotion.

Observe.

And right now, he could observe such things as no one else had seen, except Mai behind him. He rode on a dragon! That startling realization finally surged through the worries about what he'd become during his odd life.

Mountains, trees, and snow spread out below them in a view that made him wish for wings of his own. A waterfall cascaded over a cliff and fell hundreds of feet to the stream below, but both edges had frozen as though in mid-flight. A large cat, almost invisible in the snow, suddenly darted up and ran for better cover, glancing over her head to see if the dragon followed. When they did not, she stopped and held her ground on an ice-bound boulder and raised a paw as though she would knock them from the sky.

The dragon's wings flapped, and the great tiger bounded away again.

Za suspected the snow tiger wished he could fly, too.

CHAPTER THIRTY-THREE

I was on a dragon and flying off over the snow-covered mountains.

On a dragon.

Flying.

Of all the nightmares about dragons that I had hoarded since my childhood, this was not one that had ever come up. Maybe that helped because I literally could not imagine it.

The dragon's magic kept the wind out of my face. I could look downward to the left and right at the world beneath us, all laid out in snow, trees, and rock. Had any other humans ever witnessed such a view?

We swept down over the pass, and I caught a glimpse of the trail below that had taken us days to climb. We passed it in a few flaps of the broad wings. Then with a curve, we circled to the left, over a half-frozen waterfall, and out over another plain of snow and ice that stretched so far that I could not see where it ended, and the clouds began.

Then we rose into the clouds themselves.

Snow swept past the surface of the magic bubble that kept me safe. The dragon turned left and right, wings flapping, and for a moment I thought he might be lost or in danger -- but no. Maybe it was because I was linked to his magic, but I had a sense of joy. He swept up and down on the winds, not bothered by the cold or the ice -- or the puny humans who rode upon his back.

When we came back out of the clouds, the land below had dramatically changed. We had spent so much time up in the highlands of snow, rock, and scraggly trees that I'd almost forgotten the pine-covered lower areas of the mountains. Pines stretched out in all directions, broken only by an occasional stream or lake. We startled herds of deer and flocks of geese.

What had taken us weeks to climb now took so little time to descend on dragon's wings that I began to think that we might need to enlist them in the mercenaries.

Yes, I was going crazy.

The sun started to go down, and the dragon's head swept back and forth until he found a spot to land on a long, wide stretch of snow. We came down in a glide, snow spiraling upwards around us on all sides so that I couldn't see. Would the dragon abandon us in this desolate spot? Would he devour us for dinner before he flew on?

The magic that held me in place let go. I wasn't certain I wanted to climb down, but Za had started off, and I was his guard. I leapt down beside him as the dragon folded his wings and curled back his head.

"Camp," the dragon said. "Rest until light. One more day to fly."

Za grinned. "Thank you."

The snow stood shoulder deep only a couple yards away, but where the dragon had landed, he'd cleared the covering all the way down to the ground. Za found a few pieces of frozen wood, but he was able to use enough of the *Art of Ata* to convince them to burn. We had some small supplies in our packs, enough for a reasonable meal. I worried about the others and looked back the way we had come, but the clouds and the night obscured the world. I hoped Kintansa was well. I hoped we all survived this latest madness.

"I wish I knew what to ask for when we get to my grandfather," Za admitted as we sipped a warm tisane of dried herbs and leaves steeped over the fire. "I wish I knew what to look for there because I've never been to his court at all, so I know nothing about it. People speak more of the Tiger's court than his because of the splendor. I suspect the Wolf lives in a duller place."

He looked at the head of the dragon, and so did I. The great beast watched us through one blinking eye, gave a slight grumble of sound, and said nothing at all.

We hardly needed any fire that night, and Za finally let it die away. The dragon radiated warmth and we were as comfortable as we would have been in an excellent inn. It improved my mood, and I slept remarkably well nestled up to the dragon.

I even suspected the dragon would have slept a little longer if Za and I hadn't gotten up just before the dawn. Before long, the stark blackness gave way to an almost blinding white of sunlight and snow. The wind came wintry cold when I stepped out of the protection of the dragon's side, and I scurried back in haste.

"Long flight today," the dragon said as we climbed up. Which meant I had a long time with my own company. I regretted that Za and I could not ride together and discuss what we planned to do at the Court of the Wolf. Of course, that was pretending that either of us had an idea of what we would find. Za had made it plain over our dinner that he didn't know what to expect.

The dragon had chosen his resting area well. With a lumbering run, he launched himself off over a gently descending hillside. His wings spread as we took to the air.

I think I was starting to like dragons.

There were the persistent rumors that the Wolf was losing

his hold, not only on reality, but even on his lands. Trouble sprang up too often in the west -- the Tiger had pointed that out when he spoke of Kintansa's mercenaries and the excellent work they'd done to keep the lands safe when the Wolf had not.

What were we going to find? Would the Wolf help us? No, I didn't think he would. That would present a problem.

I was not going to fail the others we had left behind. I would not fail Kintansa.

We soon followed a long, narrow river valley, the walls so steep that at times the dragon had to tilt left or right to avoid scraping along the edges. I slept a little, far beyond fear now -- and trusting to the dragon and his magic. When I awoke, the sun had started to go down so that black shadows lined both sides of the trench. Pale white fog began to lift upward from the water below, and between the two, I could not see anything. I found that I trusted the dragon, but even so, I could not close my eyes again. I rested, though. I suddenly realized that we would be dealing with more trouble soon. We were going to the Court of the Wolf.

Willoway had been designated as the middle ground between Wolf and Tiger. Eventually, the two halves were supposed to be united under one leader -- and with a start, I remembered that most people had thought that person would be Za. I didn't know what would happen now, as far as the union would go. I couldn't say I even cared any longer, as long as we were not united under the Queen and her demons.

What I did know, though, was that the power of the Wolf had weakened over the last twenty years and Willoway had fallen more and more into the realm of the Tiger. We had become increasingly Eastern in our trade and our culture.

Some of us were interested enough to even know why. As the Wolf grew weaker, his interest in the wider world lessened with each year. His Lords and councilors turned their full attention to the western lands and did their best to keep those places in order. Even so, dark tales came from the west and no one sane --

Ah, well, I'd already decided on my sanity.

Eventually, we left the river and glided out over open lands with no more than rolling hills to ripple across the countryside. The snowstorms of the high mountains lay far behind us now, and bright moonlight traced roads and illuminated an occasional, dark village. The night hid us and only a distant dog barked or sometimes a wolf howled.

I wondered how often I would look up into the sky in the dead of night and hope to see a dragon.

Just as the dawn light rose on the horizon behind us, I started to see a vast, ungainly shape rising upward on a hill before us. At first, I thought some monster sat there, ready to spring up and grab us, dragon and all.

Then the morning light defined the shape better -- tall towers, glittering windows, curtain walls, and all that went into a massive castle. The light did not make it any more appealing, though. The entire edifice was built of gray stone, so roughly cut that many of the pieces looked as though they'd merely been yanked from some quarry and shoved into place without ever seeing a chisel. I wondered how the building remained standing.

This was the Lair of the Wolf. I didn't have to be told, even though I had never seen more than rough sketches of the building. As I watched, archers began to line the wall, and I thought about what Za had said -- that dragon wings did not have scales to protect them.

We circled out wide once, the dragon's neck craning left and right as he took in the scene. Then the dragon flapped twice, folded his wings, and dived straight toward the large interior courtyard.

I couldn't even cry out in surprise or protest in the brief

heartbeats as we went over the wall and down. Arrows bounced off the dragon's scales and the magic around us. The wings fluttered slightly but it was a surge of magic that slowed us in the end, and we hit the stone pavement with a bone jarring stop that cracked stones but didn't break any delicate human bones.

The magic that had held me in place suddenly disappeared, and I almost fell off. I barely avoided grabbing the spine as I started to swing downward. Then I happened to notice that Za was dropping off on the opposite side, so I changed direction and climbed down just a moment behind him and took my place as his guard.

Black-clad soldiers rushed into the courtyard. Za ignored them as he walked beside the neck of the dragon and stopped by the head. "Protect yourself," he said softly.

The dragon gave a rumble of agreement. I wondered how in the name of the forgotten gods we were ever going to get him back out of this small area.

A problem for later. The soldiers -- several hundred of them -- were the more immediate trouble. They were not well disciplined, which made them far more dangerous, but they were too afraid to come close to the dragon. That saved us from the swords, but I saw bows coming up.

Za stepped out away from the dragon. I kept at his side, one step back.

"I am Prince Zaron, and I am here to see my grandfather. Take me to him immediately."

That stopped everyone. Words whispered around us, but the accents were so strong that they might as well have been speaking another language. Za glanced from right to left, so much like a prince who had come across something unpleasant that I found myself straightening to attention and remembering his father.

Someone of rank finally showed up. I could tell before I

could see him because the mass of soldiers began to move out of the way and then stood at attention while making a wide corridor down which a short, fat man with a bushy beard walked.

He glared. He glared very well.

If he thought such a scowl was going to worry us, he hadn't considered that we had just arrived on a dragon.

"Sir," Za said with a slight nod. "I am Prince Zaron, and I am here to see my grandfather."

"That is who you say you are."

"Yes, it is who I say I am. Is General Inash available? We have met, though I was quite young."

"I don't see why we should bother him with such a ridiculous --"

A young man darted up to stand by this one. He gave him a nod. "General Inash is on the way, Lord Skiris. He has ordered everything to be on hold until he gets here."

"The General does not order me," the man said with a worse glare turned on the soldier. Apparently, it didn't affect him, either.

"No sir, of course not. The orders are for the soldiers who will do nothing until he arrives."

Lord Skiris started to say something. He stopped and looked at the dragon who had turned his head to watch. He might have made sounds of impatience, but he said nothing aloud.

The General arrived only a few moments later. He had taken the time to dress neatly and brush his hair. When he stopped by Lord Skiris, he didn't so much as give the man a nod of acknowledgment.

"So," he said and looked Za over. "I suppose you do look like him, but he'd never cut his hair --"

"I don't give a damn about the hair," Za said. He was, I could tell, starting to get annoyed. "I am Prince Zaron. You and The Wolf were at my coming of age. Grandfather told me specifically to never trust his daughter. You were there."

The man's eyes narrowed. "That is a treasonous thing to say here, boy."

"About my mother? Queen Taranis has called in demons, General. I assume you have heard about them."

"I heard that you were responsible, and now you arrive with this beast --"

Za stepped forward and caught the man by the collar. That took all of us by surprise. "I have soldiers freezing in the mountains and waiting for the rest of the dragons to turn on them. I do not have time for this, General Inash. I have come to see my grandfather. If you do not take me, perhaps the dragon can find him, but I don't think you really want this fine castle torn to pieces, now do you?"

He let go of the man and stepped back. Inash looked more annoyed than surprised now. "Oh, do come then, boy. You and your guard. For all the good it will do you."

"I am Prince Zaron. Not boy."

I had finally realized what he was doing. I had not heard much about The Wolf, except that his court lacked the grace and style of the east. Looking around, I could tell it was true. They were brutes compared to the courtiers at the Court of the Tiger. They were wolves come in from the wild, but not tamed to human manners.

I realized that Za's ability to take in everything so quickly had allowed him to adjust his personality to this new setting. The *Art of Ata* might have saved us time -- might even have saved our lives. I glanced back at the dragon as we entered the cavernous dark building. He, I thought, would be safe enough.

A servant scurried out of a room, a torch in hand, the flame battling wildly against her movement. The place smelled of mold and dirt. I could not have imagined a place more the opposite of the Tiger's home.

"To the King's quarters," the general ordered.

"Sir," she said and bowed so unsteadily that I feared she would set her hair on fire. Then she rushed across the vast entry hall and started up the stairs. We moved steadily to keep up with her. My legs felt stiff, though, from the rather strange ride we'd had to get here. I feared it was all for nothing, and the worry that I would never see Kintansa again -- how could I have thought going with this boy more important than staying and protecting her?

I wanted to resent that he forced me into this choice.

But he hadn't. More than Kintansa was at stake.

I could not believe the answer we needed would be found in this bleak place where cobwebs fizzled in the passing torch.

CHAPTER THIRTY-FOUR

Za took the stairs at a steady step, the servant before them, Mai behind him, and General Inash last. As they left the dark cavern of the entry hall, he could hear others following them in, the whisper of words he could not quite make out.

They went up one level, and then another.

However, Za's mind danced around in his head like lightning crashing against his skull. This was far worse than he had expected. How could the Wolf live in this squalor?

Barbarians. Za focused on that word. He'd often heard it applied to the people of the west, but he had thought that phrase was only a sign of the East's disdain for anything they did not invent or control. Even his mother had shown the contempt toward her own background, but he'd taken that as a sign of her hatred at being controlled by another.

Now ... now he worried about what he could do here. Others depended on him, both the people they'd left behind at the pass and the soldiers marching on Willoway from the east. Mai wouldn't survive if he didn't handle this well. Za had to find an answer. He had to please the dragons.

Za did not let his step slow since that would have mirrored his worried mind and he dared not show weakness to these people. General Inash had a reputation for ruthlessness that he'd always considered exaggerated until now.

He found himself in a dangerous situation and made worse by a combination of factors that individually would have been bad enough. Add to everything else, one more factor: Inash might not believe he really is the heir. Or he might believe that he is -- Za realized that either one might be equally dangerous for him. And for Mai, of course.

They had, however, arrived on a dragon. He rather thought that might give them an edge and stop anyone from taking any hasty action against them.

Up another flight, but he could tell now that they were nearing the quarters. He stopped at the landing and lifted his hand giving a slight hiss of sound that got Mai to draw her knife.

"Magic," Za said. "And not good magic."

"You can feel magic?" General Inash demanded and not with any sound of pleasure.

Za turned to him, his hand held out, and brought an elemental flicker of flame to the palm. It was what he had used to make the campfires, and the ability had gotten more comfortable with practice.

Inash almost took a step back. His eyes narrowed.

"I rode here on a dragon, General," Za reminded him. "Yes, I have some feel for magic. What is going on here?"

"I don't know."

Za could sense the truth in what the man said. He'd rather have had a better answer. Za wasn't certain if the man had never considered there might be magic in the area, or if he knew and didn't understand the matter. The servant put her back against the wall, the torch flickering back and forth in her trembling hand.

"What do you know, girl?" Mai asked. She kept her voice calm and even dared a hand on the girl's arm, taking the torch away so that it cast a more even light. More cobwebs fizzled. Were there any other servants around at all?

"He speaks to things, lady," the girl whispered and cast a frightened glance at Inash.

"He's an old man," General Inash said. His voice had, surprisingly, soften. "He speaks to his past."

"But sometimes the past answers him," the girl replied, a little more defiant. "The others won't work here. They've heard things. They've seen things."

"And yet you stayed," Mai said. She put a hand beneath the girl's chin and lifted her head. "You are no servant. You are his daughter."

"Granddaughter," she corrected. "My father was the Wolf's younger child, a son who died years ago."

Za felt his breath catch, and all thought of everything else lost in that moment. Granddaughter?

Cousin?

General Inash must have known the truth. He watched with evident curiosity. Za stared for a long moment before he could find any words at all. Mai waited as well, a bit of a frown drawing down her brows. Did she think this young woman a threat to him?

"I didn't know," Za finally said. "There has always been the touch of the gods on the rulers of the east. One child shall be born to them, one child to rule, and no others. Why had I never thought that it might not apply to the West as well? What is your name, princess?"

"Oh, no princess. Not I," she said. She had steadied though. "There is only one heir, you know. That was part of the pact between the Wolf and the Tiger. Even here, only one. No matter if another is --"

She stopped and leaned away from the wall and stared into his face. Za saw too much of his mother in her face, but not in her bright gray eyes. The young woman's head tilted and the touch of a smile. Za could not guess what she saw in him.

"Prince Zaron," she said with a bow of her head. "I am Cobia."

"Princess Cobia," he corrected despite the shake of her head and the worried look at Inash. The general didn't seem to care. Za turned away from him and lifted his hand again. "There is magic here. Dangerous, I think. Mai --"

"You are not going in there without me," she said. "Let's just see what we can do."

Cobia and Inash both seemed to take her answer as a surprise, and evidently expected Za to react badly. He already had a good idea of how authority worked in this dark, dank place. He would not play their game.

Instead, Za nodded and headed down the hall. Mai took the torch and gave the other two a nod before she went on. She did not tell them they need not come along, though Za was tempted to do so. Not wise, though, for many reasons. The magic worried him, but there were other problems at hand. He and Mai were not known, and he did not want any misunderstandings.

"That door, Prince Zaron," Cobia said with a nod to the door. "Let me open it and go in first. He's used to seeing me."

That seemed wise. "Thank you. Be careful. I might have stirred something since I can feel the magic and something there might also feel me."

She gave him a worried look. Za didn't think she had quite understood that he really did mean there was magic in the room. He kept close as Cobia opened the door and he slipped in right on her heels. Mai was so close behind Za that he could feel her breath on his neck.

Inash remained at the door and he held the torch now.

The room smelled clean, and even in the little light they brought, he could tell it was well-kept. Rugs covered the stone floor and a fire, banked down for the night, gave a soft glow to the well-polished furniture that sat close by. The far corner of the room held a substantial canopied bed -- one fit for a king. The blanket was thrown back, the bed empty.

"Grandfather?" Cobia said, her voice trembling slightly. "Come out. You have visitors. Prince Zaron is here to see you."

"Dragons," a voice whispered. Za could not quite find him. "No friends. Dragons."

"The dragon was kind enough to bring me," Za replied. He stepped out into the room, signaling the others back. "I think you know why."

"No! No!"

Za couldn't tell if the Wolf didn't know or if he refused to give up what he had promised. Za had, however, found the old man, standing far back in the corner, covered in shadow -- and the shadow was not natural.

"Come away from the dark," Za ordered. He lifted his hand and cast a dozen swirling lights into the air. It was not easy, but he could imagine what he wanted, and he held to his purpose.

Za could see the face of the old man now -- gray beard, wild gray hair, and even wilder blue eyes. Black moved in swirls around him, and he heard Cobia make a sound of distress at the sight. He wanted to tell her she should go, but he had to stay focused. He heard Mai say the words to her, though.

She stayed. Inash had moved into the room, hand on his sword though he had not drawn it.

"The magic is real," Inash said, the shock plain in his voice. "This is not what you created to fool us."

"No," Za said, a bit of a gasp. He let some of the lights die and then focused on the ones closest to the old man. Oh yes, they did whisper, too. They talked to someone, and he knew where these threads led. "They come from Queen

Taranis -- my mother. I need to break the link. I need --"

He didn't say more. Mai would object to his plan, and besides, he didn't want to warn the shadows. They continued to whisper to someone else, telling tales. That would be a problem. The Queen would know he was here --

Or this might be good. It might help for her to think this was where he had run. Still, he needed them gone. He required his grandfather's attention, and he would not have it with these foul creatures putting a veil between the old man and the real world.

And he could think of only one way to handle the problem.

He leapt forward and caught hold of the Wolf by the arm and yanked him free. That sounded easy, but it was not. The moment he grabbed the older man by the arm, the Wolf began to yowl and claw at him. The shadows swarmed to attack, and he realized that they genuinely wanted him.

Mai tried to help, of course. Cobia surprised him and did the same, despite her fears.

"Grab him! Take him!" Za ordered.

They didn't pause; the two women took hold of the Wolf and pulled him toward the door. Za brought the lights to him and used them to fight the shadows away. He thought the sun might also be dissipating their powers. It would be easier for something like this to form in dark corners and at night.

They wanted the Wolf -- but they also wanted him; he only realized that after his grandfather had been pulled toward the door. The shadows tried to get there -- but Za cut them off. Unfortunately, the others were not able to get out, and the Wolf began yelling.

"Evil! Evil everywhere! Evil --"

"Shut up!" Mai ordered.

No one had probably ever said those words to the man. He went quiet, though Za didn't think it would be for long. He didn't know what to do. The magic of these creatures --

Came from somewhere else. He felt the thread when he passed through one, and he saw the beast waver for a moment. He could not catch the strings in his hands -- they passed through. The shadows had noticed his attention on those links of power, and he'd upset them. They came at him in a single wave --

Mai shouted in fear and rushed to help him, though he wondered what she thought she could do. No matter. It was the shadows that had made a mistake. By massing, they made his own action far easier. He sent magic against magic, with light that sought out the strings and burnt them.

One after another the creatures popped like bubbles until the room had lost the pall of the unnatural dark. Quieter, too.

He turned and put a hand on the nearest piece of furniture to keep from going down. Mai stepped closer, ready for any other trouble.

"Light candles," Za ordered.

"Sit down," Mai said in return.

The Wolf had gone quiet. He turned his attention from one corner of the room to another, watching for movement as Mai lit the candles. Cobia kept hold of the older man, and it seemed as though as though they both had the same look of distrust and disbelief.

"The shadows are gone," Za said, but honesty propelled him to say more. "I don't know if they'll stay away. I do know that the magic came from the east and had the taint of Queen Taranis to it. I suspect that she'll realize I am here."

"Then we have to move quickly, Za," Mai said. "We dare not get caught here. And this might help, you know. If she realizes you are here, she's not going to suspect you were anywhere else."

"Yes," he agreed to what he had already considered. "They did not have the feel of anything intelligent enough to see beyond this room. They will not have seen the dragon."

"Dragons! No!" the Wolf suddenly looked around with growing distrust again.

"Sit down, sir. We must talk."

"I don't know you. You are an assassin --"

"I am your grandson."

The old man took a chair at Cobia's insistence, but his blue eyes never looked away from Za. Mai dragged a huge chair across the room for Za, and they sat across from each other, Mai at his shoulder, Cobia beside the Wolf. General Inash watched from the edge of the doorway again, but Za had the feeling he was wary of all of them now. Magic could not have made this situation any better.

Za didn't care.

"If you are her son, why should I trust you?" the old man said, a quaver of worry and age in his voice.

"I just saved you from the shadows," Za said. His own voice wasn't very strong either. "But no matter. You need not trust me, except to help me with a problem. Sometime in the past, you made a promise to the dragons. You never completed that promise. I am here to help you finish what you began."

"Dragons, dragons," the old man said with a shake of his head. Wildness had come back to his eyes again. He looked to the heavily barred window. "You brought the great enemy into my stronghold."

"I want what you promised them," Za repeated and tried to pull some force into his words. "I need it, or very many people will die. I will not have that on my hands, grandfather. What did you promise to give them?"

"They can't have it back. I won't give it up. I can't take it, and neither can they. It is a trap, you know."

Za sat back and frowned wondering what other tact to take. He glanced at Cobia, but from the frown on her face, he suspected she had no idea either. Inash frowned, but he couldn't read that face.

"When did he go to the dragons?" Za asked looking at the general.

"I don't know. I never heard of it, which makes me think it was before the change. Twenty years or so now, when I came in from the west to take command here. Before then."

"Are there any records?" Za dared to ask. He couldn't decide if these people were even literate, given the way they lived.

"Yes. I'll take you to them," Inash replied. He looked curious enough to go along with Za for now. Given the reaction from Lord Skiris, he considered even reluctant help better than what he might otherwise expect to get here.

"I'll stay with grandfather," Cobia said. "They will be bringing up his breakfast soon. He'll calm down."

Za gave her a nod of thanks. Mai gave a frustrated glare to the older man who had begun mumbling about evil again, but she said nothing. She'd grabbed a candle and frowned at the little flame as they went back out into the hall.

They crossed back to the stairs and down a flight before General Inash stopped. "What is it the dragon wants?"

"I don't know," Za admitted and drew a frown. "The Wolf promised something to the dragons. I suspect this item must be a tangible object. Gold perhaps. Or cattle."

"We could gather both," the man said as he started down this hall.

"But if neither is what the dragon wants, we might only anger him," Za added. "I hope to find the answer, but I don't have much time. Two days at best or else we won't get back to the mountains in time."

"Huh." The man gave them both a glance and seemed to believe the worry in their faces this time. "Let's hope Sina can help."

CHAPTER THIRTY-FIVE

The library gave me some hope.

I wasn't much of a reader, but I understood the importance of books. The door General Inash pushed open showed a room with a bright window open to the dawn light and walls lined with shelves. I had never seen so many manuscripts, all bound and carefully placed and dusted.

I glanced at Za. The look of pleasure on his face made me wish that we could have stayed here for months just for his sake. Maybe we could come back. I didn't much like the Court of the Wolf, but if I brought some people to clean it up, the place might not be so bad. I wouldn't have minded doing something that helped Cobia.

If we won the war.

If we found what the dragons wanted.

If Tansa wouldn't mind such a place for a while.

Too many ifs still to plan a future.

A young woman came from the side of the room. She was tall, thin, and pale; the epitome of a western woman, I thought. Her eyes were gray instead of blue, though. She looked slightly distracted, and the cloth in her hand indicated that we had caught her during the dusting.

"Sina, we need information on the Wolf. This is Prince

Zaron. You must help him in any way you can."

"You've cut your hair," she said with a frown.

"It's only hair," he said with a sigh of frustration. I could understand why. Everyone seemed to focus on the hair as though it was more important than -- ah, but of course. They realized it meant he could not inherit the throne of the east. I wasn't sure how the people of the west felt, and right now I didn't much care. We just didn't have time.

"We need information," Inash repeated, drawing her attention. "We need to know what the Wolf did at least twenty years ago, and after he'd come to terms with the Tiger, I would think. Before that, he was always on the battlefield, so he would have had a hard time going high up into the mountains."

"Oh, you want to know about the trip to the dragons!" she said and turned away crossing to a shelf of journals.

"You know he went to the dragons?" Za asked. He sounded distrustful, and I understood. Nothing had been this easy since we started on this journey of madness.

"Yes," she mumbled. "Lord Ackri -- he kept the archives before his death -- told me about it. He said no one ever asked, and he had the impression that the Wolf didn't want the tale told. However, he was a scribe at heart and a historian. He'd written it down, what he could learn -- here you go."

She pulled a massive journal from the shelf and carried it to the table by the window, fending off any attempt by others to help her. I watched her leaf quickly through the tome. I could see pages of elegant script, with scrollwork painted at the top and bottom of each page encircling what appeared to be dates.

The sight of this book made me rethink what I had thought about the westerners. This was not a world of barbarians, though they might be slipping back to that level. There might even be better places beyond this castle which, I realized, had its own reason for darkness.

"Here. There's not much, I'm afraid."

Za leaned over and nodded. "The Wolf took only a few of his most trusted pack, and they went to the high mountains, for he needed a new challenge. Though he swore the others to silence, rumors soon spread within the castle once they returned. The Wolf had found the dragons, and he won from them some gift in exchange for his own promise, though it was never clear what he had given. The Wolf was several months away from the castle, and when he returned, he lost interest in his work and left it to the councilors."

Za looked up and shook his head. "No, that is not a lot of help."

"I don't understand why the dragon won't tell us what the dragon wants," I said and let the frustration show this time. "At least we'd have a chance of locating it. But if the Wolf won't tell us and the dragon won't, then how can we get back and save the others?"

The panic had started to rise in my voice. I fell silent, but I saw a flash of worry in Za's eyes as well. Then he looked at the book and back up -- I thought there might be a little more hope in his face.

"There were others who knew. Others who went with him and said that he had met with dragons. They knew that much, and they might know more. Someone from the group must still be alive."

"Some," Inash agreed though with a frown. "None of them here at the court, though. It will take a while --"

"We have very little time," I said. Inash looked at me with a frown, but that may have been because he didn't see me as anything more than a guard who had no right to speak out of turn. That didn't stop me from continuing. "Very many will die if we don't do this immediately. We have to know what he promised to the dragons and never delivered."

Inash and Sina both nodded. Inash went off to see if he could find others. Sina went back to her journals. Za helped her as best he could. I crossed to the window and looked down, watching the dragon who shifted uneasily now and then.

The dragon had the answer. Why would he not tell us? What did he try to hide?

"I am going down to talk to the dragon," I said and started for the door.

Za looked up with a start. "You. Going to talk to the *dragon*."

"I am hoping that we can come to an understanding."

I thought he might try to follow me, but Za stayed in the library with Sina. This was trust on both our sides. I knew he could take care of himself, but I was his guard, and walking away in this strange place left me feeling chill.

We had no time. Neither of us wanted to be the only survivors of that expedition through the mountains.

I met Inash on the way down the stairs. A few servants were moving around now as well, but they were timid things. I couldn't blame them after seeing those shadows Za had sent packing. I couldn't say I felt any safer, either.

"Sir," I said to the general who had paused at the landing and given me a nod.

"I've sent out messengers and soldiers to collect two of the men. One is thirty miles away, the other over fifty. At least that's where they should be. It's going to be a couple days before either of them reaches us here.

"Too long," I said with a shake of my head, letting that hope disappear. "I am going to try to talk to the dragon."

"Good luck," he said. He might have feared I'd end up as lunch if I were not careful. I kept that thought in mind.

The dragon took up most of the courtyard, and there was nothing else around. He had laid down, his head on his paws, looking too much like a giant cat might look before a hearth on a cold winter night.

I stared at the blinking face. "We need answers, friend dragon. The Wolf is old, and I'm not even sure he remembers what he promised. We can't even be certain it is here --"

"It is here," he answered with a low rumble of words. "I can feel it here."

"Then you could find it without us?" I asked with a whisper of hope.

"I would have to tear the castle apart, stone by stone. And if what I seek was damaged, then everyone would pay for it. The Wolf or a descendant of the wolf must give it to me or else the promise will not be fulfilled."

I didn't like anything I heard here. I also didn't like how worried the dragon had started to sound.

"I fear the only way we are going to find what you want is to know what we are looking for, my friend. No one here can help us. If this matter really is important to you, I need some clue. I need to know what we must find."

The dragon blinked several times.

And then he told me.

I went back upstairs to the library. Za, Inash, Sina, and Cobia were all there. When Za looked at me, he stood, clearly worried.

"What is it?" he asked.

"Dragon egg," I said. I took the seat across from him and waved everyone to sit down. "About the size of both my hands and emerald green -- in fact, it looks like a jewel, except you can see the dragon inside."

"Damn. I was afraid it might be something like that," Za admitted as he dropped back down into the chair. "How did he get it?"

"Apparently it's been in the hands of western royalty for generations. Hunters happened on the dragon grounds and stole it before the dragons knew what they'd done. The one who survived brought the egg out of the mountains and traded it for gold to a Wolf Clan leader who then became king. Then, generations later, the Wolf went to the mountains -- apparently thinking he could sneak to the Tiger's Court -- and the dragon's stopped him and made him promise to return the egg before they let him go."

"It could be anywhere!" Cobia cried out, looking around with worry. "Anywhere in the world!"

I had hoped that she might have seen it when she was given the description, but her worry showed she had not. Damn. So still not so easy.

"Not so bad as that," I told them. "The egg is somewhere in the compound. The dragon can sense it. He could even find it if he tore the building apart stone-by-stone."

"Maybe that is --" Ishan began.

"Not a good answer," I said, cutting him short. He didn't like that, but I didn't much care. We were out of time. "He said the egg might be damaged if he did so. That, I think, is what has stopped them from coming and taking it themselves. He let me know that would not be a good answer. And either Za or the Wolf must give the egg to him to fulfill the promise you answer gave to return it. Oh, or Cobia, now that I think of it."

The others nodded. "We had better start looking," Cobia said and stood. "I can't imagine --"

"Wait," Sina ordered, one hand lifted. "I have seen a picture of the egg, and the box it was in. In the history book, and not from too many years ago, I think. We'll take them down and look through them. It might help since I think a giant emerald with a dragon inside would have been seen by now. The box was carved with designs. We might be able to find it."

No one argued.

Cobia left a few times and always came back looking less

bothered.

"I have to look in on him," she explained finally. "I do so several times during the day. He's calmer now that the shadows are gone, but he's not any more coherent. I hope the shadows don't come back."

She looked to Za, and he stopped looking through pages to spread his hands in a gesture that conveyed he didn't know. "I'll do my best to find a way to keep them back, but that may have to wait until later, Cobia. I'm sorry."

"You have people to save," she said with a nod. "That has to come first."

I looked toward the window. The day was passing. We had so little time --"

"Here," General Inash said and shoved the book he had been looking through to the middle of the table.

The drawing had been well-done. The egg sat in the box, and the box was covered in a carved design that looked like the scales of a dragon. The box was not much larger than the egg, I was sorry to see. I had hoped for something more substantial and easier to spot.

"We need to get everyone we can looking for this," Za said and shoved back his hair with a snarl of frustration. "If we can get people checking every room --"

"Too much of a temptation to them," Cobia said with a shake of her head. "There are too many desperate people at the court now. We'll have to --"

"Tell them that if they touch the box, the dragon will hunt them down and kill them," I said. "And that only Za's magic makes it safe for him to take the box up and bring it to the dragon."

"They'll believe I have magic?" Za asked.

"They already know you do," Cobia replied. "The story of the shadows and the Wolf is already spreading, and besides -- you rode a dragon. Yes, Mai is right."

Inash nodded as well. I wasn't as confident I trusted the general, but right now we needed to believe in his cooperation because he was a link to others -- and we needed others.

Za took the book down to the main hall. Inash and Cobia worked at finding people, but they came slowly, especially those from outside who had to go past the dragon. When they had about a hundred people, Za made a show of casting lights around so that they could see. It was, I realized, an excellent way to make certain they saw the magic for themselves and didn't have to believe what others said.

We sent them off in different directions. Inash had stayed, and he waited for all but the core people to be gone.

"There is a treasury," he said. "It's empty, though. What taxes we still get delivered are immediately used to keep the court and city going. I've only been in there once when the Wolf was still ... cognizant of the world."

Za nodded. He left the book with Sina and Cobia while the three of us went down into the underbelly of the building. The rooms had been carved from living rock and the stairs worn by thousands who had passed this way, reminding me of the age of this place. It had been a mighty fortress long before the empire. We took a torch that I carried, and I kept my other hand on my knife as I watched Inash. I still didn't trust him very much.

The room had locks and latches enough to keep out any thieves. The lack of guards made me realize that the treasury had to be empty, though. Someone could hack their way through the rusting metal, and no one would hear the work so far down here underground.

Za let his fingers brush over the metal rod that had melded into place so that the flimsy locks hardly mattered. I couldn't see any way past it and had to hope the dragon egg was not here. I started to turn away --

Za drew his hand back, and the metal disintegrated into a

fine dust that settled on the floor. The magic had not been easy for him, though, since I could see him give a slight sway, his eyes narrowing. I put a hand on his arm, and he nodded. I understood why he had done so much magic, though, and why he dared not let the others know he was weakened by it. There was only the two of us, after all, against everyone else here. And the dragon, but we had no real control of him. He might turn on everyone. Za had to show he had power, and I suspected showing it especially to Inash might be important.

We got the door open. It had sealed, wood to rock, but a few yanks finally got it open enough that we could slip inside. The single torch was enough to light the small, square room. The air tasted of mold and stank.

The shelves, carved into the stone, were all but bare. A few copper coins stood in a pile in one spot. They were old and corroding away. A wooden box, not like the one we searched for, sat in another corner. Inash opened the lid and gave a nod, though not a happy one.

"The Iron Crown," he said. "That should be yours, Prince Zaron."

Zaron crossed and put his hand into the box. When he drew the crown out, I suspected it glittered more than it had when Inash first looked. A few jewels shown along the points, too. Not a pretty crown, but I thought it did well to symbolize power.

Za did not put it on but instead placed it in the pouch he carried. We went through the room and left again, not even bothering to close the door. Then we hunted through other rooms on this level and some on higher ones. I searched the kitchen, being somewhat conversant in locations to hide things in such a room. Others were checking the storage rooms, scaring up more rats and mice than anything else. No one had found anything so far. What if it had been hidden in a wall somewhere? The dragon might have to tear the building apart after all, and I had the feeling he could not do it in time. I feared we would be too late --

Sina stood at the top of the stairs when we got there.

"I think I figured out where the box must be. Come with me." She hurried up the stairs, talking breathlessly while we moved. "The drawing wasn't just the box. There was a window behind it. And a view, but not one I knew from the windows I've seen. If the box was still in the castle, I realized there was only place it could be that I wouldn't have visited. The old north tower. It has been closed off and unused for several generations already."

"Why?" Za asked.

"That is the oldest part of the castle and falling apart," Inash replied. "Why would someone hide something in an area falling apart?"

"Maybe it wasn't in that shape when the egg was first put there," Za said. "It has been in the hands of the kings for generations."

Inash gave a slight nod.

I tried to recall the whole of the picture. Even though I had looked at it several times, I could not remember anything beyond the drawing of the box and what it held. I glanced at Za and saw him frown. He'd missed it too, which was unusual.

I had to hope, though. The day had already mostly passed while we had wandered through dusty rooms. Two more to get back to the mountains. If we found it, we'd be leaving soon. I was glad. I wanted out of here. I wanted back to Kintansa. I worried about her, suffering up there in the cold, trying to help all the others. What would the dragons do if they decided we were not coming back?

I wanted to scream for the others to hurry. We walked across the castle interior and climbed, finally taking a long set of narrow stairs up into a tower that had some stones missing in the walls and looked ready to fall over at any moment. The wooden floor at the highest spot led into a room that had only small holes opened around the shutters and through those the wind whistled. Dust had been blown into the corners, and a lot of it had collected on the enormous spiderwebs that hung from the ceilings.

Something huge moved across the ceiling.

"Ah," I said and took a quick step back down the stairs, mostly so I wasn't trampled as the others retreated as well.

Sina had brought a torch. She bravely stayed at the top stair.

"There on the table across the room," she said and lifted the torch.

I looked up at the ceiling. The *thing* up there retreated from the light. When I was certain it was as far from us as possible, I dared a look across the room. The torch cast moving shadows, but I could see the stand and the table. Dust sat in piles there, but I could also see what looked like the box in the book.

"Runes on the floor," Za said. He knelt there at the top of the stairs, and I barely kept from hissing and throwing myself on top of him since that was such a dangerous position. "Someone made certain it would not be easy to get to the box."

"Not to mention adding the spider," Inash said. His voice sounded steady, but I did notice the way he jerked at every noise in the room.

I found myself thinking about the Lost Way Inn. It might not have been so bad staying there, even with the demons in the city. I could have hidden there maybe even with Za. Stayed in a place without giant spiders and held out until things got better.

Danisin would still be alive.

We had no hope of winning against the demons. Every time we took even a small step in one direction, massive problems rose up that we had to deal with first. Everything from pirates to giant spiders. Standing beside Za while he studied the runes and the creature making snapping sounds above us, made me want to give up.

Tansa, I thought. *I must save Tansa.*

And Za.

He looked at me with a frown. "I need to destroy the runes. I don't think we can kill the spider otherwise."

More snapping noises.

"Does the spider understand us?" Inash asked and took a step back.

"I don't know if she understands our words, but she knows our intentions. She's waited here for centuries, you know. She's waited for someone to try to take that box. I suspect a few tried. There are no doubt tales about people who disappeared in the castle."

"A few," Sina agreed. "And this part of the building was deemed unsafe so long ago that few dared to come here. I don't understand the point. What good is having the box here if you can't get to it?"

"Someone could," I said. I had begun to study the scene myself, pushing aside the hopelessness that had tried to take me. "I would guess that the person who ruled here when the egg first arrived had safeguards put in place while he traveled elsewhere. And he did not return, most likely. He didn't give the secret on to his heir."

"Ah," Sina said. "King Ankisi. He --"

"He died of a heart attack while on a hunt," Za said. "And oddly, his heir disappeared after he came back to the castle. The younger daughter inherited." He smiled at Sina, who looked at him with some surprise. "I wanted to know about my mother's line as well as my father's."

"Oh. Yes. Of course, Prince Zaron."

"What are we going to do?" I asked.

"Make the spider think we're leaving," Za said. "And then we are going to be daring."

"I never doubted it."

CHAPTER THIRTY-SIX

Za wasn't certain why Mai went along with his plan.
He had thought she might come up with some refinements. If they'd had time, she might have managed something with less of a risk.

Or maybe not. This wasn't the sort of situation where you could plan out a battle. She did suggest arrows, but Za knew they would not work. Dangerous runes protected the spider. He had seen such designs in the book Ardeth had brought out from the island, and they were the sign of ancient and powerful magic. A wise person walked wide around them, though there had been some words about how to deal with the trouble if it couldn't be avoided.

Unfortunately, they had not read that part, but Za had noticed the pictures.

Za didn't say this to Mai. He would have rather she wasn't the one who took this chance with him, but he knew he couldn't trust Inash, and Sina didn't have any ability for battle.

All four of them went down a flight of stairs, out of range as they prepared. He doubted they'd tricked the spider by their retreat. It would know every creak and whisper in this old tower by now.

"Be careful, Za. I have not gotten you this far to feed you

to a spider."

"And you Mai," he said. He put a hand on her shoulder, startling her. "We almost have it. Then we fly back and save the others. I look forward to a quiet hike through the mountains again."

"Yes," she said with a bright grin. "I have come to realize that I don't mind the snow so much after all."

Za smiled as well. He wasn't sure why he had won such a brave and steadfast guard. He suspected it had more to do with his father than him, but he hadn't had the chance to sit down and discuss that aspect of the situation.

Not now. Za didn't have the time, as much as he would like to have an answer before they risked death. The spider remained agitated. Everyone could hear it as they climbed the stairs.

Za didn't have much magical power left in reserve. Maybe he should have been more circumspect in what he'd done. He could have turned the dragon loose on the building, but that wouldn't have won them anything if the egg had been damaged. A falling tower would have disrupted the runes, killed the creature that guarded here -- and smashed the box and egg. He knew that truth. The *Art of Ata* had let him see the whole of the situation and to know that the only way to save the others was to go through the door.

Destroy the runes. Hope Mai could keep the spider busy for those crucial few heartbeats. Get the egg, give it to the dragon, go back to the mountains.

Simple.

As they reached the opening, Za dropped to his heels and leapt forward like a demented frog, aiming straight for the center of the runes. He kept his head low and was far too aware of the spider sweeping over him on web strands.

Za also didn't quite reach the center, and as he had expected, the runes came to life trying to trap him where he was. His hand, though, reached out and slapped the floor in the circle at the center of the intricate design.

With that anchor in place, he was able to drag himself out of the trap and into the protected area. If he had known the spell that controlled the runes, he could have probably destroyed the trap and the spider with a few words. Instead, he would have to do this in a far more difficult way.

He had to hope Mai remained both wise and helpful. Once the spider got close enough to her, she could use the sword she'd gotten from Inash.

Za stayed low to the ground while the spider made angry noises. He wouldn't have much time, and he dared not waste his magic to test out the area.

"All right, spider -- I'm here!" Mai shouted. She foolishly stepped into the room. She had a torch in one hand, and the sword in the other -- and a glance did show that she had the creature's attention. "You do not want Za."

"I think, actually, that it does," Za said. The spider looked his way. Too many eyes.

"Oh, but I am so much more interesting. After all, I have sharp things and fire. These webs look very old, you know."

"And if you set fire to them, the spider will drop down on me."

"Easier to deal with when the creature is on the ground."

"Maybe from where you stand. I might feel the same if I had an open door at my back."

She gave a little laugh, and then swung first the sword at the creature and then the torch. Both hit and the spider retreated in haste. Za could see that one leg had been severely damaged. Only seven more to go.

Bones of mice, rats, bats, and even owls littered the floor beyond the runes. The spider must sit on the box most often. The webs there were thick, oozed a sticky glaze that would make them more dangerous.

The spider shifted his way, ready to --

Mai didn't give it a chance. She leapt forward, shoved the torch into the face and cut off two legs with an awkward swing of the sword.

The screams of the creature and the scent of burning spider almost overcame Za. He had lost his path for a moment, and only survived because spider fixated on Mai. She made it back to the doorway, but she would not leave the room while Za remained there.

Look at the *truth* of the rune. Look at the essence of it. Taste the hint of power. The spider was not trapped by it. The spider moved at will, though not outside the room. What kept it here?

He found a link finally. His fingers traced along the edge of the nearest design while he did his best to ignore the battle between Mai and the spider, even when he heard her give a grunt of pain. He had found one truth, and he understood it. He traced it out until it touched another, and he worked to understand that one, as well. Life for the spider -- that meant that the spider would recover from the injuries. A third truth -- spider trap so that it could not leave.

Three truths. They had to be enough, though he knew there were more truths written in these intricate runes.

Za put his hands on the stone of the floor and forced his will against the three truths, hoping that there were not others that were worse.

The runes began to glow.

For a few quick heartbeats, the spider didn't know what to do. Mai took advantage of that moment to slice at another leg and won a blow that sent her flying into the corner of the door. The spider came at Za, and he would have had a chance with his own knife in hand if the creature hadn't spun a web out around him instead. It grabbed his arm, yanked him upward, twisted him as more web grabbed at his neck and arms.

Mai stumbled to her feet.

"Fire!" he gasped.

She didn't pause. With a wave of the torch, she lit fire to the older part of the web. It burnt so quickly that ash fell like snow as the fire spread halfway across the room and caught the spider by surprise. The creature gave a cry of pain and rage and dropped to the floor, pulling Za down with her. Even the web around him had caught fire, though it didn't burn as quickly.

Za concentrated on tearing the binding apart before the creature could catch him or before the fire left serious burns on him. Mai did her best to attract the spider, but the creature knocked her aside again. Za felt the fire catch at the binding around his arms and neck and the hold weakened. He threw it off, gasping for breath. The room had filled with evil-smelling smoke, though. It did not help.

When the spider prepared to leap at him again, he forced The Sword of Glory into his hands. He hoped he wouldn't have to hold it for long because it was draining him --

The spider did something he had not expected. It went for the box instead of for him. And then it leapt at the wall, rushed to the ceiling and threw the box down with enough force to destroy it and the egg inside.

Both he and Mai yelled and leapt. It was luck alone that they didn't collide and lose the only chance to save the egg. Za caught the box. Mai brought up her sword and skewered the irate spider as it dropped to them.

They backed away in haste. The creature thrashed several times, but it died and caught fire as well. The stench was so horrible that it had even driven those the floor below farther down. By the time Za and Mai reached that far, it was all they could do to sit down on the steps and gasp.

"Won't -- do much damage to the tower," Za said. Inash

had been saying something about it. "Mostly magic. Die out now. We -- no time, no time. Mai?"

"Yes," she said and stood. "Need to clean up. Maybe grab some food. We have a long way to go back."

Za nodded and held the box tightly to his chest. He had not looked inside. Now he lifted the lid only enough to see a soft green glow and nodded with relief.

They got him down to the kitchen somehow. He hadn't been aware of much except for Mai's steady hand on his arm, someone else making certain he didn't fall. The table, ancient and scared, smelled of onions. Cobia helped the cook.

"You did find it," she said with relief and even delight. "Well done, Sina!"

"Yes," Za said. He had felt too weak to even talk for a few moments there since the magic and the battle had taken everything from him. He wanted desperately to rest. He supposed he would do so on the dragon, which was good enough at this point. "Without your help, Sina, we would not have found it at all. I fear we must go now, though. No time -- so many lives depend on us getting this back. I'm sorry."

"Will you come back?" Cobia asked with a tilt of her head.

"I hope to someday," Za replied. "I would like to learn more about you, to maybe see if I can help grandfather. I think the longer he's away from the shadows, though, the better he will be."

"And if he isn't, you should rule. You are the heir. The lands need someone strong to get us out of this mess."

"I will not rule here, Cobia," he said. He stood and reached into his pack. "Besides, the people here don't need me."

She didn't realize what he was doing until he had placed the crown on her head. Cobia reached to take it off in haste, her face pale. He caught her arm and then trapped her hands in his own.

"They need you, Queen Cobia. They need you far more than an heir who has never been here before today. You understand this place. I'd spend half of my life trying to make it eastern."

"You will rule there instead?" she said with a frown. "We are not what you want to be?"

"I can't rule there," he said and let go of her. He ran a hand through his hair, reminding her of that break with his eastern grandfather. "I don't understand what either of them really expected, you know. I can't be part of their myths and legends -- such things should pass with them as we move on to a new age. But I was mostly raised eastern, and that's what I understand."

Her hand touched the crown. "I don't think they'll accept --"

"I think they will," Sina answered. Surprisingly, General Inash gave a quick nod of agreement and looked thoughtful.

"I will leave her in your care, General," Za said. He saw the man give a nod of understanding. If Inash meant her any harm, Za would be the one he would have to deal with later. Inash had seen enough of what he could do to take that threat seriously.

"Clean up a little," Mai said and put a wet cloth into his hands. "Then let us go deal with the damned dragons. Then we'll be back to the snow, and another long cold hike -- and then the real war. Sina, do you have anything in your books about demons?"

"Ah!" Za said with shock. "That's something I hadn't considered. Do you have anything on the *Art of Ata*, for that matter?"

Sina, who had been witness to the unusual crowing of her new queen, still looked a little shocked but happy. Za saw the way her eyes narrowed, and he imagined that she knew everything in her library. The quick nod gave him some hope.

"A book on the demon wars, Prince Zaron," she said. "Very old and long. You won't have time to read it --"

"Box it up for him," Cobia said.

Sina looked surprised by the order and gave a reluctant nod.

"I will return it to you as soon as I can," Za promised.

"An old book is the least we owe you," Sina admitted and hurried away.

Cobia looked them over and sent one of the servants rushing away to find some clean clothes and good coats. They were, Za could tell, used to obeying her already, though the sight of the crown on her head drew looks of surprise. No anger. Inash would watch over her -- he could see that truth in the man's eyes. He had served the Wolf loyally; it was time he could serve someone who was more than a fading legend.

Za realized that he had changed the world. He supposed it was only right, given that he had been born to do so, though not in this way. He could no longer be the heir to the Wolf and the Tiger. The two empires would not be held together in his hands. Having been to both courts, he knew now that they never should have pretended that they could be melded into one. He hoped that they could be neighbors without wars, though.

Still, it was up to him to save them both. He found that amusing in an odd way.

He and Mai cleaned up, ate a little, and then headed out to deal with the dragon. He had wanted to go straight to the creature, but the others had been right in some ways. He had needed a few moments of calm, so he didn't make any mistakes. And besides, once the dragon had the egg, he might not have waited even a few minutes to come out.

Za and Mai crossed straight to the dragon while the others held back. He had wanted Mai to stay back, too, but he knew better than arguing with her. The dragon lifted his head.

His eyes blinked several times. Za had the feeling that he'd been sleeping like a cat curled up in the sunlight. When Za put the wooden box on the ground, the dragon looked at it curiously.

"I bring you this to fulfill the promise," Za said. He bent, managing not to moan at the pain of bruises and abused muscles. He took the lid from the box and set it aside.

Green light filled the area. The dragon stood and then sat again with a visible sign of surprise.

"I felt --" he mumbled and stopped to take a deep breath. "I felt, but I didn't dare to hope, not after so long. You are a wonder, little human."

"Thank you." He had trouble getting back to his feet. "We must go, friend dragon. We don't have much time."

"Yes." The dragon reached into the box and drew out the egg, holding it carefully between sharp claws and looking into the depths. "Welcome back little one. We go now to where you will be safe."

The dragon reached towards his chest and pulled open an area covered in scales but that clearly formed a pouch. He -- or was it she? -- carefully nestled the egg there.

"Can you fly out of here?" Mai asked looking up at the tall walls.

"I'll climb," the dragon replied. "I think you should go out the gate and meet me outside."

Za thought that sounded like a wise idea. He was glad the dragon was as anxious to leave as he and Mai. However, when he looked back at Cobia, he saw that she had taken off the crown and held it, uncertainly, in her hands again.

He walked over and took it from her. She gave a sigh of relief, wise woman.

Then he put it back on her head.

"This is your place. It is not mine. You will do well."

"I never thought to be Queen," she said. "I am only a

servant, you know."

"Oh, more than that," Sina insisted and won a startled look from Cobia. "We all come to you for information, Cobia -- Queen Cobia. We have for years. Inash might have kept control of the army, but even the Lords, when they come to deal with the Wolf, turn to you instead. You have been his voice for half a decade or more. I wrote so in the annals years ago. It is true."

Mai was the one who smiled brightly. Za wondered, suddenly, what his self-proclaimed guard saw for the future of the prince she was following all over the world. He didn't ask. She might ask him the same question, and now he had no idea what his future might be.

The dragon began to climb the wall. Pieces of rock broke away, but no one stood in the area except for the five of them, and they headed for the gate.

"What do I do if the shadows come back?" Cobia asked.

"I don't believe they will," Za said but realized those words held little comfort. "I'll try to contact you after this mess is cleared up. If you can't reach me --" He did not say that if he was dead "-- then find a practitioner of the *Art of Ata*."

"Ardeth?" Mai asked.

He laughed. It was unexpected. "You haven't spent much time with him of late, Mai. He swears that if he can find a river wide enough to float a raft, he's taking it to the sea and never stepping on the mainland again."

"You know, he might actually be wiser than the rest of us."

Cobia, Sina, and even General Inash seemed to take the discussion well. Za thought they might realize that the world had changed for them. It gave him some hope, to see them accepting that change was possible.

He liked the village below the castle. Za had not seen

much of it on the way in, and he was surprised by the brightly colored trim and doors on the buildings. People mostly cowered at the edges of the buildings because of the dragon climbing out of the courtyard and down to what appeared to be a recently ruined building, though it had to have happened before they arrived since plants were already starting to grow through the fallen stones.

It felt odd, though. "What happened to the building?"

"The temple of Aisa," Sina said with a frown. "It fell unexpectedly, and the priestess died. They call the Goddess Aia in the east."

"Hope," he said and felt a chill. "The temple to the goddess has fallen."

Mai frowned but the others didn't seem to take note of his words. He had something new to worry about, though, as he climbed atop the dragon and sailed away.

CHAPTER THIRTY-SEVEN

The dragon lifted ponderously into the air, wings flapping frantically -- but we gained height and headed back towards the distant wintry peak. I found myself not thinking about riding on a flying dragon this time. I told myself that we had plenty of time to get back and that the dragons would not have acted ahead of time. I need not worry about Tansa and the others.

But I did worry.

However, there was a different matter playing most often in my mind.

The temples to the goddess of hope were falling.

Za had been upset by the news, though there had been no time to discuss the situation. I knew we'd seen another fallen building at The Court of the Tiger. Two fallen buildings might not be linked. Za had only jumped to a conclusion --

Or seen one that was clear to him in ways that I could not see. He'd done that before which made me worry as much about the Goddess of Hope as I did about the people we had left behind. Za had said his sister's body had been thrown into a vortex to hell -- his sister who was named after the Goddess of Hope and raised, I knew, to believe she was the Goddess incarnate. Not long afterward, we'd found ourselves caught in that fog that spread hopelessness everywhere.

There could not be a connection. And yet -- and yet --

The thought worried me.

The dragon had rested all day, and he did not stop to make camp that night. The clouds lay scattered across a diamond-filled sky and the crescent moon cast enough light to show the snow-covered edges of jagged ravines lost in shadows. The solid line of trees soon gave way to more stunted and erratic stands of pines. Wind-scoured rock reflected the feeble light, and more than once I saw mountain sheep and larger animals rise from their resting spots and race for better cover. I wasn't sure if they recognized the dragon for what it was or if they wisely fled from anything that large sailing over them.

We kept going.

I finally slept for a while which showed the total change in my life from the time when I first started on this insane journey. I felt relaxed and safe as we sailed through the air. In fact, I suspected I would not feel this well again for a long time.

I awoke in the bright light of morning as the dragon turned and began to glide down toward the snow-packed pass where we had left the others.

What I saw startled me.

The dragons had made a circle around the soldiers, their solid bodies blocking the bitter wind and snow so that it piled up outside the circle, while inside the soldiers had made a crowded but comfortable camp. As we drew closer, the other dragons lifted their heads and the one we rode let out a yell that was pure joy -- though unsettling when it rumbled through the long neck we sat upon.

We came down with a long plume of snow flying up around us so that we could barely see, even after we'd climbed down. I caught hold of Za, half afraid I would lose him in the snow. We started toward the camp which was easy to locate from the shouts. They did not sound unhappy.

Tansa found us first and wrapped me in an embrace so tight I could hardly breathe. I did not pull away, but I didn't let go of Za, either, with one hand still clinging tightly to his cloak. He looked amused. Ardeth arrived, though, and I let Za go with him. Our pirate looked better for having had a few days of rest.

We went straight to the middle of the camp where they'd set up makeshift tables of limbs and flat stones. I suspected the dragons must have helped to move the stones.

"Yes, they've been a lot of help," Tansa agreed as she handed me a cup of warmed cider, watered down but still sweet. "They even did a lot of hunting so that we have not wanted for food. The rest did us good, too. Now tell us what happened with the two of you."

We filled them in, holding back nothing about our adventure to The Court of the Wolf. Tansa's hand caught my arm again when we talked about the giant spider, but the fact we'd survived it made the tale less troubling than I expected. I did expect the spider to spend some time in my nightmares, no doubt displacing the dragons that had stayed with me since childhood.

The dragons declared that we would spend two more full days in camp preparing for our hike down the far side of the mountain. No one even considered arguing with them. Despite having slept on the journey to the camp, I still felt exhausted. I found it amusing that the people we worried about so much up here in the high mountains had done better than the two of us.

"He just handed over the Wolf crown?" Tansa whispered as we were preparing to sleep. She looked bothered. I didn't know why, though.

"Yes, of course. You saw how easily Za cut off his hair,

Tansa," I said and settled down on the doubled blankets we would share. Za was already asleep at the far side of the tent. I was between him and the exit. Ardeth had rolled up in as many blankets as he could get, and the two books sat in a pile between them. "Did you really expect him to want to rule the Western Lands?"

"No," she agreed. We both slid down into the blankets and moved closer together. I held her in my arms and curled around her warmer body. "But Mai, what is he going to do after we're done? I want him to have something left."

I hadn't considered anything that far in the future, but the words sent a little chill through me. Tansa hadn't said so, but I knew what she thought. Za was settling everything he could as though he were a dying man.

No. I would not allow it.

Za and Ardeth spent the next two days huddled around the books. They were pleased with what they found, but I thought that might be because they were both scholars and what they found might not have anything to do with the trouble at hand. Yes, it did amuse me.

We still had no idea of precisely what we'd do when we finally got down the mountain. Kintansa felt that by now the eastern army was well on the move and might be two-thirds of the distance to Willoway. If we were going to be of any use, we'd have to get close without being noticed. We still hoped that Queen Taranis wouldn't expect anyone to come through the mountains at her back.

We had to move carefully.

The dragons stayed with us the first day as we began the long climb down. They swept over the skies and filled the air with shouts that were clear signs of joy, though they startled humans and the pack animals.

Then, as we reached the edge of the thicker forest, two dragons stood waiting. Before them were piles of dragon scales, glittering in the light and set with handles so that they could be held.

Shields.

"A small gift," one of the dragons said. "May they serve you well."

The dragons took back to the sky. I suspected I would never see them again.

And I regretted it.

The shields were wonderfully light, but so hard that arrows could not pass through them, swords blunted when they hit, and rocks shattered. I had never liked the idea of going into battle, and even these wondrous shields could not make me feel better about it, but they did give me hope.

Za came up with an idea for using the shields that Kintansa and Ebru liked. The soldiers were directed to form up in what we called *The Dragon Formation* so that the shields were held at different angles, depending on where in the group you stood. It would be difficult for an enemy to get through the lines.

Going down the mountain, even with an occasional climb upward again, had gone far faster than the climb on this side. The hills on the southern flank were far less rigid, with streams to follow, and open areas where we could camp. Rain fell too often, but that was still better than the cold snow and ice.

As we drew closer to the lowlands, though, we chanced being spotted, no matter how carefully we moved. The army camped in small groups when they could, spread out over a mile or more -- bad if we were found, but the scouts had seen no sign of an army in this area. At worst, we would draw the attention of some of the hill people, and they were notorious for *not* reporting odd things.

The scouts we sent out in the area reported nothing out of the ordinary. We had other scouts heading for the lowlands, and they'd still be gone for a few days. We needed to know the positions of the two armies. Had the Tiger brought his army at all? Za was the first one to say that doubt aloud, though I suspected anyone who had come this far had considered that possibility.

"There is another possibility we haven't mentioned," Kintansa added. "The Queen and her demons may have moved on to somewhere else."

"Where would they go?" Ardeth asked with a frown.

"Probably Eastward," I said. "Toward the richer lands. She wants power, and the west is in disarray. Maybe that would make it easier for her to take over there, though."

"She despised the west," Za said. "The court was Eastern in appearance for a reason, you know. The only reason she would go west would be to lay waste to it. I should have told Cobia and the others to leave the castle and find somewhere safer."

"They'll do what they need to," I said. "If they see her heading their way, they'll decide what is best. You have to trust her to be wise."

Za nodded, but he must have worried. I almost told him that he'd given up the rule, it was no longer his problem -- but then that would make none of this his problem, wouldn't it? No, not anything I wanted to say to him.

"We'll know in the next three days if she's still in Willoway," Ebru said as we looked over the map again. We're getting closer to villages. We might need to find a camp for the mass of the soldiers until we see what is going on."

Kintansa agreed with a quick nod. "It's time Mai, and I went and checked things out. The two of us know the area best. Can we trust the rest of you to stay here and stay calm?"

She looked at Za. Ardeth found that amusing. I was glad to see him doing better in many ways, but his sense of humor was going to get him in trouble one of these days. Besides, he was not a soldier, which made him a problem if we were going into war.

Za wasn't a soldier either, but the two of them did have that odd *Art of Ata* and the abilities that went with that arcane knowledge. I had the feeling that Ardeth was not a problem I needed to worry about in this mess.

I hadn't realized Tansa intended to go right at this very moment, but it made sense. Late afternoon was a time to see people passing through an area on their way to somewhere else. We knew the main road stood no more than five miles ahead and past the thick trees where the others decided to camp.

I had almost insisted that Kintansa remain with the troops. That was her place now, not wandering around the countryside looking for things I could find as quickly on my own. Then I saw that look on her face, and I realized that she needed to get away from the others.

I hadn't thought much about it until now, but these were all regular army people, and she was a mercenary. I didn't think they had treated her poorly, but I had the impression that they just didn't want to listen to her. She had been giving suggestions to Ebru who in turn gave orders. That made sense, but it must have been awkward.

We'd left our winter clothing behind, and neither of us carried a dragon shield when we left the others. The clothing we had now was simple and though well-made, should not draw too much attention. I missed my backpack and swords, though. I rarely thought about the jewels we'd lost to the *Vagabond* when the pirates took us -- but I'd had those twin swords made specifically for me.

We were back in the land we knew, though, and that was going to count more for her. And me. Both of us had been to the villages in this area long before the trouble in Willoway, though we hadn't said who or what we were at the time. We'd always been secretive. That helped us now.

What also helped were the refugees.

"I would have thought they'd have moved on to somewhere else by now," I said as we neared the first rows of ramshackle huts thrown together from cloth and limbs. They were outside the village proper, strung out along the main road for more than a mile. The entire area smelled of humans and animals, and the few people we saw stayed in the shadows and watched as though we had come to steal what little they had left in the world.

"A lot of people probably headed east," Tansa said softly. She walked with her hand on her belt knife. I did the same and wished we had the troops with us after all. "But you know how most of the city people dislike and distrust the grasslanders."

"True. And they think everyone to the west is a barbarian. I don't suppose they had anywhere else to go."

"I wish we could turn around and walk out," Tansa admitted. She bowed her head and kept moving. "We won't learn much from here, except that the city must still be in bad shape for them to be out here."

"True."

We walked on, though. The path became muddy and so treacherous that it forced us to go the right or left side of the road, and far too close to people who probably thought our cloaks looked worth killings us for -- and never mind anything else we carried.

"Go on to the next village?" I asked as we neared the edge of the village proper. This one was barricaded against the refugees, and there was no way we were going to get inside without being tricky. I didn't think that would help since strangers inside were not going to be trusted.

"I don't know," Tansa admitted. "Whatever we do, we better get off this road. Right or left?"

I glanced one way and the other. Huts, snarling people, wailing children -- they looked the same on both sides.

Darkness started to mute the world in grays, though, and that would help us. We knew how to use the dark.

"Right," I said. "Looks like the trees are closer there."

We both turned, neither of us breaking stride, and we moved as though the right was where we'd always intended to go. Our steady steps took us past the first two huts without any trouble, but at the third, a tall man stood with a long limb raised and ready to batter us both. He snarled something that might have been words, but I couldn't make it out.

"No harm, friend," Tansa said. "We'll not trespass on your area."

We would have backed off, too, if another three hadn't moved in behind us. I sighed with frustration more than fear. Two to one odds were not going to be much trouble, but neither of us really wanted to fight these people, and any trouble was bound to bring more of the refugees. I also didn't want to drop my cloak in the muck, but the others were moving in and unless we did something quickly --

Tansa tilted her head to the left slightly -- a subtle move, but I knew what it meant. She'd found a spot where we could slip aside, and I was more than willing to do so if we could get out of this fight. I wasn't sure if they were going to follow us or not. Maybe we were just in their territory and only need worry about other such locations and other people --

Why couldn't anything be simple?

Tansa and I both moved at the same time. I had to duck low to avoid the limb. I think it hit one of his confederates instead from the dull whoop of noise and the sound of a falling body. Well, that was one down.

Tansa had gone left between two makeshift huts, then right and the left again. The others followed, but the moment she found a dark crevice, we dropped down on our heels and drew our cloaks tight over our heads. Two of the men rushed by. We waited, but the third -- and fourth -- did not show up.

We could hear a few shouts, but the noises died quickly, and soon the men moved back past us again.

"Strangers," one of them snarled and glanced our way, but didn't see us. "Strangers mean trouble, Gan."

"Well, trouble for them," Gan answered. "They won't trick us."

A grumbled agreement and they moved on.

We waited until they were well away and finally crept back out and moved quietly from the area where we'd had the trouble. We avoided any area where we could hear others, heading closer to those trees --

A hand caught my arm. I hissed a warning to Tansa and drew my knife with my left hand, ready to attack. The woman had let go of me though, and stepped back, both hands raised.

"No, Mai," the stranger said. "This way. Quickly."

Not a stranger -- Elmas, whom we had last seen leaving the city with the rest of the mercenaries. I felt my first surge of hope and saw Tansa's smile flash in the darkness. We followed Elmas, back along a line between huts. She signaled us to be silent and still a few times, and then we moved on. She took us to a hut along the western edge of the makeshift settlement, and a little bit aside, though not so much that it would draw attention. We went through the cloth covered door that she held open and found the small area inside warm, if not comfortable. There were also others there.

Once the door fell back into place, one of them uncovered a candle that hardly shed any light, though my eyes quickly became adjusted. I had automatically moved to protect Tansa who had followed me in, but she wouldn't need that here. Elmas sat down on the ground with Sirma, Kisi, and Tigis.

"You've been a long time getting here," Kisi said with enough of a snarl that I knew it was a complaint. "Some of us assumed you were dead, commander."

"And some of us didn't," Elmas added. "But we had wondered where you'd gone. We could find no sign of you in the city."

"We went east," Tansa explained. She gave one hard look to Kisi before he started talking. "Through the forest, through the grasslands, to the coast. We took a ship north to the Court of the Tiger -- well, after being slowed by pirates and a trip to their island."

"You've skipped the part about the Shadows," I said. Even Kisi was starting to look intrigued now. "At least our first encounter with them."

"As trouble went, that was nothing," Tansa said, and I had to nod agreement. "We went to the Court of the Tiger, and he listened to what we said --"

"He. The Tiger himself," Sirma said.

"Yes. And his general, Gedquin. An army is coming from the east. I suspect they are most of the way here by now, so we need to prepare for that battle. Oh yes, we dealt with assassins at the court, and lost Danisin there, too. We need information. Mai and I came over the mountains with two thousand more troops, with the hope that we can surprise the Queen and her unnatural allies."

"Huh," I said and took a cup of tea from Elmas. "You didn't even talk about the dragons and the trip Za and I took to the Court of the Wolf, flying on dragons and fighting a giant spider to save a dragon egg."

They were silent for a moment.

"Well," Elmas said. "Then the prince is still alive? Good."

"We need information about what's going on," Tansa admitted. She shipped her tea and seemed to relax a little. "What about the rest of the Company?"

"Only sixty-three of us are still in the area," Sirma said. "We dared not gather together for fear that we'd be caught all at once. A few people have been taken by the Queen's men, and they don't come back. We've tried to find out where they go, but she apparently has them taken to the castle, and it's the one area of the city we just can't get inside. The others are spread out in the other camps. I don't know how many survived, Commander. I know some of them headed west, and maybe a few even went east."

"I wish them luck and peace," Tansa said. That was the traditional farewell to anyone who left the Company of their own accord. "What can you tell me?"

"I can tell you how to get into the city and see for yourself," Kisi said. "And I think that's best. We haven't been inside for at least twenty days, and it looked bad then."

"We'll go in," Tansa agreed. "Tomorrow night? Good. Elmas, can you come back with us to the troops. Kisi, where do we meet?"

CHAPTER THIRTY-EIGHT

Za had expected both Mai and Tansa to argue when he announced that both he and Ardeth were going into the city with them. Tansa had frowned. Mai, though, gave a surprising nod of agreement. "We know there's magical trouble going on in the city, Kintansa. These two not only give us a better chance of surviving, but they also have a chance of understanding what we're seeing."

"True," Tansa agreed. She turned to Lt. Ebru and gave a grim nod. "We won't be more than four days. Elmas will stay with you; she is an excellent scout and knows the area. You should have word on the main part of the army before we get back."

"In fact, if we get lucky, the Queen and her people will learn about them about the same time," Tansa added. "That might give us a better chance of learning what to expect."

No one argued.

They met Kisi and Sirma in the woods just west of the city. Za had studied what he could of the place as they neared, and the one thing that he noticed was the quiet. He'd spent almost all his life in that city, and as they drew closer, he knew that it was all but empty.

Vultures sat on some of the walls.

Sirma looked where he did and gave a grim nod. "Many people died after the first attacks by the demons," he said softly. "They just lost the ability to survive. The first fifteen days were the worst, but even the Queen realized this was not how she wanted to live. I'm not sure what she and her unholy allies did, but most of the dead disappeared, and the vultures took care of the rest."

"Most of the people still inside have a direct tie to the palace," Kisi added with a slight snarl in Za's direction. "I suspect they either fear to attempt an escape or else she has some hold on them."

"And they are up by the palace I suppose," Za said and looked toward the slightly higher ground. Summer Clouds Palace did not stand high over the city as The Court of the Tiger and the Court of the Wolf had done, but he could see the tips of four towers.

"Some guards patrol the city," Kisi added. "If they catch anyone, they are taken to the palace, and they do not come back out."

Za nodded. Ardeth, he noticed, frowned more than usual.

"What's wrong?" Za asked as they moved closer to the wall surrounding the city.

"Other than everything, and I should never have left the high seas?" Ardeth asked. "Can you feel the tingle of dark magic?"

"A bit," Za replied and stood still for a moment. "I didn't feel it before when I was here. I don't know if that means there is more now or if it had just been so much a part of my life before that I didn't notice it until I left."

"Could be. You have a good link to the *Art of Ata.* I would suspect, because of that ability, that the darkness is stronger now."

Kisi snarled again, but he still said nothing. Ardeth had taken note of the man's attitude, and Za realized that Ardeth always made certain he stood within reach of the man. Za said nothing, though he suspected the protection was not needed. Kisi had only been pushed too far in this unnatural battle.

Kisi, despite how he might feel, led the way into a stand of bushes that grew around boulders. They were well off the road but still within view of the city walls. One of the gates would be to the left, but there had been no sign of guards even there.

The Queen probably didn't worry much about people breaking into Willoway. Anyone in the area already knew it had become a cursed place. Za supposed that daring thieves probably raided the buildings within, and some must pay a high price for it if they were caught and taken to the Queen.

There Za touched on the worst of the problems and one that he dared not say to the others. The real answers they needed could only be found in Summer Clouds Palace, and he did not want to take the others in there with him.

"We saw someone slipping out this way," Kisi said. "Pure chance --"

"Unless you believe in the gods," Sirma added.

From the way, Kisi snorted, Za suspected they must have had that conversation the two held in the past. They wisely did not continue it now. Instead, Kisi led the way to the bushes and pulled aside a clever covering woven of dead weeds.

Za slid down between the rocks, following Mai who followed Kisi. Ardeth came after him, then Sirma and finally Kintansa. The narrow opening led into a larger area, and before long they could all stand. Kisi had lit a candle. The walls were stone-lined, but the stones were not worked.

"Thieves' Path," Ardeth said. "You'll find them in most cities. This was part of an old stream bed that was closed off when the walls were built, but the depression remained. People built over it. Someone got ambitious."

"We thought it must be some sort of smuggling route,"

Sirma agreed. Kisi just frowned, but then that's all he'd done so far. "It doesn't go far."

"It wouldn't have to," Ardeth said. He seemed happier about finding something he understood. "Besides, you wouldn't want something like this winding through town and apt to give way if too many people crossed over the top. This is nothing more than a door in and out again."

They only went a few yards before the tunnel ended in a ladder. From there they pushed open a secret door in a floor and climbed up into a small hovel of a building that must have been a good cover for smuggling goods out.

"We thought about leaving someone here to keep watch," Kisi said softly. He and Mai had checked the flimsy door and looked outside. Rats moved nearby, but nothing else. "But it just seemed unwise to put anyone in such a line of danger."

"True," Kintansa agreed. Kisi took that better. Maybe his frowns came as much from having been in charge and not sure she would approve.

"Have you heard anything about the temples?" Za asked.

Mai gave him a worried look. They had not talked about it since they left the Court of the Wolf, but he worried that he'd found a link he didn't like at all.

"There was a quake," Kisi said. "One of the temples collapsed --"

"Aia," Za said before Kisi could though he did nod. "Damn."

"This is supposed to mean something?" Kisi asked with another frown.

Mai turned toward Kisi, and it was apparent that she didn't appreciate the man's attitude.

"We've seen several of the Temples of Aia collapsed, Kisi," she said, but kept her voice soft. "Yes, it does mean something, especially since the other temples close by are not damaged. It has something to do with the vision you had from the Wise Woman, doesn't it, Za?"

"I think so. I wish I knew more. All I saw was the Princess Aia killed and her head thrown into the vortex to hell. Maybe what I took as a sign that my sister had died was actually something symbolic for the death of the goddess."

"You think the Goddess of Hope has died," Sirma replied softly. "Or if not dead, at least banished from her place of power. There has been a lot of despair lately. I would think it all natural, but maybe there is more to it."

"Maybe," Za agreed. "That, I think, is not the battle we need to worry about now, though."

"However, we do need to move closer to the palace," Kintansa said. "Let's go before it gets any darker."

No one argued though Za didn't want to go out into those streets. Mai and Kintansa led the way this time. Sirma and Kisi came last, with Za and Ardeth in the middle. Ardeth made certain that Kisi was at his back and not behind Za. The mercenary would notice the mistrust soon, but he had brought it on himself.

The alleys curved and turned, the buildings packed so tightly that they could not see more than a yard or two in any direction. Za sensed no life nearby except for mice and rats, an occasional cat or dog. The places were terrible, and Za hoped most of the people from this area had escaped out of the city and found somewhere better.

After several turns, and a few times where they had to crawl, they came finally to a better area of town, but found it empty as well. These buildings would draw thieves, though any jewels and coins would have gone with the owners. No doubt plenty had been left to grab, if even thieves hadn't run, half-mad, out of the city.

"We need to get closer to the castle," Za said and gave the others a look of apology. "That's where the power lies. I can feel the essence of it still."

Ardeth nodded. He looked no happier about going there than Za. Ardeth must have also felt that odd sting growing stronger, the taint of dark magic obvious in the air.

They skulked carefully through the city, and Kisi had stopped snarling so much. He was a professional, and he kept his attention on the world around them now that they were truly in danger. They avoided people twice thanks to him. Za had not noticed them, the feel of something *wrong* having overtaken his thoughts. Ardeth kept a hand on Za's arm, and Mai looked worried, but they kept moving closer toward the palace grounds that had once been the crowning jewel of a beautiful city.

They reached the processional road that led to the inner gate and took cover in the shadows there before inching their way closer to the high walls around Summer Cloud Palace. Za could hear people within the palace precinct, but mostly that came as the sound of soldiers marching. Once something huge and dark moved as though crawling up a tower, but it disappeared. If the others hadn't made sounds of dismay, he might have believed the sight had been his own imagination and nothing more.

Za had thought to get a little closer, but he pulled back from stepping down on the rock-laid road and shook his head, waving the others frantically away. They went silently into a crevice between buildings. There seemed to be no one around in this area at all.

"A trap? To warn the others of anyone coming near?" Kisi asked and even sounded reasonable.

"Worse, I think." Za picked up a stone and tossed it out a few feet from the edge. Nothing happened. He found a slightly larger rock that had fallen from a wall and rolled it out --

The road curved suddenly downward into a black abyss. The stones disappeared -- and then it snapped closed again and look normal once more

They retreated into the darker shadows as guards appeared on the wall -- so they had a link to the magic and knew what happened, but they clearly saw no one and left again. Probably rats set it off often enough that they were used to giving it a cursory glance and nothing more.

Za signaled the others to keep moving to the back of the building where they found a door, still partially open, probably from when the owners had left in haste. They moved silently through the building which must have been a shop and found places against the wall by the window where they could see anyone coming near.

Ardeth had gone pale white and shook his head without saying anything aloud. Za knew why.

"That passage led straight to a region of the hells," Za said before anyone could ask questions. Ardeth gave an emphatic nod but still appeared unable to speak. "I could sense that much and something more: *things* waited there. Hungry things. She is feeding the creatures of hell on the flesh of the living and that no doubt gives her their allegiance, at least to some degree."

"You are still convinced the Queen is behind this," Kisi said with a slight frown. "Your mother."

"My mother," he said in agreement. "And until I find out differently, I will continue to believe she is the power here."

"Not your sisters," Kintansa said and sounded startled by the idea. "I realize that you never say your sisters are the problem."

"Oh, they are part of the trouble," he replied with an emphatic nod. Soldiers moved on the walls across from them and disappeared again while everyone went still. "However, the Queen was always the one in charge."

Even Kisi nodded agreement at that one. They rested a while longer and then moved on to look at other areas. Ardeth kept quiet and looked both pale and unsteady at times, but from the way he stared back at the palace whenever it came in sight, Za could tell that he was starting to understand the situation, perhaps even better than Za. The Prince had grown up inside those walls and had always assumed what happened there was normal. Not only that, he had come to realize how immune he was to the darker feel of the place.

How had he kept himself from falling into that vat of evil?

Endris. The *Art of Ata.* Master Drital's excellent instruction that had, for years, drilled into him the need for intense observation of everything around him until that ability became natural to him. One could not observe properly if one let an emotional curtain hang between his eyes and the world. Even in battle, the need for calm observation gave him an edge.

Ardeth didn't have the same level of calm, but he did have the ability to see things that Za had accepted as normal to the world. How could he be so good at observation, and still not truly understand what he saw?

They had a long day, working their way through different areas of the city, circling the palace precinct and getting what views they could of the place. More than once an enormous shadow swept up one of the towers and disappeared. The sound of soldiers practicing at arms came loudly at different times, and they all knew the Queen prepared an army to march. Nothing, of course, had been allowed to stand taller than the walls, not so near the Summer Clouds Palace, so they had no way to climb up and see what she might have within the grounds.

"She might have as many as six thousand," Mai said as they listened again. "She couldn't fit more in there. She has gathered more than the palace guard, though. I suspect she persuaded the City Guard into her army as well."

"Whatever was left of them," Kintansa added with her own nod of agreement. "I guess she knows an army is coming

-- but which one? Did she learn about those of us coming from the north? Or has she learned that the Tiger is marching from the east?"

"Let us assume that the plan is still working," Mai replied as they sat upon a roof crowded behind a row of tall, ceramic plant containers, everything dead or gone wild. Everyone appeared to be calmer, even though they had found more of the road traps on every street leading to the palace. "Let's also consider where we can place our own troops to surprise them."

"With an army that size, I think they'll take the main road," Kisi said. " We don't know where anyone else in this drama is placed. And we don't know when the Queen's army is going to march."

"Soon," Za said. "Very soon, because she could not keep a group that large for long. Today."

Ardeth nodded agreement.

"How the hell can you tell?" Kisi asked, but it wasn't an attack this time. He was genuinely startled by the words.

"Wagons," Ardeth said, and Za nodded agreement. "You can hear them being loaded and even the animals being hitched into place. Oxen, not horses."

"Too much dark magic," Za said. "Horses can sense it better than oxen and react to what they feel. Yes, they are preparing to leave. This is good for us. We will have a chance to see how many there are and maybe even get an idea of where they go --"

"Listen!" Ardeth hissed.

Za heard the cry go up, a scream of despair. Mai grabbed Kintansa and shoved her back. Kintansa covered her ears in haste.

"Demons!" Mai warned. "Don't listen! Cover your ears!"

Kisi looked around with fear and despair, but Ardeth grabbed him, but a hand to the man's forehead, and he dropped to his knees and bowed his head. What Ardeth had done with magic put him down as well.

That left only Sirma, but he huddled by Kintansa and Mai, and Mai had grabbed him and shoved the man's hands against his ears. Then she finally did the same for herself. Za moved so that he could keep them all in sight and react if any of them moved. He listened, pulling all his *Art of Ata* abilities to hold him in place. He needed to understand the enemy.

He watched the palace. They were not aligned with the gate, but he could see where they would come out, though he hid at an angle and had a chance of not being spotted.

Things moved. Za could see the shadows change and he could hear the demons growing louder. The cry was one of such anguish that for a heartbeat, even he had the urge to move to the edge of the building and fling himself over to the ground far below.

He held himself rigid and watched.

And listened. The sounds the two demons made -- only two now since Za had killed one -- were not what he expected. The sound overlapped, braided, cried -- but not an attack.

Sorrow, sorrow, sorrow...

He could barely watch as they moved into sight, the demons with the two princesses upon their backs. Behind them marched other creatures, the likes of which he'd never seen -- tall, slender, and red-hued as though they were living fire. They had too many arms, and a head so small that he wasn't sure if they had faces. He watched them, a hundred following the demons. By then the demons and their riders had gone on, out of sight and the sound lessened. The soldiers followed, the marching perfect. Everything moved in order -- soldiers, more of the red creatures, soldiers, more of the red creatures. Slowly the army passed.

Mai finally climbed to her feet, so unsteady that he reached out and caught hold of her.

"We should have considered that might happen," Mai said.

He nodded, not yet ready to speak. He looked to Ardeth, but he wasn't certain even he had an idea of what had really happened. They stood there for a while, but Za knew he had to say what he'd realized. The soldiers were almost all gone now, past the gate.

Then the gates to hell opened. He saw the one below them and realized the others had opened as well. The feel in the air won a cry of protest from Ardeth and Za had gone down to his knees, both out of weakness and because he did not want to be seen. He had caught only a glimpse of the hungry things that surged out, all black, long, and like nothing that lived on this world.

"The rest -- the rest of her troops," he finally whispered.

Mai must have realized as well. She gave a frantic, silent nod. The army would have trouble dealing with these creatures.

But there was something more.

"Sit," Za said and knelt with them. "Sit. We must talk. I have seen something I should have realized before now."

Ardeth looked at him, still pale. They settled in a small circle, though Kisi remained on his feet, keeping the watch. Za didn't think it necessary now, but he said nothing. The guard probably made the others feel better.

"The madness that spreads before the demons is not *their* power," Za said. He shivered at what he had felt. "It is from the goddesses who are trapped atop them."

"But -- but --" Mai began. "No. Those are your sisters."

"They were, I think, at one time. Now those sisters are only shells holding the essence of the goddess they represented. The change might have come a little at a time and I didn't notice -- or, more likely, the true transfer happened only after she called the demons to her, which couldn't have been much before I escaped. The Queen prepared them for this all their lives. Mai, Kintansa -- you both spent time at the Summer Clouds Palace. You must remember how she drenched their lives in ritual."

"And when each came of age, she named them as the High Priestess of their namesake's temple," Kintansa added. "That wasn't unusual, but I remember how people thought it odd that she sent all three into temple work."

Mai still shook her head, but Za could see the truth of the situation starting to make way into her thoughts. She probably realized how it linked to the Temples of Aia, too.

"The demon didn't scream when it came at us in our headquarters," Kintansa added after a moment. "We heard them before then. Some people fled ahead of the attack, the sound driving them mad. But when it came into the building, it was silent, and the princess was not riding the demon, either."

"The headquarters used to be a temple," Mai added. "One built at the edge of town but abandoned when the city expanded. It was a temple to Aia, in fact."

"Aia, who was thrown into hell when I killed her demon," Za said and shook his head. "I can't see that I could have done anything else, but I'm also not certain it was the right action."

"You weakened them," Ardeth said. He lifted his head and looked at Za with a feverish brightness that worried Za. "You destroyed one of their power, so they removed one of the goddesses lest she give us hope and that would make us stronger. She's not dead, you know. Demons can't kill gods or goddesses, but it wouldn't be the first time they held one."

"Yes, but in the old days a hero and companions would -- " Kintansa began. "Ah."

The others understood. They were going to take the road to hell.

CHAPTER THIRTY-NINE

We went carefully back down to the ground level. I found myself thinking about the difference between serving Za's father and serving this younger prince. King Yasidin had expected the world to bow down to him and for nothing to get in his way, neither a wild boar in the woods nor an assassin in the city. He had been dangerously careless.

Prince Zaron was just dangerous.

If it had not been for him, we would not have been standing before the gate to hell.

Tansa had a surprisingly hard time convincing Sirma and Kisi to follow her orders and *not* take the journey with us. I had never seen any mercenary argue with her, let alone two at the same time.

"No, not just the four of you," Kisi said with an emphatic shake of his head. "That would be insane!"

"This is all insane!" Tansa reminded him, her voice slightly louder than it should have been. She stopped herself, gave a worried look around, and put a hand on his arm. "You have to warn Ebru about the Queen's hellish allies. We can't let the army rush on them unawares. The chances are that they'll only see the regular soldiers at first."

"Sirma can --"

"Both of you," Tansa ordered and her voice grew stern. "Both of you get to Ebru, and if there is still time, go on to the Army of the Tiger. Have Ebru supply you with the paperwork and seals of a messenger so that there is no question of letting you through. Get word to General Gedquin about the army and about where we have gone. Warn everyone to have plugs for their ears! Go. *Do this*. We don't have time. And I am still your Commander."

The last words were a test of her power. The two might have decided that Tansa had abandoned the Lightning Company. The thought did seem to play in Kisi's face, though Sirma had already bowed his head.

"Yes. We'll go," Kisi agreed. For a moment, I thought I saw another argument in his eyes, but he said nothing this time. Good. We had reached the bottom of the stairs.

"Go carefully," I warned them.

"Take our supplies," Sirma said and began to divest himself of his pack. "Don't argue. We can get food and water along the way. I seriously doubt there will be such chances for you."

Tansa agreed. We even took the majority of Sirma's medical supplies as well. They were right; we might need them and would have no other source. We parted company at the edge of the door, Sirma and Kisi heading for war ... and the rest of us heading for something worse.

"How do we even find the goddess?" Tansa asked.

"Observation," Ardeth said as he eyed the road with obvious worry. Wise man. "The basis of the *Art of Ata*. And myths."

"Maybe you ought to tell us some of that part, at least?" Tansa suggested. She didn't look ready to leap into the hellish abyss either.

"You said something of it yourself," Ardeth said. He rubbed at his hand and arm. The poison had done damage that

I didn't think would ever go away, but I could see he'd also accepted what he could not change. He kept bandages around the hand and wrist to make a brace. "You know the tales of how humans have dared the gates of the hells to rescue gods before."

"I never paid much attention to the tales," I admitted. "I didn't realize they were going to be an integral part of my training."

"Pay attention to everything," Za said, but with a laugh. "Ardeth is right, though. Not so much about the myths, though they do tell us it can be done. What I remember of them -- my father was fond of myths -- seemed to say that no two journeys were the same."

"I had forgotten that about your father," I admitted with a tilt of my head, remembering King Yasidin sitting in the garden with his son, telling him stories. That only happened at times when Yasidin couldn't do other things. He'd never spent much time with Zaron, but apparently the prince remembered those few occasions. I had never paid attention to the tales, being too worried about what might get through to kill them.

There had been the one time, though, where I was perhaps too protective and startled them both by pulling my sword and leaping into a bush where I was about to do mortal combat with ... a bunny. A small one at that, and he got away.

I smiled at the memory. The better mood helped, too.

"There is one common string that bound the stories together that I do remember," Za said. His eyes narrowed slightly. "The god, being in such a place that was foreign to their being, left a trace of their passage and had an emanation of their power that can be felt by others. They can even transform areas around them if they have the strength."

"What good does it for the demons to hold a god, then?" Tansa asked. She had her sword in hand. We were going to be moving soon.

"It is to remove the power from the human lands," Ardeth explained and looked cautiously around again. "Tying hope to a demon perverted the power. Having lost the demon, the next step was to remove *hope* entirely. The effect of her disappearance has been slowly moving across the lands where she was worshipped. As the armies meet, hope will likely disappear, probably from all the humans. It will not be a problem for those fiends and demons that the queen had let loose. They never held to hope and tend to follow far darker beings. They'll destroy everything."

"Time to go," I said. "The armies are growing closer together."

Za agreed with a single, imperious nod. I didn't like to see him so suddenly changed, but I understood the need. "I cannot tell you what to expect," Za said as he looked at us. "Be careful. I need you."

Then he turned and waved his hand. A faint light of magic spread outward across the road, and the surface disappeared. Within that portal, I saw faint, dull light. The air smelled of hot metal and stone. Nothing moved in that opening that descended at a steep angle down into the earth. This was where part of the Queen's army had ascended to our world. Za's magic had swept the cover away. I appreciated that his magic had grown stronger, but I still felt a chill at seeing him use it.

This was not where I wanted to go, but when Za moved forward, I took my place at his side. Tansa came behind me, and Ardeth walked behind Za. My mouth went dry as soon as I found myself below ground level. I even glanced back, despite myself. The opening had started to close over us. We could do nothing but go forward.

Though before we'd gone more than two hundred steps, we had to make a decision. Caverns turned off at every angle.

"Toward the castle," Za said. "The Queen had a portal

there and threw Aia in. I hope we can find a trace of her and follow it."

"We're bound to run into trouble soon," Ardeth added. "I suspect that we've only gotten this far without a problem because the area just emptied of everything that could move."

I nodded agreement. My eyes had quickly become used to the dull light, and the smell seemed no worse than that of a smithy. Some distant sounds worried me only because they indicated that we would run into trouble soon, as Ardeth predicted. There were only four of us. This was insane.

Za chose the way. I suspected he literally looked for signs of hope. I watched for trouble, and I was rewarded with seeing the stone move to the side of us as we passed.

I shoved everyone back -- making certain the other side of the cavern wasn't moving as well -- and rushed with Tansa, our weapons up. The wall melted away like syrup warmed in the sun, the covering thinning until we could see something moving on the other side.

I thought it some sort of snake at first: a huge, demonic snake. Then I saw that it had dozens of legs and a mouth full of sharp teeth. No eyes, but it sensed us either by smell or sound. Not fast, at least. I nodded to the right and Tansa agreed. I moved that way, and the head swung towards me, those damned teeth almost catching my arm. Tansa had already moved in for the attack as I spun, sword in hand, and lopped away half the head. She took the rest at the neck.

The body flopped several times, apparently looking for the severed head. For all I knew, they could reunite, so I kicked it down the cavern opposite from the direction we would go. Za gave a nod, and we moved on. The battle had been easy, but I knew that was not going to hold true for the rest of our journey. That creature had been strange, dangerous, but still an animal. There would be enemies we'd soon face who had the cunning and intelligence of humans, and probably some of them even more so.

The cavern curved and split again. Za didn't even pause, and I had to believe he knew which way to go.

The air grew fetid, though, and the walls began to warm and glow. I could feel the heat beneath my boots. None of us said anything, but we did move faster.

The cavern opened into a larger area. Shadowy creatures moved at the far side, and I hoped that we had not been spotted where we huddled at the edge of the shadows, silent and watching. Ardeth lifted his hand, frowned slightly, and then pointed to an opening on the right.

Za nodded agreement and began to move that way, though he stayed on his hands and knees, despite the heat emanating from the floor. I saw the reasoning; the natural curve of the cavern made a rise away from the walls. I thought the rise might not be natural, in fact, and that thousands of others -- not humans probably -- had walked this path and worn it down. I didn't like to think about those things wandering around here. The others didn't move fast enough, considering what might be coming up behind us.

No warning.

The ground moved. I gave a cry of surprise more than fear -- but the fear came a heartbeat later when the ground gave way beneath us.

Falling. Falling so far that I could think about what was happening, and know we couldn't survive. I tried to grab at Tansa. I thought she did the same --

Hit.

I felt the force of the blow as my body exploded in pain and I feared every bone had been broken. I feared to try and move, not so much because of the pain, but because I could not hear anything else -- no one moving, making sounds of pain ... breathing.

I didn't want to know. Dared I hope?

That thought gave me an unexpected boost of strength. I sat up, still thinking bones must be broken. The ground beneath me seemed solid stone -- well, as stable as the stone had been before we dropped. But if I had survived, the others --

I turned and looked.

They were dead.

I gave a cry of such despair that it echoed all through the area and I thought the walls turned a little redder. I don't know why I noticed. I stared at my Tansa, my beloved Tansa with her head tilted at an unnatural angle, her eyes staring back at me as though to chastise me for not lying there with her. I crawled over and took her up in my arms, but she was no longer my Tansa. There was no feel of the woman I had loved --

Something whispered nearby. Should I get up and fight it? Why? I looked at Za, whose head was tilted, his eyes staring. I'd failed him as well, and failed Endris who had put the prince in my hands.

A whisper. *Hope.*

How dare something mock me with that word! I had failed even Ardeth who laid to the right of Za, staring at me, too...

Something was not right.

I thought the ground gave way again; the world blurred, and for a moment I thought I saw Za alive again, his hand lifted, magic in his fingers. I looked away in anger and held Tansa closer, even though she felt no more than a ghost. I stared into her empty eyes and all hope disappeared, and the whispers were gone again.

Let the world fall. Let Queen Taranis win. I didn't care. Oh, Tansa would not have approved, but I didn't care, I didn't care --

Hope.

And I saw Za standing again, this time with Ardeth at his side.

Manipulation. Za and Ardeth were hope. My lovely, dead Tansa was despair. Something here in this hell wanted us to fail, and it thrived on the darker emotions -- I understood now, but it wasn't until Ardeth somehow forced his way to me and rested a hand on my shoulder that I could accept. The emotions were like a wall everywhere around us, as thick and hard as stone. I could not have broken through by myself, and when I saw him almost collapse, I reached up and grabbed his hand.

I had let go of Tansa.

She disappeared.

For a moment, that was just as bad. The loss of Tansa hit me almost as hard as her death, even though I knew -- *knew* this was not real. Something manipulated me, and if I didn't get myself back under control, I wasn't certain what it might make me do.

I grew angry, but at least I aimed that rage in the right direction. I was aware of the feel of something brushing against me like ants. Magic, and not a good kind, I realized.

"No," I said aloud. My voice sounded muffled. "No. You will not control me, you bastard!"

Tansa laughed. That was the sound that broke the spell. Tansa's laugh was magic all its own, and I could see her now, her hand in Za's as she stood. Za, though, looked pale and shaken. I pushed Ardeth his way.

"Help him. Are all of you really alright? How far did we fall --" I stopped and considered my own lack of injuries and pain. "We didn't, did we? It was all an illusion."

"All of it," Za agreed. He looked troubled. "Hold on to hope. The demons came close to destroying us with that one."

"I would have expected more physical trouble," Tansa replied. She had a hand on my arm, her fingers tight. I hadn't realized how badly the situation had affected her.

"Maybe --" Ardeth began and glanced around, his eyes narrowed. He looked more like the pirate we had first met, and for the first time since we left the Tiger's court, I thought he would survive. Well, if any of us did. "Maybe she emptied this area to fight her war. I seem to remember reading a scrap of an ancient poem about walking through the empty countries of the damned where the creatures had gone to war. I thought they were talking of the warring countries of our world. What if they were speaking of hells in truth, my friends? Then we should be less careful and more daring. We might not have much time before the void is filled."

"The only thing that has attacked us so far," I said, "seemed to me to be more akin to an animal rather than the thinking creatures we might expect to find. Like a watchdog left on duty. And the trap may have been placed for anyone who came that way."

Za looked from Ardeth to me and back again. I could see that moment when he took in all that was said and analyzed it -- he did not, at least, take much time. "Yes," he said. " Even the creatures we saw across the way seem to have been illusions. They're gone now."

I glanced at Tansa. Her face seemed too pale still, her eyes large -- and she did not look at me. I thought I saw fear in her face for the first time since I had met the pretty new plaything that came to live in Summer Clouds.

I had dismissed her as a doll, all painted and ready to entertain King Yasidin. That had changed the day she killed three assassins dressed as servants who had come to kill her. They'd been sent by the Queen, of course. We attributed their deaths to my intervention, which had not won me any points with Queen Taranis but had started a bond between the plaything and me. We were careful that neither she nor Yasidin ever realized what a dangerous changeling lived at court.

And I had a sudden, odd realization. Something that should have occurred to me long before now: on that fateful day when they took King Yasidin to be killed, I would have gone to save her rather than the prince if there had been a choice. I felt a moment of despair at that thought, as though I had, in truth, forsaken my duty for love. But no -- the gods had been kind, and I'd never had to make the choice.

I put my hand over Kintansa's, and she looked at me this time, as though startled that I could touch her. "We've made our choices," I said. I wondered what Za and Ardeth would make of those words. "I will never regret the path we took, Tansa. I don't think you do, either."

"No," she said, her voice softer than usual. I saw her take a deeper breath. Color came back to her face, and her eyes saw the world around us again. "No regrets. And we can't say things haven't been interesting."

"True," I said and even managed a little laugh.

How odd. The light brightened and the air tasted better. Za looked around with a start and then back at me and nodded with a smile of his own. "This is a land of darker emotions. Let us bring our own light to this place. I think we shall learn a great deal about the hells before we're done."

"This was not my goal in life. They don't have a sea here," Ardeth added, but he smiled and made even Za laugh at that one. His laugh was bright and true, and not a sound I had often heard at any time in his life. He had been a wisely quiet child, drawing no attention from his mother or her people.

We left the area of that dark, horrible vision behind. The walls grew wider, and I thought the trap had been placed at an area that was perhaps easier to control than the more open ones. I said so to Za.

"Well," he said, surprised. "Yes. I think you might be right. Whether specifically set for us or not, the trap caught us at that spot where we were closest together. I had not seen that truth, but it is a good one to remember. I suppose there will be other narrow areas."

"Can you still feel the goddess?" Tansa asked. "And how do we know that's not faked?"

"Not faked," Ardeth answered. "Think about what we've felt here and what we've experienced. A place like this has no natural sense of hope, and I seriously doubt they could manufacture the feeling."

I thought he might be right. I even *hoped* so. I willingly followed as we went onward.

CHAPTER FORTY

Za wished the others had not come with him. He didn't belittle the help they gave, but the fear that he'd seen them killed had started to worm into almost all his thoughts and made him dread each step forward because of what might really happen. In that way, he supposed, the trap had worked after all.

Za would not let go of the tenuous thread of hope that drew them deeper and deeper into the dark depths. They fought things, but none of the enemies were much more than annoying.

A bat swept at them through a small opening to the side, and Mai hissed in anger as it brushed against her. Za lifted a hand and quieted the others. He could hear the rustling wings. Very many --

"Find something to cover the hole!" he shouted as a dozen bats pushed through the opening. Other bats crowded in, so many that they could not push through, tangling with each other. Tansa shoved her cloak into the opening, but it would not hold for long. The best they could do was to get clear of the small area and into a space where the bats would spread out if they followed.

Oddly, Mai still had hold of the first bat, and she looked it over with a nod. "Just a regular bat. I thought so. Wonder what they're doing clear down here. And they'd be trouble enough in those numbers."

She let the bat go. Za found that amusing -- and the amusement helped, as though fresh air had swept through the little cavern and cleared away the surge of anger and despair that had grown again with each step. For a moment, he even caught the barest hint of frustration that was not his own.

"Something smart is out there, trying to slow, if not stop us," Za said. He did not try to find the enemy, though part of him wanted to face it. Better, though, to go on to the goddess. He suspected he would find the enemy there anyway.

He was right, though not in a way he had expected. They faced no other trouble, except for a few small *things* that seemed to be rushing to get away from the area. They didn't attack anything that didn't attack them and pressed on. The feel of dread grew for a moment and then died away -- an odd change.

Light ahead. He moved more quickly -- but even before Ardeth had put a hand to his shoulder, Za had slowed. The light felt unnatural to this place, but that didn't make it something good. He had to be more careful, at least for the sake of his friends.

The path twisted and turned -- narrowed over another trap they avoided by walking close to the sides of the walls, and then the passage turned and they walked into a cavern -- not a huge one, but large enough for lights to glitter in a central pillar and for Aia to stand well out of reach of them. The pillar took his attention first: dead flowers glowed at the base, along with the bones of creatures, all of them, he suspected, sacrificed to whatever power created that glow.

Aia stood close by -- and this was his sister, not the Goddess. He could not feel the sense of hope in the flesh of his sister and realized -- oh, how could they not have thought of it -- that Aia must have been creating the sense of hope that drew them on.

She'd recovered more than her head, though he could see the scar where the blade had cut it free.

"Zaron," she said with a shake of her head. "You really are far more troublesome than we anticipated."

"Thank you. I guess I am the child of my father after all. And you, of course, are the child of a demon."

"Oh yes. It took you long enough to figure that part out," Aia said. She tossed back her hair, free from the intricate weaves and braids that she wore at the castle. He thought he saw the hint of horns just above her ears. "The flesh of human and demon and the soul of a goddess."

"Only you lost the goddess, didn't you?"

Mai made a little hissing sound. She had not realized until now.

"Not lost, exactly. But we did become incompatible after you killed my demon. You will pay for that, Zaron. I had spent all my life building that link between my demon half-brother so that we could fully trap the goddess. You have driven me here to keep Hope from the battle. I should have been fighting in the battle, Zaron. I should have ridden with my sisters, and you have denied me --"

Za had not come to this damned place to be lectured. He'd learned all he needed to already -- about his sisters, about their powers, and about the goddess. With a lift of his arm, he called the Sword of Glory into his hand. He had feared it might not come, here in the depths of this hell. It was not a weapon of this realm, but neither did it belong to the world where he had been born.

Aia backed up and hissed in anger and surprise. She had not taken him very seriously, he realized. As he stepped towards her, he saw that her body began to shift and change.

She became more akin to her demon half-brother, though

a smaller version. That only made the battle easier. Za didn't think that facing his sister in battle would have been difficult; they had never been close, and the revelations here had clarified a lot of the earlier problems. The truth was that her change only made Aia think herself more powerful, and in that she became careless.

One clawed arm swept at Za, and he blocked it with little trouble. Her elongated face snapped at him as she snarled, and he slashed the Sword of Glory across her cheek before he leapt back from more claws.

She howled in anger and pain. The walls around them glowed with an unhealthy red, and the temperature rose with the power of her rage. That did prove distracting as perspiration immediately ran down his face.

She'd called in allies as well. Za left those lesser beings to the others, and they were soon involved in their own battles. He dared not look to see if they did well. He dared not take his eyes from this creature that called itself Aia. She leapt forward and a claw caught him in the arm, ripping flesh away. He spent precious magic to seal the wound, but he hardly slowed, grateful that the nail had not caught bone and snapped it.

He had *hope* still that he could win against her.

That feeling told him something more. He let her drive him backward a step, another -- and brought him close to the pillar of light. It had not been affected by her anger.

"The Goddess is here!" he said and waved to the pillar. "Ardeth, find a way --"

He didn't have time to say more. Aia leapt at him, both arms flailing, the rage tripled -- but he sensed something else beneath this attack: Aia feared to fail. She had never expected to face a battle by herself and feared what would happen if she did not stop Za and his followers. She had not wanted to be thrown into this hell, but there would be worse if she failed again.

Za did not feel sorry for her. His sword still swung true, and another cut took her across the shoulder, and the next in the chest. She cried out in anger and pulled back, and he followed, relentless in his attack. His friends depended upon him. He would not abandon those back in world that waited, hope slipping away by heartbeats, as the two armies prepared to clash.

"You -- you cannot destroy the goddess," he said as they both pulled away from their attacks, equally breathless and bleeding. "And I won't allow you to hold her. You can walk away, Aia. Here, you are just one more demon in a world of demons, as long as you do not stand before me."

She snarled. Za could see her doubt her own abilities as she stared at him. Still human enough to understand what he offered her. Za hoped she could not sense how difficult holding onto to the Sword of Glory had become, though. He was not used to wielding the weapon for any length of time the powers inherent in this realm worked against the sword.

The little break gave him a chance to glance back at his companions. The others held off the crowd of smaller creatures -- some of them quite dangerous -- at the opening through which they had arrived. A glance at the pillar gave him more strength, though. He thought the sacrifices -- animal and plant -- might be part of a binding spell of some sort. He hoped Ardeth realized as well.

Aia took advantage of his distracted moment which he had expected. She rushed at him, but he swung the sword so quickly she screamed in shock long before the weapon cut into her shoulder. He had come close to taking her head, and she knew it.

"Stop now and survive," he said.

"No! No! You will not win here, in my place --"

She launched herself at him again, clearly beyond reason. Za brought his sword up, but she suddenly threw herself to the ground and rolled with her claws flashing. They cut viciously into his legs, and he went down.

If he failed, they would not survive. He had to --

He felt a wave of strong magic behind him at the pillar. Ardeth's work, he realized, and it drew Aia's attention, her red demon eyes narrowing as she turned that way. Za had lost the sword in the shock of the attack. He feared at least one leg had been severed --

He couldn't say entirely what happened. The binding around the pillar weakened, and Za thought they would get the goddess free at least. However, Ardeth dropped down on his hands and knees and was using even more magic to help Za.

"No," Za said, though he could barely speak. "Get her free. Go --"

"We are doing what we can. Don't fight me. We need you."

Mai had taken on Aia and held her back, but she was no match for the demon. Za still would have argued, but magic swept over him and through his legs followed by a rush of pain. Ardeth had tight hold of one leg, and Za even tried to kick him to get him to let go.

Something else took his attention. Tansa still fought the creatures trying to get in, and those creatures were losing ground, backing up. Aia had turned toward them, a growl coming from her throat as she crouched, ready to spring.

"Look out!" he shouted, and the sword flickered back into his hand. Too late though. Aia leapt.

Mai swept her plain, iron sword at Aia as the creature rushed past her. It slowed the half-demon at least, and apparently, that was all they needed.

Kintansa threw herself at the pillar. He hadn't realized Ardeth had taken down the magic barrier until the woman's hands went straight into the glowing light.

For a moment everything seemed to stop.

Something changed.

Aia howled and raced out of the room, and the other things followed her. That did not make the rest of them safe. The pillar of light didn't collapse. Instead, it spread outward in a glow that burned so brightly that Za again dropped the sword and put both hands to his eyes, afraid he would go blind.

They'd won this battle. All they had to do was get out of here, get back to the surface and the army. They shouldn't have as much trouble getting away, just following the path back up.

He realized he felt hope again.

Tansa had backed away from the last sparkles of the pillar. Her hands glowed, and her face was set in concentration, but not, he thought, in pain. Ardeth stood and even pulled Za up, though he could hardly stay to his feet as pain laced up through both legs. Blood had spread everywhere, and that explained why he felt lightheaded now.

"Thank you," he said as Ardeth put an arm around his waist and helped keep him up.

Mai stood by the opening watching for the enemy, but she looked back at Tansa sometimes, fear in her face. The waves of hope in the air could not overcome her anxiety.

"We are all right," Tansa said. Her voice had a strange -- even unearthly -- echo to it. Mai stared at her without a change in expression. "Aia must leave this place. The demon-woman held me -- held her with strong magic made by others. There are demons now who would take the goddess, and then there would be no hope of escape."

"Get away," Za said. "We have to go. Mai, I need your help. Ardeth needs to be ready with whatever magic he can use."

Mai looked away from Tansa, her face bleak. She said nothing as she took over the job of holding Za to his feet.

Tansa had already moved to the doorway. It was Tansa, he realized, who carefully looked out and nodded, ready to go. Ardeth moved up beside her. Their pirate gave Tansa a worried glance but they led the way together, Tansa with her still glowing hand holding her sword.

Magic there, but not of a kind that would do battle. Not directly. They needed only to get her out of this demon world and back to their own, where she belonged.

Or did she? He knew there were realms of the gods, just like the realms of the demons. They were harder to reach, though, because the gods were so unlike the humans.

Which, he realized, meant the humans were far more like the demons than the gods. People traveled to the demon realms far too often if even half the old tales and myths were real.

A sobering thought.

He and Mai followed the other two. Mai did not have a weapon in hand. Za wanted to reassure her that Tansa would be all right, but in truth, he didn't know if she would survive sharing her body with a goddess. He could only ... hope.

Za tried not to slow them down but he had trouble moving one leg and the other and finally settled on moving the left leg and letting the right drag. Mai noticed, finally, and shifted her hold to help. He nodded thanks. He'd broken out in a sweat by the end of a few yards, though, and feared he would pass out and make even more trouble for them.

They could hear trouble coming, the scratching of claws on stone, the howls and growls of things that were not human. Za and his companions had only one direction they could go, and he hoped they reached an area with more options before the creatures reached them. They got past the trap and headed down the passage again. Ardeth and Tansa knew the way.

Unfortunately, they did not get lucky. A wave of demon creatures had blocked the passage. They backed away in haste.

No way out. He could find no way --

Mai did something odd. She had moved farther down the passage and pulled the cloak out of the hole where they'd stuffed it. She stood there, still.

"They're gone," she said. Tansa had moved closer to Mai, and the glow of her hands lit the area. "The bats are gone. They have another way out."

"Ah," Za replied. A little hope -- did that come from the goddess. No matter. He and Ardeth retreated to the area as well, Za trying to walk on his own although his right leg still wouldn't hold him. He did not curse because he feared Ardeth would take it badly, when in fact his friend had saved his life. "Can we get the opening large enough?"

"Yes," Ardeth said. "But it will take most of my energy."

"We won't leave you behind," Mai said. "We won't leave any of you."

She glanced at Tansa and away. For a moment, Tansa looked saddened, but then the Goddess seemed to retake her. The woman's head came up, and her features steadied -- oh, but maybe that was not Aia after all.

The power she used, though, was that from the goddess. She put a hand to the wall, and the rock seemed to move aside. "Go quickly," she said, a hand still to the wall.

Za did not like that she had to remain until last since the entire journey had been to get her from this hell. He could hear the demons coming closer; no time to waste as he went through into the stinking bat cave. Ardeth came with him, of course, and Mai next, but she did not go far inside. The goddess leapt in, and the wall snapped shut, but they could already hear frantic claws digging into the dirt and rock.

Za had already turned his face into the breeze, frantically searching for fresher air. He and Ardeth started that way, no one wasting time on words. The cave remained wide and mostly flat. The bat guano made walking difficult though, and

Ardeth finally snarled and waved much of it away with magic.

"Need to make better time," Ardeth said, gasping either from the stink or the magic. Likely both.

He was right about needing to hurry. Rock crumbled behind them. The creatures would be into the cave soon, and he suspected that neither the guano nor the stink would slow them.

He had not seen the opening until they were almost below it and the breeze changed direction. Night had fallen outside. He could see stars through the boughs of trees.

Above them.

"We need up," he said, frantic. Ardeth didn't have much power left. Za wasn't sure what he could do, and he didn't know what Tansa -- Aia -- would do.

Except that he had the distinct feeling that the goddess desperately wanted out of here and not to go back into the hands of Za's half demon sister.

Tansa stepped forward. She shook her head. "This is not my place. What I've already done here -- it fights against my nature to even touch such a place. I don't know --"

"Get me up," Ardeth said. "That's all I need."

"Ardeth --"

"Up!" he ordered, frantic now because they could hear more sounds coming closer.

Za drew all the power he could and shoved Ardeth upward by at least four yards. Almost -- almost within reach, but he went to his knees, and he feared Ardeth would fall, but Ardeth's own power got him the rest of the way. Za saw him grab hold of a rock outcropping, dangle there for a moment, and then force himself to go on up and out.

What could he do up there? Za turned, annoyed that the Goddess had not helped. He abandoned that feeling in the next breath. The other two held back the creatures that were trying to get through. The Goddess did her part. But still, they had to find a way out. Ardeth was safe but --

"Get away from the opening!" Ardeth yelled from above.

Za scrambled away in haste, almost falling again when the pain rushed through his legs. What was Ardeth going to do? Send down a fall of rocks? He'd have to be ready to keep them in place --

A huge tree trunk fell through the opening, dead limbs tearing free, and rock crumbling around it. The stark, white bark looked long dead, and perhaps even fragile, but it settled into place with a loud thump.

"Up! Mai, get up!" Za shouted.

She looked ready to argue, but only until Tansa backed up to the tree. "I can give us a little time."

She brought down enough stone to cover the opening and bury some of the creatures. Then she spun and caught hold of the tree, intending to climb up and out.

The tree shuddered, and she pulled back her hand in haste, but a heartbeat later she smiled.

Roots began to grow out of the dead base. Limbs flew out so quickly that Mai and Za had to duck. Leaves and flowers sprang out in a profusion of color and a heavenly scent.

"Ah. That is better. Up, my friends. Go up and quickly. I'll be with you."

Mai went first, but only because there was no immediate danger here and they did not know what they'd find above. Za tried to get Tansa to go next, but she shook her head, and he went up. There was no use arguing with a goddess. Besides, he still wasn't sure how much longer he could go, and if he failed, one or more of them would come back down to get him.

The tree felt alive in his hands, and more leaves and flowers bloomed even as he passed over the area. He glanced back and saw Tansa not far behind him. Good, because he could also hear the others who would soon be in the area.

He scrambled up over the top and fell onto the ground.

Dark here, and cloudy with the feel of rain not far off. He lifted his head to gasp at the air, then forced himself to sit and breathe more calmly. Tansa reached the ground and scrambled out. The tree had lifted branches high into the air above them.

Ardeth had collapsed on his back, his eyes closed, his still injured hand against his chest so that Za couldn't tell if it was the hand or his heart that bothered him most. He looked pale and damp; the work of getting the dead tree down into the hole had been challenging, even with magic.

"What do we do with it now?" Mai asked and looked down into the opening. "We don't want them to follow us up."

"Leave it," Tansa said. She smiled -- not Tansa's smile, though. "They dare not touch it, a thing of pure magical life and hope. That tree will spread deep roots, and the demons will, literally, lose ground to it. They should not have tried to upset the balance of things. This is how they pay. But we -- we have other matters now."

Za could hear the distant sound of battle.

CHAPTER FORTY-ONE

I could not look at Tansa. I could glance her way, but the moment I saw her face --

The others probably didn't see the change. They didn't realize that it wasn't *her*. Oh, they noted the glow from her hands, though that power slowly died away. They could hear oddness in her voice, and maybe they felt awe in the presence of the Goddess of Hope. They didn't think about what had happened.

She was not my Tansa. My heart would break if I looked at her for too long. Why hadn't she taken me instead? Why my Tansa?

"I am still here, my love."

I looked. Tansa gave me a nod. Her movement. Her voice, too -- a whisper of words she spoke close to me. Did I dare hope?

"She isn't a Goddess of destruction. We are -- sharing this form now. It is more her than me. Things must be that way for now. Aia is our hope -- truly our *hope* -- of winning. Trust us, Mai. We need you."

I watched her as she spoke. I saw the flicker of other things in her face. I saw whispers of something inhuman in her eyes -- but they were not evil things. I even dared to touch her shoulder. Tansa's shoulder and she gave her usual little twitch. Oh yes, my Tansa. I smiled and felt perhaps, more hope than I should have felt just then. I accepted it, or else I must give up now, fall down, and die.

I could not give up since we were moving closer to the battle. I could hear swords clashing and the cries of humans and creatures. I thought I could hear that inhumane scream of the goddesses on demons, too, but they were either weaker or farther away. That, I realized, had to be our first target. I turned to Za and almost cursed. He could barely keep to his feet, and he helped to hold Ardeth up who was in worse shape. For a moment I thought we ought to retreat. Leave this war to the soldiers fighting it and hope --

Oh, yes, hope. We had a goddess with us. She had to count for something. They had Mercy and Abundance. I wondered how Mercy could work in such a situation, especially for someone who was attacking her own people. I thought the queen might not have chosen well -- if she had a choice. The three were a well-known trinity and it might have been possible to take any one or two without taking all three.

Abundance could be a problem for us. I thought I could see so already in the profusion of demon creatures the queen had called up from their special hell. Hope would have served them, too -- the hope of winning did not belong only to the side of good, after all.

We had Hope. They had Abundance and Mercy. And a lot of demons.

We had the *Art of Ata*, which I had, during this long and strange journey, learned to trust. I was not surprised when I looked back at Za and Ardeth to see that they had both already recovered somewhat. I wanted them to be ready for trouble though.

"Can't you help them?" I asked, looking at Tansa.

She blinked. "I thought -- Tansa had hoped that they

would be too weak to take part in the battle and that they might survive."

Tansa blushed. She and the Goddess must have come to some understanding, though. Aia reached out, her hand glittering with golden light. She touched Ardeth first and then Za. They both stood straighter. Za bowed his head in thanks.

"We must move carefully," Ardeth said.

I had been doing so already, though I should have said the same to the others. I hadn't realized that I was leading them until now. I had gotten used to Tansa being in charge.

We came to the top of an incline, the edge lined with brush. Beyond stood a wide valley with a river flowing through the middle. The fields of grain had been trampled into muddy battlefields, and everywhere scattered with the dead. I could read the way the battle had gone so far: the queen and her allies had been on the far side of the river, but they'd crossed and pushed the human army back toward the hills. They'd rallied, though, and held. Even in only the light of the moon, torches, and fires, the scene was too clear. The sun would be up soon, I thought.

I saw no sign of our second army yet. Soon, I hoped. The humans might win without them, but I didn't want this battle to linger and to watch the military cut down, soldier by soldier.

I could see the more massive demons and the princesses far across the field from us. People had retreated from them, and I could not hear the maddening cries. Maybe that indicated a limit for the use of that horrible power. I scanned the rest of the field to the right and picking out different companies of soldiers.

"The Tiger is here," I said. I pointed to the spot where his banner flew, higher than all the others. "I don't see any sign of Lightning Company, but I would expect them to come in with the other troops."

"What do we do?" Ardeth asked.

Tansa had moved up beside me, and it was definitely her experienced look that took in the field, the line of battle -- quiet, but ready to explode -- and back to where the Tiger had made his stand. She gave a snarling nod, and that was all Tansa. I didn't think that look came from the Goddess of Hope. At least I hoped not.

"We need to get to your grandfather, Za," Tansa said. Her voice didn't even echo much. "We need to let him know that we have ... well, that we have Hope."

Za looked startled for a moment and then laughed agreement. I thought they were both crazy and maybe Ardeth thought the same. Ah, but we had been traveling together for a long time, and I couldn't say I was surprised -- or that I wasn't just as crazy as them. Why not joke about it? Why not bring something brighter into this madness?

"There are only four of us," I said and scanned the grounds. Troops stood guard along the edges of the encampment, and those would be the ones we'd have to get past. "We won't look like a lot of trouble, but we'll still have a problem getting to the Tiger."

"I can help," Za said. "I do not want to use much power, but enough to get us inside the lines will help."

"Yes," I agreed. "Or should we find the other troops --"

"They'll find the battle," Tansa replied. "Let's make certain our side is ready for them."

I can't say I wanted to walk down there and get involved in that battle. We'd fought enough already, and I didn't like to see more of the hellish creatures aligned against us. These looked far worse than the little things we had already fought.

"The Queen," Za said and put a hand on my arm before I started to move.

She stood by the large demons, a distant figure, but easy to tell if for no other reason than her crown glittered in the moonlight. I couldn't even tell if she looked our way, but I froze in place. I had to hope she didn't sense us here.

Yes, hope.

After a while, she left the area again. Nothing came our way. We were still safe enough. We said nothing more as we began to work our way down the hillside, a slow movement that took us from the last of night and into the bright dawn. I was surprised to find a few rabbits, quail, and even a couple raccoons still in the area. Better still, I spotted a fox and took that to be an excellent omen. Even Tansa smiled at the sight.

In the next moment, she was not herself again. I looked away, but I told myself that Tansa was still there. Once we were through this madness --

I stopped that thought because I really couldn't see what would happen next. We could only move forward and finish what we'd begun.

When we reached the line where the sentry stood, Za stepped forward. The man started to give a shout, but Za's lifted hand and magic stopped him. The soldier blinked and turned away. I had the feeling he didn't see us any longer. Za appeared to be ready for any trouble, though he looked pale again. Ardeth kept close to his side while Tansa -- no, it was Aia this time -- looked around with avid interest. I wondered how much connection to humanity the gods usually had if something so familiar as an army camp took this much of her attention.

We moved into the line of soldiers. They were trading off the front line that had stood ready for trouble all night. People moved everywhere as we kept a steady pace and acted as though we were going about normal business. That had to be some magic as well and I saw Ardeth's hand move sometimes when people stared too long.

People started to pay more attention as we moved closer to the tent where the Tiger must be staying. I had hoped to find him outside, checking on troops, or else find General

Gedquin who would know us. I feared that if Za used magic directed at this group, someone would notice, and I didn't think we could take on the entire army, even with hope on our side.

Ardeth was the one who brought up another problem, though.

"He will not know where we've been," Ardeth said as we stopped for a while, standing in a small group as others did, watching the tent for a sign of the emperor. "When he last saw us, we were to go with the troops and bring them here to help. Arriving like this, without them --"

"And with a dozen wild tales of everything from dragons to goddesses," I said and even took a step back. "Do we need to wait until he has word about the other troops? Will we know?"

I looked to Za to for the answer. He stared at the tent, only a dozen yards from us now, as though he could see inside and study the situation to learn the best answer. Maybe, in fact, that was what he did in his own way. I had learned more about the *Art of Ata*, but I still didn't know everything he could do. Ardeth had looked his way as well. Tansa and Aia stared, and I wondered what went on inside that head.

"Gedquin," Za said. "There he is. We dare not wait and hold back what we know."

I gave a reluctant nod of agreement. I wasn't sure about why I wanted to hold back ... except that if others learned about Aia, I feared that would not look to Tansa for any answers, and that would be a mistake.

"General Gedquin," Za called out.

The man looked our way with a frown. People did not call out to him at random, and for a moment the scowl grew -- and then disappeared in a look that might have been a whisper of relief. He'd already been at the opening to the tent, and he stopped there, watched us for a moment, and then looked inside.

"The boy is here," I heard him distinctly say.

I expected to be called into the tent and brushed my hand over my dirty and rumpled clothing. When I looked back up, though, the Tiger had come out and so had four others who were apparently of rank in the forces. They were angry-faced men, snarling whenever the Tiger was not looking their way. Not happy people, but considering the situation, I could hardly blame them.

The Tiger nodded our way, and we went forward, the four of us, as though we knew what we were doing and had every reason to be here. General Gedquin moved to stand beside Za, an action that was not missed. However, those watching couldn't know if the man moved to support Za or to protect the emperor from this stranger. I couldn't say I was certain, either. He might be standing there to be closest to Za if the Tiger gave a sign of displeasure.

I would have liked a quieter reception for our news. What dare we say here in the middle of soldiers? Why did he bring this out in the open?

"Sir," Za said with a bow of his head. Not the kind of a bow a peasant would give, and that drew some whispers. We were the show for the moment, and I suspected that we would have to make a good one.

"You have news?" the Tiger asked.

More whispers around us -- the Emperor spoke to us himself. Yes, the others were beginning to guess that we were not beggars come to court.

"The army has come through the pass, sire," Za said. "I cannot say how far away they are, but I think they will have made good time. I have seen no sign that the Queen and her people are aware of them yet."

Implying, perhaps, that we'd been doing scouting and not that we'd left the army behind for other things. Good. I saw even Tansa give a slight nod of her head.

"Then we are in a better position than some would think," the Tiger replied with a bit of a smile.

"If you believe this ragged-haired peasant," one of the men said, and even went so far as to step closer and shove Za. "How do you know this one isn't setting us up for more trouble? He has the look of a westerner, to me. Or a mongrel."

The Tiger's eyebrow rose. Gedquin shifted position. People went silent, and they may not have realized why.

"The mongrel, General Valcrin is Prince Zaron, my heir."

"No," the man said and shook his head in denial. "He cannot be. He is a peasant. Look at this hair! How can this be an heir?"

"You judge him by his hair alone?" the Tiger demanded. He took a step forward. "You judge him -- and question me -- by that alone?"

"He cannot be the heir," Valcrin replied. "Whatever else he might be, he is not going to rule the East."

I looked at the man and wondered how anyone this stupid could get into a place of such power. I suspected he must be good at leading soldiers. Diplomacy was not his high point, though. I would have found it more amusing if we hadn't been standing on the edge of a battle that might thoroughly wipe out the east and the west if this went poorly.

"He is what I say he is."

Stillness.

"Tradition --"

I looked at Valcrin with disbelief overcoming all else. I saw others doing the same, even some who had, perhaps, been nodding agreement with him a moment before.

The Tiger crossed to him. He was still a tall man, and though age had touched him, it had not taken control. I compared him to the sad wreckage of the Wolf whom we had left behind. This was not a weak man.

Valcrin's mouth clamped shut, the lips narrowed as he fought not to say something more.

"Do you really, General Valcrin, judge a person's ability by their hair? Is that all I am?" He grabbed at his own long braid and held it out. "Is this the sole reason I rule?"

"We must have traditions," the man said, but his voice had gotten a little softer.

"Then it is time we make better ones."

He reached over and grabbed the knife from General Valcrin's belt. The man leapt backward.

The Tiger sliced off his braid and threw it on the ground.

"Am I now less the Tiger than I was?" Silence. A glance at the hair. A look at the man. "We have a battle to fight. *Prince Zaron* has done much to make certain we are ready for it. We fight here, or we retreat and fight in the East. I would rather finish the matter here. Is there any hope of that happening, Zaron?"

"Hope," Za said and smiled. "Oh yes, we do have *hope*."

The Tiger signaled us to go with him back into the tent. General Gedquin came with us -- after he picked up the braid -- but the others did not follow. I saw the Emperor brushing at the hair on his neck. He frowned.

"You get used to it," Zaron offered.

"Sit down. Tell me what I need to know."

We told him tales of mountains, dragons, Wolves, and Goddesses.

And now ... now we had to make it all count for something.

CHAPTER FORTY-TWO

Za climbed to the slight rise that overlooked the stream. The hordes of hell lined up on the farther side, a sullen red glow of power all around them, including the greater demons with their princess riders. Silent now, but he expected trouble from them soon. The sun sank toward the horizon behind a wall of blood-red clouds. Aia had pointed out that night would not be a problem for the demons, and the Queen had grown more active near sunset.

But at least Za and his companions had a few hours rest. They'd all slept despite the situation. They had reached the point where more dangers hardly mattered.

The other part of the Eastern army had to be near. Mai and Ardeth had gone out to find them. It would not be an easy journey nor a safe one, wandering back behind the enemy lines. There might be more of the Queen's troops out there, scouring the land as well. He had to hope --

Za turned to Aia. He could feel her force in Tansa's body, stronger now that Mai was not by her side. He thought Aia let Mai have Tansa when she was near, and he liked the goddess better for it.

"How much does what we hope for affect you?" he dared to ask.

"The wishes of individuals, in most cases, are just whispers around me. Sometimes one is very strong, but that doesn't mean I will take hold of it. Some hopes are simply passing thoughts, no matter how strong the wish might be at that moment. How many children, do you suppose, hope that a parent might go away and never punish them again? One must be careful, you know."

"And in a situation like this, where so many are together, hoping -- oh hoping to win, hoping to survive, hoping that the enemy will go away. And that's from both sides, isn't it?"

"In a normal battle, yes. However, the Queen has few humans on her side, and the demons do not think as humans do. The Queen alone was directing us. She has power, you know -- but you have your own gifts."

"I am trying to decide how she will use the other two demons and goddesses," Za admitted. He stared at the demons and their riders. "I suppose a person could hope for an abundance --"

And he stopped. He stepped back, looking away from the scene below and again at the Goddess beside him. She did not glow, still hiding most of her nature behind the frail human shell.

"You," he said and then took a deeper breath. "You are the strongest of the three because many people go through you when they hope for abundance or hope for mercy."

Aia gave a slight bow of her head in agreement. "Some do go directly to my sisters. They have their temples, and one might ask for abundance in the harvest or mercy for an ailing friend. Fewer people come directly to my temple because hope seems nebulous to them. However, out in the world, beyond the walls of the temples, I am the more powerful. People keep me alive with their hopes for better things. Oh, and some hope for evil to fall on enemies -- the Queen is such a person -- but they are not usually so strong. In the world, people hope for many good things."

Za gave a bow of his head to the goddess. Until now he had not realized the power that stood beside him. He had a thought, then. Something that would have to be carefully done. Then he smiled at another thought.

"I hope that Mai and Ardeth remain safe," he said.

She smiled: Tansa's look at that moment. "Yes," Tansa agreed.

Za thought the goddess might be amused, but he also believed that their friends were safer for the wishes.

As they walked back to the tent, he became too aware of people bowing to him. He'd left that life behind in Palace of the Summer Clouds so long ago now that seeing them bow left him uneasy. Living in the palace had been a lie that he did not want reborn here.

The Tiger had given orders that Za could come to him at any time. He and Tansa walked into the tent, glad to see only Gedquin there with the Emperor. What he was going to propose would sound like insanity, but it was a little thing.

Za brought a chair over for Tansa to sit at the table and then settled beside her. The Emperor and the General had remained silent, and he saw interest in both their faces.

"Goddess Aia," Za said and leaned closer to her. "I wish -- I *hope* that you can teach us a simple prayer that will help in this time of our need, and that we might have mercy and abundance to help us."

"Ah," she said. "Not such a simple hope, you know."

"I know," he admitted. "But if we can spread this prayer to the soldiers with us --"

He surprised her. She looked toward the tent opening. "Right now, they hope mostly to survive, but they are random wishes. If you could direct them all toward one hope --"

"It must be simple wording," Gedquin said. Za had been aware of how uneasy the general was in the presence of a

Goddess. Za even thought that wise. Now, though, the General leaned forward and stared into her face. "Something that can be learned quickly, spread from person to person. Some will ignore this. We haven't the time to tell them the reason, nor would it be wise to show that we have you in our camp. We must do this carefully."

"Not much time," the Goddess said and looked again to the tent. "Night will come. Still, you have another way to spread such a prayer. Za can help me."

"*Ata*," Za said. "Magic. A compulsion? But it cannot be anything complex. I haven't that ability."

"And what you truly hope for must be wise. My ability with the demons is limited."

They had to plan. "You understand that this will not win the battle," Za said to his grandfather and the general. "You must still be ready, General Gedquin. Oh, and it would not hurt to *hope* Mai, and Ardeth can get the other troops here in time."

Za and Aia worked on the simple prayer, but she did not guarantee that it would work.

With the very last light of day, the enemy army began to show signs of preparing to do battle. General Gedquin gave his own orders, and people quickly took their positions on their side of the river. They did not like to fight at night, but they didn't argue. Za was aware of the movement everywhere around them, but he and Aia focused on the few words. No more than ten or else there would be no time for others to memorize them.

Ten words of power.

They might change the battle.

CHAPTER FORTY-THREE

At least the weather wasn't horrible. That was what I told myself as Ardeth and I made our way through the underbrush with burrs sticking to my clothing and twigs tearing at our skin. Ardeth mumbled very many things under his breath, but at least they were not in words I understood -- though I did get the implications.

"We'll be out of the woods soon," I said as a warning. Something might be on the trail. I would hope for the troops we sought, but I could hear no sound of them. They had to be near. I desperately wanted the battle over and for Aia to go back to her own realm, to leave Kintansa --

"Careful!" Ardeth caught my arm. I'd dislodged a large stone, not paying attention to where I stepped, and nearly went down. Ardeth surprised me by holding on and looking into my face. "I trust Aia. I believe that she will do what is right, Mai. You will have Tansa back again."

The words annoyed me in one breath and then brought tears to the edge of my eyes in the next. He said no more and let go, giving me time to turn away and get my emotions in check before I dared to speak.

"I tell myself that saving the goddess and winning the war, those are more important than any single life. But she's *my*

Tansa, not some stranger --"

"Like I am," Ardeth said. "I'm sorry that the goddess took her. If I had been able --"

I turned to him, shocked by the words. "No," I said. "I would not wish this for you or Za either. I would have taken her, but I suspect we would not have been a good match. Tansa is handling this. Tansa is still there. I have never been close to the gods, Ardeth. I can't make myself trust her."

"It is difficult," Ardeth agreed. I found that comforting because I didn't like to think the problem was only my personal fears and weaknesses. "What do we know about the gods? How can we trust that what she has told us, about being trapped, is even true?"

I sighed agreement. We went on in silence for a while. When I glanced at Ardeth, he still frowned. I wondered if he thought more about this situation but had not said. He practiced *Ata* just as Za did, but I suspected they might still see things differently. I wanted to ask him and decide if perhaps I'd been relying too much on Za's view.

Not now. We came to the edge of the woods with the road only a short distance away. Empty now but I knew this road was well-traveled, and even with the battle not far away, I suspected there would still be some people around. They had to go on with their lives, no matter the wars fought around them.

"Should we stay in the bushes?" Ardeth asked.

"Not now," I said. "Anyone hearing noises in the bushes might be apt to attack, thinking we are there hiding and preparing to do harm. We'll just be careful. I have to believe that our people are somewhere along here, moving as quickly as they dare."

He didn't look convinced. "I am better on the ocean, you know. I understand what is happening there. Here you can't even clearly guess what the weather is going to be."

"I suppose this has all been less of an adventure and more of a tour of hell ... even before we made that little side trip."

"I miss the ocean. I fear I will miss it for a long time."

"You aren't going back?" I asked, so shocked by the words that I stopped walking and put a hand on his arm.

He looked at me, dark eyes blinking. I had the suspicion that he had not considered the truth of what he must have already been thinking. "I still have a great deal to teach Prince Zaron," he said at last. "I can't say how long it will take, but this is not a duty I can abandon until I'm certain I have done all that I can."

"You have helped get us through this mess," I said and started on again. "Za has needed you. None of the rest of us really understand what he's doing, you know. We can play guards, but we can't help him."

Ardeth said no more. We walked in silence along the road. I wanted to find something more to say to him, to help, but --

But I saw someone coming our way and had to fall silent. The person had been quiet as well, but now began to whistle a tune -- and I understood. I stepped out of the shadows, and the song stopped.

"Elmas," I said and greeted her with a slap on the arm.

We had located the others. In fact, we had found more than I expected. Half a mile farther on we joined up with all the surviving Lightning Company, who had in turn joined with the soldiers from the east who had come through the mountains with us. Lt. Ebru all but embraced me. I don't think I had ever seen anyone so happy to find someone to lead them to battle.

Ardeth and I explained the situation. By now the sky had gone dark, and only a few lanterns showed our location. That still made me feel as though we stood out in the middle of an open field holding stars in our hands to make certain everyone saw us.

"We can make camp and start at dawn," Ebru said after she'd heard the tale. "We don't dare get too much closer, because they're bound to realize --"

"We have to go now," Ardeth said. He was not looking at either of us but stared off into the direction of the battlefield. "We must go immediately. The demons do not rest."

"Ardeth?" I said and dared a hand on his arm.

He looked at me and blinked. Then he nodded. "They're starting to attack. We have to get back."

"Fight at night?" Ebru said with a frown.

"You can wait until morning," Ardeth replied. "If there is any battle left, we'll still need your help. But I must get back and help Za."

He turned as though he would rush off into the night without even me. I snared his arm. "Hold on, Ardeth. Just a moment. I'll go with you."

"We have no time," he said and looked frantic. "I can sense the demons moving. The army will have to fight, night or not. The demons don't care."

"Damn," Ebru said. She looked steadier. "In fact, they'll expect it to be easier for them at night, won't they? Not tired like humans."

"Yes, this is true," Ardeth agreed.

"Then we go with you. Or at least follow behind as quickly as we dare."

"You can't miss the battle," I told her. Part of me said it was my duty to stay with the troops, but I didn't think Ardeth should go off alone. The troops knew what to do and Ardeth, alone, might run into trouble. We needed his magic as much as we needed the troops. "Good luck to you. I trust that you'll look over the battlefield and do what will work best. Or I should stay --"

"Go with him," Ebru said. "Gedquin sent me for a reason."

That made sense. I looked at the dozen members of Lightning Company and thought about telling them what had happened to Tansa and taking them with me, but there was no time. "You do what is best as well."

Kisi nodded. They might not work well with the trained troops. Ebru would understand. I hoped that they all did well, though. I hoped that --

Ardeth pulled away from me and started to jog back down the trail. I gave one last nod to the others and rushed to catch up with him. He did not slow for some distance, leaving the others far behind.

"We must -- we must get there far ahead of the troops," Ardeth said, mostly out of breath but still moving. "Warn our side that they are coming so they can be prepared. This is the battle we must win, Mai. If we don't -- well, nothing will be won again in our generation and probably several more."

I felt a chill at those words. Ardeth couldn't know that to be true, could he? How much could the *Art of Ata* tell him about now, let alone about the future? The Tiger had brought an army, but other armies would rise --

I realized then that they might not. Who would lead them if we lost the Tiger? Lost Za? Who would lead a new army and prepare for a battle that others didn't even know about yet?

Ardeth was right that a loss in this battle would mean generations under demon rule. I'd been so focused on the battle that I'd failed to see the larger picture of what would happen if we lost. The idea had not been possible. This was not like the East fighting the West. We were humanity facing the demons, and if they won, the world would change.

How could the queen do this? How could she turn against humanity? For power? I had my doubts that she would survive to enjoy anything she might win. I had never liked her --

We reached the edge of our lines again, having made a wide circle and come up on the eastern side of the camp. The guards were ready for us, and they looked worried.

"The others are near," I said. We had to spread the word. "Be ready."

"Yes," the woman said with a bow of her head. I had never rated a bow before, but I supposed being associated with the Tiger, and Za rated me a bit above tavern keeper these days.

I would miss those simpler days.

"Something going on," Ardeth said with a wild look around.

I could see that the enemy, already poised to move, pausing before battle when both sides sized up the other, breath held. I looked around frantically for Tansa and Za -- and found them at the front line.

"No!" I cried out in the near silence.

I started to rush forward. So, did Ardeth, but we were far from that area, and the demons raised up their heads and gave a cry that would be the challenge before they surged forward --

Then, above that demon cry of war, came thousands of voices joined in one prayer.

"We pray that Aia will keep Hope in our hearts and win us Mercy and Abundance!"

"Oh, the tricky bastards," Ardeth gasped, but he was grinning as he caught my arm and stopped me. "Look what they've done!"

The two huge demons and goddesses who had been in the front of the line were in disarray, turning and snapping at their own. Some of the smaller creatures still crossed the stream, which did not seem to slow them in the least as it would have humans. The mass plowed into the right and left wings of humans, but the demons at the center had already fallen apart. I could not clearly see Za or Aia now -- but I knew exactly where they were in the next moment. The ground moved by the stream, a ripple outward and fell, covering the stream bed in a road that the humans already rushed across.

"I need to help Za," Ardeth said and charged forward just as I had been going for Tansa.

We were still some yards away when we reached the first line of battle. I had known Ardeth was good with a sword, but I had not realized how good until he pulled his and moved forward through one block after another. I decided to guard his back -- and to stay out of in front of him, because I wasn't entirely sure he knew friend from foe right then. Some humans fought with the Queen, but I thought they held back. I wished them to go away and let us fight the real enemy.

That would be battle enough. The demon creatures never seemed to tire. Wounds hardly slowed them. They had to be utterly destroyed while the humans on our side fell to injuries and death alike. I heard the prayer repeated still and found myself taking it up as well. I couldn't tell if it gave me more power or not. I fought off anything that came at Ardeth's back, and he cleared the path before us. Magic, I realized. I could feel it like a fever burning from him and feared that he would destroy himself.

We crossed over the blocked stream. I looked frantically around for Za and Tansa realizing they must be on this side already, or else Ardeth would not have kept going. Where would Za and Tansa go? Were they trying to reach the Queen and kill her? No, I thought. No. They were trying to rescue the goddesses.

I anticipated Ardeth's change of direction, which probably saved us both. I wasn't sure he even realized I fought behind him, but we managed to keep moving forward. The demons here were far fiercer than what we had faced on the other side of the stream. I felt worn. I didn't think we could make it to my beloved's side.

I had no idea what happened with the rest of the battle. I

didn't care. I had focused on two things -- keep Ardeth safe and reach Tansa. Ardeth was my only hope of getting to that second goal. While I could fight off claws, teeth, knives, and swords, it was still his magic that kept us moving forward.

"*Aia, don't let her fall,*" I whispered and then gave a start of surprise. That had been the prayer I had whispered whenever Kintansa had gone off to battle. I had always held on to hope. I pulled it closer now as we pressed on.

CHAPTER FORTY-FOUR

Za forced his focus to stay on the goddesses, both the one beside him and the two others that they hoped would tear free of the demons. This was no easy task. He'd never been in battle, and the cries of the dying along with the stench of demon and human blood would have driven him far away from this madness if he'd had a choice. He was not a prince trained for war. He'd been a court pet, the peacock raised up with fine foods and fawning attention, but always intended for the sacrifice when spring came around again.

Oddly, he did not feel bitter about the realization. Amused, he supposed, that the peacock was now splattered in mud and worse, and all his pretty feathers gone. Amused that the peacock had found he had teeth and was not opposed to biting.

Za had never realized he had an ability for fighting, even under the tutelage of Endris. As much as he felt honored to stand with a goddess on his right side during this battle, he would have appreciated having Endris on his left and Mai at his back.

The Goddess of Hope neither killed nor destroyed, but what she touched -- human or demon -- turned away from them and did not attack again. That did not mean that the two of them weren't without injuries. Both had cuts, scratches and in Za's case, a bite that had gone deep into his right shin. He used what magic he could to ease his wounds, but that weakened his own powers.

Aia might not even be aware of how dangerous the wounds were to Tansa. That worried him. He did not want to be the one to tell Mai that they had lost Kintansa. How odd that this singular worry should drive him on more than the fear of losing the battle.

Aia touched those who came too close to her, but mostly she moved toward the other two goddesses and the demons that still held them captive. That left Za to deal with the enemy creatures, both large and small. When they had gone well more than halfway to the demons, he brought the Sword of Glory to his hands. The magical weapon took power to wield, and he feared he would not be able to hold it for long --

Then he heard the prayer go up again. The humans must have realized the power of it and that Aia was with them, though they probably didn't realize that she fought beside Za. Za felt the surge of energy and thought it might even have helped him. The demon's army did not much like it, and some backed away with their teeth bared in long faces and their clawed arms raised as though to protect themselves from something in the very air around them. Za had a moment of rest. He dared not release the Sword of Glory for fear he would not get it back, though. Around him, the others still fought.

He realized one truth: they might still lose, even if he and Aia won their special battle. However, if he and Aia lost, it wouldn't matter what the others did.

So, the peacock had to pretend to be an eagle. He knew nothing about war, strategy, and maneuvers, but that work would be in the hands of his grandfather and the generals. He had only to stand guard for Aia and fight at her side.

Magic came towards him, and he worried until he saw Ardeth cutting his way through the enemy lines, the fool. Za wanted to step that way and help him, but he dared not leave the goddess. He prepared to use magic to help Ardeth if he needed to, but so far, his friend had not slowed.

Not alone, either; Mai fought at Ardeth's back. They looked as though they'd practiced this for years.

"Ardeth and Mai are almost here," he said to Aia, glancing to the side where she stood, watching the demons a hundred yards away.

"Yes," Aia said. "Good. I hope that Mai..."

She didn't finish whatever she had started to say, and Za wondered what it was that Aia worried over. Or was it Tansa? He wanted Tansa back. He wanted to believe that they had not really lost her. The chill that thought brought almost dimmed his power, but he overlaid the worry about Tansa with *hope* for her instead.

A shift ... that was what he felt when Ardeth arrived at his side. His friend looked pale and shaky with all the power he'd used, but he kept to his feet and he held up his own, normal sword. Mai appeared no better even though she had not been expending magic as well. The battle drained them all in its own way.

They stood together, all four of them who had taken this journey together. Za refused to think that Tansa was not here.

"We must take the demons," Za said. The creatures were reforming their lines and his little group had a moment between battles. The rest of the war still pressed on behind them and a little to the sides, but few were close enough to help. "They will not easily give up the goddesses. I killed one with the sword, though. I can do it again if I can get to the head. Aia? Is this attack wise?"

"I cannot say," she said. "But I do think it will be necessary."

"Can you help?" Mai asked.

"In some ways," she said.

She reached out and touched each of us in turn. Za felt not only stronger, but he had hope again. Oh yes, that did help. Rather than wait for the enemy to prepare, Za started forward almost at a run, the sword bright in his hands. Ardeth and Mai kept pace with him, and the Goddess followed.

Za's sisters sat atop the two demons. He supposed they were also half-demons like the human Aia had been. They were not his father's children, unless he, too --

No. He would have known. Endris would have known. That was not the doubt to bring forward in the middle of this battle. He dared not find any self-doubt lurking in his thoughts, not about his own nature.

Za had almost reached the two demons whose front legs were as tall as him, their heads the sizes of small huts. The teeth were more massive than the Sword of Glory, and when he swung at the nearest head, he barely scratched the creature.

The demon almost took his arm. Mai leapt in and knocked the head aside by brute force of a kick to the cheek. Za moved back and gave her a nod of thanks.

How could he get to the top and shove the sword down through the head? No handy stairs here. No trees, even, or he might have been tempted to climb up and leap down, hoping to drive the sword in. His sisters would try to stop him, though, no matter what --

He had to take the chance.

"I need up top," he said to Ardeth.

Ardeth shook his head, although he didn't argue. Aia, still standing back, looked worried. Perhaps it only now occurred to her that they might lose. What would happen to the goddess then? What would happen to Tansa?

Za didn't intend to find out, one way or another.

He started forward, not at all surprised to find Ardeth

move with him. He decided to try his luck with Mercy rather than Abundance. He raced straight for the demon, Ardeth at his side, while Mai made a shout of surprise and probably annoyance. They should have told her the plan.

Neither the goddess nor the demon expected them to climb up the side of the creature. Neither had Mai who yelled something rather rude and then leapt in swinging her sword at the other demon who tried to move closer and pick him off. Ardeth had made it halfway up the demon and held onto one scale while he swung his sword at the head that whipped around, snake-like, to try and catch them.

Za did not pause. He climbed straight up and found himself kneeling at the juncture of the neck and body and faced Hasana who lifted her hand and power came to it as she smiled. He'd never liked Hasana who was his mother's chief ally. Just as well to take her on now.

He pulled up all the power of *Ata* and put as much truth in his voice as he could. "I pray to the goddess Hasana and ask that she show mercy to me and my companions as we fight to free her."

A cry of surprise came from Hasana's lips; not a human sound, that bird-like screech. The power that had been building in his sister's hand died down, flared, and died again. He left the goddess and the half-human to fight out that battle within the same body. The demon he had climbed had begun to leap up and down, trying to dislodge him. Ardeth, he realized, had already fallen, but a glance to the side showed him struggling to his feet again and helping Mai to hold the other demon back.

Za spotted his mother as she rushed at them, and he feared she might have some magic of her own. He dared not let her retake control of the demons.

One chance.

Za turned from the Queen lifted the sword and shoved it

into the base of the skull. This was not a quick kill, though. The demon tried to shake Za and the sword free. If he let go, the sword would disappear. But holding on --

Mai arrived. He wasn't sure how she had climbed the raging beast. Ardeth followed -- and then Tansa. He hadn't expected her, but he saw how she moved to deal with Hasana.

Za had freed Aia, or at least severely weakened the hold on her, by killing the demon she usually rode. They'd exiled her to a hell because she had been too dangerous to leave out in the world of humans with so little demon left to control her.

Za understood that truth. He held tight to the sword.

Abundance rushed towards them. His mother had climbed up with her and shouted, but Za didn't distinctly hear the words. How long? How long could he hold on?

Ardeth caught hold of the sword's hilt with him, his fingers wrapping around Za's. He said nothing. Blood ran down the side of his face and Za could sense pain pulsing through Ardeth's arm.

The battle's focus had turned to them. The lesser creatures screamed and rushed toward the wounded beast. Za thought his mother summoned them. They would climb up, hundreds of them, and the battle would be done.

Why did the demon not die?

Because Mercy kept it alive. He'd killed one demon, but only because Hope had not been on it at the time -- had not dared to come inside the mercenary's headquarters because it has once been a temple to Aia. No temple here. Nothing to do but remove the goddess.

"Hold to the sword. Hold tight," Za said.

"I can't. I don't have your power -- the sword is your weapon --"

"You are stronger than I am," he said.

And he let go because there was no more time.

Ardeth gave a cry of surprise. Somehow Mai heard it and

looked in shock as Za pulled away from the sword and crawled up the neck, clinging to the scales and skin. Aia had a hand reached out to Hasana, but from the look on her face, Mercy fought her.

"She must -- off --" Za gasped. He looked back to see Ardeth clinging to the sword, but he feared the work would kill his friend. He was not willing to let anyone else die in this useless war.

"Off," Aia said with a quick nod. "Yes."

The goddess of Hope threw herself forward with a shout that must have taken Hasana by surprise. Who could have expected Hope to be so vicious as she caught Mercy by the hair? Or maybe that was Tansa? Za wasn't as certain of what he would do now. Go back and help Ardeth? Stay and help --

Za had no chance to help. Aia wrapped herself around the other, held while waves of power, blue and green, rushed over the two of them like tame lightning. The blue light grew less and less and finally a sharp flash of blue knocked Hasana from the demon. The great creature shuddered and fell as well. Dead. Za and Ardeth tumbled to the side, landing hard on the ground. He feared the other demon and goddess -- and his mother -- would be on them before they could even stand, but he saw that they were in fast retreat, and the lesser creatures, the ones that had survived, raced out after them, abandoning the battlefield.

Za struggled to his feet, knowing they had to go after the queen and Kwana. Knowing --

The ground opened beneath the running demon and queen, and it tumbled downward; he could not see where it went, but his mother screamed either in fear or protest. This had not been her plan. The lesser demons leapt into the cavernous opening, probably to escape to their hells. The Queen might survive. Za knew that he should follow.

But he looked at his companions. Aia, thrown aside from

the other goddess, and now lay too still, her face slack, her eyes open: Tansa's face. Mai had fallen a few steps from her, face down in the dirt. Blood covered her back. Ardeth, the closest to him, did not breathe. The only movement came from the retreating army and the soldiers on the other side of the blocked stream. He thought they celebrated.

Za looked again at his companions.

Only Hasana, on the ground by Tansa, moved.

"No," he whispered and then grew louder. "No!"

Za dropped to his knees by Mai, but he could not quite reach her. Gone. *All of them gone.* He was aware of the Tiger coming closer and stopping either at his shout or at the sight of the goddess Hasana as she stood. The body that had been her shell and prison, the one who had been his sister, seemed to be made of mobile stone now, the skin hard and cracked as though something tried to get out. The core within glowed with unearthly power.

"Peace, Prince Zaron. Peace," she said, but her voice sounded like two or three people this time. "We are still here. You have lost neither Mercy nor Hope."

But he had. He had lost his friends and his faith.

Except when the light of the Goddess spread around him and over the others -- then he dared, for one more time, to *hope* for a miracle....

CHAPTER FORTY-FIVE

The forest trees gave way to stumps and new growth. Through the scatter of wild bushes, I could see a small village and the wide spread of the grasslands beyond. The weariness of a few moments before disappeared and even the horse moved faster. Busy villagers worked out in their fields and waved now and then reminding me that I was not a stranger here.

I slowed the horse as I reached the western edge of town, observing the building I still considered buying for a tavern and inn. The Lost Way Inn might live again, though I didn't pretend it would be the same.

I slowed even more. I had no reason to race through the town, risking the chance of literally running into someone. I didn't want to hurt or annoy any of the locals. We'd tried to be good neighbors since we bought the cottage and farm at the edge of Edgeway.

I'd been away for nearly a full turn of the moon, though. I wanted to get home to the cottage. I wanted the peace I hoped to find there.

"Mai!" Sirma shouted and waved at me. "Good to see you back!"

A weight lifted from my heart. He would not have greeted

me so happily if anything had gone wrong.

"Still here, I see," I said and slowed to a stop. Sirma wouldn't keep me for long, and if he had anything I needed to know, he would tell me now.

"I found out I like the work of being a medic better than I expected," he admitted with a shy smile. "Your trip went well?"

"Well enough," I said. Most of what I'd seen was not something to discuss out on the village streets. Nor would Sirma ask for details, not out here in the open. "I'll let you know when we need a meeting."

He nodded. Word would spread of my return to the others who had also settled in the area. Only a handful of Lightning Company had survived the battle that had taken place not too far to the south. Those survivors were not in any hurry to rebuild the mercenary company. No one wanted to go back to war.

I felt a chill again. It always came when I knew that Tansa and I had not survived, either -- but the power of two goddesses had brought us back, along with Ardeth. We were, I thought, a gift for Za. Of late, I had made a study of old myths and children's tales. I had found such a *gift* only once before, and that had been to someone whom the gods would need again.

I was not surprised that we might yet be called back into battle, though there had been no sign of the demons or the queen. Even the priests and priestesses I'd talked to had said that the hells themselves seemed calm these days.

No, I did not trust that calm at all.

I waved to a few others as I rode on, all locals who shouted their own greetings. Then I was at the edge of town and pushed the horse a little harder. The mare was glad to be heading home and didn't mind racing the last quarter mile.

The cottage had beige walls, green frames (they'd been red

when I was last home) around the windows. Flowers bloomed in wild profusion in a garden that had spread from one side of the building across to the other. I caught the scent of food cooking.

As much as I wanted to leap off the horse and race inside, I took the time to put the animal in the coral, remove her saddle and blanket, and make certain she had food and water. With my duty done, I leapt up over the fence rather than use the gate and headed for home.

Tansa had come outside. She smiled as I neared and then wrapped me in her arms. That startled me, though I felt myself melt into her arms and gladly accepted the kiss that welcomed me home.

"Where is she?" I asked. Aia was not with Tansa, who never would have kissed me with such passion if the goddess still shared her body.

"Our lovely goddess of Hope has developed a fascination with sheep. She's off with them."

"Sheep?" I repeated. I looked over at the sheepfold and then to the field where four of the white and black animals danced through the grass. "We need more sheep, Tansa. Lots and lots more sheep."

Tansa laughed as she gave me another hug and then took my hand. We sat down on the bench by the door. Two cats and a half-dozen kittens came at a run. Four peacocks strutted and sunned themselves in this foreign place, as happy to be here as I was. Home.

"Tell me about Willoway," she said. "I'll tell Aia later unless there is something she needs to know now."

"Nothing that important," I said, grateful that I could hold her hand and relax. I had never gotten quite used to Aia, but we accepted each other. And the Goddess did say she would move on when the time came. I had to believe her. "Za is still trying to talk his grandfather into sending a mayor for the town rather than leaving him in charge. He truly does not want to be there. Ardeth remaining has helped, though. Za has someone who understands, but at the same time, someone with whom he can discuss the art of becoming a pirate. I'm serious. We had more than one meal delving into such a possibility."

"Good," Tansa said with an emphatic nod. "Za should have his chance to sail the seas and know some freedom. What of Hasana?"

"She stays mostly in the temple, which is the safest place for her, especially in that less than human form. Like Hope, she says she could go, but the link to this world would lessen, and that might not be wise just now. I don't much like that Hasana is still in a body that is half-demon, but she can control those impulses in the temple, and I got the odd feeling that the link to the demons might help us in the future. Za did say that they have confirmation that the Queen and Kwana are somewhere in the hells. She's lost power, though. Hope and Mercy can make up for what we've lost in Abundance, as I understand it. We might have some lean times in the future, but Mercy says she will do her best to mitigate any suffering."

"Aia has kept that tenuous link with Kwana," Tansa said and gave a wave of her hand that seemed to take in the plethora of flowers, kittens, and probably those birds singing in the nearby trees. "But someday we might yet have to recover Kwana and the gift of Abundance."

"Not until Aia and Hasana are ready for that battle," I said. "And neither of them seems to be in a hurry to rush into hell after her."

"And when they are ready, we go back to war."

"Yes," I said. I held Tansa's hand tighter, and she looked at me, fear and worry in her eyes. "We would even if we didn't owe the goddesses our lives, Tansa. We would fight the battle for the same reasons we fought before we became so embroiled in the wars of gods and demons. We'll fight if this war comes to us because we will always fight for what is right. Now ... is your food burning?"

"Damn!" Kintansa leapt to her feet and rushed inside.

I followed her, pushed the door closed, and hoped that the goddess found the sheep fascinating for at least a few more hours.

THE END

ABOUT THE AUTHOR:

Hello!

I am an eclectic and prolific author who has published in several genres, including Young Adult Mystery, Contemporary Fantasy, Epic Fantasy, Science Fiction and numerous works on writing. While I started on the outer edges of traditional publication with sales to small press and magazines publishers, I have since moved most of my work to the Indie world and I am madly in love with the new world of publishing and the direct contact with readers.

I live in Nebraska with my husband, my cats and a small but entirely useless dog.

I also own Forward Motion for Writers and the ezine, Vision: A Resource for Writers.

Connect with Zette:

Web Site:

http://lazette.net

Facebook:
http://www.facebook.com/lazette.gifford

Joyously Prolific Blog:
http://zette.blogspot.com/

Smashwords:
http://www.smashwords.com/profile/view/Lazette
G